Sarah Ann Walker

My Dear Stranger

Sarah Ann Walker

Sarah Ann Walker

Copyright © 05/09-1 2014 Sarah Ann Walker

All rights reserved.

ISBN: 0991723120
ISBN-13: 978-0-9917231-2-6

Sarah Ann Walker

DEDICATION

To Jakkob

You are the greatest blessing I have ever known.
And I hope every single day I have given you the love and
strength needed to make it through life happily.

There will always be bullies baby, but one day I hope they
don't hurt your heart as much as they do now.

All my love,
Mommy
xo

Cover Design- James Freeburg
Cover Synopsis- Sarah Ann Walker & Cheryl Shockley-Dent

This book is a work of fiction. Any reference to real people, or real locales are used fictitiously. Other names, characters, places, and incidents are the product of the author's imagination, and any resemblance to actual events or locales or persons, living or dead, is entirely coincidental.

Sarah Ann Walker

Sarah Ann Walker

CONTENTS

Acknowledgments   I

This was the beginning...

... Of the end.

Sarah Ann Walker

ACKNOWLEDGMENTS

I want to thank my husband once again for the beautiful book cover. It's exactly what I wanted.
I want to thank my parents for giving me their support once again.
I want to thank my sister Brennah for the funniest, filthiest line ever- I'm glad I could write it into this book (Patrick loved it.)
I want to thank Paola for being my best friend for a quarter of a century (Holy Shit!)
Thank you Chris Carmillia always for your support and excitement.
Thank you Brenda Belanger, my Boston Bruins Beauty.
Thank you Anayis Terzian from Indigo Books for all the opportunity.

Thank you Deniro, Paula, Christina, Megan, Jodie, Randi, Diane, Tara, Joan, Sleepy, Jen, Stephanie, Diana, Darcy, Sandy, Katica, Gladys, Crysti, Peggy, Shanyn, Sam, Briana, Cori, Glenda, Ashley, Jessica, Goldschool, April, Laura, Dena, Lisa, Rosanna, Suzy, Carla, Alanna, Michelle, Hayley, Tracy, Melannie, Whitney, Lou, Lynn, Glenda, Manda, Michelle, Leisa,
Triple M Books, A Literary Perusal,
Wine and my Kindle, & A Pair of Oakies to name a few...

I want to thank my many friends, fans, readers, and bloggers who have supported me this last year. I wish I could name you all.

Thank you Cheryl Shockley-Dent for being a kind, patient friend when I was stressed.
And thank you Kim Rinaldi for giving me great advice, and for *always* having my back.

Here goes... my third book.
And potentially my last.
xo
Sarah

Sarah Ann Walker

Sarah Ann Walker

This was the beginning…

Sarah Ann Walker

CHAPTER 1

I was cleaning out the spare room this morning and I found my old hatbox filled with my special stuff. You know, the stuff you think is important. The stuff you keep year after year, move after move, man after man. The stuff filled with weird memories, and nostalgic little tidbits which you truly believe at the time are the most important treasures you have. Yes... *those* things.

After running out to the garage with my hatbox for a cigarette which I still hide from my husband, I lifted the lid and was transported back in time to a place where these useless things, photos, and pieces of scribbled upon paper actually meant something to me.

When I found pictures of old friends I thought were going to be my BFF's I smiled. Where the hell are they now, and why don't I actually care about them anymore? It's amazing to me how once upon a time these friends were everything to me, and now I don't know where they are or what happened to them. And sadly, I really don't care. They were important to me then, but they have absolutely no importance to me now.

Sifting through the papers and notes; the little love notes and messages from potential boyfriends, the catty notes in high school from my girlfriends trashing another girlfriend behind her back, I'm humored and enlightened.

I truly never thought I was a teenage bitch, but I guess I had moments like everyone has in high school. You know the moment- the moment where you suddenly follow along and decide to hate the one girl you actually do like for a week because everyone else decided to hate her. A week where she struggled with being disliked, and you thrived on being with the group who disliked her. It's amazing how truly brutal teenage girls can be with one another. Well, until it's your turn to be hated for that long week. After that week of being hated, trashed, bullied and emotionally tortured I know I never followed again.

Even when my little group tried to pick one of us to hate again, I *know* I didn't follow along even once after I had survived my turn, because I remember being the one in the middle. I remember walking with the 'good' group, but still talking on the phone to the 'bad' girl who everyone hated that week. I remember talking to the good *and* the bad until the week was over and she was back in the fold.

Thinking about it years later, I realize teenage fear and insecurity for girls really is intense, and I find it amazing how many of us actually survive being a teenage girl.

I remember being a teenage girl. I remember the confusion and desperation and fear all the time. Everyone wanted to be liked, and everyone wanted to be popular. I was liked and popular, but at a heavy cost.

I had secrets that hurt, and I hid my real personality for years. I was too afraid to just be myself, like most girls are I think, because being a teenage girl can be awful. That I clearly remember.

Looking through my hatbox, I finally pull out the dreaded two books I've been avoiding. One is a thick notebook, a diary I guess, but it doesn't look like a diary so I'm fairly sure my mother didn't read it. It's more of a full sized spiral notebook with 'English Lit' on the front cover as its disguise. I remember thinking I was so clever because my mother would have never read an English Lit notebook hidden among real school notebooks, so I think my secrets were safe from her.

Anyway, it's a scrapbook diary. It's my diary, but I only wrote the important stuff in that book though- not the day to day 'dear diary' stuff some girls used theirs for. My diary held only the important stuff; like the deaths of musicians, or the deaths of fellow high schoolers from drunk driving accidents. In that book I only wrote the really big stuff. It started when I was 15 and I kept adding only truly *important* information until I was 22.

Really, it's more of the social history that created me.

Skimming through I find I'm shocked by just how much tragedy I believed personally affected me at the time. It's weird how in my teenage brain I thought the death of 4 students from a different high school, whom I had never met, was my tragedy to mourn. Yes, the death of 4 teenagers affects the whole community, but somehow I made it about me, though I had never met them, nor really cared about them at all. Yet there I was attending the massive funeral at the other high school- our rival high school no less- crying dramatically in my school uniform to show MY school's support. But really, it was absurd and highly dramatic, though I think that is the way of high school girls sometimes.

Flipping through pages I see the events that DID truly affect me personally. The sudden death of a close friend from a rare, acute sickness that stunned me and the city I live in, making her front page news for 4 days straight. The death of my grandfather which absolutely broke my heart. The death of a teacher who I had a major crush on also making the front page headline because of his stupid car accident when he fell asleep behind the wheel.

Death.

It seems I've always been afraid of death, so I've often found myself dancing with it as close as I could. I did things, and I experienced things. I tried things but I always survived, though sometimes I was shocked by my own survival- Not that I actually wanted to die when I was a teenager, because I didn't. And NOT that I wanted attention through my hidden dramas because I never told anyone at the time about them. So, no one else knew what I was doing, or feeling, or experiencing, or imagining for myself at the time. But I knew.

I danced with death for years, and I don't know why. I was so afraid of death, but I pushed my body to do things, take things, experience things that could only imply I had a kind of death wish. But I didn't. I have always been afraid of death, and I still am actually.

Some days it's amazing to me how far I've come. I did things no one knows about, and I lived things I've never spoken of. But to the people around me now, I'm a wonderful, accomplished, loving person, and no one knows just how far I've come. But I know.

I'm a wife to an amazing man, and I love him for making me amazing in the eyes of others. I love him for knowing there is more to my past but never asking about it. I love that he has never asked me to speak about my past.

He wooed me, married me, and he allowed me to become the woman who would be married to someone like him, no questions asked. Even though I can be very lonely some days with him, I never take for granted the fact that he helped me become all I ever wanted to be in other people's eyes. And he's good for me.

I'm a mother as well. I'm a mother to a beautiful son who I adore. I am a good mother and I truly love being a mother. Other parents think I'm a terrific mother, and I'm proud of that.

I love being a mother to my son, and I love knowing I'm doing everything I can to make him feel valued and secure in his little life. I want him to know that he is an amazing person as he grows so he never feels the sense of fear, insecurity and sadness that I felt growing up. I want him to know he's amazing, so he *feels* amazing. And so far I've raised my son well.

He's happy and well liked. He has everything he needs but he's not spoiled. My son possesses an intelligent, beautiful soul which I'm proud to say I helped create. My son is everything to me. He is the strength that tethers me to this world I live in.

Lighting my 7th cigarette in our garage, I'm glad I'm alone. My husband knows I sneak a smoke or two once in a while, and though I know he disapproves, neither of us actually acknowledge I smoke, therefore we can't ever really argue about it. I think that's the best thing about my husband; He knows stuff but he never acknowledges it, therefore it's like my hidden stuff doesn't play out in our wonderful life together. My husband doesn't acknowledge anything bad, therefore I'm not actually doing anything bad.

*****

I'm alone this weekend- My very first alone since the birth of my son. My husband took my 6 year old skiing with his whole, huge family, and I opted to stay home, which is an absolute first for us.

After much discussion around our dining room table, I finally agreed to let my husband and son leave me alone so they could go skiing with my in-laws. And I know my son will be fine. I know he will. He may be the youngest of my husband's huge family, but that's going to work in my favor, I think. My son will have all his aunts and cousins watching his every move. Plus, I honestly do trust my husband with my son anyway, so I really shouldn't feel nervous. But I do. I can't help it.

My son is my blessing on this earth, and this is the first time we will be apart since he was born. This is the first time I will not kiss, and hug, and giggle with my little boy. This is going to be the longest 3 days of my life, I think.

I am alone, and this is the first time being alone in over 8 years. I'm alone, and this is why I've decided to rid myself of my hatbox today. It's time.

My husband knows my hatbox lives under the spare-room bed, because my husband knows I took this hatbox with me when we moved twice. My husband knows this is private, and I know he has never opened it, nor snooped. My husband is too good a man for snooping. Plus, my husband doesn't want to know certain things about me anyway, which is good. He doesn't want to know, and I no longer want to tell him, so we have a mutual understanding. He doesn't ask, so I never have to tell. Ignorance in this case truly is our bliss.

Opening a lounge chair in the garage is strange, but I have a feeling I'm going to be here a while. Walking back into my kitchen I brew a whole pot of coffee while wondering if my son and husband are almost at his family's resort. My son is probably drawing in the backseat, and my husband is probably listening to one of his conservative, long-winded talkshows on the radio. My son has an amazing ability to tune everything out when he's concentrating on his art, which is just another reason why I love him so much.

Opening the treat drawer, I pull out a fresh pack of cigarettes. Pouring the whole pot of coffee into a huge hockey mom thermos, I wait. I know what I'm going to do, and I know I have to prepare myself. I know what I'm going to do and I'm scared to do it. But I will. It's time.

Walking back into my garage, I walk right to the waiting lounge chair, take a large gulp of the hot coffee which burns all the way down my esophagus, and I settle in. With shaking hands, I light another cigarette, because its time.

Opening the hatbox one last time I reach in and slowly graze my fingers along the teal blue silk of my special journal. I remember the feel of this silk, and I remember caressing the texture of red and yellow thread within the Asian blue silk. I remember resting my cheek against this special journal throughout my endless nights alone, and I remember the texture of silken thread imprinting my cheek as I held on tight and cried around it.

Rubbing my cheek against my journal, I can't help but smile. I wonder if the adult me even remembers what it felt like to be the teenage me. I wonder if the words will still hold the same weight for me now that they held for me then.

Sitting back in the lounger with my thermos of coffee, my pack of smokes, and my mind buzzing, I settle in for this.

I really is amazing to me where I ended up when I think of the years I spent with this special teal blue silken journal keeping me alive.

Opening the cover of my special journal I see my teenage girl handwriting and smile again. My writing is cute and decorative with circles on the i's and a little heart on the top of each page. God, I was so young and naïve.

My Dear Stranger I

I'm lying here staring at the silhouettes upon my bare walls as the stars glow, reflecting light through my windows. The world seems audacious, bold and daring.

You promised to call me to see if I'm still alive, but if I wasn't alive, would I answer the telephone? I can't believe how much I drank tonight. I can't believe how much I threw-up. I can't believe how you took care of me tonight at that nasty bush party. You're such a good friend Petzy, and I know I'm safe with you when I drink like that. I know you are my friend even if I don't want more than friendship with you.

My room is so dark tonight, even with the moonlight glow through my window. And I can't help but just lie here. Why can't I sleep? Probably because I passed out in Petzy's car for a while when he left to collect all his friends. Maybe this is a second wind or something.

Why am I crying? Maybe I'm hung over already? I don't know, but I feel wide awake and sad, and my tears are spilling all over my purple pillows. What's wrong with me? Maybe I need another drink.

My Dear Stranger

Looking, I see the man again. The man in my dreams. He follows me around and He enters my soul. With His dark eyes, He lets me weep quietly in my bed while He watches me silently. Why does He stand there in the corner all the time? Why does He take my crying silences and make them His own?

When He just stands there while I write, I feel kind of paranoid or threatened, I'm not sure which. I know He tries to appear real, but He must be a dream. He has to be a dream because I know I'm okay, even though I'm awake.

Lighting a cigarette, my parents are still pretty cool about me smoking in my room and I love that. With my white hardwood floors and minimalist furniture, there isn't much to burn. And as long as my window is open, and I don't smoke in my bed, my parents stay cool. Though right now I'm technically lying in my bed, which they forbid, I'm sitting up, sort of, so they can't be mad at me if I'm caught. Grabbing my ringing phone quickly, I'm glad my parents bought me a private phone line for my birthday. Answering, I smile. Petzy does care, and he did check in. Petzy questions my health, and asks if I'm still living. I speak sarcastically, uttering reassuring words to him, but I'm honestly happy he cares enough to call. And when he is satisfied, he says his simple goodbye as we end his conversation.

I see the man again. He stares at me from the corner as He waves his ghostly hand. Why does He come to me? What does He want from me?
I close my eyes, trying to leave Him absent from my room, yet when I reopen my eyes He sits at the end of my bed.
Quietly, softly, He hums to me a lullaby as I slip into a comforting trance of early childhood. This lullaby is familiar, yet I can't place it.
I lie here with my cigarette burned to the filter, creating a stench hidden by beautiful streams of white fading smoke, while He sits at the end of my bed watching me write.
Who called on this man to enter my soul? Was it a guardian angel, or a friend? Why has He come to me again? Why does He always return when I show Him such little affection?
I should probably stop writing now because it seems a little rude writing, trying to ignore the man who waits at the end of my bed for something from me, I think.

Last night I decided to do something. I was holding my diary and pen and I tried to stand from my bed but my knees buckled and I fell to the floor. I remember just as quickly as I fell, He stood and picked me up delicately in his arms. Placing my limp arms around His broad shoulders, I finally felt a sense of tranquility in the night.
He carried me to the washroom and filled the tub with warm relaxing water while He stared at me. Eventually, He placed me in the water, with my body slowly stripped by Him and cold, but once in the water I became startled by my situation.
Massaging and cleaning my body with a sponge, He gently caressed my breasts and thighs, and I remember it felt heavenly. I had never been bathed before by a man, and I couldn't believe how good it felt. I felt relaxed and beautiful.
Once again, I felt an intense internal déjà vu with Him while I was bathed. Who is this man who touches my skin with delicate lips and hands?
After a time with Him in the bath I began to feel my eyelids grow heavy. I remember I tried to fight it but my body took control, and slowly I fell into unconsciousness...

This morning, I am alone. There is no one around. All is quiet.
Once again, I am lying painlessly in my bed, while my hair is wet, and my skin in damp, and I don't know what happened.
But as I rise from my bed and peer out my window I see him. He is tall and dark, waving His ghostly goodbye again.
I am still alive somehow. And as I remember Him, I wish He had kissed me goodbye. I find I already miss my dear stranger.
April 1996
16 years old

CHAPTER 2

Looking at my makeshift ashtray, a coffee tin cast off, I'm surprised. Who knew someone who doesn't *really* smoke could smoke so much. What the hell am I doing?

I think I'm sad, or scared, or maybe just struggling with the fact that this was our beginning. I don't know, but I'm glad my neighbors can't see me, or even smell me from the angle of the garage window toward my back property. I think my whole neighborhood would be shocked to see me like this.

Sadie Hamilton would never be chain smoking in her garage, lying in a lounge chair in her pajamas by 10:40 on a Saturday morning. Sadie Hamilton should be dressed, on her way out shopping, antiquing, or going to a sporting event with her husband and son.

Rising from my lounger, I know I have to get dressed, and I want to get dressed. I need to be as normal as possible for this. I have to remind myself I am normal, and I *can* do this.

Why did I always sign my own journal with my name, the date, and my age? Why did I think that was so important at the time? I didn't want anyone to ever read this book. I didn't ever want this to be found, and yet I signed, dated, and submitted my age to each entry. I don't know why I did that, but it's hard remembering clearly my younger me. It's hard seeing my younger me through these older eyes. It's hard seeing my teenage writing, and my teenage tear stains in the blurred ink on the crinkled pages of this journal.

*****

Dressing, I think I'm surprised I look the same as I did when I woke up this morning. I don't really feel the same. Actually, I feel a little nauseous, which I think is to be expected for someone who hasn't had breakfast, and for someone who drank an entire huge thermos of coffee while chain smoking. It's funny how I did that for years with no effect, yet now I'm nauseous.

Looking in the bathroom mirror as I brush my teeth, I'm relieved to see I still look the same as I did earlier. I've always been attractive, not gorgeous, or even stunning, but attractive, yes. I still look young, and I take care of myself. I eat properly and though I don't work out at a gym, I do go for long brisk walks every single morning before my husband leaves for work, and once again in the evening when my son is settled into bed. And so far, these walks are all I've needed to keep my body at a low weight without having to do much more, though I'm sure as age creeps up, this too will change.

Waiting at my front door, I'm not sure what I'm waiting for, but I feel something forcing me to pause. Jumping, my house phone suddenly rings, and running for the phone I can't wait to hear his beautiful little voice.

"Hello?"
"Hi, mommy. We're here at auntie's chalet. I miss you."
"Her chalet?" I grin.
"Daddy says it's a chalet, not a cottage, and that people who have these chalets have lots of money so they get to call them chalets, not cottages, if they want to. Right, Daddy?"

Hearing my husband in the background makes me smile. He is so good with our son. He is always so patient and loving, and I'm really happy they're together for their first 'alone' trip, though alone is really not the case with all my husband's relatives around. I'm sure they feel they're alone though without me there to mother them and monitor everything, like I tend to do.

"What are you going to do first, baby?"
"Hot chocolate." And there's my little boy. Forget the skiing, and all his cousins and aunts and uncles, and even his daddy, my baby is headed right for his aunt's world famous hot chocolate.

"Okay, but don't drink too much. You're going to be skiing and running around and I don't want you to get a sore stomach, okay?"

"I won't, I promise." And then there is the silence I know of my son. He hates speaking on the phone, so he always just waits for the other person to speak so he can answer.

"Okay. Have fun baby, be safe and I'll call you later. I love you very much, Jamie."

"I love you, too. Here's daddy..." And that's it. My son is gone, probably running for his Aunt Mary's delicious hot chocolate.
"Hi. We made it, and he talked my ear off the whole time."
Smiling, I knew Jamie would. "He's excited."
"I know. But man, he can talk. What are you up to?"
"I'm not sure yet. I was going to go grocery shopping, then clean the house later. I think it'll be a boring weekend for me, so I'll probably call you way too often."
"No problem. I like talking to you. But not now, Jamie is already forcing Brady to take him outside, so I better go. Have fun. I'll call you later."
"Okay. Have fun, but please watch him okay? I'm very nervous he'll get hurt."
"I know Sade, and I'll watch him. Nothing'll go wrong, I promise."
"I know, I'm just scared..."
"I have to go, but try to relax. I'll call you every hour, okay?"
Smiling, I know he will. "Okay, have fun."
And that's the end of our call. My husband and son are safe, and I know they'll stay safe, but I can't stop my fear. I need Jamie to be safe. I need Jamie.

Walking out to my car, I see the Nickels family across the street with football equipment. Ugh, I don't think I'll ever be okay with Jamie playing football- it's just too violent. Not that hockey isn't bad enough, but somehow it feels less violent.
Waving at her, Karen waves back looking exhausted. She has 3 kids which means sports, and meals, and house-keeping, and mothering for 3 kids, which looks to me like it equals pure exhaustion. I don't envy that kind of manic existence because I like my life.
My life is almost entirely quiet, with only Jamie's voice in my house, which I never get enough of. If he isn't speaking with me, Jamie plays quietly, and my husband watches television in the lower family room which I never hear. So thankfully my house stays pretty quiet all the time. We even had a clock in the living room that tick-tocked too loudly which I hated, so we replaced it with a totally silent clock.
I really hate noise, especially ambient noise. I hate when people jingle keys or make the change in their pockets rattle, or tap their fingers or feet for no reason. It just seems so stupid to me. I always want to tell them to stay still and enjoy the quiet like I do.

*****

Driving toward the grocery store, I'm just not in the mood. I'm not sure what mood I'm in, but a grocery store seems like way too much work today. I don't want to, so I'm not. Turning toward the coffee house I love, I wait in line and order 5 extra-large cups of my favorite coffee to go. I can always microwave them later when they've cooled.

Once I've left the coffee house I know what I want. I know I want more cigarettes. I know I do, but I'm scared someone will see me. We live in a huge city so the chances of being caught are slim, but I find myself driving far away from my house anyway.

Finally stopping in the next town over, the suburb of our city, I pull into a gas station. Asking for a carton of smokes seems wrong, so I ask for 8 packs of smokes which IS actually a carton, but the attendant doesn't correct me, instead just handing over 8 packs for me to buy. Neither of us said the word 'carton' so it feels different somehow, maybe even okay.

Arriving home, I pick up my carton of 5 coffees, and my noncarton carton of smokes and enter my beautiful home. I love my home. It's colorful, but soothing, and I love the silence of my home.

Walking into my kitchen, I leave my four extra coffees on the island, and walk to my bedroom. It's only 12:30 and I have a whole day ahead of me for this.

Undressing out of my nice appropriate public clothing I throw my hair in a ponytail, and change into a t-shirt, my comfy leggings, and a huge sweater. The weather is sunny but definitely cool, and since I've decided to spend my day in the garage, I should probably dress for warmth. God knows, a damp, cool garage can wreak havoc on muscles.

Entering my garage, sitting back in my lounger I light a smoke, exhale slowly, swallow a gulp of my favorite coffee, and simply relax.

I'm not sure what I'm doing and I'm not sure why I think I have to do this today. I'm not sure why I'm doing this today, but I think I'm ready today. It's time.

Exhaling again while getting comfortable in my lounger, I finally open up my silken teal blue journal.

My Dear Stranger II

Last night I awoke to my dear stranger again. Quietly and peacefully He stood, watching me sleep as He had so many times before.
My stranger is so beautiful, yet I think He is completely unaware of the pain and loneliness I feel when I'm alone. Each time He visits, the tranquility I feel with Him is overwhelming, but too great to live without once He leaves me- as He, Himself has become too great to live without.
No harm, nor upset comes from His visits, only love and adoration surfaces. And though I wait patiently for His visits, and each visit becomes more intense than the previous, still I feel only at peace when He comes to me.
I began to cry as He wrapped His warm arms around me, giving me a sense of wonderful strength and security in His warmth. Many nights have been spent in my stranger's arms, as His strength sets my pain and anguish free. Without words, He lets me know He understands and loves me, as I love Him.

After an hours' worth of tears, I found myself drifting easily asleep with less heartache and misery than before His arrival.
But once I was asleep, the dreams of sadness and loneliness conquered all the happiness I had previously felt with Him. Yet as I woke with my heart racing, and my tears dripping down my face, my stranger stood over me smiling, holding my hand in His own.

Gently, He placed a cool wet cloth across my forehead and softly kissed my lips. Raising a glass of water to my mouth, His eyes mirrored my image, which caused me to become upset once again. I looked horrible, but still I knew He loved me- all there was to me.

I feel He was certain my fever would break, yet I could see the concern and fear in His eyes. For the first time I saw myself give to Him all the reassurance and love which He had always given to me. Within this reassurance given, tears trickled down my pale cheeks, because I became tragically aware that my dear stranger was not invincible. Like myself, He too had fears, though He chose never to show His own vulnerability to me.
Whether through conceit, or simple intelligence, I knew He would never again let me see His face of fear and vulnerability because it has become His quest to heal all my fears and sorrow. After only minutes of smiles and peace within a warm

hug, I began to fall asleep as my dear stranger knelt by my side.

I am convinced that it was at that precise moment of sleep, with His gentle smiles, and delicate kisses that my fever finally broke. With Him by my side, I finally became well.
I often wonder if my dear stranger is only a continuous dream within a dream. Yet as I awoke this morning with a dry facecloth on my pillow, and with lips fully quenched, I knew He had come to me again.
Filled with love and hope, I will await His peaceful return.

April 1997
17 years old

Smiling, I remember that night vividly. I remember feeling loved. I remember His beautiful concern and I remember how He cared for me. I was sick with a fever and my parents were away again, but I wasn't alone. He came to care for me.

I really don't know how many times He visited. My memory likes to believe it was every single night but I know that's not true, because my memory also feels all the loneliness I felt when He didn't visit me at night.

Rising from my lounger, I stretch my aching back and find one of the patio furniture pillows to help the ache. Looking at my gross makeshift ashtray, I think I'm shocked by how full it is. What the hell do I do with it now?

Seeing a grocery bag with a muddy pair of sneakers in it, I throw the shoes in the garbage and empty the coffee tin into the bag. My husband won't see the bag low in the garbage bin, and I'll make sure there's plenty of garbage on top to hide it.

Finishing the last of my first cold coffee, I contemplate grabbing a second, but I want to space them out. It's only early afternoon, and this day may become long for me yet.

Sitting back in my lounger with the pillow placed behind my back helping me sit up better, I'm ready. It's time.

*****

Reading the first lines, I'm struck with the strangeness of my writing as a teenager. I was a 17 year old young girl, and I wrote such descriptive words within a poetic style. I remember at the time NEVER wanting anyone to find this book. I remember my constant hiding of this book until I found the absolute best spot ever for it. I remember how much time and effort was spent keeping this special silk book out of the hands of others, and yet I also remember wanting it to sound adult-like and intelligent.

I remember that. I remember looking up a few words to be very descriptive or dramatic. I remember using my thesaurus. I remember thinking I needed to relay this information intelligently, like an adult would so it would be taken seriously. I remember wanting to sound like an adult with my words, but I didn't know the actual reason why at the time.

It makes no sense to want to fake your own 17 year old speech patterns for a book that you never, ever want anyone else to read.

But I remember now. I remember why I faked an intelligence of speech that I honestly didn't have at age 16 or 17.

I thought I was going to die young.

I was sure I would be dead within a few years. I was sure I would die, therefore, I wanted to sound adult and intelligent when I described my relationship with Him- just in case.

I didn't want anyone (especially my parents), finding my blue silken book to think I was a child living a bizarre life with an older man. I wanted them to know I was an adult too, should my book be found when I was dead.

I was sure I wouldn't survive a few more years, so though I didn't want anyone to find my book while I was living, I did want them to be impressed with it should it be found when I was dead. I wanted my book to sound mature and poetic and beautiful when it was finally found after I died.

Death.

Again, I functioned almost exclusively within the realm of death. The thoughts of, the reality of, the knowledge of... my death.

I was sure my death would be young, and I was sure it would be an awful death. So I spent my reality surrounded by thoughts of my post-dead memories for others, and how to carry them forward positively to the few people in my life.

I wanted to be loved, respected, and thought of fondly in my death. Therefore I wrote in a romantic, poetic manner all which my young life tried to comprehend in my living world.

Everything I wrote at the time was not *for* that time, or even for myself. Rather, everything I wrote was for my post life non-reality which others might find and read after my death.

My Dear Stranger III

Last night, I saw my dear stranger again.
Slowly, gently He waved His ghostly hello from the dimly lit street below. Strangely, I felt slightly threatened, though deeply loved, as I watched through my bedroom window as He approached.

Minutes later, I crawled back into my warm bed and fell asleep easily, once all the confusion, and memories of painful screams fell dead, immediately upon His arrival.
It's so strange to me that my heart knows when He has come to me.

Throughout this sleep, nightmares of loneliness and injury haunted my rest until I woke to my dear stranger standing over my bed. He greeted me awake with a warm smile and a gentle touch, as He had so many times before. And in that moment I knew He would never harm me, but only love and fill my heart with the great love and security I have come to know only through Him.

The time He spent watching with understanding eyes, as my heart bled and tears fell, allowed me to know without words that He felt my pain. Each time He has visited, His presence fills my heart with hope and wonder as to our future, because my stranger knows me, and He knows all there is to see in me, and still He loves me and returns. Inevitably, I find sleep easier and peaceful when He comes for me.

So again, I fell asleep with His eyes watching and protecting, only to awake in a bubble-filled bath of soothing relief. Softly He bathed and massaged my body, as only He could. And as each time before I felt no embarrassment nor insecurity with Him, I felt only pleasure from His gentle care of me.

Once bathed, He carried my damp body back to my bed, placing me gently under my soft sheets. And then it happened!

My stranger began kissing my body, softly, sensually, filling my body with an ecstasy to rare for words. His hands were so gentle and comforting as He touched me as I had never let anyone touch me before. With His fingers He explored me and entered me until His body edged into mine. His kisses lasted an eternity, while His embrace felt warm and inviting. He touched me and kissed me, and I found myself bracing for more.

Staring up at my dear stranger I noticed for the first time He appeared to want to speak to me, though when open, no words escaped His lips. Only a loving smile was able to reach me- a smile so beautiful I welcomed him into me, because my dear stranger was so new to me last night.

Hours later I found myself completely content as I watched His silhouette stand and easily walk across our bedroom to the same corner He always watches me from. And watching Him, I realized the love I felt for Him in that moment was simply overwhelming. I couldn't contain my love for Him. Crying gently, I felt myself falling asleep while He watched me from across our room. Once again I found myself slipping into unconsciousness within my blood stained sheets, as His eyes watched me silently.
And though my dear stranger is still a mystery to me, as He waved his ghostly goodbye I found myself anxiously waiting for His return.

And this morning I don't care that my virginity is gone, and I don't care about all the pain I had to endure for Him. I barely remember it now. I don't even care about all the pain between my legs this morning. I remember when I cried out in shock and pain He gently covered my mouth with His mouth to take in all my pain. I remember how He took my pain into His body as I struggled with His size thrusting inside me. What an amazing thing to do for me. He loved me enough to force my pain into Him as I screamed and fought His painful intrusion.
October 1997
17 years old

*****

Well, that was the beginning. That morning I was never going to be the same. I couldn't possibly know then what I know now. I couldn't even comprehend what was to become of my life. I don't think a 17 year old virgin is able to understand the complexities of a sexual relationship. I know I wasn't able, though at the time I honestly believed I was.

Reading my words now, I still don't honestly understand our beginning. There are words floating in my mind. There are labels for the act. There are bad words associated with what happened that night, but I still can't say them or think them because of what became of us afterward. I find our lives were never easily labelled.

I can't help but wonder about us now though. I can't help but wonder; if the start of a relationship is forced but the situation of the force changes, is the relationship still tainted forever?

CHAPTER 3

Standing, I feel cold. Its afternoon on a cool day but I still feel very cold. My limbs are achy and my skin feels tight. Maybe the sun is no longer beating down on the garage brick. I don't know, but I think it's time for another hot coffee.

Entering my house, I suddenly feel like something's wrong. Turning and checking the front door, it's locked as it should be, but I jiggle the locks and double check anyway. Turning to the windows I begin making sure every single one is locked on the main floor. Walking into my kitchen, I pull on the sliding glass doors, but they don't budge. Pulling out the metal door safety bar, I place it in its slot against the bottom of the glass, and feel better. Looking, I decide what the hell, and pull out my huge butcher knife to rig above the glass doors, just in case. Surely the knife will fall on an intruder and if not impale him, it will certainly scare him into not entering my home... I hope.

Walking down to the basement next, I check the bars on every window to make sure they're secure as I reengage each lock. When I'm done I know the main floor and basement are totally secure. Upstairs, I turn off quickly and reengage the alarm system for everything, including the garage glass-break sensors, except for the actual garage door into my house. When each of the 42 panels, minus the garage door are red, I exhale.

I'm not sure why I feel like something is wrong, but even after checking everything is as it should be, I still do.

In my kitchen I place my second coffee in the microwave and decide a bathroom break is needed, and my teeth definitely need a good brushing. I have that awful smoky, coffee breath nastiness going on and my tongue feels thick with it.

I wonder why I'm smoking. I mean I *do* smoke once in a while, like when I'm super stressed, or nervous about something, I might have one or two, but that's usually every couple months, and certainly not frequent enough to think of myself as a smoker again. Today is different though. Today feels like I need the nostalgic comfort I once gained from smoking, so I'm happy my husband isn't around to see me.

Oh! My husband. That's what I'm forgetting. Crap. After grabbing another sweater to fight off the cold I feel deep inside, I run downstairs to the answering machine. Shit! There are 6 messages.

"Hi Mommy, I'm good and safe. Daddy says hi." Oh, his voice. God, I love my baby's voice.

"Hi Mommy, I'm done skiing for now, but Brady and Tyler say I can go again later with them and the big kids. But Daddy and Aunt Mary and Aunty Kim will be there to. Where are you? What...? Oh, daddy says hi again and wants to talk to you... but it's not mom, dad." Still listening I hear the shuffle on the phone. "Hi honey, we're good, and Jamie's having lots of fun. Mary wants you to call her later about a food trick she learned for Jamie because He. Wont. Eat. His. Veggies..." I can almost hear Jamie groan. "Anyway, we're going to go into town soon for an early dinner, but I'll call you after. We miss you."

When the phone suddenly hangs up, I miss them terribly. I've never been away from my baby, and beside the very infrequent medical conference, I'm rarely away from my husband either.

"Hi Sadie, its Randi from Dr. Marlott's office. I'm just calling to remind you of your dentist appointment on Wednesday. I hope you have a great week-end. See ya next week."

Yuck, I hate the dentist. Even though my dentist is a nice older man, it still feels gross going to the dentist. I hate the feeling of being trapped in a chair with a man over me, in my mouth, while I struggle to not obsessively gulp and gag as he fumbles in my mouth- especially when I want nothing more than to push him away from me. I really hate the Dentist.

"Hi Sadie, its Meg. I'm not sure what you're doing later, but Mike and I have decided to have a last minute get together tonight. Bring Jamie if you want, Melissa and Morgan will be home to play with him and to watch him while the adults have a little fun. Anyway, let me know if you guys can make it. Sorry for the short notice, but I needed to do something tonight, and I decided a small party was what I needed. I hope you guys can come over. Call me and let me know either way. Thanks."

Um, nope. No little get together with the '4 M's' as they call themselves. To deal with all her sickeningly perky and all her imaginary competitions with me over everything, I need my husband for sure. I think even my 6 year old realizes Meg is just too much for anyone, but especially for me.

"Hi honey, where are you? Jamie says hi again, and he's so hopped up on junk food, I don't think he's gonna sleep at all tonight. We're back from our dinner and I thought I'd check in. It's weird that I haven't heard from you all day. Usually you call me all the time, even when I'm around the corner, so this is a little weird for you. Are you okay? Call me Sade."

And he's right, I usually do. I love my husband's voice. I don't know why, but I always call my husband to hear his voice. I call him when he's at the store. I call him when he's at work. I call him sometimes if I'm upstairs and he's downstairs. I don't know why, but I always need to hear his voice. I love my husband's voice.

Grabbing the phone, I sit at the kitchen table and dial my guys.
"Hi, honey. How are you?"
"Good. Where's Jamie?" Suddenly, I'm just desperate to talk to my son.
"He's right here. What's wrong?" He's right there. Good. Okay.
"Nothing. Sorry... I just miss him. Are you still having fun away from the old ball and chain?" I grin.
"Yup. It's been great without *her* around," he laughs at me.
"I can see that. But can your old ball and chain speak to her son now?"
"Sure. But I want to talk to you before you hang up with him, okay?"
"Sure."
When I hear Jamie called, I finally relax. Everything is okay now. Jamie is safe. And hearing him talk in the background, I smile. My son can talk and talk when he's excited.
"Hi, Mom!"
"Whoa. Hi. How are you? Are you having fun?"
"Yes! Brandon and Brady and Tyler are taking me outside to build the world's biggest snowman, and I'm not tired at all. So I don't have to go to bed yet, Aunty Kim said so because she's making a big fire in the fireplace with real wood. Not like ours with the button on the wall, but a real fire and we have long steel sticks to make s'mores, and I ate all my dinner, but I'm really hungry, so I think s'mores is a good idea to fill my stomach before bed like you always want me to do so my stomach is full when I

sleep, so I don't ever feel hungry, right?" I can't help but grin as he tries to justify s'mores as his bedtime snack.

"Um, I don't think s'mores before bed is the same thing as toast to fill your tummy, but for tonight it IS okay. Just don't think this will be your new bedtime snack, okay?"

"Okay..." And I can almost see his pout.

"Have fun making the world's biggest snowman, but make sure you tell an adult if you start to feel cold, okay? I love ya to pieces, Jamie."

"I love you too. Daddy wants the phone now." And that's it. I hear the phone placed on maybe a table from the clang, and I hear his little voice running away.

"Hi. What are you up to?"

"Nothing. Cleaning," I lie. "He's pretty jacked up, huh?"

"Totally. Every time I turn around he's eating something sweet, or drinking juice. I finally had to give him the mommy look about a half hour ago when he picked up another brownie. I think that's it though until his bedtime s'more," he laughs.

"Uh huh. You know he's going to try for that bedtime snack every night for the next week, don't you?"

"Yes, I do. What are you doing tonight? Anything good?"

"I think I'll pamper myself in the tub, then watch a movie."

"That sounds good. I'll call you when Jamie goes to sleep so you can say goodnight, but I'm warning you it's going to be much later than 8:00. And as his dad I've given him permission to stay up late and reckless with his cousins. Okay?"

Smiling, I know he's teasing me. "Okay, but just remember you get to deal with the cranky, tired kid tomorrow."

"Done. I love you, Sadie."

"Love you, too. Have fun."

And that's it. My son is fine. My husband is watching him closely, and they're having fun. I can relax a little. I want them to have fun, and I want them to be safe, but a small part of me hates the fact that they're having fun there without me. It's like I'm expendable, like they don't really need me to function like I thought they did. I feel like they don't need me anymore.

Okay, I'm being stupid.

Grabbing my nuked coffee I make my way back to the garage. And settling in, I light a smoke, lift my knees to tuck my sweater around my legs for warmth, and I begin again. It's time.

*****

My life during these years was almost a bi-polar existence.
During the day I lived life like a typical teenage girl. I survived by spending all my extra money on clothes and makeup. I had the best shoes and killer purses. I bought endless CD's and I went to the mall every week-end with my girlfriends. I was normal... on the surface.

But then I had my other life. I had a male lover who greeted me in the night. I had a man who came to me and taught me the act of being with a lover. He was a man, and I was his girl. He loved me and I waited every night to be loved by Him.
Every single night I showered, shaved, and wore only my best pajamas to bed while I waited in the night. My parents probably thought I was vain or too obsessed with cleanliness, but I didn't care what they thought as long as they didn't know the truth of why I had a marathon shower every single night before bed.
 If I went out with friends I always came home and did the same thing. I kept my nightly ritual, whether I crawled in at 2:00am drunk, or was home on a school night going to bed by 11:00 for an exam the following morning. I didn't care what time it was, I showered, shaved, and dressed for him each and every night before bed.
I was lucky that my parents really didn't care what I did. I was lucky that their bedroom was across the upstairs landing, with the bathroom on my side of the house so they couldn't hear me hop in the shower every night regardless of the time. I was lucky they weren't that observant, but I wouldn't have cared anyway. My only concern was making sure I was always physically ready for Him to come to me.
I was half crazy with the need for Him, and I was always edgy at bedtime waiting for Him.
I remember when I had my period I would freak out every night. I was lucky that my period was always very light, usually lasting no more than 4 days, but for those 4 days I could think of nothing but my period at night. I was so scared He would come to me when I had it. I was so scared He would come to me and I wouldn't be able to do anything with Him. I was young enough that my period was still embarrassing to me, and not something I could easily discuss with anyone, but especially with Him.
For years, I HATED my period because it had the potential to stop me from being with Him.

In hindsight, I realize He only came to me maybe once a month, or sometimes even less frequently than that, but my anxiety for Him was so great I couldn't imagine not being prepared and ready for Him should He actually arrive on any given night.

And so I obsessed with my personal hygiene, and I always prepared my body for Him to love, in case He came to me in the night.

My Dear Stranger IV

Last night my dear stranger came to me again. It had only been a few weeks without Him, yet His arrival was just as thrilling for me as each time before. When I awoke to His shadow standing over me, I couldn't help but notice His disappointment as the companion beside me lay asleep completely unaware of my visitor.

Quietly, I stood and took my stranger's hand, leading Him outside. The cold, soft breeze sent shivers up my spine and though it caused my nipples to grow instantly erect, I wasn't embarrassed or ashamed.
I looked into my stranger's eyes- the eyes I had come to love and worship, but they were new to me. They looked so sad and betrayed, and for the first time I felt I had truly hurt Him with my actions.

Within seconds, a tear trickled down His cheek as I wrapped my arms firmly around Him. Once in His arms, we both began trembling as we warmed each other with our love.

Minutes seemed to turn to hours in His embrace and with each passing moment a new emotion surfaced, until I felt the need to confess to Him.

And I spoke. I told my stranger of the great love I felt for Him, and I told Him of the tremendous pain I feel each time He would leave me and fade into the night. I explained that I felt no harm from His visits, but only relief and reassurance. And I admitted that the only misery I felt came when He would leave me.
Once seated in each other's arms, wrapped so tightly, I began to explain my

companion's presence in my life. I spoke of the physical closeness this boy brought to me when I was alone, but that there was no sexual intimacy. I told my dear stranger that my heart and soul were given completely and only to Him, but sometimes I felt very physically lonely, so I allowed the boy to lay with me.

With these seemingly apologetic explanations, a beautiful smile surfaced on His face, replacing all tears previously fallen. I knew He understood, as only He could understand all my mistakes and anguish. Mistakes which ultimately kept me from sleep on many nights such as this one.

And with His smile came the most beautiful sound my mind had ever heard. It was the sound of my dear stranger's voice. I had finally heard His lovely, soft voice speak my name out loud.

The cold dark night with its whispering breezes also heard His voice speak my name, so magical was this moment between us.

In the near two years of His visits no feeling or touch was as perfect and fulfilling as the moment His voice rang out into the cold winter night around me. When He began speaking to me, my heart felt an even greater love- a love I thought never possible. My body ached for His touch, and all the loneliness I often felt disappeared at once. His soft lips kissed mine passionately as His gentle hands touched my skin, allowing me to feel all the pleasure between us. With few words, He told me of His complete, intense love and acceptance of me. My dear stranger also explained how this love we share will never change nor die, no matter what I do to hurt or destroy it.

And though I know we experience a love so rare, hearing His words utter this truth caused my heart to bleed and my tears to fall. I knew we could never be together physically but that our hearts and soul would be together always. And this truth of our love brought upon the painful reality I had chosen to ignore. We will always be together but we will never BE together.

With these final words He kissed my tears away and held my hand close to His heart. Slowly He stood and with another beautiful smile, I knew He would be back for me soon. I knew He would again take me away from all the misery, and He would return to love me, as only He could.

Once down the street, He turned and blew one final kiss goodbye for the night, and at once I felt such guilt and shame toward myself, thinking of the boy sleeping in my bed- a bed which craved only my dear stranger's touch.

And though the walk to my room took only seconds, these seconds gave me a chance to forgive myself as my dear stranger had.

Once he had woken, I asked my companion to leave peacefully and when questioned, I told him of my undying love toward my dear stranger. A love no man could ever fill, nor understand, and I again begged him to leave me.
And when my companion left minutes later I stripped my bed of its sheets and rested painlessly on my bare mattress thinking only of my dear stranger's love as I dreamt of His next visit and slowly fell back asleep, alone.
February 1998
17 years old

*****

I remember that boy. He was popular and I was popular, and it made sense. We made sense.

My parents were away again. They were traveling as always, and I was very lonely. I remember one of my friends telling me Kyle wanted to date me. I remember being confused about being wanted by him. I remember my girlfriends thinking I was stupid to not invite him over, especially since my parents were away again.

And so I did. I called Kyle and invited him over. I remember being afraid he would want sex, which I didn't want. At all. But I also remember that I didn't want to be alone anymore because my stranger hadn't visited in the night for quite some time.

And so I invited Kyle over, and I was desperate and pathetic. I was trying to be a posh adult. I raided my parent's liquor cabinet and found champagne. I bought strawberries and h'ordevres. I bought a sexy little negligee. I was trying to be anyone but me.

When Kyle arrived a little after 8:00 he was pretty drunk already. And as he entered our family room, he tried to kiss me but I casually moved just in time. A half hour later he kissed me while we looked at my dad's music collection together but his kiss was gross, sloppy, and I remember he tasted of stale beer.

When I brought out the champagne and strawberries he chugged from the bottle as many eighteen year old boys would have, but I was unimpressed and depressed. We didn't feed each other the strawberries while sipping champagne like I had imagined. We didn't gaze at each other with passion and intensity. We weren't posh adults, and we weren't romantic lovers.

Eventually, I worked up the nerve to ask a very drunk Kyle to come upstairs with me, which he did. We walked upstairs side by side and entered my spotless bedroom together. We each paused on the side of my bed, and then he passed out- just like that. The second he stumbled to my bed he was out cold. I remember being surprised someone could sleep so easily and so quickly, no matter how much alcohol they had drank.

I drank all the time. I was drunk often, but I could never easily fall asleep.

Anyway, I changed into my negligee to feel adult and sexy and I curled up against a passed out Kyle for his warmth. I lit a smoke and exhaled deeply any disappointment I felt. I was disappointed that the night wasn't filled with adult intensity and passion, but I was very relieved too. I didn't want to have sex with Kyle and I was afraid I would give in if he had tried, just so I wouldn't be alone anymore.

But that's the end of our story until He visited me.

And I was lucky. He forgave my almost infidelity, and Kyle was a good guy about the situation when I woke him and asked him to leave.

And at school on Monday Kyle told everyone what *really* happened, not what could have but didn't happen. Kyle admitted to all his friends that nothing happened at all between us. He actually admitted he was too drunk to do anything and that he was sorry about it. And I was relieved again.

As far as anyone knew I was a virgin which was important, because in high school sleeping with someone, even once, could be a life sentence to Slutdom. Unless the relationship was a long high school relationship, a girl putting out was a slut- plain and simple. At least according to the standards of my uptight school, she was a slut.

So Kyle was a good guy and my reputation was saved. The only drawback to his honesty was I became more sought after. Boys became way more interested in me because I 'might' put out. I was a good girl, but I *might* become a bad girl with the right guy. And so I was suddenly more popular with the boys, which annoyed some of my girlfriends- as catty high school girls typically feel when someone else gets some attention.

But after the Kyle debacle I never dated another boy from school again. That was the choice I made. Girlfriends pushed for other boys, some in high school, some even in college, but I abstained. Never again did I date anyone.

And for prom I went with Kyle under the absolute understanding that we would not be having sex, nor even making out. And he was cool about it. I even joked with Kyle about one girl who WAS slutty wanting him. So at the hotel that forty of our friends rented after prom, he left us to go have sex with her while I got drunk with my girlfriends. And that was the end.

My young life continued filled with my huge secrets hidden. And no one ever knew about my strange, often lonely, little life.

CHAPTER 4

My Dear Stranger V

Last night as I lay asleep, dreaming lonely dreams, my dear stranger once again came to my room. His visits have become more frequent than just even months before but the excitement and passion was just as great with each visit.

When He sat on my bed the sense of elation I felt became overwhelming. I wanted His delicate hands to touch my body and I wanted His sweet lips against mine. Looking into my stranger's eyes brought upon such intensity and fulfillment, I barely felt sane.

Within seconds, He took me into His warm embrace and rocked me gently as my heart pounded and my mind raced from my terrors. I wanted to hear His voice. I wanted Him to love my body as only He could. Yet He did nothing.
For hours I stayed silent in His arms as emotions rushed to the surface, often creating tears and just as often smiles. I wondered how my dear stranger could bring upon every emotion with no words, but with only a gentle touch.
Soon after, I felt tears trickle down my face and I realized His eyes cried for me. His tears tasted like sweet wine on my tongue and His heart seemed to bleed with each tear of my own.

Finally, I asked Him why He cried but no words escaped His lips. Looking closer at His eyes I saw such sadness.

Suddenly, my stranger grabbed me and forcefully pushed me flat on my bed. With His eyes looking wild, He pushed my pajama bottoms down my hips until He gasped and stared at my thighs. Oh god, I tried to fight Him. I tried so hard to pull away. I grabbed for my blankets and I grabbed for His wrists. I tried to push His face away but He was just so much stronger than me. So I just stopped fighting.

As my stranger looked at my thighs, I cried. What else could I do? What could I possibly say? I didn't know how to explain away all the marks.

So staring at the wall I whispered, 'I'm sorry.'

When He gently turned my face back toward Him He no longer looked wild. His face had calmed. His eyes weren't crazed or sad. He simply looked at me fully as only He could. He looked at me completely.
Raising an eyebrow, He once again asked without words.
'Um, I don't know why. I didn't mean to do it. Sometimes I don't even know I do it until I'm bleeding or until I kind of wake up to what I've done. I don't know why, I really don't. Sometimes I don't even remember picking up the knife, or the razor, or the sharp things. I just see it after and I kind of feel better. I don't know. Um, I don't know what to say. Are you mad at me?'
God, I was so desperate, but He didn't speak.

Frightened, I stood and held Him in my arms, rocking ever so slowly, humming the numerous tunes He had always given to me.

The last few visits He had seemed sad and confused like myself. He no longer looked to have the impossible strength which used to comfort me in the night. He seemed so sad and terribly weakened.
Immediately following these tears, my dear stranger stood and took my hand into His own. Together we danced to the darkness of night, and I knew we were completely together once again.
Seconds later, He raised my chin, wiping away any trance of tears while I looked into His eyes, until suddenly His voice rang out.
And I felt ecstatic. My heart began racing once again. I wanted so desperately to hear His words of comfort and reassurance.

When He finally spoke, my stranger told me of our love so rare, and of the felicity achieved by His visits through our passion and surrender. And He even admitted He was often frightened by the intensity of our love, but He wouldn't change it.

And this confession left me bewildered, though completely sympathetic, for I too felt this same fear.

After those few words, He gently placed my body back into my bed and left me for mere moments. When He returned He once again stripped my thighs of my blankets and slowly, gently, He began cleaning my wounds. Once He seemed satisfied with my care He rocked me until I fell asleep.

When I awoke this morning, my heart ached for my dear stranger and for all the hope and love He gives to me. I feel embarrassment for what He saw and I feel a heavy sadness in His absence, but with swollen tear-stained eyes I wait for Him, knowing He will return to me soon.
April 1998
18 years old

*****

I was cutting myself often then. I couldn't really control the urge to cut myself, at least not when I was alone at home. Sometimes I did it at school with my metal ruler down my thighs, or sometimes with my keys, but usually I could refrain at school so no one could see what I was doing.

At home alone was different though. At home there were too many implements available to me. Alone at home there were too many sources of release. Alone at home there was too much freedom to refrain from fixing myself.

At home, I could sneak my parent's alcohol and drink alone in my room, or I could use the knife under my bed to cut my legs until I felt better. So I did.

I don't know why I had to do either, but I know I always felt better afterward. The minute I felt the physical pain and saw the blood I was instantly better. If I was stressed, or tense, or scared or lonely, it helped. And afterward I was distracted from my feelings because I had to take care of the wounds. I had to focus on hiding the injuries. I had to think about what I would say if someone actually saw the wounds, so I was distracted by mending my body and focussing on any explanations I may have to come up with as an excuse. The wounds were a release and an escape for me.

Thinking about it now, I'm pretty sure I wasn't a 'Cutter' though. I didn't cut myself because I liked it. I didn't crave the cutting itself, but rather the feelings that occurred afterward. I think I just used cutting myself as the means to the release I needed.

If there had been anything else I could've done I'm sure I would have tried it. And alcohol helped. So if my parents were away and I could get drunk in my room, I did that for the release I needed instead.

But I know I was never a Cutter per se, I was just an escapist who used cutting as the means to the end.

CHAPTER 5

Stretching my arms overhead, I'm aching. I have no idea what time it is, or how long I've been in the garage. I feel like I just started this thing, yet I'm pretty sure I've been at it for a while.

Walking into my home I realize a bathroom break is definitely needed and another coffee is mandatory. I'm cold and tired, but I really want to finish this tonight.

After nuking my coffee and using the facilities, I realize I've been at this quite a long time. I don't know the actual time of night, but I'm sure it's nearing midnight. I should probably check my messages, but I don't really want to hear Jamie's sweet little voice tonight, especially knowing I didn't wish him a goodnight at his bedtime, which would also be another first for me.

I have never been without my son, and I have never not fed him at bedtime, nor tucked him in and kissed all over his little face before he slept. I have never been without my son, and after this weekend I know I never want to be without him again. Jamie is mine, and I love him too much to ever be without him again.

Grabbing a blanket from the hall closet, I wrap it around my waist and prepare for more of this. I know I have to complete this. I know I have to get this done this weekend. It's time for us.

Entering my garage, I'm a little disgusted by the smoky smell but I ignore it. There's always time to air it out before my guys return to me. So grabbing one more outdoor pillow I prop it in the lounger and sit back down while sipping my favorite coffee.

Thinking about my past is weird for me. I don't really feel like this was my past because my present is so different. Everything in my world is so wonderful now. Everything is totally planned and scheduled, and I don't ever walk around aimlessly like I did back then. I know these were my earlier years but I feel very much removed from them.

This is a very strange feeling for me, but eventually I light another cigarette and settle in for more. It's time.

My Dear Stranger VI

Last night as I screamed within my nightmare panic, your haunting image increased my suffering. I wanted you to be with me. I needed you to be here for me.
I have moved again. Unsteady in my homes and unlikely to stay for long, I have moved once again. Yet, with the move before you had found me. Creeping quietly into my room, gently into my new bed, you finally came home to me.

When you found me you smiled at my fear. When you found me we held each other in my new residence. Should I again fear your absence with this move? Should I question your ability to find me? Should I question your love? Should I cry as I wait for your arrival?
I want to smile at my insecurity but I can't. Where are you? Where have you been for so long? What has taken you so long to find me?

Together, we have never been so absent from each other. Love used to hold us so close. Each challenge and each brutality strengthened our love. You used to cherish each moment we spent together. You adored my neurotic insecurity. You comforted my pain. You caressed my untouched body. You pushed my inability to express myself. You loved my body. You loved my breath. You loved me, completely.

My tears are again streaming. My mind is again screaming. Where are you? Why have you not come to me?
Time endures. Days are blurred. Your absence depresses. My life is pain filled and my heart suppresses… this agony.

I will attempt sleep once more, though I know this sleep can only be torture and pain without you here as you haven't been for more than half a year.
I love you and I miss you, my stranger, my dear.

November 1998
18 years old

*****

I had started college by that time and I had moved out of my parents' home. I was alone, officially. I was now completely and totally alone in my own home.

It's funny to me now how I thought of that time as being truly alone, but in reality I had always been alone. I had an independence my friends didn't have, but envied. I had an independence from the emotional attachments some friends needed with their parents. I didn't need friends or family, and I never needed attachments... except to Him.

And I remember that apartment so well. I loved it. It was the perfect apartment for someone like me. It was in a small building, but a four-square type building with a landing in between each neighbor therefore we were only beside one other neighbor, allowing for a certain amount of privacy that I loved. And with very high ceilings and thick walls, I never heard the neighbors above or below.

It truly was a wonderful apartment for someone like me who wanted her privacy desperately.

So I was officially alone, but my friends from high school still visited and partied with me. They came over. They drank with me and danced and sang. We were young enough to still feel like kids partying like adults. We felt young and free and we loved the fact that one of us had an adult apartment to party in. So we partied. And while I partied I faked being a typical 18 year old very well.

I drank with my friends, and I acted like any other 18 year old girl on the surface. I was normal. I went to college and I came home and crashed in the afternoon to prepare myself for all my friends arriving at my door by 8:30 to start pre-drinking before we hit the bars we loved with the fake ID's we cherished.

And overall I was truly okay. I was lonely at night, waiting on His visits, but the loneliness of the days were filled superficially with being 18, hanging out with girlfriends, drinking in the evenings, and having a certain amount of fun to occupy my time.

But my nightly ritual continued. I showered and shaved, while I waited for Him to come for me. I begged in my bed and I cried in my living room. I said pseudo-prayers, and made deals with god. I was desperate at night. I was the desperate version of myself that I hid in the day from my friends. I was always waiting for Him to come to me with a desperation that was numbing.

I was always waiting with a certain anxiety based on fearing He didn't know where I was. When my parents moved the year before to a nicer home around the corner from our previous home, I was afraid. I thought for sure He wouldn't find me. I went into full panic mode every night while I waited to tell Him of our quick move. I waited but didn't see Him again before we did actually move into my parents' new home.

Amazingly, the very first night of our move He came to me though. Amazingly, He knew where we were and He came to me happily. He came to me that first night and I didn't have to suffer the *what ifs* or the *oh no's* of Him not knowing where I was. He came to me immediately after that move.

Yet this move was different. I had lived in my new apartment for nearly 4 months and He still hadn't come to me. I spent every single night torn up in knots of anxiety based on the fear of His absence. I spent 4 months with the same hygiene ritual, waiting for the night He came to me. I waited each night for my stranger to come back to me.

Until finally He did come to me.

*****

My Dear Stranger VII

As always desired, my dear stranger came to me last night with opened arms and a beautiful smile. Waking from a light rest, I was delighted to find Him in my room waiting for me, as I often wait for Him.
This visit I so desperately needed, because my heart ached, and my body craved my stranger's touch. I had felt like He hadn't touched me in years. And though it had only been a few months since He had last come to me, I was unsure and frightened that my stranger no longer knew where I lived. Upon my quick departure from my house I was unable to tell Him of my move because of the suddenness with which I had left. However, with no reason to doubt, He had known where I now stay and He had come to me once again.

Moments were given to only gazing at each other, as our eyes filled with tears of joy. For me, my stranger is so unbelievably beautiful, I find I often have no words to describe His strength and love for me. And I have tried. I have tried to describe this great man in this book, but I have yet to find words which can describe with worthiness all that He is to me.

Jumping from my bed in a desperate attempt to feel Him, I ran into His opened arms as He held me so tightly. When our lips kissed passionately time stood still for us.

Slowly my stranger lifted my gown and stared contentedly at my naked body. Touching and caressing, His hands roamed my body as only His hands could- As only His hands I would allow.

He cupped my breasts gently as His eyes held my own. Gently, He held my back and laid me onto our bed. And in that moment I felt so anxious, my body trembled and my breath became short and hard. God I loved Him, every part of Him.

He began touching my skin slowly like a gentle interlude as to the pleasure that was to come for us. He kissed me slowly down my nape, around my breasts, teasing my erect nipples with His tongue. Moving slowly, my stranger made His way between my legs. And frightened, I held still. I trust Him completely, and I trusted Him then, but I was nervous by this intimacy. Silently, I held my breath as He opened me up with His fingers.

When I felt His warm tongue move around my body as His fingers plunged inside me I found myself moaning and crying out for His love. Never could I have imagined this feeling. Never could I have imagined this pleasure. There was something so brutal in its beauty for me. That moment between us was something I couldn't understand, but I didn't care. I didn't care because love and trust plays such a powerful role in this amazing passion we share.

After a time, with my body heightened and sensitized beyond my ability, I begged my stranger to love me. I begged Him to make love to me.

And as the intensity of that moment had nearly given me over to climax, His lips devoured my body and His tongue left only a trail of eroticism in its wake. Eventually, my heart raced and my soul screamed out for Him, as my orgasm flowed freely for Him. Hours escaped from the world and they stayed only between us.

Weakened, my heart beckoned for my dear stranger as my lips covered His entire body. I felt manic and intense as I grabbed and kissed Him everywhere, but no love making occurred.

Staring once more into my eyes, my stranger smiled as one beautiful tear fell for me. And I knew how He felt. Sometimes our love just couldn't contain itself. Often my own heart felt like it would explode, or simply stop from the intensity of our love.

Eventually I realized I had been repeating over and over, continuously in a gently whisper, 'I love you, I love you, I love you...' until He lay down beneath me, wrapping His arms so tightly around me.

Finally, after minutes of silence I heard His beautiful voice speak to me as he whispered, "I love you as well."

His words. God, those five words echoed in my mind, creating a hallucinatory effect on me. Suddenly crying within my happiness, He held His arms tighter around me, and feeling such tranquility within His embrace, I found sleep was inevitable.

When I awoke this morning to a bright warm sun, my smile gleamed like that of a small child, but my heart ached too. I could still feel my stranger's arms holding me tight, safely protecting and loving me, even in His absence.

God, He is so beautiful to me, words could never describe, and I love Him more than my own life.

Rising from our bed, I will hold His memory close as I wait for my dear stranger's return.

January 1999
18 years old

Oh, I remember that night. I remember Him loving me like that. I remember my shock at the act and my shock at my reaction. Before that night I didn't know what oral sex felt like and I didn't know how amazing it could be. But I remember learning all my firsts with Him.

And it really was amazing. Even my memory is as clear as it was then and I can still feel it. I remember the desperation, and the building, and the fear, and panic, and then the insane, ultimate release. I remember screaming and crying and pulling Him to me. I remember it today as it was then.

And I know I have never had a feeling quite like that since Him. Of course I have felt, and I have experienced pleasure, but not like that. I have never had that kind of intensity with another. I don't even know how to. I'm much too reserved in my adult life to release like that, and I'm much too adult to submit to a pleasure as carnal and physical as that release was for me.

Remembering that night I'm suddenly aware of myself and my surroundings. I'm stunned to find myself on the edge of orgasm, with my hand in my leggings and my knees wide on the arms of the lounger and I'm almost there. Thinking back, I remember the intensity of His eyes as He watched me come undone. Watching, He waited until I was barely coherent before pushing me over the edge. I remember the feeling... *Oh god...*

I can't believe I've just orgasmed and released in my garage in a lounge chair. Laughing, I'm a little stunned at my behavior. I hope I was quiet. Oh god, if my neighbors heard me I think I'll have to move. My husband wouldn't even believe me if I told him what I've just done and why we have to move. Actually, he wouldn't believe any of this at all. Nothing. None of this.

God, I need another smoke. A total cliché I know, but the truth nonetheless. Horribly embarrassed, I have to use the little sink in the garage to wash my hands of my release, and drying them on my huge sweater, I shake while lighting another cigarette.

Pausing, with a cigarette in hand I just can't seem to stop myself. I need another hit of Him.

My Dear Stranger VIII

Last night my dear stranger came to visit me. It had seemed like an eternity since we last touched and I feared He had lost my love far away, but finally He had returned to me.
Quietly, He crept into our bedroom, as I awoke slowly to His gentle kisses on my thighs while His head lie nestled between my legs. Slightly startled I stared at Him as I settled. Moments faded between us until finally He looked into my eyes

in return. And oh, my stranger's eyes were wide and clear and no sadness came with Him, only His love was present in His eyes.

Kissing my thighs, His mouth made its way up my body. Slowly, tenderly I shuddered with sheer excitement. How long had it been since His kisses? How long since His warm embrace held me tightly?

Moving slowly toward my lips, my stranger lifted my silken nightdress off my shoulders as our lips met. Crawling until He towered over me, He kissed my lips and eyelids, while my heart pounded under His touch.

The cool night air brushed against my skin hardening my nipples, while sending a shiver up my spine. And I watched Him smile at my anticipation.

Pulling me upward gently, straightening His legs around my waist, my stranger met my smiles with His sweet kisses. Stripping my stranger of His clothing, I touched His chest with my anxious fingers as we stared at one another, until suddenly my dearest lit a lone candle next to us.

And though the light was dim, I felt something new. Something of panic. Something I had never felt before with my dear stranger.

Tightening my grip on His waist I lowered my head as I tried desperately to hide my breasts and stomach, and my face. I was desperate to hide all of myself. Confused and looking a little saddened by my sudden insecurity, my stranger gently raised my chin as He stared deep into my eyes. Moving my arms to my sides, He smiled a beautiful reassuring smile, as He touched my breasts and kissed my lips once again.

Gradually looking down at my naked body, my stranger helped me feel beautiful in His eyes again.

Leaning backward, I rested my head upon my pillows as I watched my stranger touch and love my entire body.

My stranger's firm yet delicate hands held my neck still as He slowly eased downward. Across my breasts He teased my nipples. Resting His head upon my stomach He kissed my navel until His tongue eased lower and His hands roamed. Suddenly, my body thrust uncontrollably with near climax against Him as His fingers entered me quickly.

My stranger then pulled me upward, watching my face carefully until I sat in front of His sculpted body- a body which had come to please me, as no other could. Sliding His hands under my body, He gripped me firmly, lifting me gently, while lowering me onto His body. With eased penetration, I moaned and grasped for His body as He held my gaze so intensely.

And the ecstasy I felt was amazing. Every part of my body, every sense, every *muscle felt Him within me. Stretching and burning, I felt Him engulf me. I couldn't remove the smile from my lips even as we kissed.*

Our eyes were wide, looking for one another's soul. Our hearts were pounding in sensual rhythm. But all I felt was His body deep inside me.

My dear stranger was gentle and loving. He touched my body softly as I rocked against Him and cried out in pleasure. Tears began trickling down my stranger's face as we grabbed and held each other so close.

Eventually, I lied backwards as He moved His strong legs back so He once again towered over me.

Bracing His arms and kissing my lips, we danced to each other's desire with thrusts and sweet sighs.

And no pain was felt. No laughter was cruel. No insecurity resurfaced. Just beautiful love-making occurred as hours were spent together.

With His hands so gentle on my body, I screamed my climax as I kissed my stranger and groped at His flesh. Nothing could have been more perfect last night. Sometime later, holding me tightly against His chest my stranger leaned on His side and carried a flower up the back of my thighs, across my backside, as He gently caressed my bare skin. Placing the flower against my lips, I turned and kissed Him with such passion, I felt my heart actually swell within my chest. After long soothing kisses, I felt my body growing weak as my eyes grew heavy. And after receiving one last sweet kiss from my stranger, I fell quickly asleep in His arms.

When I awoke this morning I felt the same momentary loneliness and confusion following all His visits. As always my heart ached for His delicate touch and soft kisses. Confused, I panicked for a moment wondering if He had come to me at all, or had the memories been merely another dream of Him in the night.

However, when I picked up my folded nightdress, a sweet smelling flower fell from the silk and I knew my dear stranger had come for me, as He would again soon.

February 1999
18 years old

And those were our times together. Countless. Endless. I was only 18 years old but I made love like an adult. I never suffered the backseat shame my friends did. I never lived through the drunken debacles of my peers. I was a teenage woman who made love with her adult lover.

And no one knew. I was the pretty, popular, smart, fun girl who got drunk at college parties but kept her legs tightly closed. I was a challenge to some and a mystery to others. I was Sadie who didn't put out, but had fun regardless.

I lived in a strange world where everyone thought I was a prude and a certified virgin for life, but I knew the truth. I was loved and adored. I was a woman who understood passion with a man, and making love with a soul mate.

And then my world ended.

CHAPTER 6

After the Attack

After the attack he walked away with a clean conscience and dirty hands,
While I crawled painfully in dirt.
I begged, he laughed.
He taunted, I screamed.
I fought, he won.
He was victorious, I died.

After the attack he was left with satisfaction and hate filled denial.
While I was left with a desperate reality to deny.
I pleaded, he punched.
He hit, I hurt.
I struggled, he oppressed.
He was victorious, I died.

After the attack he stood and walked easily away with a grin,
While I was left to walk without ease covered in his sin.
I detested, he loved.
He adored, I hated.
I begged, he deafened.
He was victorious, I died.

After the attack few words were spoken but horrendous thoughts threatened,
While I lay in silence and neighbors listened.
I tired, he strengthened.
He overpowered, I cried.
I decayed, he replenished.
He was victorious, I died.

After the attack he began a new loveless challenge,
While I contemplated my new loveless existence.

After the attack, he was victorious... as I died.
And now I am no more than a small broken i.
August 1999
19 years old

If only my sad words had been able to adequately express how I had really felt that day. If only those sad words on the tear-stained page could have adequately expressed the absolute anguish I had felt. If only I could've told people what that day had really been like for me. But I didn't have the words for the people. And I didn't have the words to write on paper. There were no words I could write to adequately express that day. And there were no words I could speak to give voice to the horror of that day.

People tried though. People tried to help me.

My parents stepped up and offered help. The police offered help. The Doctors offered help. The therapists offered help. Everyone offered assistance but I couldn't be helped.

I was gone.

*****

Looking around my garage I'm disgusted with myself. I stink and I'm dirty and I should really stop this. This doesn't change anything. Opening another pack of cigarettes doesn't change anything. Reading another page doesn't change anything. Nothing changes anything. I know I should stop, but I just can't.

Walking back into my home, I use the little washroom near the front door and scrub my filthy hands, but I refuse to look in the mirror. I don't want to see this sad Sadie. I am married, and wonderful, and smart, and an excellent mother. I am not that young Sadie anymore.

Microwaving another coffee, I flick on the outside light and stare at my yard. The pool is closed up for the winter and the backyard looks lonely without all the furniture on the deck. My backyard looks lifeless. Funny, my back yard looks a little like I feel right now.

I'm missing something.

When the buzzer sounds, I grab my favorite coffee and slowly make my way back to my garage.

Stopping I decide to make sure. Checking all the locks on all the windows on the main floor feels good. I'm being secure. I'm taking care. I'm being smart. Running downstairs, I double check all the bars are in place and all the windows are locked by unlocking and locking them again just to hear them engage. Looking at the closest of 8 main panels in my house, I see all 42 lights are red. Everything is armed except the door into the garage from my home. Everything is as it should be.

Now, I can proceed to my lounge chair.

Opening my smoky garage I decide to open the side door, just a crack. I know I can't be seen unless someone walks way down the side of my garage, just inside the fence gate. I know that, but I'm still nervous someone might.

I cannot have someone see me smoking in my garage. I can't have anyone see me like this. I know I don't look the same right now, and that's okay. It's okay to not look the same when doing this. I know I don't really feel the same while I'm doing this either. I know that, and I'm okay with that. I think I'm rational enough to know that anyone under these circumstances would look and feel a little off. Anyone would feel tired and gross when finishing this. I rationally know it's okay that I probably don't look very good and I'm okay with that right now, but I still don't actually want to be seen looking tired and gross. That is not okay for me.

My Dear Stranger IX

Last night my dear stranger came to my bedside once again.
Waking from a light rest, my attention was drawn to His eyes- eyes so lovely and filled with hope, instantly my own eyes wept. Instantly, i reached out for Him, as His arms drew me tightly into His embrace.
As time passed, my stranger did nothing but hold my weeping body. A body so recently damaged and brutalized, i had thought i could never recover. But then He came for me.

But my mind began a whirl-wind of questions. Questions i didn't speak but mentally obsessed over. i wondered if He knew what had happened, and if so, i wondered how much, or how little He actually knew. i wondered what He had felt when it happened to me, or what He felt when He had found out. i wondered what He thought. i wondered if He had bled as i did, or if He had screamed when my body screamed. i wondered if He felt the sadness and humiliation i did. i wondered if He felt the desperation and horror i did. i wondered if He felt the same about me now, as He once had.

Such a whirl-wind of questions, my heart broke once again. And though i had desperately wanted Him to come to me, i must admit there was a part of me, a very small part, which felt resentment toward Him.
Why had He not protected me? Why did He not know of the events and stop them before i was left to scream? Why had He not come sooner? Why had it been nearly 2 months since His last visit?
Such a whirl-wind of questions and resentment, my mind lost consciousness.

After nightmares of the brutal events, my body lay battered and torn on my sheets. Healed bruises ached and invisible scars bled. My heart raced as my tears and sweat collided on my face. And during this panic, my dear stranger watched.

Once i collected myself and focused my tear-filled vision, i saw in the corner my stranger's face looking somewhat sad, and yet still so filled with peace. Looking i was astounded.
Looking, i suddenly became enraged!
How could He looked sad yet peace-filled at the same time? Did He feel sad for my torn body but filled with peace for His own flawlessness? Why did He look at me so simply?

Finally, i screamed...
'What is it? Why are you looking at me that way? Where have you been? Why didn't you help me? Why didn't you SAVE me?!'
Tears poured down my face and my lungs gasped for air. But my stranger just watched me and said nothing in reply. A few minutes passed and slowly He walked back toward me.

As He sat on my bed, again i collapsed into His arms and wept. With my face buried deep in His chest, He rocked and soothed me into silence.
Minutes later my stranger kissed any trace of my tears away. Within His warm embrace, all my anger and sadness faded away, as i was slowly filled with the security He had always given to me. Slowly, a peaceful calm engulfed me. And in that moment i knew i was still alive, and the world remained audacious.

Resting in His arms, i knew in moments such as these, during His visits, i was safe. No brutality would threaten and no hands would savage. Knives could not graze my skin and my panic would eventually settle. My stranger was here and for the first time since the attack He would protect my body and my mind.
His visit was once again thrilling, yet it was completely different from all His other visits. i didn't crave His touch, and i couldn't be with Him sexually. And with no words, He understood not to touch me intimately.
Hours were spent as i wept away the memories until i fell soundlessly asleep- a sleep which i knew would lack the horrific realities i had lived through while His arms held me tight. It was a sleep of dreamless unconsciousness...

When i awoke this morning, i felt warmed and a little more stable. Sadness carried less weight and my humiliation slowly turned to anger. i felt lonely and i actually missed my stranger's embrace, but i was happy to feel a little stronger. Breathing in the morning, i know my dear stranger will wait for my return into our world, just as i will await His next visit.

October 1999
19 years old

*****

I remember that time. I remember what I felt like. I couldn't talk to anyone anymore- I trusted no one. To be fair, my friends did try for a while. They put in the time. They made the calls and they attempted a few visits, but I refused to see them. I refused to talk to them. I refused everyone because I trusted no one anymore.

He was my friend. And he was vicious.

He said unbelievable things as he hurt me. He made confessions of love. He confessed his insanity for me. He said every single thing every single woman ever wants to hear under different circumstances, in a different situation. He loved me. He adored me. He was *in* love with me. He wanted to have a life with me. He wanted us to be together. Forever.

He was my friend. And he was brutal.

I think that's what I struggled with the most. The act was brutal, yes. Within any reality being forced is brutal, I know that. But it was the brutality in which he took me and the instruments he used, the scars he left, the injuries he caused unnecessarily, all while telling me he loved me.
And that was my struggle. He was my friend who I trusted and I have been encased in my confused shame ever since.
I could never understand what I did to provoke it. I was a good girl, and I treated everyone well. I was fun and young, yes. But other than hugs hello or goodbye, I never touched anyone or allowed anyone to touch me. I never dick teased or flaunted any sexuality at all. I hung out with friends. I drank and danced and laughed and had fun. But I was a good girl. I was *always* a good girl.

He was my friend. And he was deadly.

He was a friend I trusted, and he did the unthinkable. He confused our friendship with love. He confused my simple hugs with a want for more. He equated unrequited want with the need to force my love. He was confused, and I became lost.

And so I pulled away.

I didn't discuss what happened with anyone after the first day I lived with it. I told the Police about the factual events. I told the doctors and the nurses about the factual physicality's of the events. I told my family the basics. And then I never discussed it again.

I lied to the Police and said I didn't know who he was. I told the Police he was waiting in my apartment. I told the Police he was an unknown intruder because I didn't know how to discuss what really happened. I didn't know what to say, and I was afraid of telling the Police the truth- I had opened the door to my FRIEND. I had allowed my friend into my apartment *because* he was my friend. But I didn't want what he did to me.

I didn't discuss my friend, and I didn't tell the whole truth. I didn't know how to tell. Everyone I knew knew him. Every single friend I had knew him well. And I was afraid. I thought others might blame me for letting him into my apartment as a FRIEND, not knowing what was about to occur to me. I was afraid people might think I wanted his love originally but that it got out of hand. I was afraid no one would believe me. I was afraid people would think each scream, and each hit, and each kiss, and each moment of force was what I wanted. But it wasn't. So I told no one who he was.

I told NO ONE the truth of who hurt me because I was afraid, and I trusted no one anymore.

And it was okay because my family had a very successful outlook on life- Don't talk about it and eventually it goes away until it never really happened in the first place. And I was glad for that outlook. That 'don't acknowledge it so it never really happened' outlook saved me from discussing the un-discussable.

But to be fair, my parents did try to help. They offered counselling, and they offered to have me move back into their home. And when I refused to move back home they helped with the security issues in my apartment.

They are good people, just not the best parents, but they have never really been neglectful. They aren't wealthy, but they are certainly comfortable. So I never went without, nor did we ever really struggle. We three were just comfortable, and this comfort was what I had known my whole life.

So I stayed comfortable. I told what happened because the Police already knew what happened based on my neighbor's account and based on the physical evidence left all over my apartment. The Police knew, so I closed off my emotions and I told them accurately what had happened. I told them everything I could, except his name.

And then I stopped speaking. I didn't speak of it, and I tried to make like it never happened.

I think my denial of events ironically helped me move past them eventually.

CHAPTER 7

Lighting my hundredth cigarette I'm a little stunned by my sudden image of my parents. I think I see them differently than I used to. I think they may not have been quite as good as I thought they were when I was younger. Or maybe because I'm a really good mom to Jamie I think they aren't as good as I thought they were. But maybe it's only *because* I'm such a good mom that my parents seem less so. I don't know. But I do feel a little differently toward them since the birth of Jamie, I think.

Sitting here thinking about my parents I feel a little uneasy. I feel like I should be mad at them, or tired of them, or indifferent toward them at the very least, which really I think I am. I think I am indifferent toward my parents, almost sadly so.

I'm not sure how I feel, but regardless if the feelings I have are positive or negative, I think I'm mostly indifferent. I don't think I cared if they lived or died, but not in a bad way. They were just my parents, and though we were never particularly close, they did seem to care for Jamie enough to acknowledge his birthdays with huge presents and lots of fanfare when they weren't traveling.

My mother was the second wife for my dad; a slightly older man who had had a wife and child before her. But my mother was smart. She had me immediately, to secure her place with my father. She was smart because she birthed his only daughter and then never had another. She was smart to quit when she was ahead. And it did work out. My parents were actually pretty great people. They were well-liked by many, and they had a very good life together. My mother picked the right man to 'trap', because she somehow knew that they would actually love each other past a forced marriage. And they did.

My father had his previous life before my mother, and then he had this life with her, and rarely did the two mix. From what I understand, my father's first wife was a high school sweetheart he fell out of love with within only a few years of marriage, but he stayed for their son. He stayed until he met my mother. And though it seems like my mother was a home wrecker, apparently my father's first wife was relieved when he finally left her as well.

From what I understand she moved on quickly after my father and she too is very happy with her second husband.

And so it all worked out. When I was born I had a teenage half-brother I really didn't know, but I had 2 parents who loved each other very much.

Overall, I would say I had a good childhood, though a childhood often lonely because of the independence they gave me so they could be independent *of* me.

And so I chose the 'don't acknowledge it so it never really happened' outlook of my parents about everything in my life. I chose to ignore that which hurt me so that it would eventually stop hurting me.

And as I said my friends did try after the attack, but I couldn't really understand them anymore. My friends were young. They still partied. They still got drunk at college parties and slept with strangers. They still acted like fools, and that was okay. I was happy they could just be normal. I was okay with wishing them well. I was okay with walking away, because I wasn't a party fool, I didn't feel normal, and I didn't trust anyone anymore anyway.

I remember a month after the attack 3 of my girlfriends showing up at my apartment unexpectedly. They brought alcohol and lots of smokes. They planned to help me out of my funk. They planned to liquor me up, make me get on with life, and they planned to make me live again.

Or that's what I thought, at least from what they first told me.

In reality, within 45 minutes of them drinking heavily, skirting around the giant issues I had, they laughed, gossiped, and talked about shopping, parties, and the guys they wanted to bang, to my discomfort. They all talked and I listened silently. They all talked about all things every girl our age talked about and I sat silently with nothing to add.

And then it happened. My one friend Cassie just blurted out, "So what happened, Sadie?" And as I froze she continued. "Seriously. Like, what happened? I mean I know you were raped and cut up, but what did he actually do to you? I mean, if you don't want to tell me actual details, fine. But I just thought maybe you would want to tell your best friends what happened. So you feel better or something..." And then she waited. They all waited. Carey and Heather sat there with their smokes, and drinks, not talking, or moving, or really even breathing, I don't think. With wide eyes, all three of my high school best friends sat waiting for me to tell them what happened.

But before I could react or freak out, or speak even, I looked back at Cassie and she was almost bouncing in her chair. She looked so excited about the potential of me telling her all about what happened. She looked so excited, and in that moment I realized I had never been more hurt by a friend in my life.

Staring at Cassie, I couldn't speak. I was shocked and tired of my life, and just hurt. Yet just as quickly as the hurt hit me, I became angry. Looking at her wide, expectant, gossip-laden eyes, I was disgusted with her. I hated her in that moment. I hated all three of them. I hated everyone anyway, but now I officially hated my old girlfriends as well.

Taking a deep breath, I asked the question calmly. I wanted to embarrass her. I wanted to embarrass them all. I was angry, hurt, but mostly, I was disgusted.

"What would you like to hear, Cassie? What details do you want?"

And looking, I could see she was a little uncomfortable. She thought for only a second before stammering, "Oh! I don't need any details, I just thought maybe you wanted to tell us, to help *you*. That's all." But she blushed and gulped, so I knew she was caught. I could see her trying to get out of looking like an insensitive bitch to me.

Bracing myself, I actually found my voice and as I stood and leaned over my table I yelled with that voice. I couldn't even control my voice if I had wanted to, because I had no control in that moment.

"Well, Cassie. Thanks for the offer, for MY benefit. I appreciate your kindness, really I do. So here you go. He raped me, fought me, fucked me, cut me up with a knife, but he didn't stab me, because he didn't want to 'hurt' me. He was just a little out of control when he casually flicked at my body with the knife. He-"

And then Heather jumped in and tried to stop me by calling my name, but I continued anyway.

"So he nicked and cut me, but not on my face, well, except for the little one above my lip, but that was an accident. He didn't mean to cut up my face, because he thought I was pretty, but when he grabbed my mouth to kiss me on the kitchen floor, he mistakenly nicked me above my mouth with the knife, until he threw it on the floor beside us. Then he proceeded to make me kiss him, over and over again, even though I struggled and pushed, and tried to turn my head away from him over and over again, until he finally got mad and punched me hard in the face. Right here Cassie!" And turning my cheek toward her I grabbed at the side of my temple and cheek to show her, even as Carey jumped up from the table and started walking toward my front door to grab her purse.

"So I was a little out of it by then, but I remember still screaming and fighting as much as I could, but it was hard cause I'm kind of small and my arms were really weak and he was sitting on my legs so I couldn't kick him or anything, but-"

"OKAY! I'm sorry. I didn't mean-" Cassie screamed, but I cut her off again.

"No it's good! This is for MY benefit, *right* Cassie? Anyway, he bruised me all over and torn my clothes, and then he picked up the knife again and tried to cut off my pants and underwear- that's how I got this!" I screamed as I raised my shirt and showed her the dark red line down the side of my hip. "And then I remember him hitting me again really hard in the face and actually in the stomach which made me not breathe very well, and then he told me he loved me. That I really remember. He told me he was in love with me, Cassie. He actually said that. He said 'I love you, Sadie. I really do.' And then he hit me again when I couldn't speak and he told me he loved me again and then I remember-"

"Fuck! Okay Sadie, I'm sorry! Nevermind! If you're gonna be a fucking psycho, forget it. Fuck this!" Cassie yelled back at me as she grabbed her booze and smokes and started getting her purse ready to leave.

But I couldn't stop. "What's wrong, *CASSIE?* Too much information for you? You don't want to miss the best part. Honestly the best part comes next. There was a dick and a wooden spoon handle involved. There was more punching and lots of other stuff! Don't you want to hear it?" I screamed to her back as she was almost opening my front door.

"Fuck you! You're a fucking Psycho! Maybe you deserved what hap-"

And that was it, I screamed as loud as I could as I ran for her. Making contact I began hitting and punching Cassie even as Heather hit me and Carey tried to pull me away from Cassie. I was out of control for the first time in my life, well, at least physically. I was absolutely blinded by my rage wanting to kill Cassie. I wanted her dead in that moment. I really did.

But the tables quickly turned and I suddenly had to fight Cassie, Heather AND Carey in my hallway. I found myself fighting as best as I could. I tried to do everything I wasn't able to do to him. I kicked and punched and bit. I think I even head-butted Heather. I don't know what I did, but I was deranged and getting really tired, very fast.

And then, unbelievably, Patrick pushed my door open and he shoved Carey back and ripped me from Cassie's arms, even as he yelled and kicked at Heather to get the fuck out of my apartment. He went ape-shit crazy defending me. He looked as out of control as I felt.

Gasping for breath, I tried to fight my way back to them, but Carey and Heather were out the door fast, and Cassie was seconds behind, pausing only to snatch up her purse from the floor in the hallway, but Patrick didn't stop.

Patrick went completely He-Bitch on them, screaming and swearing, and spitting at them. Yelling in the doorway while the three girls kept screaming about me all the way down the stairs, even as Patrick yelled right back behind them.

Trying to focus through my adrenaline delirium I heard Patrick yell, 'twat waffle' and I was stunned silent. Becoming slightly coherent, I heard a final scream of 'Fucking Psycho' I think from Heather which had Patrick dive for the banister to yell, 'Fuck off! You cock juggling thunder cunt!' back at her.

And then he exhaled and smiled at me. He actually turned off all the verbal sparring in a fraction of a second, turned and smiled at me like nothing was wrong. He smiled like he had fun. He smiled like the events that just took place were nothing at all.

Stunned once again, I leaned against my doorway and smiled back.

Holy shit! I had no idea what just happened, or why it happened, or how it could happen. I had never been in a fight in my life. I had never hit anyone in my life. I didn't even know I was capable of fighting, but somehow I kind of felt good. Well actually, I felt like shit, and my body ached everywhere, and my head was pounding and my hands shook and hurt, and my face was killing me, but mentally I felt pretty good.

Patrick looked me over, straightened my shirt, took my hand and led me back into my apartment. He locked and alarmed my apartment like I needed, then he walked us back to my kitchen table, sat me down and said, "We need a drink."

Looking at him like he was insane, I just smiled and nodded as he grabbed my vodka and poured us each a huge half glass of vodka with a drop of orange juice, handed me mine and walked into my bathroom. Joining me seconds later, he began wiping away the violence from my face with a cool, wet cloth as I sat silently watching him.

When he lifted the glass to my mouth I remember flinching as the Vodka burned my lip even as I gulped down half the glass.

Sitting beside me, Patrick breathed, "that was fun..." and I burst out laughing because unbelievably, it WAS fun. I don't know how, and I'm not supposed to like violence or fighting, but up until I started to lose the physical battle against my three friends, I did enjoy myself. Illogical or not, I couldn't deny it. Actually, I still can't deny it. Attacking those three bitches was fun for me. Lashing out at them was enjoyable that day. And though I haven't really fought someone since, I remember that physical battle with a kind of pride, because I almost held my own, and I almost beat them. I almost knocked Cassie on her ass for being a total fucking bitch, and it felt good.

Smiling, I remember that day so vividly. Patrick made me lift my shirt to my bra so he could look for any bruises, then he stayed the rest of the day with me. We ordered a pizza, had a few more drinks, and we watched a movie together.

Hours later, beside me on my couch, Patrick tugged my hair lightly and asked, "Do you want to talk about earlier?" To which I whispered, "Not really..." And that was it. He asked me and I answered, then he dropped it. He wasn't looking for gossip, and he wasn't fishing for the scoop. He was just a friend who asked in case I wanted to talk, and he dropped it immediately when I didn't. He was never a Cassie in my life.

Patrick was amazing, and he made me feel special to him. I had really only known him at that point for a month. But for that one month he had pushed his way into my life, invaded my solitude, and after that day I wanted him in my life as a friend, even if some days it seemed otherwise.

Only one month in, Patrick was willing to go all He-Bitch on three girls just to defend me. He defended me without knowing why I was fighting with 3 girls in my apartment, and I adored him for it.

A short while after he had asked, I finally spilled, by my own mouth the events and why I went psychotic on my old friends. I told him about Cassie fishing, and I told him what she tried to say about me deserving it. I spilled and Patrick listened until he eventually smiled and said, "Good for you, Sadie. They're fucking bitches and I hope you never speak to them again." Which I never did.

And so after a time I enrolled back in college for the second term, left my apartment infrequently- except to go to class. And I continued, alone.

My phone stopped ringing, and my friends stopped dropping by. I assume the rumors of Psycho Sadie made the rounds. I was alone with the exception of my one male neighbor who always stopped by- unexpectedly and frequently. He stopped by and he was male, but he was gay, so I was safe from him.

My neighbor Patrick stopped by frequently, and though we never discussed the attack, he did admit once that it was him who finally heard my screams and called the Police. I even learned later it was Patrick who convinced our Superintendent to let him in to clean up my apartment when I was in the hospital. It was Patrick who scrubbed away all the brutal evidence of what happened to me from 4 different rooms in my apartment. It was my gay, safe, male friend Patrick who entertained me with his frequent drop-ins, whether I wanted them or not.

It's funny and wonderful for me when I think of Patrick.

He and I lived across the hall, and other than one time when he and his gorgeous boyfriend stopped in for a quick drink after a party on a Friday night when we were all stumbling into our individual apartments drunk, Patrick and I were essentially casual acquaintances, until that day.

After that day, he never left me alone again. I woke up to Patrick in my kitchen making breakfast, and I would startle to Patrick sitting on my sink when I was in the shower as he waited to tell me some amazing adventure he had had the night before. He was safe, and he had absolutely NO boundaries. He was just this awesome, funny, charismatic, gay man who was safe for me.

Patrick was older than I was by 6 years. Patrick called me his 'pretty girl'. Patrick invited himself into my world, but he never asked the questions I was supposed to forget. Though I really doubt he had to ask for details- he did see me taken out by ambulance after the attack, and he did clean my apartment while

I was in the hospital. I think he even saw the Police remove the knife that nicked and tore at my skin while I was being 'loved'.

So I went back to college. I lived alone. I had a Patrick and his usually gorgeous boyfriend of the week for entertainment, and I stopped talking. Eventually, I even trusted Patrick enough to not be armed with a small knife in my pocket when he was in my home with me alone. I slowly learned to trust Patrick.

But after the attack I was different. I was very quiet in class. I suffered anxiety attacks in large auditorium lectures and I suffered anxiety attacks in small little rooms with bodies pressed in all around me. I started taking night classes, so I could be alone all day watching television or scrubbing my apartment, and I came home from my night classes with less night to fill in darkness and silence.

I actually preferred night classes which most would think odd I'm sure. But what happened to me, happened in the day, so nighttime wasn't psychologically affected by it. I didn't feel a psychological fear of night. Daytime was when I felt most lost.

Night was a time when I ran to my car quickly which was parked in the first spot right outside my apartment front door. I locked myself in and checked my knives under the seat and in the glove compartment to make sure they were still in there waiting so I was safe.

And after class I had male and female buddy system escorts who walked me back to the campus parking lot. Once home, I parked in my spot beside the front door, grabbed my little knife and ran for the door of my apartment. And 36 steps later I was in my alarmed apartment leaning against the door safely inside.

My dad had generously paid for an entire alarm system on every window and on the 2 doors to my apartment- the front door and the balcony door. My apartment was on the second floor of a four floor walkup, but it had a fire escape ladder attached to the end of my balcony, therefore it was alarmed too.

My 8 windows, 2 stories up were also alarmed because the old brick walkup building had decorative ledges and artistic little niches and footholds that someone could actually climb if they were so inclined. And so I continued in my apartment- anxious by day, sleepless by night.

And when I would return from night classes, I would enter and check both security panels, making sure no window nor the balcony door had been disturbed. I would continue living, knowing only my parents and Patrick had the code. Patrick- only having the code when it was installed because he scared the shit out of me the morning after it was activated.

That next morning after its activation, Patrick didn't know about it and he entered my apartment to make me breakfast. And once the alarm tripped, and after I ran at him from my bedroom with a knife, he fought me until I realized who he was as he gently coaxed me sane, calming me down until the code slipped out of my mouth as I released a post-adrenaline cry on the floor with Patrick holding my hand.

Patrick. He was the lifeline holding me afloat in the murky sea I was slowly drowning in.

I remember that time, and I know if I could have loved then, I think I may have loved Patrick forever.

*****

Lighting another cigarette and finishing my freezing coffee, I can't help but laugh. I think this is my two hundredth smoke today. My husband would have a heart attack if he could see me now.

Pausing, I think I hear someone outside my garage door. Jumping, I dive for the door and slam it shut as I twist the lock and freeze. Pausing against the wall beside the door I try to listen. Pausing, I try to breathe again.

Jesus Christ! I'm sure it's no one but it sounded like footsteps walking along the side of my brick garage. I'm sure it's no one, but it sounded like someone. I'm sure it was no one. I'm sure of it.

Oh my god... trying to catch my breath I can't believe how afraid I am. I know I'm being irrational. I know I am, but I'm scared. Plain and simple. I'm afraid and my body is freaking out with the sudden change in my mood.

I hate this fear. Thank god I don't feel it often, because this is killer fear. I'm shaking and sweating and chilled and I can't breathe very well. My heart is pumping, and my mind is racing. My hands are shaking and my legs feel weak.

Sliding down the wall in my garage, I'm trying to relax my body. I'm too tense and I'm going to get sick from the tension soon. I know I am. When I get this much intensity of fear I usually become sick until I experience a full post-adrenaline dump. I get sick from this much fear which weakens me further.

Reaching with my legs, I hook my foot on my lounger and slowly pull it towards me. Grabbing my smokes out of the little cup holder I light one and try to soothe my nerves while calming my body. I remember a smoke always helped me with this fear. I always remember using a smoke to help with the fear.

Inhaling deeply, and exhaling slowly, I sit back down on my butt on the floor against the wall, and almost instantly I feel a slow, steady spread of relief throughout my body.

I haven't been afraid like that in quite a while. That one was quick and nearly debilitating, but I only have those ones maybe once a year now.

CHAPTER 8

    I remember one of the very worst post-attack freak outs I had. It was a bad one. I remember how crazy I looked and I remember how crazy I felt. It was a crazy moment I have never forgotten.
    Patrick had convinced me to go around the corner with him to this tiny little restaurant because he had a crush on one of the waiters. And though I rarely, *if ever* went out, I always found Patrick and his begging and whining hard to fight, so eventually I gave in.
    And at the restaurant, seated in the lone window seat, Patrick proceeded to charm the pants of the waiter, or almost charm his pants off. Actually, I think if Patrick had told him to right then and there the waiter would have dropped his pants for him.
    Anyway, we did have a lovely meal, and I tried very hard to be as social as I could be with Patrick and the waiter, until it was finally time to leave. And 6 drinks later for me, and 3 glasses of chardonnay for Patrick, with one phone number for him, we both stumbled out of the restaurant happy.
    With only maybe 50 yards on the main road until Patrick and I turned onto our street I felt safe and really just happy after our fun dinner out.
    And then I saw him on the corner of our street and the main street. I saw him, but I don't really know what happened.
    I remember the event but the details are fuzzy and kind of tunnel-like. I remember the sounds of the street, and I remember the hum of Patrick's voice chatting away. I remember pain and confusion as I walked slower and slower until Patrick finally turned back to me.
    And I remember the fear.
    When Patrick began shaking my arm and snapping his fingers in front of my face I knew he was speaking to me. I knew he was trying to get my attention. I knew he was with me, but I felt nothing but the fear in that moment.
    Staring straight ahead, I was watching him watching me. I was watching him as he stood still staring at me. I was watching... until Patrick damn near broke my wrist.

Screaming out at the pain, I was shocked back into the world of the living. My attention was turned to Patrick. He and the pain were all I knew in that millisecond.

Trying to function again I mumbled something to Patrick. I think I asked him 'What did you do?' I think I asked him something until he grabbed me hard around both upper arms and shook me.

I remember looking past Patrick's shoulder but he was gone. He was no longer watching me watching him. He no longer stared at me. He was no longer there. I was alone again with Patrick and the fear in that moment almost crushed me.

I remember the hum of Patrick's voice as I tried so hard to return to him. I remember trying so hard to focus on words while I looked at Patrick's face. I remember his lips moving but no coherent sound reaching me. I remember the car taillights blurring past us and I remember pain.

Everything hurt me suddenly. Everything was on fire in my body. Everything was spinning and shaking and moving within me. And then the post-adrenaline dump hit me and I threw up on the sidewalk with Patrick rubbing my back as I hunched over vomiting.

I remember Patrick pulling me off the sidewalk to sit on a step of a closed lawyer's office. I remember sitting as he spoke words I didn't really understand. I remember the chaos in my mind as I tried to understand why I had seen the man who had hurt me at the end of our street.

Eventually I found my voice and moving slowly to Patrick as he leaned closer to me I whimpered, "We have to get home now. We have to set the alarm."

And I think it was then that Patrick finally understood. Actually, I'm sure he understood based on his sudden movements. With my spinning head and blurred vision, I watched Patrick jump back on the sidewalk, and I watched him try to find something out of place. I watched him try to find the man who hurt me

With my head still between my knees, sitting on the step, Patrick finally understood. Placing his hand on my head, with his body blocking me from the street as best as he could, he whispered, "Where is he Sadie? Do you still see him?" And shaking my head no, I just sat there trying to breathe as my world continued to spin around me.

"Let's go back to the restaurant and call the police. Now, Sadie."

Quickly taking a look back down the street I knew he was gone. I knew it. So I didn't want the nightmare to continue. I didn't want to be interrogated. I didn't want counsellors asking me questions again, and police victim specialists asking if I remembered any more details that could help find him. I didn't want more of all this nightmare.

And I remember looking back down and finally seeing myself. With a sudden awareness of myself, I was stunned. Looking at myself still sitting on the lawyer's front step I was bleeding and covered in quickly cooling urine. I had actually urinated in my pants.

Stunned, I looked at my pants and leg and couldn't comprehend what the hell had happened. And it was that lack of comprehension that finally freed me from my trance of fear.

Jumping up, my humiliation and fear drove me to race for my home. Running, I threw my shoes in front of me, bent quickly and scooped them up as Patrick grabbed me from behind.

Fighting him, I screamed to let me go. I screamed at Patrick to leave me alone. I screamed at Patrick to not touch me. I screamed and screamed until the scene blurred all around me again.

Gasping and fighting, I shoved him away as 2 college looking men crossed the busy main street to come toward us. Watching in sudden silence the scene play out, I was so afraid of the men I began running again. I ran until I could hear them yelling for me to stop. I ran hearing them yell at Patrick to stop. I ran and ran down our side street until I made my way up the front steps of our apartment.

But once there, I realized I no longer had my purse or keys and I began ringing every buzzer on the door panel. Smashing the buzzers, I waited as Patrick approached me slowly.

Whipping my head toward his voice, I saw his hands extended offering me my purse, as the 2 other men walked up to him.

And I was afraid. In that moment I was afraid of everything. I knew they might hurt me and I knew Patrick might hurt me. I knew they could hurt me and I knew Patrick could hurt me, though I honestly didn't think he would. Looking at him, with his arms still extended, holding out my keys in one hand and my purse in the other, he blocked me from the men.

Looking, I realized I wanted Patrick. Looking, I really saw Patrick. Looking, I finally understood.

Shaking my head to clear it further, and taking my keys and purse from him, I turned and unlocked the front door of our apartment.

When one of the guys stepped forward and asked, 'Are you alright?' just as he touched Patrick's shoulder I knew I had to fix this.

"I'm okay. He hasn't hurt me yet. Oh, I mean ever. We're friends. But thank you." And throwing myself into our building, I bolted up the stairs to my landing and fought my shaking hands preventing me from unlocking my front door. I fought the shakes by holding the key with both hands. I fought and eventually won as my door pushed open and the alarm sounded its warning.

Pushing inside, Patrick followed, even as I tried to shut the door behind me. Pushing his way in, Patrick was the one who disengaged the alarm then quickly reset it. It was Patrick who made the beep-beep-beeeeep sound of my reengaged alarm. And once I heard that sound, I knew I was okay.

"Don't talk yet." I told him, and he nodded as I leaned against the wall and tried to breathe.

It's hard to say if my lack of breath was because I ran for the first time in years, or because I was so out of shape, or because I smoked a pack a day, or because I was too keyed up by the adrenaline. Whatever the reason, I knew I needed silence as I leaned against the wall and fought to catch my breath.

Eventually, I turned from Patrick and entered the bathroom. Closing and locking the door behind me, I stripped off my soiled, bloody pants and underwear, removed my sweater, pulled my hair up in a ponytail and ran the shower. Looking down at my leg, I was surprised to see all the little cuts against my thigh. I was surprised and clueless as to how exactly that happened.

But once in the shower I sat on the tub bottom and just tried to warm myself. I cleaned my body and squirted antibacterial soap on my thigh cuts which burned brutally. I was freezing and shaking, and really, just so tired from all the mental aerobics and physical exertion, I needed to relax and warm myself, so that's what I did.

However long later, I remember Patrick gently speaking to me from behind the shower curtain.

"Are you ready to get out now? You've been in the shower for an hour."

"Not really. I'm still cold."

"I can help you get warm. Why don't you get out now, and I'll help you get warm. We can just chill out if you want?"

"Okay... Can I have a towel?"

And then the curtain was moved slightly at the end, and a towel was handed to me by a hidden body.

Standing, I took the towel offered to me and dried myself. Covering up, I remember inhaling before opening the shower curtain because I was honestly afraid of Patrick in that moment. I was afraid of him, but not physically. I was almost one hundred percent sure he wouldn't physically hurt me, I really was. It was in that moment I truly feared his reaction to me. I feared the look on his face and I feared the way we were probably going to change. I feared the ending of our friendship.

So opening the curtain, I braced myself, but I shouldn't have worried. With arms wide open, Patrick had a look on his face that I'll never forget. It was sympathy and *love*.

Staring at him for mere seconds, I just took in his face. And he loved me, I could see it. In that moment, I saw everything on his face that he felt for me and it was that look of love that was my undoing.

Not waiting for me to embrace him, Patrick pulled me hard and fast into his arms. Grabbing my hair he forced my head to his chest. Gripping my toweled back he forced me tightly into his arms, and I cried.

I'm sure it was another post-adrenaline dump, or maybe exhaustion, or maybe relief, or maybe just life. I don't know, but for whatever reason I stood still in the tub with Patrick's arms wrapped around me, and I cried.

Eventually, Patrick made some silly comment about me getting snot on his sexy silk shirt and I pulled away with a grin.

Stepping carefully out of the tub, Patrick kept a hand on my elbow as he made me to sit on the toilet seat. Seated, I didn't really know what to say, so I waited for him to take the lead, which he did.

Bending down on the floor, Patrick raised my towel slightly and looked at my thigh. Looking, I still didn't know, so I asked.

"What happened?"

And waiting for an answer, he sat his butt on his heels, looked up and exhaled. "You started stabbing your thigh with your pocket knife while you were on the sidewalk. I didn't know what was happening at first, until I did know, and then I took the knife from you." And taking my wrist into his hand, Patrick showed me the bruise around my wrist. And it was a dark bruise. A perfectly shaped bruise of a hand wrapped around my bony wrist, with finger marks and even gaps in between. It's funny, but I remember being almost mesmerized by the hand print bruise. It truly was perfect.

"Oh. Why did you bruise me?" I asked gently because I didn't want it to sound like an accusation.

"I'm sorry. I tried to get it away, but you were so still except for your hand hurting your leg and I tried to get it away, but I had to squeeze your wrist hard to make your fingers open. I really did try to get it away, see..." And raising his own hand I see a bunch of nicks and cuts on this fingers and inside his palm.

"Oh! I'm sorry. I didn't mean to hurt you."

"I know-"

"No, I really didn't mean to hurt you. I wouldn't hurt you on purpose. I didn't realize what I was doing."

"I know. I could tell you were kind of in a trance or something."

"I didn't mean to hurt you." And I really didn't. Seeing Patrick's injuries bothered me very much.

"I know, Sadie. Look at me, pretty girl. It was *my* fault. I tried to get the knife from you by grabbing at it, instead of your wrist. It was totally my fault. It really was. I know you didn't mean to hurt me. And don't worry, I'm clean, and I assume you are as well. So it's over now."

"What do you mean...?" And then I understood. "Oh, I AM clean! I never thought of that. Sorry."

"I am too. I'm kind of the condom Queen in this here town, no matter how much I put out," Patrick grinned at me. "Plus, I'm tested regularly anyway, and I'm clean. So we're okay, and it's over now. You didn't hurt me, I did because I was stupid, and we're okay. I'm just going to put some band aids on your thigh, okay?"

And nodding, I waited as he nursed my thigh in silence. Reaching out, I placed my hand in his hair and pulled him toward me by his nape. Leaning in between my legs, Patrick wrapped his arms around me and rested his head against my shoulder. Embracing him, I tried to make sense of our terrible night out together.

I couldn't believe I saw my rapist. I couldn't believe he was standing at the end of my street. I couldn't believe he seemed to be watching me. I couldn't believe he was waiting for me. I just couldn't believe I saw him again.

"I saw him..." I whispered.

"I know. Can we call the police now? I really want them to know, Sade. I'm going to call them anyway, but I think you need to tell them, too."

"It doesn't matter. He's gone now."

"It DOES matter, and I'm calling them anyway. But I want you to tell them what he was doing and wearing, okay. I mean it, Sadie. I want you to tell them everything that happened. I still have Detective Monroe's card so I'm calling him. But I want you to talk to him as well. I mean it, Sade. If you don't, I'll get all Queen, and bitchy and Drama on you until you do, so you may as well give in." And pulling away from our hug, Patrick stared at me with a mixture of humor *and* seriousness until I knew I wouldn't win this battle with him.

"Okay..." And we did.

Patrick took me to my room and pulled out my clothes to wear. He walked into my kitchen and poured us a drink, and made a pot of coffee. Patrick sat me at my dining room table and called Detective Monroe, who amazingly, was actually on duty that night.

And close to two hours after Patrick's call, Detective Monroe was sitting across from Patrick and I, as Patrick told the tale. With little help from me, Patrick filled him in on our night out. Patrick explained that I rarely went out. Patrick explained that me going out was an anomaly, and therefore extra scary and strange that I saw the bad man the one rare night I actually went out. Patrick explained everything he could, until it was my turn to explain.

But I didn't really have a voice. I didn't know what happened. I couldn't explain the panic and fear or the knife or the urine. I couldn't explain the sounds and sights. I didn't have words to express what that moment was like for me- what it had felt like. It was too weird and too messed up in my head to explain.

I didn't really see his features or anything specific. It was more like I saw him as a whole. I thought he had on a dark blue sweater and jeans, but I really only saw him as kind of a blue-ish whole. It's like he was backlit, or glowing, or the only thing illuminated on the street.

But I tried to explain what I saw and how close he was to us, and what happened, I really did. And Detective Monroe said he understood, and that my description was common and typical of a victim experiencing a vision of their attacker. He said most victims suffer this tunnel-vision type memory of the events. He forgave my inability to accurately describe the man who hurt me thoroughly, as I tried to stop shaking.

Patrick and I didn't tell about my the knife, and we didn't mention me urinating myself. Or maybe he did. I don't think so, but I found myself very distracted while Patrick spoke.

I was tired. It was well after midnight. I had had a long night and all I wanted to do was sleep.

And when Detective Monroe and Patrick both looked at me in silence, I realized I hadn't heard the question, because I really didn't know anything at that point, except my exhaustion.

"I asked if you'd like a victim counsellor to call you in the morning, Sadie."

"Oh, no thank you. I'm okay. I just want to set my alarm and go to sleep. I'll be fine," I stated automatically.

When he eventually rose from my kitchen chair I remember the relief I felt. I wanted to sleep. I wanted to be safe. I wanted to be alone. I wanted my stranger to come to me to make my fear go away.

After Detective Monroe left, it took me another 15 minutes to get Patrick out of my apartment. He was so stubborn and adamant about staying over. He wanted to sleep on the couch. He wanted to stay with me. He wanted to be here if I needed him. He wanted, he wanted, he wanted...

Eventually, almost angrily, I convinced him to leave me alone. I told him it wasn't about what he wanted, but about what **I** wanted- and I wanted to be alone. So he left, begrudgingly.

And once alone, I rewashed my body and changed into an attractive nightgown, made my way to bed, and then I waited.

I waited all night for my stranger. I waited up. I forced myself to not fall asleep. I stayed up waiting for Him, but He didn't show up that night.

I spent an entire night thinking and waiting until it was morning and I finally fell asleep. And I did sleep until Patrick forced me to get up in the early afternoon.

And that was the last time I ever saw the man who hurt me. I think that was an unconscious decision on my part to protect me. I think I never wanted to see him again, so I didn't. I think my mind simply blanked him out.

Eventually, his face disappeared. And eventually his body disappeared until I never saw him again.

I could never make the sounds go away. And I ALWAYS heard his voice uttering his disgusting words of love and affection for me, but I didn't see him ever again. It's like my mind blanked out his physical appearance from my life. My mind stopped remembering his hair, and eyes, and body. My mind couldn't erase what happened to me or all the gory details, but it could erase his physical memory from my mind.

And so I stopped remembering what he looked like, and I never saw him again.

CHAPTER 9

My Dear Stranger X

Last night my dear stranger came to me again. It had only been a month since His last visit, but as i woke to His beautiful eyes, my longing seemed unbearable.

Suddenly, i remembered our last visit together lacked the physical and emotional commitment which we had built over the years, due to my own resentment and sadness. However, when i looked at His face i knew He had forgiven my previous hostility, just as i had forgiven His absence throughout the brutality i had endured.

Running across my room i greeted my stranger with a hug so tight i could barely breathe. Being held tightly in return, i realized my love had grown stronger than i could've ever imagined.
Kissing my forehead, my stranger came alive with happiness. i could see the pleasure on His face at my forgiveness. And i could see the pleasure my forgiveness gave through the embrace that followed.
We were together again. And though my own recent brutality still threatened, in my dear stranger's arms, the torture eased while He remained with me.
My dear stranger took my body into His arms and gently carried me to my bed. He lay underneath me, allowing my body to fit neatly into His embrace. Initially, i felt a slight uneasiness at this intimacy because of the recent savagery i had endured. However, just as quickly as it came, my uneasiness faded into the night because i was with my dear stranger and nothing could have made me feel more peaceful or secure.
My stranger held me, caressing my face and hair, so soothing and calm. He made my body feel light as i fought my mind for sleep. Inevitably, my body won the battle and sleep claimed me.

But the nightmares struck and the brutality tortured. i was alive but unable to stop the pain. Crying and screaming i tried to fight it but i couldn't. i was

powerless against him. Again.
Suddenly, i found myself awake fighting my dear stranger for seconds until i realized the pain had all been another nightmare memory to torture. My newest brutality had been dreamed memories, but this time He was there for me. He was there!
i was safe and alone no longer. He would alleviate my pain and wipe away all my tears. He would make the pain distant, at least until He left me again.

And i just couldn't help myself. i couldn't contain my desperation. "Please don't leave me again. i'm begging you! Please don't leave me this time because i can't cope with all of this alone!" i screamed these words surprising us both. And with no reply, He took me back into His arms for another tight embrace.

And we lay together for hours while all the horrific felt afar. No words were spoken though i knew one day soon i would tell my dear stranger all that had occurred. i would tell Him all that had happened to me. i would tell Him how hard i fought. i would tell Him how i had screamed for Him to take me away from the pain. One day i would show Him my scars just as i showed Him my tears. But not last night. Last night was left only for security and devotion.

As the hours passed and daylight approached, again my eyes begged for sleep. Again, i tried desperately to fight it but sleep had become such a luxury in the past months my body couldn't resist the newly found security it felt within my stranger's presence. And as my eyes grew heavy, and my stranger kissed my eyelids so softly, i was no longer able to fight. Quietly, i fell into unconsciousness holding my dear stranger tight.

When i woke this morning i was astonished to find my stranger still awake next to me. He had stayed for me. He had stayed all night. He had heard my pleas, and he had stayed just for me!
For the first time since the attack He was here when i awoke. For the first time i could kiss His sweet lips good morning. For the first time there was no morning sadness nor sunrise loneliness. For the first time i could breathe after sleep

because He was here for me completely.

As i turned to kiss my stranger's lips i saw His eyes of pain, and i instantly wondered what i had screamed in my sleep. i wondered what secrets of brutality i had told.

But before i could panic at my unintentional confessions my stranger kissed my lips and smiled a smile so beautiful for me, my anxiety rested. All my questions didn't matter because He was still here and He had stayed for me.

Sadly, my stranger stood and bent to kiss my forehead. He walked slowly to my bedroom door. But wanting to scream 'Don't leave me!' i didn't speak. i remained silent as tears fell down my cheeks and my heart cried. He was leaving me. And even though i believed He would return to me again, my sadness was overwhelming.

i watched His body walk from my room and down the hall. i watched my dear stranger turn and blow one final kiss. i watched... until I couldn't see His body anymore.

Desperate and motionless, my mind raced and my body ached. i couldn't control my stream of tears from falling. i couldn't control my thoughts of finality and panic from surfacing.

What if He left me forever? What if He never returned to me? How could i live without the love shared with my dear stranger? How could i continue...?

Minutes after His departure i let the fear and desperation take me as I fell asleep once again. i knew what horrors were about to abuse me, and i knew the pain that was about to destroy me, but i simply didn't have the strength to fight any longer.

i allowed the exhaustion to take me. And just as I fell into the darkness, I suddenly exhaled as i realized He would return to me and He would return for us.

November 1999
19 years old

My Dear Stranger XI

Last night my dear stranger came to me.
i had awoke from a light, haunted sleep to find His beautiful eyes watching my body in agony, as He too looked agonized. My heart broke when i saw His horrified face, but my love grew even greater when i watched His horror turn into a beautiful smile for me. In that one moment i wanted to be held so tightly, i could barely contain my excitement. God, my stranger is so amazing, and He loves me wholly!
Once i was fully awake and no longer suffering my nightmares, my stranger slowly walked across my room as He greeted my longing with a warm embrace. In His arms i was filled with happiness, as tears fell down my cheeks when He kissed my lips and breathed deep into my body.

Again, we were together. Again, i wanted only my stranger to take me away from all my pain. Again, i wanted His sweet lips to caress my sorrow away. And again, i was comforted by His love so great and so amazingly rare, i often lost my breath when He was near.
While embracing, i pressed my lips so firmly against my stranger's that from His lips escaped a little moan. Slightly pleased by my own aggression i smiled and held Him even tighter. Grabbing His body, i squeezed and groped until finally He broke our embrace seemingly confused and frustrated by my sexual aggression. And staring into my stranger's eyes i questioned His actions, but there was no reply.

I remember wondering why He looked so unimpressed with me. Was this physical pleasure not what He desired? Did He no longer desire me? And as my heart began to race i wondered was He finally leaving me?

Every insecurity of every year we had been together surfaced. Every inhibition screamed. Every memory of past brutality cut deep into my soul. Every single peaceful moment between us ceased. Every shared kiss suddenly faded away. The pain of His rejection had become so great that my heart died in that very moment inside my chest. My mind became shattered with thoughts, fears and memories. My body simply couldn't stand the pain. My breath left me empty.

And suddenly i collapsed, watching my dear stranger's face fade away...

When i became conscious my stranger smiled so beautifully, i had forgotten why i had become so stricken. But just as quickly as i woke, the memory returned. Sobbing uncontrollably, i looked to my stranger for answers- for a reason as to His distance. And as He wiped my tears, my stranger began a horrendous journey of unforgiving thoughts, desperation, and regrets with me.
Crying Himself, my stranger told me of His own broken, bleeding heart. A heart filled with angst over the brutality i had endured He thought it was impossible to recover from. He spoke of the great pain within His own soul and of the intense need to avenge my life- my life taken from us and shattered by another.
My stranger screamed in agony and He cried with remorse. And throughout i tried desperately to accept His words without feeling for my own pain as i wiped His tears and held Him softly. But again He became distant toward me.

When i questioned Him again, my stranger shook and suddenly apologized for needing me when it was i who should be depending on Him. When I understood, i smiled for him. i suddenly understood His distress clearly, as i battled my own resentments and hostility toward all around us. In that moment I knew my stranger was weak and completely dependent on me for release and understanding. And it was an amazing feeling in that moment to know He truly needed me as well. It was a moment in which i was the strength for us.

Sometime later, my dear stranger asked the questions i had been dreading for months. He wanted to know what happened. He wanted to hear from my very lips the horrific truth. He wanted to sit and hear my words relay to Him all which i could possibly bare- all that my heart would allow. He wanted every detail i could detail and He wanted to bleed just as i uncovered all that had caused my own blood and humiliation to flow.
Suddenly, my body ached and my mind raced. My tears flowed and my heart pounded. My soul screamed and my throat tightened. My insanity retrieved what my sanity had fought for.

i did want my stranger to know everything. i did want Him to fully understand my new sadness. i did want to give Him all the answers He craved. i did want Him to hear each word fall from my lips as i held back the wretched screams of slaughter... But i was unable to speak.

So silently we sat together. Silently, we both fought the pain and anguish. Silently, we each waited for my words.
And when finally my words surfaced i was surprised by my own restraint and eloquence. i spoke clearly and as delicately as possible, wanting no added pain for my stranger or for myself. Hours passed as i told my tale but time stood still between us. Both my stranger and i breathed deep and fought so strongly. When i had told all that memory and personal suffering would allow, i looked to my stranger for some meaningful words. But instead of words, He held me so tightly my strength subsided and a mental collapse beckoned me home.
Tears and wails. Shaking and vomiting. Hysteria and fatigue. Silence and wordiness... All surfaced in my mania.
My breakdown, my release, my homecoming was complete. Where i was going to end up was unknown and unquestioned. What was to become of me was also unknown. What was to become of us was feared, but undecided.
The truth was known. The story had been told. The brutality now had a living audience. And my dear strange delved into silence.

Together, He and i would never be the same. Together, we would have demons and nightmares. Together, promises of safety and security were rendered invalid. We would either recover or we would surrender to the pain.

The silence that followed was overwhelming and yet completely expected. Neither my stranger nor i could find words to release the demons and nightmares inside, nor could we distinguish between our new reality and the reality of our past pleasure and loving naïveté.
We were together and now we carried each other through the nightmares. The demons which slaughtered now had the two of us to fight.
Hours faded away and sunrise glory climbed. My dear stranger was alive for me as i am living only for Him.

When i awoke this morning alone my heart broke, but then I remembered our night together. My dear stranger has been given my life just as i cherish His life within my heart.
i know He will again visit just as i know He has not left me. i know, but i'm a little frightened by the demons and the effects they will have on my dear stranger and i.

But until He returns i will dream of only His beautiful eyes watching me in my darkness.
November 1999
19 years old

*****

Looking around my garage, I'm disgusted again. I haven't slept or eaten in a long time, and I feel weak with the physical neglect of my body.

Why do I feel like a really good mother but crazy at the same time? Aren't those two concepts truly mutually exclusive of each other? How can a good mother be crazy as well? I don't know.
And if I wasn't me, I would think it wasn't possible. But I am me, and I do think it's possible. I KNOW I'm a good mother, just as I know I'm not normal, or okay, or really, even truly sane anymore.
I know that but somehow where Jamie is concerned, I am a terrifically together, loving, supportive mother.
It's like my personality shifts, or I just lose myself completely in loving and caring for my son. I look at him, and I forget everything *but* him. He is my world, and I love him, and because of my love for him, I'm able to put all my insanity and neurosis and insecurities, if not completely away, I can at least hide them so they don't affect Jamie in any way.
At least that's what I tell myself. And I think I'm right. I think I do a great job mothering my son with little to none of my crazy past around him.
Sure, I can be a little obsessive with his health, and yes I panic about any potential danger he may suffer from time to time, but overall, I think I hide my real true intense panic from him quite well.
Jamie seems very well adjusted and happy. He knows his mommy loves him, and he knows he is very special to his mom.

He knows he is loved and cared for, so I think I've done a good job. Actually, I *know* I have.

From the day he was placed in my arms I put all my stuff aside so I could focus on being an amazing mother to him.

That's what I think, honestly. And completely objectively, I'm pretty sure I'm right, too.

*****

My Dear Stranger XII

Last night as I slept with nightmares to interrupt and confuse, I woke to a soft tap against my bedroom window. Once fully woken I raised my blinds and was shocked and surprised to stare into my dear stranger's eyes.

The night was dark and the streetlights dim, but amazingly I could see every contour of His face- A face which had brought such joy and fulfillment to my life. Running for the panel, I turned off the alarm and returned for Him. Watching; our hands mirrored each other's as we opened my window. God, I could feel His hands on mine even as the glass separated us.

And once our worlds joined the cool air sent shivers down my spine as intense desire began to control my thoughts.

When He entered my room, I tried to hide the effects the cool air had on my body, yet just as quickly as my body heightened, my stranger raised my arms and lifted my nightgown over my head.

For minutes there was no movement nor sound. My stranger merely stood and stared at my body with such adoration I felt neither insecure nor unattractive.

When my stranger took me into His warm embrace the cool night instantly disappeared. The night became full of hope and peace.

In little time His hands wandered my body as His lips kissed all of my flesh. I felt an eager ecstasy as my eyes held His face with my gaze. I wanted Him fully and I knew He wanted me also.

Recently, our time together had been filled with agony, fear and never ending questions of my sanity. However, last night we knew there would be few questions, suppressed pain and little confusion between us.
My dear stranger gently carried me back to my bed as He kissed my lips passionately.

Throughout our re-acquaintance i felt inadequacy threaten yet each smile and kiss from my stranger relieved any insecurity momentarily felt. Our passion had been long awaited and often feared never to return. However, i knew He was my love and i His. So after much trial and agony our passions were finally welcomed home.
Minutes turned to hours, and hours felt like days. My stranger pleased all my desires and turned all my recent cravings into reality. Never did I feel physical discomfort or sexual pain. And though I hadn't been touched in nearly 2 years, my stranger was careful with my body.

With each kiss our love grew stronger. With each touch our hearts mended for each other. Our love may seem obscure to most but I need not know a name or past as He knows mine. We are fulfilled and completely content with each other. As my dear stranger once expressed, 'our love is divine and we will never need another.'

When our passions were quenched and our hearts stronger He held me in His arms and caressed my bare skin. Many thoughts raced through my mind- so many things I wanted to say, yet I said nothing.
Minutes later I sat up and looked down into my stranger's eyes and within this glance of mine He smiled and enough had been said.
So to the gentle beat of His heart and to the rhythm of His breath I slowly fell asleep.

When I woke this morning I felt such love my heart ached. I wanted my stranger back in my arms. And though He had left me again in the night I know my dear stranger will return again. He will return and wipe away my tears, comfort my soul, and He will return to love me passionately forever.
October 2001
21 years old

After 2 years of suffering, struggling through life with only my one friend, and a loneliness that had made me hollow inside, I was finally able to make love with my stranger again, and it was perfect.

I had healed... relatively speaking.

CHAPTER 10

My Dear Stranger XIV

Last night my dear stranger saved me.
i had not rested nor slept in days. i had kicked and screamed as all the demons surfaced and threatened. i was alone in our world with death surrounding me. i was hiding in a darkened corner, hiding from the demons, hiding from myself. i begged my stranger to come to me. i begged Him to save me. Through terror and panic i rocked back and forth with closed eyes while i dreamed of my stranger's warm embrace.

And finally i felt Him. With a soft touch on my cheek, i opened my eyes to face Him. Kneeling, my stranger was in front of me. And then i froze. i was frightened. i panicked at the sudden intrusion into my solitude as fear and horror gripped me again.
Was my dear stranger only the demons in disguise? Were the demons using my love as the weakness in which to kill me? Was i being manipulated into believing they were Him, so they could take my body with ease?
Pushing and fighting i punched and kicked. Screaming, i begged Him to leave me alone.
Firmly, my stranger grabbed and held my wrists until my vision cleared and i could finally see. The beautiful eyes staring could be no one else's but His eyes loving, worshipping, and pitying me.

In that moment of clarity my relief created a great rush of emotion. Sobbing, my breath became strained and weak. But holding me tight, my stranger cradled me until the demons ceased and i was finally free. Inevitably, my sobbing became desperate hiccups of breath until i fell into unconsciousness...

When i awoke seemingly minutes later i was alone on the floor. And confusion and fear resurfaced as it had before. Where is He? How could He leave me so desperate in need? Where are the demons? Have they killed my love, to torture

me?
And then i saw through my tear-filled eyes Him coming for me.

Quickly, my dear stranger ran and kneeling again He wiped His own tears, as He smiled for me. He slowly raised a glass of water to my parched lips, while He washed my face and brow with a cool wet cloth. And as he performed this ritual i could only stare at His beautiful eyes which gave me my reason to breathe.
Too weak to stand on my own, my stranger raised my arms around His neck as He tucked my body into His arms and easily lifted me from the floor. Walking toward the bathroom, He took me from my darkened corner, my hiding place. And in that moment i suddenly understood, i was barely alive but the world remained audacious.

In the bathroom my stranger sat me on the side of the bathtub, using his hand against my chest to keep me upright. Lifting my chin, He smiled deep into my dying eyes, and that simple moment became the most overwhelming moment of my life.
Oh god, i wanted to weep. i wanted my stranger to understand. i wanted Him to know i WAS sorry for what i did but i desperately needed some peace from my nightmares because it was too hard to always fight.
And with a voice low and strained i explained why i did what i did.

After my confession, moments passed between us in silence. My stranger looked at me and spoke not a word. Still being held up against the bathtub wall, i had no strength left. i was exhausted beyond anything i could've ever imagined in this life.
And then He spoke.
'My love, I am here for you and I will never love another. I will feed you and bathe you and comfort you and hold you. I will defend you and keep you free from your demons. I will kiss you and love you like no other can. I will save you and help you whenever you're in need. I will worship our love for the rest of our days, but never again will I love you in vain. Do you understand my words?'
And i did. i heard Him, and i understood clearly. In that moment i was made to see what i had attempted to do.

Weeping, i tried to kiss my stranger, but sickness prevailed and i nearly fell to the floor. Yet as always, He caught me quickly in His arms and smiled to reassure us both i think. Weakened, i knew He held my entire life in His arms. Moments later He gently raised my arms and discarded my blouse. Slipping my skirt and panties from my body, i watched in blurry fascination because i was unable to help.

Once my clothing was removed, He suddenly knelt between my legs and rested His head against my chest. Oh, how i tried to hold Him but my body simply didn't function anymore. Alone, He held me tight.

Rising from the floor, my stranger turned me and lowered my body into the water, until startled my body came alive. i grabbed for him. i kicked and flailed. i begged. i screamed. With my eyes i pleaded but He just wouldn't listen to me. He ignored my pleas until i eventually gave into ice cold submission.

My stranger bathed my body and cleansed my soul. He smiled as His bright eyes reassured me i would survive this. And though i shivered uncontrollably, as He kissed my forehead i felt warmed in His presence.

And within this warmth and cold, because of my demons and my attempt, because of the exhaustion deep within i began another journey. i began to fall.

Frantically, i fought and screamed. Gagging and gasping for breath, my panic resurfaced. The demons returned, haunting and laughing at me again. The demons were hideous and insatiable. Creeping closer and closer to me i was alone and i knew they wanted to torture me.

One demon grabbed me, squeezing tighter and tighter until i choked and vomited. i was beaten. i was tortured. The pain on my chest was unbearable. With closed eyes i felt the demon kiss me and i couldn't fight any longer, i had to give in. I was just too tired to continue like this.

And then it stopped.

Once i finally opened my eyes i searched for the demon but only my stranger's face could i see. Still choking and struggling, He forced His breath into me. And i understood. Catching His breath, i followed His eyes around and was amazed by the scene. i was lying naked on the bathroom floor with my stranger still straddling me. With His hands on my chest and with flushed cheeks, He was fully alive forcing His life into me.

Seemingly relieved by my return my stranger suddenly collapsed onto me. And i held Him close to me while my deadened body shook horribly as my stranger's breath coursed through my body.

When my stranger sat up and examined my broken body i could see the pain and devastation in His eyes. Suddenly filled with remorse, i tried to take His hand into mine, but He angrily pulled away. In that moment of rejection i felt so alone and confused. I begged, 'forgive me please!'

And then my body hardened and convulsed. Too weak to fight i was thrown into my stranger's lap as my vomit and regret spewed forth. And i felt utterly alone until He finally reached out to me.

He wrapped my dying body in his arms while i shook and trembled. He held my hair clear. He kissed my neck softly. He rubbed my back delicately- All through my toxic release.

And when terror and confusion joined my body's suffering i could feel Him. Through each convulsion i was covered in the warmth of His love. Each time i believed i could no longer continue or fight, i think He recognized my surrender and He forced His will into me. Yelling often, He would wake me from my numerous trances. Kicking walls and shaking me He forced me to stay conscious for Him.

And amazingly, He stayed with me. He chose to stay. He caressed my aching body even while my excretions covered the floor. Minutes turned to hours as i slept and i woke, but never did He leave my side.

With my vision blurred, i woke to my stranger standing naked in front of me. With my mind confused i wanted to question His intensions. i was shocked that He planned to take me under such tragic circumstances. All i could reason was maybe He wanted some peace through love-making. Suddenly feeling hostile, i was disturbed by the image of such an act during such horrendous emotional weakness. Looking in my eyes, i saw comprehension in His face as He acknowledged my hostility. And with His sadness so great, i could actually see the hurt and distress He felt at my wrongful conclusion.

God, i felt such shame. How could i have ever doubted His intentions?

My stranger once again picked me up off the floor and holding me He placed us inside a warm shower. Still too weak to stand my stranger let my limp body rest against His as He sat me in the corner. Holding me up firmly with one hand He again cleansed my broken body. Turning me toward the wall, my face rested against the cool tile. i tried to hold Him but my body was incapable. i wanted to help but i couldn't, so i began to weep from the sadness that overwhelmed me.

My Dear Stranger

i needed to be forgiven for my attempt. i needed to express my love for Him. i needed my stranger to understand my actions. i needed His love forever...

When i awoke this afternoon, daylight threatened to blind me. But i squinted and searched frantically through the light, and to my great surprise my stranger was still near watching me.
His eyes were bright and His smile was beautiful. Walking toward me, He pulled down the shade and sat down beside me. Raising a glass of water to my parched lips, my stranger still helped me. Desperate for rehydration, i gulped as the water poured down my chin until He pulled the glass away from me.
My stranger sat the glass on the bedside table, then suddenly turned back to me while grabbing me tightly in His arms even as the pressure threatened to destroy my body. Releasing me seconds later from His embrace, i stared at the fear etched upon His face.

And gently He spoke.
'You almost killed us last night. Look, I understand demons and nightmares abuse, but I'll never again save you if my love means so little to you.'

Such simple words. Such glorious instructions. Such love given so freely. Alive, we were together. And suddenly a peace grew inside me. Never had anyone saved me before. Never had anyone truly loved me before. Never had i believed in anyone before.
And this newest of realities caused a great physical pain in my chest, as He kissed my forehead and left me quietly in my bed.

And i think i understand.
He will return to me because i now know and see, just as i live for my dear stranger, He lives to kill the demons inside of me.

December 2001
21 years old

*****

I drank then. A lot. I drank heavily and frequently. But I wasn't an alcoholic. Well, I *was* by some definitions, but not really. I drank because I didn't want to feel, not because I craved alcohol. Does that make sense?

I honestly don't think I was an alcoholic because the drinking was only the means to the end for me. If there had been another way in which to stop myself from feeling, and fearing, and missing, I would have tried anything else instead. But there wasn't anything else, so I drank and sometimes swallowed pills with my alcohol to really numb me out.

Again, I don't really think this made me an alcoholic per se. I think it made me an escapist who used alcohol as the way in which to escape.

I did many other things as well. Whatever it took. Whatever was required to make me not feel, I did. From self-mutilations to ingesting various substances. Whatever I could do, I did. And usually I did it well, though there were a few times I went a little too far. There were a few times I once again danced with death a little too closely.

I remember sitting in a little cafe once that sold alcohol. I remember a male blues singer strumming his guitar as he sang in the coffeehouse. I remember drinking both at my table from the waitress and at the bar with the bartender so neither knew how much I was actually drinking.

Then I remember waking up in the parking lot, throwing up, moaning on my side while 2 men tried to help me. I remember becoming conscious, seeing the men, fighting and screaming in between vomiting, and I remember a small crowd gathering after my screams. I believe a couple talked to me and called an ambulance. I don't remember for sure how it happened, but I ended up in the hospital that night and the following day with a case of alcohol poisoning.

But by the time I left, I had lied to each and every person I spoke with, including the Psychiatrist for the required Psych visit. I convincingly blew off the whole incident as a one-off, until I quickly left AMA and hopped in a waiting cab to take me the few blocks to my apartment. But I knew that time was close.

Oh, I remember this other time I woke up topless on my balcony one morning. I have absolutely NO recollection of how that happened, but I do remember the fear I felt waking on my balcony topless and wondering why the hell my door was wide open with no alarm set, and why I was lying on the cold wood of my balcony.

I remember looking at the high rise apartment across the street and wondering if anyone saw me or was still watching me. I remember thinking how lucky I was no one walked up the fire escape to my balcony to get me. I remember crawling back into my apartment, closing the balcony door and waking up hours later still on the floor beside the door in my living room with the alarm still not set, covered in vomit.

And though those 2 times I remember most, there were many other lesser incidents. Like waking up vomiting, and barely able to turn myself onto my side as I vomited in my sleep. Or waking up in the bathroom around the toilet unsure of how I got there. Once I even woke up *on* the kitchen counter, balancing precariously with my head and neck in the sink covered from head to toe in my own vomit.

Those times were frequent, but again, not because I was an alcoholic. I never craved the alcohol. I never thought of alcohol with affection or thirst. I never thought of pouring a glass of alcohol because I wanted or enjoyed it. I poured the alcohol because of my need to numb the horrible feelings inside me. I poured to wipe out all the feelings that threatened to suffocate me.

Even now, drinking my first alcoholic beverage in 8 years straight from the bottle, I honestly don't like it. This doesn't taste good to me, nor do I feel good drinking it. I don't want it, but I'll drink it anyway. I'll drink it because I need this liquor to numb me from what I'm doing, because I really can't do this sober. I cannot do this with a clear head because it hurts too much.

So walking back into my kitchen, I'll grab a tall glass from the cupboard and pour. I'll drink this vodka, as I wait for the soothing relief of numbness to calm me.

I'm not an alcoholic because I don't want the liquor. I'm an escapist because I want the effects of the liquor only, not the alcohol itself.

CHAPTER 11

My Dear Stranger XV

Last night my dear stranger came for me once again.
i had only experienced one afternoon since His last visit but i had missed His embrace so much i had believed my heart would break without Him.

Our last night together was spent with such trial and fear, i had thought Death would surely come to claim me. But death had not won because my stranger had saved me from Death's vicious hands. Today, i am still alive, and the world remains audacious.

Last night i was incapable of leaving my bed. Though inner peace had recently found me, demons were again trying to penetrate my soul. And my sleep was feared but inevitable. So when i woke, i was delighted to find my stranger lying next to my broken body. His eyes were so full of love as His fingers eased through my knotted hair. He was here for me. He was here and in His smile i could see He would love me forever.

My lips desperate to speak were so parched and cracked, blood began to surface. So my stranger took my face into His hands, softly kissing my lips moist. Looking into His eyes i believed my stranger had forgiven my attempt, my hostility towards life, and my desire to end all the brutality and nightmares. My stranger then sat me up propped by pillows and He began to quench my thirst with sweet juices and warmed soup. He began to fill my sunken body with nourishment as He watched my skin slowly color.
But suddenly my body convulsed and all i felt was its rejection.
Vomiting, i cried for my stranger as He held me tight. He held a bowl to my mouth like He had known i would again be ill. He held me while my body ached with vomiting repulsion. Crying, my stranger held me as He kissed my bleeding, dying body.

And in that moment my anguish was truly overwhelming. Paranoia surfaced and the pain swallowed any peace i had momentarily felt. Slowly my mind began to question His actions.
Had my stranger poisoned me? Had He joined the demons who were trying to kill me? Was He trying to punish me for taking our love in vain, as He had previously claimed? Did He no longer love me?
And so i tried to fight Him. i tried to break free from Him, but my stranger held me tight.

And when no vomit remained and i could finally see, i was thrilled to feel Him still holding me. Relief surfaced so quickly, i surrendered to Him. Smiling, my stranger acknowledged my return. And with a kiss on my brow, He again forgave my delusional hostility.

Leaving me for mere seconds, my stranger returned and again He lifted me into His arms and carried me to the bathroom. Again, He had run a bath. Again, He had planned to cleanse me. Again, He planned to wash away all traces of my horrid, self-induced journey.
And once I was in the soothing warm water, He smiled and kissed me. He forced me to receive all of His love and attention.

Quickly undressing, i watched His beautiful body sink into the warm water with me. Sitting behind me, He pulled my body against His own. Taking my hands into His, He kissed my dry brittle nails and fingertips.
And in that moment i loved Him so completely, my mind fully grasped the selfishness of my attempt.

Once the water had cooled, my stranger stood and helped me from our bath. Even brushing my teeth, He took care of me. Drying me He held me so firmly that even as my legs were unsteady, i wouldn't fall or collapse. He held me up once again.
Returning to our bed, i reached for my love's body. Though physically weak, i wanted sexual love to heal me. i wanted to touch His body and i wanted to give Him great pleasure as my apology. But sadly, He wouldn't allow me.

But before i could panic with insecurity, He gave me a sweet reassuring smile as He turned His lips close.
'I want you to feel my great love for you,' he whispered in my ear.
And kissing my neck, He slowly eased down my body.

Still weakened i tried to guide His path with each of my longing sighs, until my stranger then slowly eased His body into mine. And i could see He didn't want to cause any damage to my broken body as He moved gently and penetrated my body slowly. Oh, but I could feel Him.

He strengthened within His own muscle contractions and like a slow tease He delighted my body. He held and kissed me while my body replenished within the soft movement He gently provided.
"Together we are alive. Together we are our pleasure. We were born for each other," He whispered in my ear.
And when i tried to touch Him to give Him pleasure as well, He still wouldn't allow me. Whispering, He told me i was to be the sole recipient of this production. And firmly, He took my hands into one of His and raised them to the pillows overhead. Then He slowly moved. His other hand moved. His tongue soothed me.
Staring at my face, He watched my inhibitions dissipate within His performance. He watched me writhe within His seduction. i was too weak to control myself and climax nearly threatened to overwhelm me. But with my slight movements, i too watched His face enjoy my pleasure. And then i felt my climactic release, surrounded by His sensual attention.

Afterward, He finally released me and i grabbed for Him so tightly with a strength that surprised us both. Embracing Him, He smiled at my reaction to our love, while my kisses devoured His lips.
Escaping my embrace, my stranger examined my rejuvenated body with a delicate caresses. And overcome with my happiness, i tried to speak.
In a soft voice, i managed to whisper, 'i'm sorry for my attempt, but i promise to live only and forever to love you.' And confirming my words with a smile, His own relief was evident in His eyes.
As we each wept, my stranger held me so still and warm that comfort and peace revisited. No panic surfaced, nor confusion threatened, because together we would face the night in each other's arms.

When i woke this morning i was physically alone, however the sweet scent of our love-making lingered in our bed. And quickly rising, i ate and drank to nourish and heal my body's broken remains so i could love my dear stranger once again.

December 2001
21 years old

I took pills frequently then. Usually, I mixed them with alcohol to numb my feelings. Usually, they were prescription. Not necessarily MY prescription but a prescription nonetheless.

I wasn't bad or dirty though. I wasn't the kind of girl who hung out and did drugs. I didn't smoke up with stoners, and I didn't purchase my pills from some seedy dealer. I was a good girl who just took some pills when I needed them.

Once, I found some pills of my mother's from a minor car accident, so I tried them. Sometime later I found some old pills of my dad's from a broken leg he suffered during a skiing incident, so I tried them.

I found pills here and there. But I wasn't a junkie. And I wasn't a drug addict. I didn't crave the pills, and I didn't think of the pills fondly, or with craving. The pills were not attractive to me as pills. Rather, I took pills so I would stop feeling. That's all. That's what they were for me. They were merely the means to the ending I desired.

They could have been anything. The pills were just that- little pills that helped me achieve the results I needed, nothing more.

I didn't take pills badly though, and I didn't take them for no reason. I didn't take them when I wanted to get high. I NEVER wanted to get high. I just didn't want to feel all the pressure I lived with, so I took pills sometimes alone, and sometimes with alcohol.

But it was never the pills. I never wanted them; I just had to use them so I wouldn't feel all the pressure all the time.

My Dear Stranger XVI

Last night my dear stranger came to me once again.
Alone, and feeling great despair, my stranger entered our room just when i believed i could no longer endure my sadness.
Smiling, His eyes were bright and warming. Staring at Him, i was amazed at how beautiful and alive He was, and i knew He had come to save me again as He had so many times before.

Welcoming my stranger with an embrace, i sobbed as i held Him so tightly i began to lose my breath. Fighting for me, i saw how He tried to ease my anguish.

Pitifully, i suddenly begged the questions i had always struggled with.
'Why must i always feel this pain? Why must i struggle with this continuous sadness? Why is peace only a short-lived reality for me?'
Struggling, i asked the most important questions i held.
'Why do you always stop my attempts? Can't you see my pain? Don't you want me to be free from all my demons of despair?'

But once i exhaled, my stranger stood and walked away from me. Alone again, i was left to question the hostility and anger of my words. Saddened, my stomach convulsed as i sobbed within my desperation.

Minutes later, my dear stranger returned. Sitting gently beside me, He smiled and slowly leaned forward, gracing me with the sweetest most passionate kiss we had ever experienced, until we eventually parted lips. And in that moment, that glorious moment, my heart was full and all my sadness seemed to lessen.
Then a sudden clarity hit me, and i knew- i couldn't handle this pain any longer if my stranger wasn't here with me.

Moving His hands from behind His back, my stranger held them mere inches from my face. He then opened His palms and began to laugh hideously. Panic stricken, i sat up and looked at His gifts.
In His right hand He held the mixed array of my sleeping pills i had lined up ready, and in His left hand He held a razor blade so firm He had caused His

own palm to bleed.
Shocked by His find of mine, i looked to give my stranger an explanation.
Maliciously, He glared at me in return.
Screaming suddenly i begged Him, 'why are you doing this to me?' Desperately i tried to explain, 'i'm sorry you found those things!'

Suddenly, my stranger stood and picked me up in His arms. Fighting, i tried to break free but His strength was too much for me.
Arriving in the bathroom, my stranger forced my clothed body into the filled tub even as i fought Him until he had me helpless and frightened.
And again i screamed, 'why are you doing this to me?' Until His laughter quickly silenced me.

All my confusion turned to panic and fear. My stranger looked at me with such hate i felt my heart break.
And then He spoke.
'My love. You don't love me enough to live for us. You are too selfish and you do not care for our love because of your own pain which has made you blind and callous.'
And breathing deeply He continued.
'Please understand, I DO recognize the demons who haunt you. I do know of the despair which overwhelms you. And I do know of the forces that abused and brutalized your body and soul. But I once told you I would never again save you if my love meant so little to you. So please never doubt my love for you, as I am left to doubt yours.
You see, I'm going to stay here. I'm going to help you preform our greatest production. I'm going to stay right here. I will stay and I will watch the beauty escape your eyes as the love leaves your heart. I will stay here until your last breath graces my trembling lips.'
And choking back tears, He continued.
'I will do this because unlike you, I love you more than my own life, and I want you to see and remember this love of mine which you abandoned in your last moments of life.'

Oh, god... My stranger said these words to me with such calm conviction, i barely noticed the steady stream of tears which followed His words. But I felt them. Instantly trying to take my love into my arms, He instantly forced me back into

the water as He grabbed and held my wrists tight. Crying, i begged Him. Fighting, i tried to free my hands, until He suddenly plunged into the water in front of me.
Angrily, my stranger looked into my eyes and shaking His head feverishly He reached for the razor blade and pills.
Screaming, i tried to push my stranger until kneeling, He pinned my wrists under His weight. Enraged my stranger glared at me until brutally He grabbed my face with his hands.
And i knew unconsciousness soon threatened because i wanted release. i wanted peace from this newest brutality, but i also knew i couldn't give into the darkness. So pleading with my eyes, i begged to be released, but again He ignored my cries for freedom.
Shaking my head, i tried to break the stranger's grasp. Clenching my teeth, i tried to fight the stranger's attempt, but i didn't succeed.

The stranger looked at me with such anxiety and madness, tears poured down His cheeks while His chest gasped for breath. And with insane concentration and strength, the stranger forced my mouth open as i tried to fight Him still, but i failed. And filling my mouth with my pills, the stranger again laughed deliriously.
Panic and agony. Fear and sadness. Life and death.
My throat nearly swallowed, while confusion and desperation turned my fight into near submission.
But my eyes begged Him. My eyes pleaded to Him. My eyes... became blurred and frozen.

Suddenly, the stranger relaxed and released my face from His grasp, as He allowed my wrists to pull free from His weight.
Frantically, i spit the pills into the bath water. Desperately, i pushed His body off of my own. Angrily, i beat at His body with a ferocity that left me speechless. Weakened, He collapsed onto my body.
Sobbing, the stranger raised His head as He looked into my eyes.
Screaming, the stranger tried to pull me tightly into His embrace.

And then He spoke.
'Never forget the intensity in which you just fought me. Never forget your strength- a strength I know and watch with amazement. The despair which

swallows your peace must never again blind you, because even as sadness threatens your sanity, you must believe in your strength as you also believe in our love.'
And wiping away His tears, He continued.
'I'm sorry I scared you, but I have begged and pleaded. I have loved and adored. I have offered you my life of love, but I can't continue to fear your potential actions and attempts. I can't continue to fight your despair alone.'
And smiling, He continued once more.
'I will do anything for you because we were born for each other. I am sorry for the brutality which I have just inflicted upon you, but I needed you to fully understand the depth of your attempts on me. If ever you have loved me as I have loved you, please, I beg you to give me some loving peace. I don't want to fear your actions every single day of our lives.'

And the stranger's words were so gentle and heart wrenching my mind raced, even as i felt all my sorrow and shame. But no words seemed appropriate, even as i clearly saw the depth of His love and adoration for me.
Taking my stranger into an embrace i felt His heart beat within the furious rhythm of my own. i could see the relief in His eyes and i could see Him clearly in our desperate silence.

Eventually, my stranger stood and with eyes so bright He extended His hands to my own. With movements so slow, He lifted my trembling body from the cold water into His warm arms. Stripping each other of our cold, wet clothing, we walked back to our room.
And in our bed we both lay still, wrapped tightly in each other's arms, while the world crept continuously audacious, until sleep came soft and secure.

When i awoke this morning i was graced with a smile from my stranger, as His hands caressed my bare skin. But no words are necessary. No forgiveness needs to be sought. No apologies need to be given. No anger remains, and no despair threatens. My dear stranger is here, living for me always.
And as the day progresses, my dear stranger continues to embrace me, while He watches these very words escape my soul, living to rest eternally upon this page of ours, in memory.
April 2002
22 years old

*****

Sitting in my lounger with my last coffee and my endless smokes, I feel overwhelmed with sadness for my younger self during those dark years.

I remember the feeling I had every single day. I remember slowly fading away. I think I even knew I was fading, but I didn't care enough to stop it. There was something so dark and painful inside me I simply didn't know how to live with it. I didn't know how to shut off the pain and darkness, so I tried to numb it instead.

Those years were horrible. Those years were deadly for me- they were deadly to me. There was little left of the high school Sadie I had once been; young, happy, normal, and typically high school melodramatic.

I was a normal girl until I was 16. I may have had too much independence and been granted too many freedoms by my parents, but I never abused it. I always maintained good grades and a typical healthy demeanor of a teenager. Actually, if I'm being really honest with myself, I maintained the facade of healthiness until I was 19, and then I couldn't pretend anymore.

After I was attacked, I changed indefinitely. To this day I'm changed. I know I moved on enough to have a wonderful, loving sexual relationship with my husband, but I was changed.

To this day, I look over my shoulder too much, and watch my back, and fear everyone around me, always. I constantly fear everyone and everything which has never changed; I've just grown better at hiding it.

But I wasn't good at hiding anything for those few years. I was awful and ugly and just broken, no matter how much I loved my stranger, and no matter how much I tried to be better for Him. There was just no helping me at that point.

I remember sometimes seeing myself in a mirror and being shocked at my own appearance. To say I was thin is misleading. I was very thin but it was a thinness based on looking concave and undernourished. It was the kind of thin that tells people you're sick. The kind of thin-bodied, grey-skinned face of someone with a terminal illness.

I looked terminally ill, and to some I may have even been

described as such. I may not have been terminally ill, but I think I was sick nonetheless.

I was sick with my life and my past, and with my reality. I was sick and I didn't know how to get better.

CHAPTER 12

Sitting in my garage I hear the phone which won't stop ringing. Christ! It's so annoying. Everyone knows I don't like noise, so why do they keep calling me?

Sitting, I try to wait it out but they just won't stop. The ring is constant with no break. They don't even hang up and call back. Why isn't the machine picking up?

Standing, I make my way inside. Oh, I didn't realize how cold it was outside. I didn't even realize it was dark outside. Actually, how long have I *been* outside?

"Hello?!" I ask with annoyance.
"Sade! Sadie. Where are you?"
"At home. Obviously."
"What's wrong Sadie? I've been trying to reach you for hours. I've called you a hundred times. Where were you?"
"Why? I'm not doing anything bad."
"What's wrong, Sadie? You sound upset."
"Why did you call so many times?"
"Honey, what's wrong? Is everything okay?"
"Yes." But it isn't, is it?
"Sadie? What's wrong? You sound upset, and I've been trying to reach you all day. Jamie even called and left messages. Where were you?"
"Why?" And then there is silence.
"Sadie, are you okay? Are you alone?"
"Of course! What does *that* mean?"
"Jesus, not that. You just sound so strange, I didn't know if you were being held by someone, or if you couldn't talk because someone was there... That's all. Are you hurt? What's happening? You never ignore the phone, especially if Jamie and I call."
"I didn't want to talk to you..."
"What?! *Why?*" Alex actually yells at me, and Alex rarely yells.
"No reason. I just didn't. How's Jamie?" I ask suddenly missing him very much. Actually, my heart is beating really fast, and I

feel like I'm dying without my little boy. "How is he, Alexander?" I beg.

"*Alexander?* What's happening Sadie? Are you mad at me for something?"

"How's Jamie?" I beg again as I start crying. I don't know what's wrong, but I suddenly feel like I'm dying on the inside. Everything is tight in my chest and my head is pounding.

"Why are you crying? You can talk to me, honey. I'm here. What's wrong?"

Growling, I ask again, "How the *fuck* is Jamie?"

"Good! He's good Sadie. He's sound asleep in the bunks with Dylan."

"He's good?" I whisper.

"Yes. Jamie is safe and sleeping. He had a great day, tobogganing and skiing, and he ate a huge pasta dinner and too much dessert, but he's good, Sadie. Everything is fine with Jamie, I promise. I would tell you if anything was wrong, but there isn't. I'm in the room next to his, and he's fine."

The relief I feel from his words is instant, because Alex *would* tell me if something was wrong. He would never keep Jamie from me, or not tell me if he was hurt. Alex knows better than to keep my Jamie from me.

"Okay. Thank you Alexander for everything. But I have to go…"

"Sadie! What's wrong?"

"What time is it?"

"I don't know. Um, 12:40, why are you-"

"In the morning?"

"Yes, in the morning. What are you doing, Sadie? We tried calling you the entire day and night. Jamie begged you to call him back. He misses you. Jamie misses his mommy, Sadie. Didn't you hear his messages?"

"I miss him too…" I whisper crying. God, this feels awful. I shouldn't be away from Jamie. He is everything to me. He makes me so happy. I think I'm not happy anymore.

"I don't think I'm happy without Jamie. Can you not take him away from me again? Could you promise me, Alex? Can you promise to not take him away from me again?"

"I promise. But I didn't take him away from you. We all talked about it and you said he and I could go to my sister's without you. You said we could go and that you would be fine for 3 days. You *wanted* us to go. Do you remember that, Sadie? Do you remember when you said we could go?"

"Not really. I remember you taking him away..."

"I didn't take him from you..."

"You did because he's not here, is he? You took him from me because I love him."

"I didn't take him from you, and you know it. Deep down you know I didn't take Jamie away. We're coming home tomorrow morning and you'll have Jamie back. Right, Sadie?"

"Okay. I have to go."

"Wait! What are you doing? Where are you?"

"Why?"

"What's going on Sadie? You sound so upset and strange right now. You never cry, and I can hear you crying. What's going on, honey? Please tell me."

"I'm doing nothing wrong, I just can't really talk right now. I'm sorry Alexander, but I have to go. Please bring Jamie back to me. Please..."

"Wait! Honey, what *is* it?"

"Nothing. I'm fine. I'm sorry I didn't hear you calling earlier. I'm sorry..."

"Where are you right now?"

"Why do you ask?"

"Sadie, please. Where are you right now?"

"In the kitchen. Is that a problem?"

"No, of course not. I'm just trying to figure out what's happening. You won't talk to me. And you've ignored us for 2 days, and you seem really sad and I'm just trying to understand what's going on with you, that's all. Why won't you talk to me, Sadie?" He whispers.

"You *know* why."

"I don't! Tell me why you won't talk to me."

"Because you're you."

"What does *that* mean?"

"I can't talk to you about this and you don't want me to, and I shouldn't anyway 'cause it's bad."

"What's bad? What's happening? Sadie, you can tell me. I promise I can handle anything you need to tell me. What is it, baby? *Please...*"

"It's nothing. I'm okay. I'm just saying goodbye. That's all. I have to say goodbye now."

"To me? I don't understand."

"No, not to you. Never to you. Right, Alexander? I can never say goodbye to you. But I have to go now."

"Wait! What are you talking about?! What do you mean? I really don't understand. Why can't you say goodbye to me? Why would you even want to? What the hell is happening?"

"Thanks Alexander for making me Sadie Hamilton. I truly appreciate it, but I have to go now."

"Sadie! What are you talking about!?"

Knowing I'm freaking him out, I have to make this better. I have to or he'll come back too soon, and I'm not ready for him.

"I'm good, Alex. I'm just tired. I'm going to go to bed, and I'll talk to you in the mor-"

"Wait! Jesus, you're really scaring me-"

"Don't be scared Alexander. I promise everything is fine. Just call me before you leave tomorrow, okay? I'm going to go to bed now, but I'll wait for your call in the morning. Please hug Jamie if he wanders out of his bed tonight. He might get scared there. He might need me. He might need a hug, so can you please give him a hug for me? Please?"

"Of course. I always hug Jamie, Sade. You know that."

"I know. You're right, I'm sorry. I just miss him. I'll see you tomorrow."

"Do you miss me?" He asks quietly.

"Of course. You're Alexander. Of course I miss you."

"Okay... I love you, Sadie. Very much. And I miss you, too."

"Good night, Alex."

"Sade... Do you-"

"I really have to go now. I'll see you later."

Hanging up, I'm shaking and struggling, and tired and wired. I feel so out of sorts, like I'm desperate for something. Anything to make everything back to normal. I don't want to talk to Alexander anymore. I don't want to talk anymore.

When the phone instantly rings again, I click the on/off button quickly, and shut the ringer off. I don't want to keep doing this with Alex. I don't want to have to pretend with Alex right now. I don't want to be perfectly together for Alex right now. I'm tired and cold and I need a smoke.

I need to finish this. Finally.

My Dear Stranger XII

Last night my dear stranger came to me again.
Waking from a deep drug-induced sleep, I was pleased to feel Him thrusting between my legs. Trying desperately to open my heavy eyes, I smiled as I grabbed hold of my stranger's body, pulling Him harder into me as my fog slowly lifted.

The night was hot and I felt need all around me. I was sweat-covered and aroused. I slept with molten dreams of our sexual history. Through the drugged haze, i dreamed of His body moving inside me until I felt Him in my reality. Moaning, I felt Him leave my body, only to have the vacant feeling replaced with the wet sensation of His mouth on me. Writhing, I felt His hunger and my sexual need as i begged His tongue to bring me to release.
Forever I moaned my need as the sensation increased. Turning and panting, I held His tongue deep inside me as I arched and struggled with my impending release. And He knew. Moaning into my body and pushing my thighs further apart, my stranger knew I was close and He loved bringing me my release. He knew, and He worked me until my sexual frenzy nearly eclipsed our love. As my body trembled He knew my climax was going to reward Him soon.

With an agony and ecstasy my body was tattered as I succumbed to the agony of the ecstasy I felt. Screaming out, I grabbed Him close to me, as I panted and tried for coherent words. But I was unable to speak as He kissed me deeply. And it was beautiful. Tasting myself and feeling His pleasure for my release, i reached for His body to aid Him. Wanting Him to know the pleasure i had, i stroked and fondled Him as our kisses increased.
Suddenly turning me onto my stomach, my stranger's body weighed me down. And feeling His weight on me was thrilling and new. Usually, my stranger faced me, like He was always aware to let me see it was Him with me and not a demon. But last night, as He rested on my back i knew it was Him, and I excited more.
Lifting my hips, my stranger towered over me. Being so small, and He so large, my stranger was able to engulf my entire body, resting His face beside my own. And grabbing my hands, He held me tightly to Him as He quickly entered me from behind.

Screaming at the sudden intrusion, He paused as I relaxed for Him. Knowing He waited relieved me. Knowing He wanted my pleasure and not my pain comforted me. Knowing He wanted this position excited me.

And then He moved. Hard and fast. Heavy and demanding. He pushed inside me as His weight crushed me to the bed. Feeling His hands crush my own, I exhaled and tried to feel all the sensation He provided me. And He did. Oh god, the movement was hard, followed by other movements- in and around me. Teasing and increasing in strength, I could barely breathe with my need, but He waited for His release.

And then I felt it build again. Shocked, I heard myself begging again. Fully aroused, I felt myself tightening on Him. Desperately, I tried to move against Him for more feeling, but He held me still.

Groaning, I actually found myself bite His lip. Shocked, I was scared until I saw His eyes light up. And then He moved again, harder and faster, crushing me under His weight. Intensifying every feeling of passion I had ever felt. He moved, and I was pushed higher.

And then it happened. My body exploded on a rush. I couldn't contain my scream, or my shuddering movements beneath Him. I screamed, and moved, and gasped for breath and nearly died in His arms.

Feeling Him still above me, my stranger then moved, again hard and fast. Painful and exciting. He powered into me as I clenched my teeth in reaction to my sensitivity until I felt Him grow harder while still above me.

With no words, I knew when He released inside me. I knew from the feeling, and I knew from the silent stillness. I always knew my stranger inside me. Turning us suddenly, I was spooned with Him deep inside me. Struggling for breath I didn't dare move. No part of my body felt like my own. My muscles ached and my body was exhausted. Exhaling, I pushed harder against His body as He wrapped His arms tighter against me.

I felt loved and abused in a good way. I felt like my stranger didn't hold back with me. I felt like He finally took me as He wanted without fear of my reaction. I felt happy that He did take me as He wanted. And it was as it should be.

When I felt my stranger kiss the back of my head, I smiled. Even as my eyes grew heavy once more, I was content in His arms. I felt loved and cared for. I felt peaceful and exhausted. I felt good in my stranger's arms while I felt sleep keep dragging me down.

When I woke this morning my body ached. But with a smile, I inspected the bruises on my wrists and body, and the nail marks in my palms. I was sore, and tired, but happy still. I felt good. I felt right. I felt like my stranger scrubbed away the bad memories with good ones of Him and I.

I feel like I might be okay now.
July 2002
22 years old

CHAPTER 13

Thinking back on what followed I'm astounded I lived, honestly. I suffered so much I can't believe I didn't kill myself. I can actually think on that time now and realize I was either too afraid to die, or I was stronger than I thought. Probably mostly afraid with a little bit of strength mixed in. I don't know how but I survived, and amazingly I didn't become a strange early 20 something suicide statistic. I still don't know how, but I lived.

After the last time we were together I became pregnant.
I was pregnant by Him and I was lost.
I was suddenly pregnant by a man no one knew about, and I was alone.
I waited every night for Him to tell me what to do. I waited for Him to tell me what would happen. I waited for Him to come back to me so I could understand what the hell I was going to do. I waited for Him to come back to love me so I would be okay. I waited for Him to come love me so I wasn't alone anymore.
I waited. But He never came back.
And I was lost.

And it was more than my typical lost. I was devastated and panicked and just completely lost. I was still evading school as much as possible. I only went to school when I knew final lectures were going to be given before final exams. I showed up to final tutorials before final papers were handed out. I showed up if the Prof was a jerk and actually took attendance and then I left through the back doors as quickly as possible.

I was a ghost in my school who spoke to no one. I ghosted through the halls with my head down when and if I attended school, for those brief sessions which were required so I would pass.

I was alone and waiting.

Eventually when I hit 3 months without Him and 3 months of pregnancy, I knew I had to do something. I had to tell someone. I had to go to the doctor or take vitamins, or decide what the hell I was going to do about my life. I knew I had to do something, but I had no idea what to do.

I had been hiding my sickness from Patrick, and I was afraid to tell him in case he asked me the question I couldn't answer.

And I couldn't even imagine telling my parents I was pregnant, especially since I couldn't tell them who the father was. I couldn't imagine the shock and confusion on people's faces when Sadie the Virgin Prude was suddenly knocked up and appeared to not know who the father was, or simply wouldn't say who the father was. I didn't know what to do. So I did nothing.

And amazingly, or thankfully, or tragically, depending on my mood, I woke up at 4 months pregnant having a miscarriage in my bed. I felt crampy and absolutely exhausted before I went to bed, and I woke up covered in blood. I woke up barely able to move from the weird exhaustion I was drowning in.

I remember reaching for my phone on my night table and calling an ambulance for myself. I remember moaning because I was uncomfortable but not really suffering pain. I remember feeling so tired when the dispatcher spoke to me, but that's all I remember about my physical being. I was losing the baby physically but all I felt was unbelievable exhaustion.

My mind was filled with pain though. I was lying there lost and confused. There was a part of me that wanted the baby because it was His, and also because I thought I wouldn't be lonely anymore with His baby. But honestly, the bigger part of me was simply relieved.

And then of course I felt the guilt of being relieved and I was more depressed. It was a strange little circle of worry, relief, guilt, and despair wrapped up in a body that was bleeding all over my bed with unbelievable exhaustion weighing me down.

So the ambulance came and I remember I couldn't make it to my locked door which was embarrassing. I couldn't even make it out of my bed. I heard the knocking and I heard the dispatcher on the phone telling me the EMT's were there to help but I just couldn't get out of my bed, which was of course the furthest room from the front door in my apartment.

And then they were suddenly there in my room with my wonderful Patrick, of course. While not talking to me or interfering, Patrick stood in my bedroom doorway while the 2 men moved my comforter and looked at me and my sheets. They started prepping me for transport while taking my vitals. They started asking me questions, but I looked at Patrick.

I watched him watch them until he finally looked at me. Waiting for something from him, Patrick finally leaned against the doorframe casually and then he smiled at me like everything was okay. What he did that let me know he was freaked out was suddenly push his hand through his hair, which he never did. Patrick's hair was always perfectly in place with tons of hair product; but without thinking he pushed his fingers and hand through all his hair which just killed the look he probably spent 2 hours perfecting before this rude interruption.

But he smiled his charming smile at me in a kind of, 'it's going to be okay Sadie' sort of way, and then he turned toward what the EMT was doing to my body, and we never made eye contact again.

And I was so embarrassed. After the EMT removed my sheets, he actually snapped on a rubber glove and touched me. He seemed totally clinical, not even looking at my vagina as he touched me, but he did anyway, and I wanted to die.

No one touched me there except for the bad man once, and always, my stranger. No one had ever looked at my vagina, and suddenly a gloved hand was feeling around and Patrick was watching with a clinical eye all that was happening to me while I cried.

Eventually, my cries turned into sobs and I could no longer answer the questions posed to me.

How far along? 4 Months, because I knew the last night He had visited me. Any previous spotting? What's spotting? I didn't know. Last Doctors appointment? I hadn't made one yet but I was going to. Due Date? I don't know for sure.

And then we left. They carried me out of the main building, with our few neighbors curiously watching. But Patrick had covered me totally with a blanket over the gurney sheet, so no one saw where I was bleeding from, and then he followed in his car behind the ambulance.

I was told in the hospital the miscarriage was incomplete and a D&C was required. The fetus was gone and I felt grief, and relief, and guilt. And I felt lonely.

Doctors spoke to me. Nurses spoke to me. Even a chaplain spoke to me about my grief. Patrick waited inside my room when he could and outside my room when he couldn't, but I was alone.

I was placed on IV's, given meds, tested and examined. I was beyond humiliated by my circumstance. I was beyond humiliated by just how many people looked, touched, examined and invaded my vagina. I was alone and humiliated.

I was also severely anemic. And that's how my parents found out.

I needed real medical attention, and a D&C. But I never would have told them about the pregnancy and miscarriage. I would have had the procedure and taken the medication but I would have done it alone. I wanted to be alone. He wasn't here, and I had lived and breathed alone for so long that having people around made me uncomfortable.

Patrick betrayed me however, and called my parents.

When my mother walked into my room hours later the procedure was already complete, and I remember looking at her thinking she must be shocked. My mother must be embarrassed that I had screwed up so totally. She must have been humiliated by me, but she wasn't.

My mother came in, walked right up to me, and took my hand. She didn't cry, or say anything negative, but she held my hand and smiled at me. She was cool, and I was relieved. This is what I knew of my parents; calm and cool. So if she had acted any differently I would have lost whatever was left in me.

Whispering, my mom asked, "Why didn't you tell me, Sade? I would've helped you. I would've helped you fix this."

Stunned, I had nothing to say. What could I say? I didn't know that. I didn't know she would help me. It's not like I was particularly close to my parents. I couldn't have known she would help me. I didn't know what to say, so I shrugged.

"Did you want the baby?" She pushed.

And again, I had nothing to say. What could I say? I did and I didn't. I wanted it so I had Him, but I didn't want it because I didn't have Him. What could I possibly say to my mother? I didn't know what to say, so I shrugged.

Minutes passed between us in silence until my dad walked in. Looking at the door, I burst out laughing at him. Covered with balloons and stuffed animals, and even multiple bouquets of flowers, my dad looked like an idiot.

Smiling at him affectionately, my mother shook her head. And in that moment when my dad looked at her and shrugged while smiling back, I felt like an interloper. They had a good marriage, and they clearly loved each other. They could still smile at each other affectionately while their daughter was a mess in front of them.

Watching my dad enter my room further, I realized I didn't know what to say. So I said nothing.

Clearing his throat, my father asked, "How are you, Sadie?" But again I had no words, and I didn't know if I should tell them anything. I didn't know if I *could* tell them anything. So with no words still, I shrugged.

In the silence that followed, my parents stood beside each other while my mother unloaded my father's arms. Placing the flowers everywhere, and tidying up the little bedside tablet of post D&C pamphlets, and miscarriage facts, and anemia information, my mother tidied up everything. My room looked nice, and it looked like I wasn't alone.

My parents sat beside each other, not speaking but holding hands. My parents looked at me, but we didn't speak.

Finally, "When are you going home?" My dad asked.

"I don't know yet. They have to monitor the anemia, and make sure the IV's are working. So I may have to have a blood transfusion tomorrow if I'm not getting better. But if I'm good by tomorrow night, I can probably leave."

"Oh, that's good," he exhaled. "So Patrick will probably bring you home then?" He asked. But I didn't know. Looking, I wasn't sure if Patrick was until my mom confirmed she had spoken to him, and Patrick wanted to bring me home.

And that was it. My room looked good. My parents sat in silence with me for another half hour, until my mother mentioned the parking meter, and within seconds they stood to leave me.

Looking I didn't know what to say, so an 'I'm sorry' whispered past my lips.

My mother took my hand again and kissed my forehead, while my dad patted my leg. They were being supportive, I know that. This was their support.

"We'll be back from Florida on December 19th, so we'll all have a good Christmas together. And by then this will only be a memory. Don't be sorry Sadie, this happens. Just be smarter next time, okay?" My mom smiled her words as my dad nodded his head.

"Okay," I agreed quietly.

And that was it. My parents left the hospital. My mom did call my room that night however to tell me she loved me, and to reaffirm that 'everything would be okay'. And I agreed because what else could I do?

It was the end of November and my parents were leaving for Florida like they did every single year on either the 1st or 2nd of December since I was 12 for 3 weeks. But they always returned a few days before Christmas so they could prepare for the holidays and buy my Christmas gifts. They always left, but they always returned so I wasn't alone at Christmas.

My parents did visit the next day telling stories about some of their friends and their families. They spoke about light subjects, while ignoring the reason for my hospital stay completely. When they left my room they did however offer reassurances that I would be fine by the time they returned from Florida.

And Patrick stopped by. He was very busy with his own school work. He was finishing his PhD thesis and I knew it was very important to him, but still he made time to visit me for a few hours the couple days I was in the hospital. He made time to be with me while he could and I was grateful. Patrick understood I wouldn't talk so he filled our time together with stories of his weekend and the new guy he met. He told me about all the crazy and the fun that was his life so I wouldn't have to think about the pathetic and lonely that was my life.

Patrick was amazing but acted like he wasn't doing anything special for me. Even when I found myself suddenly whispering 'thank you for trying,' when he took a much needed breath from his escapades, he simply shrugged and smiled.

So my parents came the morning I was to be released and then they left knowing, or rather stating, that I was in good hands with Patrick. They were acting the same, so I figured I had to act the same too.

I'm not sure if I ever really was the same though.

As usual with me there was always drama and upset. There was always depression and suffocating despair. There was always this need to escape from myself. There was a desire to be anyone but myself... and this didn't change. It just became more pronounced.

I left the hospital with Patrick who brought me clothes and shoes and thought of everything I may need.
When I was wheeled to the doors, he pushed me. When I was slow to stand from my exhaustion, he aided me. When I sat in his car gingerly, he drove slowly the 4 blocks back to our apartment.
Patrick was amazing that day and I felt such affection for him, I sat in his car and cried. For maybe 20 minutes I sat in his car out front our cool walk up apartment and cried, and he said nothing. He held my hand and shushed me a few times when I cried too hard and nearly threw up, but otherwise he did nothing but sit beside me while I cried.

After I returned home, I continued the next 7 1/2 months of my life waiting. I attended school infrequently, and I lived in my silence alone, except for the random calls from my parents and the frequent drop-ins by Patrick, and maybe a boyfriend of his.
But otherwise, I was completely alone, waiting.

CHAPTER 14

So I continued.

I went to college, then University. I was very smart and maintained very good grades even though I almost never attended school. I sat in my apartment all day and I waited every night for my stranger to show up. I waited every single night, just like I had spent my years waiting.

I did have a slight friendship with a woman named Silvana who I had met in school, and she tried to form an actual friendship with me over the course of a semester. Often we drank together in my apartment while she tried to be my friend. She really tried to engage me in my 'story', but I had nothing to tell. I would never tell anyone anything about myself. I'm not even sure I knew what to tell about my life, so I told her nothing.

Once a week, my female friend Silvana came to my place for dinner, we ended up drunk every time, and I even had a little fun with her. I kind of lived around her once a week visits, but that was all she was to me- a once a week visitor, which was much more than even my parents at the time, but that was just their way.

Throughout the semester I enjoyed Silvana's pseudo-friendship until I went out with her socially once. After incessant begging to go out, one night I felt drunk and secure enough to actually do it. So we went out. We went to a dance club and I was ridiculously quiet and drunk, until I wasn't so quiet anymore.

And I looked like a fool, I know I did. At the club, I danced my ass off and I had fun until a man wrapped his arm around my waist and started dancing against my back. And that was all it took to turn me into a psycho. Admittedly, I can't even deny it; I behaved like a total psycho.

After screaming, turning around, slapping his face, throwing my drink at him, I kicked him, and before he even had a chance to defend himself against some tiny little 20 something, I had grabbed and twisted his penis in my hand.

And I was repulsed. I know I looked like a complete psychopath, but I was more repulsed by the feeling of him in my hand than by any embarrassment I should have felt at my behavior.

And my new friend Silvana was mortified, I could tell. Originally, she jumped into the fray thinking he had caused some offensive injury to me, but when he pushed me off him and she screamed 'what happened' I replied the truth. I said such simple words but I spoke them like I had been repeatedly stabbed.

"He touched my waist and danced behind me," which he had. And then through the thump of bass beats, and the thrill of the music inside my stomach, I saw her look at me like I really was insane.

And the man stood there with 2 of his large male friends in front of me. He looked at me like I was crazy. He looked at me like he wanted to hit me. He looked at me... And then his face changed to some weird expression I had never seen before and he leaned in closer to me and quietly asked, "Are you okay?"

But I wasn't. Obviously. I was not okay, and really I didn't know if I had ever been okay. I actually don't remember a time when I was truly okay. I know I spent years depressed, and I know I had lived with undiagnosed depression for years. I know I hurt myself with razors, and knives and really anything I could find to help me release the pressure inside me. And I know I hid everything from everyone because I was never okay.

Looking at the club guy for mere seconds in silence, I remember I had no words. I couldn't answer his simple question. Like a deer in headlights I stood still staring at him as I tried to find my words. The music continued and the mood was wild all around us, but we 5 stood completely still among the chaos of the night club as I stared at him speechless.

So slowly shaking my head no, I finally exhaled. Strangely, I almost wanted to kiss him which was insane to me. I never wanted to be touched by anyone ever, but here I was looking at this stranger in a dance club and all I wanted to do was kiss him in that moment. But I did nothing.

When he slowly reached out his hand I actually found myself leaning into his palm as he took my face in his hand, and it truly was one of those surreal, out of body, bizarre moments when everything just stops all around you. The sounds faded, and the atmosphere vanished. I rested my cheek in his hand and I closed my eyes. And I felt something, until I woke up.

When reality surfaced seconds later I pulled away just as quickly as the moment had occurred. Turning abruptly, I left Silvana and the 3 guys as I stormed through the throngs of people pushing and shoving until I made my way to the long corridor where people made-out against the dark walls before hitting the exit doors.

Leaving the club, I ran from the doors, hailed a taxi, and was home within 10 minutes. Locking my door quickly, and rearming my apartment, I quickly stripped myself of my velvet little purple dress in my front hallway and stared at the wall as I stopped everything and sat on the floor.

And then I cried. Like a big, ugly, awful cry; I bawled my eyes out and wished for all the pain in my chest to stop. I just wanted to be normal and not sad all the time. I wanted to be normal so badly I didn't know how to make the craving for normalcy stop. I didn't know how to be normal, and I didn't know how to stop wishing I was normal.

I realized that was my one and only night out with my one and only female friend in years, and I ruined it because I was NOT normal once again.

But Patrick found me shortly after that.

Apparently, he and his boyfriend heard my sobbing in the hallway, which I still find hard to believe, but that's what I was told. Days later Patrick told me they heard a loud, keening-like cry coming from my apartment and he almost threw up from the intense instant upset he felt when he realized it was me making the awful sound.

So Patrick and his boyfriend used his key, opened my door, and quickly shut off the alarm. And as I looked up at him, his knees gave out and he fell into me as he grabbed for me.

And that I remember clearly. A very beautiful, highly dramatic reaction from my very beautiful, highly dramatic Patrick as he collapsed around my body and took me into his arms.

Crying still, I let Patrick hold me forever. I didn't even care that his boyfriend was watching us silently, and I didn't care that I looked like an ass. I didn't care that I was 23 years old and a complete mess, and I didn't care that Patrick knew what a mess I really was, until suddenly I turned my face and kissed him.

I don't know how I did it, but I know why. I needed a connection that was safe. I needed to not be lonely. And I needed to just feel something with someone. And thankfully, Patrick kissed me back.

When I remember it now it's funny because Patrick was gay, and not just a little gay, but totally and completely gay. He wasn't bi, and he had never, ever been with a woman because he always knew he was gay, but there he was kissing me passionately because I needed it so badly.

So we kissed. We kissed nice and softly, until it became heavily. We kissed and eventually I felt him touch me a little. Slowly, he took my breasts in his hands, and he played with my nipples. He explored my breasts and my neck and my face as he kissed me. And it was good. I felt good and safe in his hands.

When I slowly became aware of my surroundings I was amazed to understand Patrick and I were being watched by his boyfriend Stephen. Patrick; all post club sexy, and there I was in my bra and underwear only, because I had stripped my dress off before my crying jag in my hallway.

I was having a nervous breakdown and Patrick was here with me throughout it. And so we kissed, and explored, and slowly I found myself touching him back. Amazingly, I even justified in my head that I wasn't cheating on my stranger because Patrick was gay, so it's like it didn't count or something.

I don't know. But I do know I felt an attachment to Patrick without any fear, and that's what I needed then and there. I needed to feel. And I needed it safely. And he was good to me.

I remember vaguely thinking at the time, not only are all the good ones gay, but man, they know how to kiss, too. I was distracted and I didn't care about anything, and he was so good, I was lifted, and I was walked into my bedroom. I was kissed against a wall, and I was held tightly by him as he wove us through my apartment to my bed.

And I still didn't care. I kissed him like my life depended on it, which quite honestly it might have that night. I'm not sure, but with the way I was feeling had I not been distracted, to this day I feel like I may have done something very bad to myself, and finally succeeded.

But Patrick saved me that night. He kissed me back when he knew I needed to be kissed back before I did something very bad.

He kissed me, and soon he touched me too.

Amazingly, I had a brief moment of clarity, and in my brief moment of coherency, I saw Stephen lying on his side beside us watching as Patrick and I made out. And no one spoke or acknowledged the unthinkable between us. I'm sure I knew what was happening but I chose to ignore it so that I wouldn't stop it because I didn't want to stop it. I desperately needed a connection with someone. And I needed it with Patrick because he was safe.

But for one brief moment I did panic though and everything stopped. I was suddenly aware that Patrick was pushing my panties down my hips, and I felt Stephen's hand on my other hip trying to help. I felt it and panicked, and everything stopped as Patrick looked at me.

Begging for something I'm sure, he smiled at me and kissed the tip of my nose, like he always did and I relaxed instantly, and that was all it took.

Really, I should have felt like a whore, but at that age, Patrick was the first man I wanted to sleep with who wasn't my stranger. He was the only man I could allow to touch me without fear. He was gay, therefore safe, and I knew he truly was my friend. So gay or not, I really did trust him with my body.

Succumbing to our situation, Patrick entered me with his fingers as I watched his face study me. He looked at my naked body and didn't seem disgusted which I'm sure would have killed me in that intense moment. He looked at me like he loved me- not like a man in love, or even like a man in lust, but just like a man who loved me and was willing to perform an act to help heal me. Remembering his look of love, it was really very touching.

And so we did.

For one awkward moment, I saw Stephen reach over and give Patrick a condom, as they smiled at each other. For one second I almost came to my deluded senses, jumped up and ran from the room, but just as quickly Patrick, and presumably Stephen, sensed my panic and he shushed me gently while he applied the condom, as Stephen leaned over me and gently kissed my lips.

Shocked, my lips barely moved, but he wasn't kissing me aggressively or even sexually. He was soothing and comforting me, and then Stephen whispered against my lips, 'It's okay, Sadie. Patrick loves you and you're safe.'

So naturally, or maybe unnaturally, I burst into tears again as Stephen kissed me for real- like a grab his hair and hold him in place against my lips kiss, even as I felt Patrick slowly make his way inside me.

Kissing Stephen, I didn't care about Patrick entering my body. I didn't care that I was actually having sex with someone who wasn't my stranger. And I didn't care that it would probably become a huge mistake in the morning when I coherently realized I had had sex with my GAY friend and neighbor while heavily kissing his boyfriend on the lips throughout.

But time continued, and though it was nice, there were no fireworks or even an 'oh my god' moment, but I don't think there needed to be. I wasn't looking to have raise the roof sex, and I wasn't looking for orgasmic bliss to whisk me away. I wanted a connection to someone, and that was all. I wanted to feel something other than nothing. And I did.

When Patrick was finally ready to release, Stephen seemed to sense it and he stopped kissing me. While Stephen was looking at his boyfriend, I was mesmerized by the look on Patrick's face. He looked so different than my stranger did in this moment of release.

He looked beautiful and peaceful, or like content. Maybe because this wasn't back arching screaming sex he didn't look like my stranger did during His intense releases, or maybe Patrick never looked like that upon release. I didn't know. I had been with my stranger and I had the bad time, both which looked so different to me.

And thankfully Patrick had the sense to look at me as he released and not at his boyfriend, which would have humiliated me I think. Actually, I'm sure had he been looking anywhere other than at me, the sense of uselessness and loneliness would have been so complete as to throw me over the proverbial edge. But he didn't. He smiled at me, leaned in, and kissed my lips as he had his orgasm.

Shuddering after his release, he didn't flop on top of me, or even say something stupid and pointless. He merely leaned down and turned us so we were spooning. Rubbing his chest against my back he cupped my right breast in his left hand more like a comforting caress than a sexual act, and then he whispered, 'I love you Sadie, and I'm glad I could be with you.' And that was it.

Stephen left the bed, walked to Patrick's side, presumably to remove the condom from Patrick and he left the two of us alone. Patrick pulled the covers up over us, and unbelievably I fell asleep soundly, quickly, and without the constant pain in my chest I lived with each and every night of my life.

Hours later, I woke up to Patrick still asleep in bed with me, and no other sound in my apartment so I fell back asleep for another few hours.

Waking again around 11:30, I actually had to shove Patrick to get him out of my bed, which he did, eventually. And as he walked out of my bedroom, he didn't say a word, which was good because I had a feeling words were going to mess with my head and cause my sudden peace to crash down all around me.

When I heard my alarm disengage, I wondered about Stephen until I heard them quietly talking in my hallway as they closed my door. Unbelievably, Stephen must have slept on my couch to leave me and Patrick alone. Unbelievably, they had both made a kind of love to me that night. And unbelievably, I felt warmth deep inside me for the first time in years.

So when Patrick yelled from my door he'd see me later for dinner, I smiled. I didn't feel awkward, and I didn't feel like we had made a mistake that we could never come back from. More amazing still, I didn't feel like my life was going to be over soon, nor did I feel the soul-consuming depression I lived with constantly, in that moment.

And we were fine. Patrick came back over around 6:00 to make dinner in my apartment.

Walking in, he leaned over the back of my couch and kissed my cheek, as I lay snuggled up in a blanket. Then he prepared dinner for us.

And I remember walking into my dining room thinking 'here we go...' when he called me for dinner, but Patrick smiled at me and asked instead, "Do we need to talk about last night?" And shaking my head no, we didn't say another word about the night we kind of made love together as friends.

And even now when I think back, I realize Patrick really was a little miracle to me at that time. Remembering how handsome and charismatic and charming he was makes me ache with missing him. To this day, when I think of my Patrick, my heart breaks when I remember our sudden end.

CHAPTER 15

3 months after the bizarre night I had sex with Patrick, which was 3 months after the miscarriage, which was 4 months after Him, I entered Patrick's apartment for my morning coffee. He and I had an open door policy for food and coffee, so I helped myself once in a while.

Walking to Patrick's counter, I saw his thesis. And I don't know why- maybe it was fated. Maybe I was meant for this. Or maybe I was just nosey. I don't know why, but I looked at his thesis with pride.

Opening the first page I read the dedication to SMA- my initials, and I was so surprised, I smiled instantly as I snatched it up. After the title followed a 2 line synopsis.

'The Story of S' was the title, and that's when I knew.

'The Story of S- A tragic tale of a woman drowning in misery through years of undiagnosed mental health issues, suffering through life with Borderline Personality Disorder.'

This was me. Sadie Madeline Adams. I was 'The Story of S'.

Running for my home, I took Patrick's thesis and I grabbed my purse and fled my apartment. Unsure of what I was doing or where I should go, I drove hysterically to a park near the high cliffs of our city. I drove to the edge, and sat on the edge, while I lived on the edge, holding my story in my shaking hands.

And so I read.
And it was all there, too. Everything. From my rape right after I moved into my apartment, to last month's crying jag over the rigatoni I had burned. Everything was there, and I realized I had been an experiment, and a test. I was his 4 year PhD thesis.

I read things from his perspective. I read things from my perspective. I read things from an objective perspective. I read everything. And I WAS a woman drowning in misery.

Hours passed as I sat on the edge with my legs dangling, looking at my life from this new perspective.

To say I was devastated is an understatement. To say I was hurt means nothing compared to the despair I felt that day. To say I was embarrassed is also an understatement. I was humiliated, and I was destroyed. Plain and simple.

I was 'The Story of S' and I couldn't function as I sat on the cliff.

Reading pages and pages of me was stunning. Literally, I was stunned by Patrick's observations and insights. I was amazed by how much manipulation actually occurred between he and I in those last 4 years. I was simply stunned reading the story of me.

So I read and reread for 9 1/2 hours the history of those last 4 years of me...

By 5:30 I was done all but the last chapter. But for some reason I was waiting to read that chapter. For some reason I thought my last chapter would be important, so I waited.

Eventually, I stood and stretched my aching body as I walked back to my car at the cliffs. I drove completely numb to a corner store nearby. Once there, I bought a pack of smokes and a dreadful coffee, then I returned to my spot on the cliffs.

My cellphone had been shut off hours before when Patrick had called but I refused to listen to my voicemails. I was homeless and alone. I couldn't return to my apartment, and I didn't know what to do. I was utterly alone. Again.

Walking back to my cliff-side perch, I lit a cigarette with remarkably steady hands, sipped my gross coffee, and picked up Patrick's thesis for the grand finale.

And after previously reading his opinions and views of me, I thought little could shock me. I thought there was little else that could hurt me. I thought, what could he possibly write that he hadn't already written?

But I was wrong.

Flipping to the final chapter I was again stunned by the graphic descriptions of me and my life. From his observances of my neurotic tendencies, to borderline agoraphobia, to suicidal tendencies to my complete lack of trust in anyone, Patrick nailed me.

Patrick painted a picture, or rather wrote a thesis, describing the most pathetic woman that had ever existed. Patrick painted me as the most weak-minded, mentally unstable person walking around unmedicated and free of psychiatric assistance ever.

Patrick painted me as a complete lunatic capable of nothing in this world except for a complete decline into madness and depression.

In chapter format with subtitled text, he gave a psychiatric condition followed by endless examples of how I fit within the definition of said condition. And he told everything.

I was stunned. There were so many psychiatric terms mentioned, and though I knew the definition and example of almost every one of his descriptions, admittedly there were a few which stumped me.

Suicidal, depressive, neurotic, borderline personality disorder, emotionally unstable personality disorder, social anxiety, social psychosis, etc., I understood all too clearly.

Fits of self-mutilation and excessive alcohol addiction I understood as well. Inability to relate to others was another I knew, and agreed with totally.

He described how I felt emotions more easily, more deeply, and for longer than most others do. Therefore, he wrote, I have a harder time getting over situations which most people could get over or move past, quicker and easier, causing me to suffer an abnormal amount of time over one specific crisis than the majority would. He even gave percentages and references of the things that occurred to me as basis for his conclusions.

And it was all there. Everything... well, except for the sex.

Amazingly, though I had lived under a microscope for 4 years and had all my mental inadequacies highlighted for purpose of a PhD in Psychology; evidently, Patrick did leave out how he and I had had sex while his partner looked on and aided in our debauchery. I figured *that* little fact probably wouldn't have sat well with his Psychology professors.

He wrote of my miscarriage as another example of my inability to cope with my outside world, and as an example of my sexual promiscuity because of my lack of social morals and inability to recognize social norms and practices as pertains to relationships.

And that's when I finally lost it. Reading the part about my 'promiscuity' made me laugh. Actually, I laughed out loud sitting on my cliff thinking of the 2 men I had ever willingly had sex with for which he was one of them.

I found it hilarious that he said I was promiscuous when I had only ever slept with 2 people my entire life, yet he slept with 2 different people every weekend for the 4 years I had known him.

At that point I had hoped he embellished slightly so that he could simply use another example to pad his thesis, because no one would ever call a 23 year old who had sex with one man, and one friend *once,* a promiscuous woman. At least I didn't think so.

Anyway I read my story until the last sentence. I read with an amazingly clear head and with a complete lack of emotion. I wasn't crying or hysterical anymore. I wasn't dying or thinking up new ways to die. I was just a woman reading a very interesting thesis on a sad, pathetic stranger... Until the very end.

And then I lost it.

Patrick went on to describe the depth and very problematic degree of my delusions as based on my alleged sexual relation with an 'imaginary' man. He went on to describe how I would look and speak and act after my supposed affairs with my imaginary lover. Patrick described seeing me post delusion and almost believing *himself* that a sexual act had occurred, based on the physical signs, and even scents which accompanied these delusional relations. He went on to describe the nightmares and dreams I had, culminating in sleep walking and sleep talking about an alleged stranger who came to me in the night.

Patrick wrote of the confusion he himself felt after my nightly confessions in my sleep about a beautiful stranger who came to me in the night. He spoke about the depth of my delusion, bordering on schizophrenia, but only as it pertained to my sleeping issues and inability to mentally shut down in my sleep, often causing a sleep-deprived temporary psychosis.

And there it was. My dear stranger as a delusion. A great delusion I'd spent 7 years suffering through, according to Patrick and his thesis.

Patrick finished his thesis by basically saying if I lived another 5 years he would be surprised because I was so emotionally and mentally unstable. Patrick didn't believe it possible someone as weak-willed and emotionally unstable as I was could possibly live much longer than that.

He stated that though he would watch and do what he could to help me, with a complete absence of sentimentality, Patrick had faced my inevitable decline and probable death from a variety of suspects.

He even gave hypothetical examples starting with my easy suicide, to a delusional accidental death, and ending with an alcohol related overdose because I drank excessively and alone.

He seemed so objective and heartless in his assumption of my death, I found myself as heartless and unemotional reading it. I read everything amazingly with an almost clinical objectivity. I read it all like it didn't pertain to me, except for the part about my dear stranger, because that was where my objectivity ended.

So I closed the thesis and sat with my cold coffee and half pack of cigarettes and tried to understand, or rather digest, everything he said about me.

I was finished the 'The Story of S' and I desperately needed to understand where I went from that point forward. So I sat, and thought, and smoked.

Eventually I walked back to my car at dusk and wrapped a blanket around myself and grabbed another safety knife from my trunk, but I honestly was clueless. I didn't know how to proceed from there. I didn't know what I should do, but I knew I couldn't do it from my home.

After falling asleep briefly, I heard people playing outside my car, probably teenage lovers and their friends hanging out, so I started my car and drove to the last place I thought I would ever go- my parents' house.

Pulling into the driveway, I was surprised to see my mom on the porch having a cigarette. I just stopped still and stared while she smiled at me and shrugged. I stared and eventually smiled back.

"You're dad doesn't know I smoke when I'm stressed, so please don't tell him, okay?" She grinned.

"No problem," I grinned back and lit my own smoke.

Sitting on the porch I asked if we could go to the backyard which she agreed to. Walking through the side gate there was a very heavy silence all around us, and I didn't know where to begin.

"What's going on Sadie? Patrick has called like ten times, and he said you took off and he was worried, and he said he really needed to talk to you and explain everything. He even told your dad he was worried you might hurt yourself, which freaked him right out."

"Where *is* dad?" I asked instead of answering her.

"He's driving around looking for your car." Waving her hand outward and shaking her head she smiled, "And I know it's weird that he thinks he can find one little silver car in a city as big as this one, but that's all he could think to do since your phone was off."

Smiling and looking at my lap, I realized that felt good. My dad cared enough to drive around aimlessly looking for me which was really sweet.

"I would've gone too, but I was holding down the fort in case you came here and needed me," she said as I quickly looked up into her pretty green eyes.

"I'm okay. I just had a major shock today, and my *friend* Patrick isn't such a good friend, and he betrayed me and I'm hurt and I hate him, and I will honestly never speak to him again as long as I live. That's all," I mumbled.

Suddenly laughing, my mom mumbled, "...that's all," as I laughed too. That did sound fairly dramatic, even for me.

"I really do NOT want to ever see him again, so can I stay here tonight, and then go to my apartment with dad tomorrow and move some stuff out for a little while until this blows over. But I promise I won't stay here long. I'll get an apartment real soon, but I just need to stay away from Patrick until I can move away and guarantee I never see him again. Is that okay? I don't mean to intrude, but I have nowhere else to go."

Looking at me, my mom took my hand and rubbed her thumb back and forth across my knuckles. Looking at our hands, I remember wanting to cry so badly, but I fought emotion in front of my mother. That was never her thing- emotions or tears.

"Sadie, you don't have to ask us permission to say here. Ever. This is your home too for as long as you need it. Honestly. And you know I don't lie or give fake smiles and empty words. I'm too direct for that. But what are you going to do? What do you want to do?"

"Just like I said. I'll ask dad to take me home tomorrow so I can pack a few things. I'm changing my locks so Patrick can't get it, and then I'm moving on. I do NOT want him in my life for a minute longer. He used me, but I don't want you to ask how, okay?"

"Okay. But you can tell me anything. I'm really terrific with other people's drama. You can tell me or ask me anything."

"No, I can't. At least not yet. But I might, just not today. I'm so tired, I'm going to pass out. Do you mind if I just go to bed now?"

"Go ahead. I'll call your dad and let him know to come home. Go to sleep, honey." And in that moment my mother actually leaned forward and hugged me, which was very awkward for me.

Panicking, I jumped up and replied quickly as I turned to enter the kitchen sliding doors, "Thanks. But NO Patrick, okay? Promise me. I really will never forgive him for this, so I need you to promise you'll keep him far away from me, okay?"

"I promise. No Patrick, ever."

"Thanks. Um, and good night mom," I almost choked because it felt so weird to feel like my mother had my back then.

"Night Sadie," she spoke as I darted for the stairs.

And that was it. I crawled upstairs, barely able to move from the exhaustion suffocating me, but I made it to my old bed and collapsed on top of the covers.

Lying there, of course I thought of my stranger and I actually prayed he wouldn't come to me. For the first time in years, I didn't go to sleep begging him to come to me, or praying I wasn't alone anymore. For the first time, I actually wanted to be alone in my drama.

So I spent the night thinking. Literally, the whole night I thought and planned. By sunrise I know I closed my eyes and I remember I slept until mid-afternoon in my childhood bed. I slept soundly because I was pretty much unconscious.

If my parents checked up on me, I didn't know or wake. If they spoke to me I didn't hear them. I was beyond exhausted, but I had a good reason to be; I had decided to fix my life in the course of my night thinking.

I made the plans, and I thought of my future for the first time in my life.

*****

4 days after leaving my apartment in a scramble, I made an appointment and I met with 2 of Patrick's psychology Professors. I told them I was SMA. I told them 'The Story of S' was me. I told them my life in short form. I told them I was an unwilling participant in Patrick's thesis. I told them I was the unknown subject of Patrick's future career.

I spoke about everything to the 2 Professors as they listened carefully, and I was fair, though through his betrayal many would argue fairness was not expected of me, I gave it anyway. I gave credit to Patrick for many of his observations and diagnosis', and I applauded his tenacity in studying me for nearly 4 years of my life, though again it was without my knowledge or consent.

Winding down our 3 hour conversation, the Profs did have certain hard questions for me, and I answered them honestly, though they both said I absolutely did not have to. I chose in that moment to admit to many of my emotional shortcomings. I admitted to the suicide attempts, and excessive alcohol intake, and even to the cutting. I admitted to most of what Patrick described and analyzed, and I was remarkably calm throughout.

Sometimes I was reduced to tears, and sometimes I was pretty shaken by my own honesty, and sometimes I almost drowned in my truths, yet again these 2 Profs were very kind in a caring, professionally detached sort of way. They prompted me to speak without pushing me to answer, and it was good.

I think I woke up a little more that day. Well, actually I woke right up and acknowledged the half-life I had always been living. I woke up and tried to figure out a plan for my future.

Dr. Synode, one of the 2 Profs even offered me counseling, either with himself or with another Psychiatrist at the University, but I declined his kind offer. I even explained that because of this shock, I *was* going to make some changes and I was going to seek the help I needed but at my own pace, and by my own choosing. And thankfully, Dr. Synode and Professor Willis wished me well and extended the invitation indefinitely, which was very kind of them.

After 3 hours sitting with them, there was one last thing I needed to admit to them. One thing that was crucial to my story. One thing that had made me the adult I was. So I did.

Looking at both men seriously, I told them my stranger was in fact real and that I had in fact been having a relationship with him since I was 16 years old. And then I exhaled.

Waiting for either to speak, I felt like I needed them to understand that Patrick's assertion that I was promiscuous AND delusional was wrong. I told them I had willingly slept with only my stranger, and then I dropped the bomb- I had slept with only one man *until* Patrick. I actually told them Patrick and I slept together once, and I told them the circumstance as well.

To a stunned silence in the little conference room where we sat, I admitted that the very gay Patrick found me having a nervous breakdown, and admittedly, I wanted the connection, so he and I had sex. I explained that though clearly he left that part out of 'The Story of S', I thought it was crucial to understand just how lonely I was. I explained that though I was a physically willing participant in the sex, emotionally he may have taken advantage of me, which was further confirmed by his refusal to admit to it in his thesis.

Finally, I questioned not only the betrayal and the manipulation by Patrick in attaining his thesis but the means in which he presented himself in order to gain the knowledge of my life which he needed to use, as the basis for his 4 year PhD thesis.

I asked the 2 Profs if the means in which Patrick attained his subject matter was less important than the end result. I asked if Patrick knowing I was a 'woman on the edge' was a good choice as PhD candidate when he was willing to watch someone slowly dying without stepping in or offering assistance or at the very least attempting to get me help- all so he could watch me unravel for his selfish need to attain material for the very thesis that could have killed me had I continued on that path I was on, even as Patrick sat back and observed me.

And then I stood before I said any more. I didn't want to destroy him, because I honestly believed he looked out for me overall, and because I was honestly grateful for his friendship. A friendship that was absolutely dead to me the minute I read the dedication to SMA.

And as I turned to leave, Dr. Synode stood and offered me his hand, which I shook with tears in my eyes. Looking past him to Dr. Willis I thought these 2 men were really good doctors. They could see what I needed, when I needed it. For 3 hours they mostly listened and spoke only when clarification was needed, and they even offered to help me afterward.

When I left the room, neither Professor told me what would happen to Patrick, nor did they even imply he was to be penalized by the means in which he found and used his thesis material, but I knew. I could see on their faces that each man felt anger, frustration, and sometimes dread as I relayed the story of my life to them, and Patrick's part in the last 4 years of it. I knew he would be penalized to some degree for the betrayal.

So I left the university. I remember walking to my car in the early evening and I remember shaking uncontrollably when I sat in my car. I remember thinking this must be some kind of post adrenaline rush or something, because the shaking was killing me. Sitting there, I took my time. I lit a few smokes, and I drank some warm Pepsi I had in my purse. I sat there until I was steady enough to drive to my parents' house.

And when I returned to their home, my mom was waiting in the kitchen for me. It was 7:30 at night, and she was still waiting. Looking at her I didn't want to cry so I gave her a lame smile and said, "It's done, and the Professors were really nice." And that's all I could say.

Blessedly, my mother nodded and said nothing else, like she knew I was incapable of further speech.

And that was the end of Patrick and my 4 year 'friendship'. I did see him again, once at my apartment, and 3 times on campus, but I was very, *very* clear that if he so much as spoke one word to me I would start screaming, so he left me alone.

I received one letter under my door from him which I found one of the times I went home for more clothes before I moved out of my apartment for good. I received a letter, but I threw it away. Amazingly, I actually threw it away without reading the content because I didn't care what he said, or whether it was good or bad. I wanted to move on and reading his letter wasn't going to help me move on, so I threw it away unopened.

Because of Patrick I had to leave the apartment I loved, and I had to find somewhere else where I felt safe, which was proving difficult. Because of Patrick I trusted no one, though to be fair I never really did before him. It's just his betrayal confirmed for me the absolute truth of people- Anyone can and *will* betray you if given the right opportunity or circumstances.

So Patrick and I never spoke again. I know he didn't graduate that year as he intended so I assumed he did receive some penalty regarding his thesis, but I know he did graduate 2 years later, a year after I should have graduated with an Honors BA, so

I also assume he didn't have to actually start his thesis from scratch.

And I don't know anything about him anymore. I don't know where he ended up, or if he slowed down. I don't know if he ever fell in love, or if he ever found a soul mate. I know nothing, and I'm okay with that because I try not to think of Patrick if I can help it.

Patrick has become nothing more than another name to throw into my hatbox. He is a footnote in my history, and I need him to stay there.

*****

After the colossal meltdown that followed me with The Patrick Affair as I referred to it, I did start attending school semi-regularly. I won't lie and say I went all the time, because I didn't. Between living at my parents, looking for an apartment and just trying to function, I went as often as I was emotionally able. I went as often as I could which was a big step for me.

And 3 weeks after The Patrick Affair, I saw Alexander Hamilton near the Psych buildings. Walking from an appointment I made (and kept) with Dr. Synode, I was nearly back to my car when I saw Alex sitting near a fountain. Looking, I remembered him from high school. Looking, I remembered he was very attractive, popular, and always nice to me when our group of friends intertwined at various parties. Looking, I realized he was still good looking. Looking, I realized he recognized me.

Smiling at me, I fought the unbearable urge to run from him and cover my head. I fought my natural tendency to look the other way from a man. I fought being afraid of him. I fought being *myself* as I had been for years.

With a strength I didn't know I possessed, I smiled back. That's all. I didn't stop and I didn't try to speak to him. I didn't do anything but continue walking to my car as I left campus. But I did smile back at him, which I was pretty surprised by.

When I returned to my parents' house, my mom was in the kitchen cooking dinner and she motioned to the paper where she had circled a few apartments for rent. And I took the hint. I had been with my parents for weeks, and though they were supportive and kind to me, I could tell they wanted their lives back. They wanted their freedom, and quite frankly I wanted my freedom back as well.

So I apartment hunted seriously. I thought of the student loan I'd been granted for the summer session, and I tried to find another apartment I could afford. I thought of how far I could make my loans last. I thought of where I wanted to live, and *how* I wanted to live. I looked hard for something new to fit the new me I wanted to create.

And a few weeks later I found my new apartment, perfectly situated closer to my University, but far enough away that I was still a single woman living in her own apartment, instead of a student living in a student housing apartment. I was close to school, but far enough away to be myself without being confused for a typical student.

So my parents moved all of my stuff out of my old apartment with me, and my dad promised to keep Patrick away should he attempt to talk to me again, which he did. I moved in 2 weeks after that because being a University City meant many apartments were available all summer while students broke leases from their previous year of school.

I was enrolled and started the summer session so I had more credits in fewer time, plus a major distraction from all the changes I was trying to make.

If I kept moving forward and was distracted, I found it easier to actually take these forward steps.

And then I finally spoke to Alex.

Alexander seemed to always be near me on campus. Well, the days I actually went to school, Alex was always around. Alex smiled and said hello, and made light banter with me while I fought running from him to my car.

Eventually, Alex began walking with the security patrol to my car with me. Eventually, Alex's conversations made me give one or two word answers in reply. Eventually, I began speaking back to Alexander's conversations.

And he was good. There was something so soothing about his voice. There was something so calming and warming, that I often found myself silently listening to his tone of voice, rather than to his actual words. There was something so lovely about Alexander Hamilton.

After maybe a month of hit and misses, Alex finally asked me if I would like him to accompany me to all my classes, and I remember looking at him like he was joking. I thought he was being sarcastic because of the bizarre inconsistency of my school attendance, but he wasn't. Alex honestly wanted to walk me to and from whatever classes I attended, and so a phone number was exchanged.

With NO pressure, Alex asked for my phone number and gave me his. Alex asked me to call him when I planned to attend class, whenever that was, so he could meet me in the parking lot to escort me to and from my class if he was available.

He asked me to let him know when I would be at school because he was concerned with my safety. He told me he didn't like thinking of me alone in the evening on our huge campus. He told me he thought of me frequently, and he wanted me to be safe. He told me he liked me and wanted to know I was safe.

So 7 weeks after the first smile, I called Alex and actually told him I would be attending the evening class, and he thanked me for telling him and said he would meet me in the parking lot. And I remember hanging up the phone and thinking of his voice. He was just so calm and cool and he spoke so honestly with a touch of humor and with an ease I had never known.

There was something about Alexander that was soothing to me.

After all the shit I had dealt with the previous 10 ½ months of my pathetic little life, I actually wanted to bask in the ease Alexander's voice provided me, and so I did.

After that first phone call, the seal of my silence was cracked wide open. I found myself calling Alex just to say hello and nothing else. I found myself waiting to see if Alex would return my call. I found myself waiting for Alex to call me, and he always did. Once that seal was broken, he called me often.

Alex still did all the talking, but I found myself drinking in his voice as I sat listening.

Alexander's voice was wonderful for me because he didn't ask for anything in return. He never demanded anything of me. He asked questions but when I paused, or swallowed hard, or closed down completely, he moved on. He didn't push me to go to class, and he didn't question why I didn't go to class some nights. Alex just called to tell me about his day, while I sat silently listening.

Alexander was this tall, handsome man who simply walked with me. He spoke to me kindly, and with a gentleness and ease of tone which I never feared. He was a lovely little light who gave me some calm when we walked. I found that Alex brought me a little peace in my darkness.

And I found myself warming up to Alexander in a way I didn't think was possible. He wasn't as intense as my stranger, and he wasn't crazy in my face wild like Patrick had been. Alex was somehow in the middle of the 2 men I knew and loved and hated the most.

And then the moment that changed my life forever happened.

The moment that rebirthed me. The moment I started the journey to all I've ever wanted to be. The one moment in time that defined absolutely everything of my life afterward.

CHAPTER 16

9 weeks after our smile, 4 months after Patrick's betrayal, 8 months after the miscarriage, and 12 months after His last visit, Alexander kissed me in front of the campus museum.
Alexander kissed me, and I loved it.
I was stunned. Shocked. Confused. In awe.
I loved Alexander's kiss. It was deep and beautiful, and romantic, and loving. It was the kind of kiss that weakens knees, and makes a body press in against the other person.

Alexander.
Alex kissed me and everything stopped for me. All the worries and the loneliness and the horrors and the fear... *stopped*. Everything I had felt for as long as I could remember stopped. Alexander kissed me, and I forgot who I was in his arms.

Alex walked me to my car as usual. He talked and I listened as usual because I loved his voice. Alex spoke and laughed and walked beside me toward the parking lot.
But Alex stopped suddenly and took a step in front of me, turned to me, slowly raised his hand to my cheek, took my face in the palm of his hand and leaned into my lips. Slowly, like he was asking permission he leaned in. Gently, like he didn't want to frighten me he held my face. Softly, like he was afraid I'd run he kissed my lips.
And it was amazing.

Alex kissed me... and eventually Alex broke off the kiss. Unbelievably, it was Alex who stopped the kiss from escalating because I couldn't stop it. Unbelievably, I was almost disappointed when he stopped the kiss.
Unbelievably, I *loved* Alexander's kiss.

When he pulled away from my lips, Alexander ducked down, leaned his forehead against mine and exhaled. Waiting, neither of us spoke. Waiting, I didn't know what to do or say. Waiting, Alex stayed firmly pressed against me.

After forever, I turned my head slowly and kissed the inside of his palm. And then the dam broke.

When Alex whispered, "Sadie..." I burst into tears.

Standing together, I cried and Alexander wiped my tears as quickly as they fell. With no words between us, I was lost. Shaking my head, I heard myself moaning as I hunched over and grabbed for my hollow stomach.

Everything ached in that moment. I was happy and miserable at once. I was moving on and regressing in the same second. I was experiencing my first kiss and I was cheating on my only lover. I was new and I was used.

I was in agony.

After forever, Alex stopped trying to wipe my tears with his fingers, and instead used his sleeve to wipe my face, eyes, and nose. But he didn't flinch, and he wasn't repulsed. He acted like my behavior was normal and perfectly okay. He didn't seem remotely shocked or scared, or horrified by my horrific behavior.

And when I finally caught my breath and stood back up to look at him, Alex smiled at me- he actually smiled.

Grinning at my confusion, Alex whispered, "I've never made a woman cry after kissing her. This is definitely a first."

And smiling at his light humor, I whispered an 'I'm sorry...' as I stood still in my confusion and pain. "I don't know who to be when I'm with you," I confessed.

"Sadie... you can be anyone you want to be with me. I promise."

Pausing to take in his words, I stared at his face and I believed him. I could be anyone with Alexander and I wanted to be. I just didn't know how to change me. And I really didn't know who I wanted to be.

So making a decision, I told Alex I had to go. I asked him to give me some time. I asked him not to call me, and amazingly he agreed.

Alexander walked me to my car in silence, and he paused at the door as I sat in my car. Leaning against the opened door, he waited until I finally turned my face toward him.

"Sadie, you can be anyone you want to be with me. Just ask me for help and I'll give it, or tell me what you need and I'll do it.

Anything at all." Stunned again by his gentleness of tone, I looked at Alexander Hamilton and I believed him.

"Okay..." I replied. "But I need a little time."

Smiling, Alex leaned down, kissed my cheek, and said, "You've got time. Just let me know when you're ready, and I'll be right there. Call me when you're ready for me, Sadie. Okay?"

And nodding my head yes, I waited for Alexander to shut my door as I slowly backed away from him. Driving slowly, I didn't know where I was going. Driving unaware, I didn't remember which turns to make, or which streets to drive on. I didn't know my own name in that moment.

Eventually, I found myself parked in my old apartment's spot- the spot by the front door. The spot I had parked in for years. My old spot to my old apartment. The apartment of my trauma, and youth, and abuse, and love, and horrors, and Him, and of Patrick.

Sitting in my old spot, I wanted to see Patrick so badly, because I wanted to ask him what I should do. I wanted to admit to everything that had been my dear stranger. I wanted his guidance, but I couldn't do it. Patrick was dead to me, and I needed to leave him buried. And so I left.

Pulling out of my old spot, I drove to my new apartment near the University and I started again.

For 11 days I stayed in my apartment. I didn't go to class and I didn't leave my apartment. For 11 days I spoke to no one. And Alex almost made it, but finally on the 11th day after our wonderful kiss my phone rang.

Sitting near my phone which absolutely never rang, I knew it was him. I knew Alex was calling, but I just wasn't ready for him yet. I had spent 11 days struggling with my 2 realities.

I had my waking potential with Alex, and of course I had my sleeping reality with my stranger- A reality with my stranger which was all I had known for nearly 7 years of my life.

Waiting near the phone, the machine finally picked up and I heard Alex's lovely voice for the first time in 11 days.

"Hi Sadie. I know I said I wouldn't call, and I won't again, I promise. I just want to know you're okay. That's all. Call me and say 'I'm okay' and you can hang up. That's all I need from you, nothing more. We don't have to talk about anything else. I don't want you to talk to me until, or *if* you're ready. I just want to know you're okay. I care for you, and not knowing if you're okay is driving me crazy. Just an okay, Sadie. That's all. I promise."

And I believed him.

Sitting on my couch beside the phone, I believed Alex wanted nothing more than to know I was okay. He had never asked for anything from me- he didn't try to enter my apartment, and he didn't try to force visits with me after class. He didn't ask me to hang out with him before or after he walked me to and from my classes. He didn't push himself into my life. All he ever did was talk to me and make sure I was safe coming and going to school.

So leaning for the phone, I dialed. Shaking, I waited. But after only one ringtone he answered.

"I'm okay," I spoke quickly before he could even say hello.

"Thank you. Is there anything I can do for you?"

"No... but thanks."

"Will you let me know if there IS anything I can do for you? Anything I can do to help you?"

"Yes..." I whispered.

"Okay. Good night, Sadie."

But pausing, I was wordless. I wanted to hear him speak. I actually wanted his voice speaking quietly to me. I wanted to talk to Alexander Hamilton *because* he was Alex.

"*Anything*, Sadie."

"Thank you. But not now. There's some stuff. Um, I can't talk about it. But thank you Alex for caring."

"I do care. But I won't call you again. I'll just wait for you, okay?"

"Okay. Good night, Alex." And then I hung up before he could say anything else.

Sitting with the receiver in my hand, I found myself cradling it to my chest as I cried. I couldn't even tell you what I was crying about. I didn't know what I was crying about. I missed Alex, but I missed my stranger more. I had feelings for Alex, but I loved my stranger totally. I liked walking with Alex, but I *lived* for my stranger.

There were so many things going through my head. There were so many emotions ripping through my chest. I was sad, and lonely, and unhappy. I felt guilt for liking the kiss with Alex, and I felt guilt for liking Alex's kiss but not telling him about my stranger. I liked Alex's kiss but I felt guilty for not telling my stranger about Alex.

Everything was surrounded in guilt, and I was desperate and disturbed because the guilt was quickly killing me.

So walking to my bathroom, I found some of my pills. Walking to my kitchen, I found a cold bottle of vodka in the fridge. Swigging right from the bottle I downed some of my pills with the alcohol. And gulping hard, I leaned against the counter as I struggled with my reality.

*****

When I woke up, I was under the table staring at the empty bottle- the large bottle- lying on its side. Crawling to a stand against the table, my body was in agony. Walking slowly, with my pounding head leaning to the right, for some odd reason that helped, I eventually made it to the bathroom. Running the water and turning on the shower, I could barely undress. I was a mess and I knew it. This time I had gone a little too far, I could tell.

Sitting slowly on the edge of my tub, I let myself slide to the tub bottom as the water poured over my head. I remember wanting to wash my hair, but my hands wouldn't work very well. With a shaking that was pretty obvious, I gave up trying to reach for the shampoo.

And then my body began dying on me. I could actually see it happening. My stomach started moving strangely, almost like something kicking its way out from the inside. My legs started shaking badly against the bottom of the tub. I actually watched my hands cramp into claws that I couldn't straighten. I suffered cramps all over my legs, and my feet felt tight and stuck in their horrible position.

I was lying there on the bottom of the tub with a body in agony, and I couldn't help myself at all. Even if I could've yelled, I didn't think my neighbors would have heard me. Even if I could have attempted to get help, I didn't think I would have made it to the front door which was closest, or to the phone which was much further away.

Watching with my head lying in the water, cocked to the side, as my body continued to move and cramp, I realized I was pretty far gone that time.

I remember knowing I was dancing my final dance with death. And in that moment of acknowledgement I closed my eyes and gritted my teeth to all the physical pain, and then I thought of my stranger. I thought of our years together and all I had gained from Him. I thought of all I had gained. I thought of the benefit to all the years of my stranger's visits, and then I thought of nothing.

What had I gained? Sexual knowledge never to be used with another? The ability to orgasm with only Him? Loneliness? A life half lived? Love and obsession? Insecurity and pain? Unbearable loneliness and suffering?
What had I gained from my years with my stranger?

I remember waking hours later on the floor beside the shower. I remember waking in the midst of vomiting. I remember my body vomiting and shaking but I did very little to aid myself. Actually, I remember not being able to help myself. And so my body lie dying as my mind succumbed to the fact that I was probably dancing with death for the very last time.

When I became conscious again a few hours later I remember my confusion. I remember looking around the bathroom wondering how long I had been there. I didn't even know if days had passed, but what I did know was I was disgusting. Truly, I was undeniably disgusting.
I was lying in my own vomit and excrement. I was laying in filth. I was covered in the unimaginable. But at the very least, I was alive.
Waiting patiently as the smell assaulted me, I was eventually able to move my arms and then my legs. Slowly, I crawled my way 2 steps back to the shower. Looking at my disgustingly filthy hands as I tried to turn on the taps, I saw everything my body could expel all over me. I saw it all. I even saw my blood.
I remember as the shower warmed waiting and wondering where exactly the blood came from. Based on the agony of swallowing, I could have torn my esophagus while vomiting, or I could have bled out the remains of my stomach lining. I could have simply

expelled all I was able to, until blood was the only thing left in which TO expel. I don't know, but I do know I was in pain, sad, confused, and yet relieved that I was alive in that moment.

Where was He?

After all the times He had magically appeared when I was this near to a death, He had always come to me and saved me. Where was He? I hadn't seen Him in nearly a year and when I really needed Him, He wasn't there for me... again.

He wasn't there again. Like every other day and night of the last year, He wasn't there, and yet I waited. I waited and cried, and begged, and agonized over His absence. But again, just like every other day and night for the last year, He wasn't there.

When I was able, I remember struggling to take my shower. I remember having to lift my legs over the tub and nearly crashing onto the floor. I remember pumping the anti-bacterial disinfecting soap all over my face and hands and body. I remember scrubbing under my nails and between my legs. I remember reaching slowly for my shampoo. I remember using soap and lather to wash away the smell of my death. I struggled, but after an hour at least, I was finally sitting on the edge of the tub clean as the water poured down my head and face.

I was clean, finally. I was no longer crying and I could breathe deeply. I think the hour of steam even helped my breathing even out.

And when I was able, I made my way, slowly, unsteadily out of the shower and bathroom, grasping my towel, and using my other hand against walls as my guide, forcing my way to my bedroom. I fought and struggled, but eventually I made it to my bed.

I made it and then I collapsed. And I remember the exhaustion was so great, and the pain in my entire body so intense, and the throbbing in my head so powerful, my body could do little more than collapse. And so I landed in my towel, pulled my blankets over myself and collapsed into the exhaustion that was my life.

When I woke a few hours later, my body felt the same. I remember feeling all the aches and pains, while the throbbing of my skull seemed unbearable. I had the worst hangover head I had ever known, almost like I could actually feel my brain move independently of my skull.

But I was alive.

With a strength I couldn't believe, I slowly made my way to my kitchen, and nearly collapsing again, I leaned against the cabinet next to the fridge as I found some apple juice.

Gulping the juice, I forced myself to stop. Waiting, I held my stomach and breathed deeply through the growing nausea. Waiting, I held on as the juice settled. And as I forced my body to slowly live, I also forced all thoughts out of my head. I pushed each thought of Him out while I struggled to just live.

After the juice, I grabbed a whole box of Melba toast, a bowl, my apple juice and a bottle of water. Making my way to my living room I refused to think. I settled myself in an inclined laying position on my couch and I slowly fed my body the nourishment it needed to survive this round of mistakes. And though I still vomited here and there, eventually I felt myself slowly become stronger.

And I survived.

10 hours later I was well enough to attempt plain toast, and a few hours after that a grilled cheese. I spent 2 full days recovering, which was pretty amazing to me, and pretty shocking too. But I did survive.

And by the third day, I lit my first smoke and finally allowed myself to think.

So I thought of my stranger. I thought of nothing but my stranger. I thought of the years my stranger had visited, and I thought of the years my stranger had NOT visited.

And for the first time ever I found myself growing angry with my stranger. I felt betrayed by His absences and hurt by His neglect. I was angry for all the years I had spent waiting on His visits.

I was angry, but just as quickly as the anger surfaced it left me with a hollow sadness in its wake.

And I WAS sad.

I cried heavily and often when I thought of Him. I cried for all the years wasted. I cried for all the life not lived. I cried because even in that moment of anger, I missed Him so much my heart broke again and again, but I couldn't change that.

I loved Him. I remembered loving Him. I remembered the depth of the love I had felt and I remembered the struggle to love Him.

He had made Himself everything to me, so without Him I had nothing, even though I was nothing with Him as well.

He was the beginning and the end of my days. He was my every thought and my every feeling. He was all I had, and all I was. My stranger was all I had ever known of love and I ached for Him.

Yet even as He was a ghost in my life, I realized I was the one who floated from one day to the next, empty and yearning. I waded through the murky depths of my despair as I waited for Him to come to me. I was alone but always waiting for more. I was alone and lifeless because He wasn't with me. I was lifeless and alone because He hadn't come back to me in a year.

A year I spent with constant trial and upset. I spent a year alone. I spent a year with mistake after mistake. I spent a year with pain after pain. I spent a year filled with misery and upset and loneliness and betrayal. I spent a year alone. A fucking year!

*****

5 days after my accidental overdose my phone finally rang. And even though I knew who it was, and I did think of him from time to time, he was not who I loved. I loved my stranger. Plain and simple. I was in love with my ghostly stranger.

And over the course of my waiting I'll admit some moments were spent regretting my love for Him. Moments came and went when I resented the love I had. Moments washed over me in a tide of hostility, loneliness, and regret.

But then the other moments came. The moments when I remembered our passion and beauty. The moments I remembered us filled with love and hope. The moments I remembered He and I spent together loving each other wholly.

And so my days continued.

I didn't call Alexander back, and I waited for my stranger. I waited, as I always had.

Eventually, I came up with a plan of action- a test, if you will. A groundwork for how I would proceed with my stranger. And suddenly I felt stronger.

I felt like I had the upper hand though it was still me waiting. I knew I was waiting which was essentially a weakness, but it was a weakness wrapped in a new found strength. I knew what I was going to do. And I knew what I was waiting for.

I wasn't sitting back waiting aimlessly anymore. I had a plan and ultimately I had a decision to make based on my plan.

But it was still in His hands at that moment. He still had to come to me. I still had to wait for Him. But once I knew what I was waiting for, I felt remarkably better. I felt stronger. I felt less lost. And so I waited.

With the sadness I had always known, I waited. With the sadness that consumed every part of me, I waited. With the sadness that had defined my entire life to that point in time, I waited for my stranger.

Inevitably, my sadness bounced from soul-consuming to numbing.

I would walk about my apartment in a trance of pain and craving. I would watch television blindly. I would listen to music with deaf ears. I was a zombie walking in a state of misery, waiting day and night for His arrival.

I left my apartment twice during those weeks I spent waiting. I walked 2 doors down to the convenience store to purchase a few cartons of smokes, and some food. I didn't eat much then, but I found myself truly without anything edible. My cupboards were bare and my fridge was a graveyard given only to housing liquors and the accompanying mixes. I had no cans of soup, nor boxes of Kraft Dinner. There was nothing left, and so I walked 2 doors down and struggled to carry back 6 bags of supplies twice in 5 weeks.

I even called a local taxi service who picked up liquor for customers so I didn't have to leave my apartment again. And I waited.

I had enough soup, alcohol, coffee, and smokes to live. I had everything I needed to sustain myself until He came to me. And so I waited.

Every single day I dressed and ate and made myself live. I went through the motions of living, even though I was nearly dead.

And I knew it. I knew I was a corpse merely filling out clothing. I knew I was lifeless and I looked it. But I waited every single night for Him anyway.

Every time I saw myself in a mirror I saw the lifelessness I had become. I was sallow and grey, and thin, and haggard-looking. I wasn't attractive anymore, and I wasn't pretty. I was a hundred pounds of lifelessness. I was a ghost of my former self, even as I waited for my ghostly stranger. But I continued to wait anyway.

Every single night I performed my ritual still. I showered and prepped my body for Him. I dressed in my nicest nightgowns. I made sure my body was ready for Him. I did everything I had always done for Him. And I waited.

I waited, but I had a plan. I knew what I needed. I knew what He needed to do. I knew what He needed to say, and I knew what He needed to be.

I had a plan, and it was that plan that kept me sane and made me continue living. I had a plan. And I waited.

And then 36 days after Alex had kissed me, 15 weeks after our smile, 5 ½ months after Patrick's betrayal, 9 months after the miscarriage, and 13 ½ months after His last visit, finally my dear stranger came to me.

CHAPTER 17

My Dear Stranger XIX

Last night, my dear stranger finally came to me.

I had not seen, nor touched my stranger in over a year. I had not been seen nor touched in over a year. A year I was alone. I had spent an entire year alone and waiting.

Last night as dreams came and went, I slept and woke in misery. In my dreams horrors crept and peace faded as I slept and woke in desperation. My nights are filled with nothing but this- my nights are spent alone and waiting.

For over a year life had passed lonely and desperate. For over a year filled with sadness I had swallowed my heartache and hopelessness. For over a year I had endured an emptiness sheltered by pain and endless trial. For over a year I had suffered hollow energy mixed with the exhaustion of my loneliness. And I have waited through it all, alone.
Life has passed me by. I have met people at school. I met a man I couldn't befriend. I have had opportunity I did nothing with, because I am meant to be alone and waiting.

Last night I slept and I woke, just as I had for over a year. I woke as usual. I woke battered and betrayed by unseen nightmares and endless fear. I woke scared and unsure. I woke filled with pain and loneliness. I woke alone and waiting.

Last night I woke in the bathroom, sitting on the side of my tub utterly confused in my sleep-walkers trance. Looking around, I soon realized I had run a bath in my sleep. Placing myself back into my surroundings, I realized I had had a plan. Maybe my unconscious needed to cleanse myself of the nightmares, or maybe my body simply needed to be cleansed. I don't know, but I rarely understood my intentions when I woke from my sleep-walking trances.

Undressing, I eased into the hot water and relaxed. Aware of this most simple pleasure, I closed my eyes and allowed the heat to engulf me. I waited for the heat to warm the coldness inside me. I waited in the silence as peace settled in and I found myself falling back asleep.

When I woke seemingly minutes later, I was cold and shaking as hours had escaped me while I slept. My chest once again felt the curious weight which burdens me through each of my days, until suddenly I saw movement. Suddenly I was not alone and waiting. Suddenly... with a scream and a jump I saw Him. Sitting casually with a towel across His knees, He seemed to wait for my comprehension. And I did comprehend.
I looked at Him. I looked to Him. I looked, but I felt nothing but confusion in that moment.
Who was this man who sat with me? Who was He to be so still beside me? Who was He to me? And I knew...

Horribly aware of my nudity, I tried to cover my body from Him. Searching His face for answers, I tried to cover my exhaustion of Him. And slowly His smile faded. Slowly, He held the towel out to me. Slowly He moved, aware of my trepidation.
Seeing me still, covered by my desperate hands and unsure of Him, He turned His body from me and slowly He inhaled.

With a movement so fast and so full of purpose I escaped the water. Clothing myself in the towel I stood beside Him, waiting. But no sound came. No movement came. No acknowledgment flowed between us. There was just nothing left.
When I stood in front of Him, as He sat so still, I wanted to weep. I wanted to hit Him. I wanted to love Him. I wanted to hate Him. But there was nothing. What had become of us? What had passed between us? What had survived, and what had died within us?

Finally, I gently touched His shoulder as He shuddered and turned back toward me. Catching the look in my eyes, the stranger grabbed me so quick and intense, my body threatened to break under the strain of His embrace. With His arms wrapped around me and His face buried deep into my chest, I heard Him slowly exhale against me.

But in that moment I didn't know what to do. Unsure of what I felt, and unsure of the stranger holding me tight, I attempted to leave the room. And though He held me for seconds too long, gently He released me from His grip.
Walking to my bedroom I waited on my bed. Walking to my bedroom, the stranger stood at the door waiting for my cue.
Unsure of my desires, I made a gesture so deliberate and forgotten over this past year, the stranger immediately walked to me and sat next to me on my bed. Turning from Him I laid down on my bed. Turning to me the stranger laid down beside me.

And I was confused. I loved Him and I hated Him. I was alive, but I felt dead. I was warmed but I was empty. Unsure of my desires, I waited. Unsure of my desires, He waited. Waiting, I eventually turned my back to Him as I lay on my side.
Engulfing me in His arms the stranger lay beside me, holding me so tight, breathing into my neck as we waited.
Waiting, I realized over a year had passed for me alone. Over a year had passed for me sad and only half alive. Over a year I had waited to tell Him our secrets. Over a year I had waited for Him to come to me.

So closing my eyes, I began to weep. Tears streamed down my face as misery flooded my chest. The weight of my soul felt heavy and destructive as my tears continued to flow from my body. Trembling, I had no more control. I felt nothing but sadness as He held me tightly in His arms until the exhaustion and sadness pulled me back to sleep.

When I woke this morning my sight was blurred and my body ached. I felt no release or peace. I felt only misery which I desperately didn't want to feel anymore. And He still held me tightly in His arms. He held me in a way that used to bring me peace, but now only felt like a heavy weight on my body crushing my chest.
When I turned to Him, He smiled at me in such a way as to make me almost forget the waiting. Almost. But then I suddenly remembered the year I had spent alone.

Who was this man who came to me with delicate smiles and hands? Was He a guardian angel or friend? Or was He the man born to destroy me finally?

I didn't know, and He didn't explain our love or even His absence. Again, He gave me nothing as excuse or explanation. Again, He gave me nothing.

Unaware of what I wanted or craved, and unaware of my feelings and beliefs I lay in silence. I was unaware of my life and my love, until I slowly raised my face again to the stranger. And in a whisper so sad, I asked Him to leave me forever.

I asked Him to leave me. I asked Him to rise and walk away. I asked Him to leave my room and my home. I asked Him to please leave me forever alone. And pausing for mere moments, with eyes so beautiful swimming in tears He looked to me. But before He could look through me, I turned from Him and us.

Eventually, I heard His soft cries as His body left my bed. I felt His warmth ease from my skin. He turned the music off and He left my world in silence. I felt Him leave me physically though I could no longer really feel the absence of warmth for the surety of my decision.
But I did feel the weight which threatened to crush my chest. I felt my loneliness and sadness. I felt my misery and pain. I felt, but I no longer waited.

"I'll be back for you because you were born for me to love," I heard Him whisper as He left my room.

And so I cry as I write these words. I am living half alive. I am still alone, but I'm no longer waiting for His return.
My life is here, wrapped in these sheets, barely able to breathe, alone and desperate, though my heart no longer waits.
I am here now, half alive but alive. I am no longer waiting for the world outside to let me live, slow and sure, as I finally learn how to breathe alone.
August 27 2003
23 years old

*****

And that was our end. There was no big drama, nor dramatics. We didn't make love as a final act of unnecessary suffering. We didn't kiss goodbye. We did nothing. That was our end. That was the simple ending that has haunted me for almost 9 years.

I am haunted by the complete absence of anything. After nearly 7 years together I feel like we deserved more. I feel like a grandiose gesture was required. I feel like the almost 7 years we spent together needed the dramatic ending which the relationship itself had strived on.

Our entire existence was based on our drama, and the end was based on the words 'please leave me' followed by the leaving of me. I was left after living for Him for nearly 7 years of my young life. I was left as quickly as He had come to me in the night.

And I have been haunted.

Years have passed with Him always there. Each milestone, each accomplishment, each everything I have done in the last 8 years are secretly wrapped up in Him.

Maybe not every single day, but certainly every few days I have remembered Him. I have been caught unaware and He has assaulted me. I have smelled a flower and He came to my mind. I have made my bed and remembered Him soiling my sheets with my virginity. I have even taken the dishes from the dishwasher and remembered a glass of water He once placed at my bedside.

8 years I have waited, which is really unfair to my husband and son. Well, maybe not my son because he has all the love I could possibly give him. But for my husband? I'm not sure. I think I hold back. Actually, I know I do. I love him, and he's a good man, but I still hold back part of myself from him.

And I just can't handle all this pressure anymore. There's too much pressure on my chest weighing me down.

CHAPTER 18

Looking around my garage I'm disgusted. Everything is all messy. There is stuff everywhere and I hate it. It's all so messy, I feel like *I'm* messy.
But He never came back...

I don't understand what I'm doing and I don't understand what I've done. What have I become? What did I do wrong?
But He never came back...

I no longer live a half-life. I am fully alive with a large life surrounding me. I am alive and happy.
But He never came back...

*****

Why do I feel like this? What's wrong with me? Everything hurts and yet I feel nothing.
Oh god, I miss Him. Where are you? What are you doing? Crying out, I can't seem to stop myself. Where did you go?

No, that's not fair. I made Him leave. I made Him go. I did this. Oh god... I miss you.
Where are you?

I can believe He left. I can't believe He actually left me. Sobbing, I can't seem to stop myself but I know I'm not making sense. I KNOW it, but it just doesn't feel right to me. I made Him leave me, but He left me. Why?
No. No, no, no. I needed Him to leave me because I wanted a good life. And I have a good life, I know I do. Oh, god. What is

my life?
 I can't breathe...

Pulling and tugging at my collar, I rip my sweater off but I still can't breathe. Tugging and pulling at my collar, I rip my t-shirt off but I still can't breathe. Everything hurts. And my chest is so tight.
 Pulling and tugging, I rip my bra off, and I inhale as deep as my lungs will allow. Why can't I breathe right anymore?
 Rounding my spine, holding my knees, rocking back and forth, I can finally breathe a little.
 Please. Please make this stop.

Why did you leave me?

Reaching, I crawl across the floor and grab for a smoke, I light up with shaking hands and wait for the peace to envelop me. Waiting, I wipe my face of tears and breathe in deep my nicotine dream. Waiting, I need the peace to take me. I need to remember to breathe.

Why did you leave me?

Crying and begging, I feel nothing but His loss in this moment. Where are you now? Do you love someone? Are you happy with someone else?

I can't seem to fight this desperation. I need to know. I need answers. I don't know, but I need to know if He loves someone else. Why? What does it matter?

> He left me because I asked Him to go.
> He left me because I told Him to go.
> He left me because I wanted Him to go.
>
> Why? Why did He leave me?

My Dear Stranger

... OF THE END

Sarah Ann Walker

CHAPTER 19

Freezing, sitting in my garage I remember that time so clearly. I remember how cold I was all the time. Even in the summer I froze. It's like my skin had a layer of ice underneath and I could never get warm. In the shower I warmed until the second I got out and then my body froze to the core once again.

For years, Patrick used to make jokes and poke fun at me, lightly of course, about me being a cold hearted bitch. He would wrap a blanket around me and rub my arms briskly to try to warm me up when I shivered. He would crank the heat, even in May so I could get a little warmth into my skin. Once he even joked that I must love seeing him all hot and sweaty and that's why I insisted on blasting space heaters in my apartment.

But I didn't. I was just cold. Always. My body froze, no matter how hot the outside temperature or the temperature inside, it didn't matter, I was always cold.

I remember finding out years later I was always anemic and I also had Raynaud's phenomenon, which caused me to be cold. Learning I wasn't suffering from coldness because I was emotionally unstable was helpful. Learning I was actually cold and it wasn't just my imagination or because I was dead inside made me feel remarkably better. I actually didn't produce enough red blood cells to warm me, so I was emotionally okay- just physically cold.

Like right now. I'm freezing. Well, actually I *am* outside in the garage and it is late fall and I'm barely dressed, but still... I'm freezing. But it's not my fault and it's not my imagination- I have an ailment that makes me cold. I have chronic anemia which may have even caused the miscarriage as some suspect. I don't know. I just know I freeze all the time.

*****

2 weeks after He left me, on the second Saturday of September, I received a call from Alexander Hamilton.

The University summer break was over and classes were to commence on Monday. After exiting a midday shower, I saw the blinking light and I knew it was Alex. I just knew. And I couldn't believe he still cared enough to call.

My absence from the world had been thorough. I had spoken to my mother once and lied about everything going on in my life. I told her the summer session of school was fine, and I was fine. I had pretended I was University attending Sadie, when in reality I was next to nothing Sadie. I blew off anyone and everyone including Dr. Synode. I became a ghost in my city, a ghost to my parents, and a ghost in the world.

I was lucky my student loans covered my summer session. So when I lost my mind, I called in and withdrew from my classes, and that withdrawal afforded me a credit into my bank account in which to live on over my summer of mental and physical vacancy. And though I knew I'd have to pay back those summer session loans one day, it wasn't then, so I was okay. One day the weight of my excessive student loans would crush me, but it wasn't that particular summer. Therefore, after my withdrawal I had enough money to stay in my apartment for 2 months, paid in full, with nothing to do but ghost about my life while I tried to figure out my reality.

10 minutes after his call, I was tightly wound when I pressed play on my machine. I didn't want Alex to be mean, but I also understood he was a twenty four year old guy who kissed a girl who vanished on him. I understood he was probably angry, and likely to tell me to piss off. I understood he was likely telling me to leave him alone, though admittedly I really didn't want that. I didn't know what I wanted, but I knew I wanted Alexander Hamilton's light and ease in my life, in some small way.

So sitting on my couch, I leaned over, prepared myself mentally, and pressed play.

"Hi Sadie. I'm not sure what's going on, or if you're coming back to school, but I wanted to say hello and check up on you. I promised I wouldn't call again and I didn't, but schools starting up and I had hoped you would be attending this year. You're so smart, and I would hate for you to tank your University studies. Plus, I miss walking with you. If nothing else, could you call me back and let me know you're okay. I just want to know you're okay, even if you don't want to be my friend anymore. That's all, I promise. Um, I'll wait for your call."

Listening to his message over and over again I was truly surprised by the relief I felt hearing his voice. Alex seemed so sincere, and kind. He wasn't pushy or demanding, and he didn't stress me out. He seemed like just a nice guy, and I found myself wanting just a nice guy in my life.

Bracing myself, I pulled my wet hair from the towel, put on my housecoat, and lit a smoke. With shaking hands, I eventually dialed the phone number I had never forgotten.

Waiting out 2 rings, Alexander answered the phone a little breathless, like maybe he had run for the phone.

"Hello?"

"Hi. I'm okay," I breathed huskily. But my nerves were shot, and I felt almost nauseous with my anxiety.

"Hi, Sadie. Thanks for calling."

"You're welcome." And then we suffered an awkward silence.

"Are you going back to school on Monday?"

"I'm enrolled."

"That's good. When is your first class?"

"Tuesday afternoon." And then we suffered another awkward silence. Maybe it would help if I gave proper answers versus the bare minimum I replied.

"I'm going to be there Tuesday. Would you like me to meet you in the parking lot?" Would I? Yes. I realized I did actually want to see him. Well, more I wanted to *hear* him speak, but that required seeing him, so I guess I did want him to meet me.

"Yes, thank you. I should be there at 2:45, for my 3:00 tutorial."

"Okay. I'll see you then." And then we suffered a not so awkward silence while I figured out what to say next.

"I'm just going to walk you to class, and I promise not to kiss you. Kissing you, though great for me, turned you into a mess which was pretty hard on my ego, so no more kisses for you. Okay? Really, I am NOT going to kiss you, so don't even ask me to. I mean it, Sadie. Even if you beg me, I'm not kissing you, so forget it." And I could hear the humor in his voice. I knew he was being playful, and I realized he didn't resent me, or think I was a jerk. I realized he wasn't going to tell me to piss off, and he wasn't angry with me. And amazingly, I felt relief.

"Fine, Alexander. I'll try not to beg you to kiss me," I teased back. "I'll see you Tuesday. And thank you."

"You're welcome. Take care, Sadie."

And when he hung up, I felt okay. It was so strange for me to feel okay. I didn't crave Alexander like I did my stranger, and I didn't ache for him like I ached for my lover, but I did like him, and I did like listening to him speak to me.

Alexander seemed like such a plain, straightforward good guy, and for that I was grateful. I needed a little straightforwardness in my life. I needed to not want, and fear, and crave, and obsess any longer. I needed to move past my years of waiting. I needed to let my stranger go. But not to be replaced with Alex- far from it.

I needed to let my stranger go for me, because ghosting through life was killing me, and I was smart enough to know it. There was a reason I hadn't visited or been visited by my parents in months. There was a reason I hadn't left my apartment in months. There was a reason I closed myself off from humanity. I pulled away from everyone because I looked like death, and I didn't want to look like death anymore.

So I spent the next 3 days trying. I felt terrible; all weak and exhausted. I know I looked like a victim of some horrific illness, but I tried. For 3 days I ate and drank coffee, I tried to smoke less, and I didn't have anything to drink, at all. Every time I thought of alcohol, I made myself have a coffee or apple juice instead. I did everything I could to avoid being pulled back into my despair.

Struggling, I fought the anxiety that threatened to keep me in my apartment on Tuesday. I was neurotic, insecure, and socially awkward to say the least, and the thought of being surrounded by students everywhere scared the hell out of me. I was scared, and this fear made it harder not to drink, but I didn't. I was petrified of all the noise in the halls, and on campus, and throughout the lectures. I knew there would be people everywhere, and because I hadn't had any human contact in so long, I was struggling with copping out and staying home.

And I honestly wanted to. Staying home felt like the best thing I could do, but I wouldn't. I had decided I was tired of ghosting through life so I had to make myself attend school because I no longer *wanted* to be a ghost.

So 3 days later, on Tuesday afternoon I found myself smoking back to back waiting in my car until I was finally able to turn on the ignition and make myself move. And it only took an hour and a half. Honestly. An hour and a half of sitting in my car, nauseous from chain smoking, shaking, and fighting my nerves, until I was finally ready to drive to school.

Arriving at 4:15, I actually laughed at myself when I pulled up. My class ended at 4:30, so my first intro class was pointless, but I made it to school. I was actually at my campus, sitting in the parking lot, laughing at myself for working up the nerve to get there, but then being too late to actually attend my class.

Lighting a victory smoke and exhaling through the cracked window, I startled when Alexander suddenly knocked gently on my window. And I knew he was gentle, but the noise seemed so loud in my deathly quiet. Checking the lock on my door again quickly, Alex smiled at me. He didn't look offended and he wasn't angry with me for making sure the door was locked. Instead he hunched down and rested his arms against my window, smiling.

And I was relieved again. Alexander's smile made me relax. He was smiling and waiting for me to calm down. He was waiting on me. Without asking a thing, or trying to force his way into my car, he just hunched down and smiled as he waited for me to get a grip.

As we each waited in silence, I looked at Alexander and I felt calm wash over me.

Alex was very good looking, with tanned skin, and brown hair, and with lovely blue eyes. He was so good looking on the surface, but it was his voice and his kindness that calmed me. Alexander would smile and speak to me, and everything dark seemed to faded away for me.

Looking at Alexander waiting for me calmly, I decided to act. I rolled down my window halfway and finally tried to speak. Embarrassed, all I had was a 'hi' and a blush until he took over.

"You did well, Sadie. I knew you would show up... eventually." And smiling again, I couldn't help my grin.

"Sorry I'm late. I tried..." I mumbled.

"Better late than never. Do you want to just walk to your class so you get the feel of it? Obviously, you're too late to attend, but you might like to walk to class anyway."

"Do you mind?"

"Not at all. I'm done for the day, so I have nothing I'd rather do. Are you ready?"

"Yes..." and I was. I wanted to get out of my smoky car, and I wanted to walk beside Alexander again. I wanted to hear him speak, and I wanted to join the land of the living again.

Standing up, Alexander actually asked, 'may I?' before attempting to open my door, and I appreciated his patience. I didn't want to feel rushed, and I didn't want to feel overwhelmed. It seems so stupid to me now, but getting out of my car was this hugely monumental event for me. But I did it.

Taking a big breath after grabbing my purse, I unlocked and opened my door as I inhaled the summer campus air into my lungs. I had forgotten what summer air felt like, and I couldn't believe how warm I felt immediately. It was nice to be warm. It felt amazing to be warmed by the air for the first time in months.

Standing, I waited for something, *anything,* but nothing came. Treating me like some wounded animal, Alexander waited for me to proceed. Walking forward, he walked beside me, not touching me or even invading my personal space. He walked beside me until eventually he began speaking.

As if nothing was strange and my behavior was normal, Alexander began speaking about his classes, and the campus, and the improvements which were made, and about anything, and nothing at all. He spoke, but not obnoxiously, and not about himself ad nauseum. He spoke and I listened to the soothing, warming sound of his voice as I made my way to my potential classroom, turned around, and walked back to my car.

Even when others students, friends of Alexander's approached him and I tensed up, he gave curt little nods, or simple smiles of greeting, but he never left my side, and he never engaged anyone else, but me.

When we found ourselves standing beside my car again, I remember thinking, *oh god, please don't do anything stupid, Alex. Please.* But I shouldn't have worried. He did nothing stupid, or wrong. Actually, he did nothing- which was exactly what I needed.

Opening my car door, I felt awkward for a moment until Alex asked if he could walk me to my class the next day. Smiling at me he waited until I was in my car, then as I rolled down the window he sat right back down on his haunches and waited. With a look that screamed friendly and safe, Alexander waited for my answer.

Looking closely at him, I replied, "Yes, please. I would like to walk with you," and I meant it. I *would* like to walk with Alexander Hamilton.

"Okay. Same time tomorrow?"

"No. My first class starts at 11:00 tomorrow but I'll try to be on time." And I knew I would try harder.

"Sadie, just try. I don't care if you're late. We can always ask someone for the intro notes, or you could even ask the Professor. Just do what you can and I'll be here waiting, okay?"

"Okay. Thank you, Alex. I'll see you tomorrow." And I knew I would.

Starting my car, Alex stood back up beside me and smiled as I began reversing from my spot. Waiting, he stood still until I drove away and then he waved at me. Seeing him in my review mirror I felt happy as I left the campus to drive the few blocks back to my apartment.

When I finally arrived home and made my way inside my secured apartment, I actually allowed myself to smile and I felt good. I wasn't quite giddy, but happy definitely. I felt alive-ish. I felt like I might want to try to walk with Alexander as often as possible. I felt something inside me.

So 2 hours after I returned home, I dialed his number. I couldn't believe I was doing it, but I made myself.
"Hello?"
"Hi. It's Sadie."
"I know. How are you? Is everything okay?"
"Yes. I just wanted to thank you for walking me to class, and for waiting for me even though I was really late, and for not making me feel bad for being late, and for not commenting on how awful I look. And for being nice to me."
"Wow. Slow down. I was happy to walk you to class. I don't care that you were late, just that you eventually made it. I didn't think you looked awful. And I like being nice to you. Okay?" Smiling in my living room, I murmured an 'okay', and suddenly felt pretty stupid.

Embarrassed, I continued speaking. "I'm sorry I sound so dumb, I just don't talk to many people, well anyone really, so I don't know how to talk to you. Um, I should go. I just wanted to thank you for walking me to class," I spoke quickly and awkwardly.
"Please speak to me any way you want. Whatever you want to say, I'll listen. And I'll always walk with you, Sadie."
"Okay. Thanks. I have to go. See you tomorrow," I gasped hanging up the phone.

And suddenly, I started crying again.
Actually, I sobbed. I felt good and bad, miserable and happy. I felt torn. I felt even more unsure of myself than I ever had before. I felt conflicted and sad. I didn't know if I was making a mistake trying to rejoin the world, or if this kind of sobbing reaction was normal for someone trying to live.

I felt everything in the span of that evening, and when I finally stopped shaking and crying, I fell asleep heavily on my couch.

Afterward, I remember being stunned that I had slept through the night without my nightly ritual, which I had never missed except for the times I was in the hospital. I was stunned that I had a day old uncleansed body, and that I wasn't as freaked out by my dirty feeling body as I thought I would be. I was stunned that I was awake, alone and functioning at 7:25 in the morning.

But I did think of my stranger. I would be lying to myself if I said I didn't wonder if He had come to me in the night to watch me. I would be lying if I said I didn't want to see Him still. I would be lying if I said I didn't still love Him, because I did.

Getting up eventually, I made coffee, hopped in the shower, and applied makeup to my hollow looking face. Afterward, I dressed as best as I could with my ugly, loose-fitting clothing while I made another huge decision.

Reaching for my living room phone, I made another huge step when I made a call to Dr. Synode. Leaving him a desperate sounding message, I asked to see him again. And after I hung up, I was pretty proud of myself again because I knew I had made a few huge steps in the course of 2 days. I was trying, and I was surprised by how easy these steps actually felt to me after I committed to them.

I was still freaked out, and neurotic as hell. Insecure and totally paranoid of my safety. I was sad, and hopeful. I was struggling, but I was also kind of thrilled by the reality of my attempt to live.

I felt; which was pretty new for me at the time.

At 9:30, an hour before I was going to leave for school, my phone rang. Waiting out the rings, I finally jumped for it at the last second, and I listened as Dr. Synode spoke quickly and abruptly. Telling me he had spares all morning, and a TA to cover his 12:30 class, he wanted me to come see him as soon as I was able. So I agreed.

Driving to the campus, admittedly, I was nervous. I had spoken to Dr. Synode about most of my issues before, but not all. He knew the Patrick fiasco, and he knew my suicidal tendencies, but he didn't know the true depth of my issues. He didn't know about the brutality of my attack, and he didn't really understand my stranger. He knew about my life in point form, and strangely, I was looking forward to telling him about all or part of it in depth. I remember knowing I needed to speak with someone to help with all my confusion.

And so I did. Within 2 1/2 hours of walking into his office at 11:00, I had spoken more to him than to any other person on the planet. And it was weird. It was a floodgate-type scenario. I sat in a chair across from him in his University office and I spilled my guts. I spoke endlessly; and I made sense sometimes, and other times he had to try to reason what I was saying. I spoke quickly and quietly, and with upset and devastation. I spoke with a tragic sense of loneliness deep inside me. I spoke about it all for 2 1/2 hours.

In hindsight, I find it amazing that my life fit into the span of 2 1/2 hours, but it basically did. I told Dr. Synode about everything I could. I told him about my years and years of waiting, and loneliness, and restlessness, and pain. I told him everything, sometimes in graphic detail, and sometimes simply breezed over. But I spoke while he listened intently.

And never did he rush me, or ask invasive questions. He rarely pushed me for further explanations. He never seemed to judge me, nor reprimand me for the things I had done in those years to myself.

Rarely did he speak though, which left me to just spill my secrets. All over his office, I spilled everything that made me me. I told him the details and events which slowly created this shell of a woman. I told him why I felt the way I did, and what made me feel the way I had felt for the better part of my life. I spoke honestly for the first time in my life about my life.

By the end, I was absolutely exhausted. I felt an unbearable heaviness on my chest, wrapped in fear and confusion. I felt weak and lost. I felt like total shit, actually.

Afterward, Dr. Synode looked over the notes he had scribbled down throughout my 2 1/2 hour spillage and placed the phone back on the cradle. Watching him, I had a vague memory of the phone ringing once, him picking it up, hanging up, and placing the receiver back on his desk. I think he thought I was important enough to ignore all calls, which was actually a wonderful feeling, because I realized I was important to him in that moment, and I needed that.

After he glanced at his notes quickly, the silence of the room started to close down on me and I found myself shaking and breathing with difficulty, but quickly he looked at me and leaned forward across his desk to take my hand. Rubbing his thumb back and forth across the back of my hand he looked at me, and started breathing slowly in and out dramatically until I found my body copying his movements breathing slower in and out.

"I want you to come see me tomorrow morning, Sadie. I want you in my office at 9:00 tomorrow morning. Can you do that?" He asked me calmly.

"Yes..." I replied just as quietly.

"Okay. Go home now. Don't attempt classes today- you're not ready today. I want you to go home, get comfortable, make yourself a healthy dinner, and I want you to try to sleep tonight in your own bed as early as possible. I want you to sleep Sadie, but if you can't sleep don't stress out about it. We'll deal with any sleep issues tomorrow."

"Okay."

"I have a series of issues I need to explore with you before I can help you, but we need to talk more. I need a few answers to some important questions-"

"Like what?" I interrupted.

"Not today. You're done for today. You have made remarkable steps today speaking with me, and I want you to stop for the day. If you have anything important to add, I want you to write it down in a journal tonight so we can go over it tomorrow morning. But you are done for today. I need you to go home, make yourself comfortable, eat a healthy meal and I want you to sleep. Can you do that?"

"I'll try," I promised. "Will you tell anyone anything I told you today?"

"Never. I promised you multiple times today that I would never repeat anything we discussed, and I meant it." I didn't remember him saying that to me.

"I didn't know."

"I told you multiple times that I would not repeat anything we discuss. I told you that I had privilege as a practicing Psychiatrist at this University hospital and that I was taking you on as a patient, therefore confidentiality is not only implied but legally binding."

"I didn't remember you telling me that."

"But I did. And I will continue to do so each time we meet until you remember."

"Thank you, Dr. Synode," I mumbled. "I'm scared of talking."

"I know. But I plan to help you learn to speak. You have many issues to work through and many issues to deal with. But I plan to help you. We'll meet frequently at first, and we'll discuss medications and therapies along the way. As for today, I just want you to go home, get comfortable, make yourself eat, and try to sleep. That is the only requirement for today. Will you do that, Sadie?"

"Yes," I agreed. And I would.

When Dr. Synode slowly stood from his desk, he walked around until he was standing in front of me. But feeling overwhelmed, I pushed my chair back slightly, until he wasn't hovering over me.

"Sadie, I will not hurt you ever. You are my patient, and I will only help you from today forward."

My Dear Stranger

"Okay," I whispered as I rose from my chair. Taking a step backward, I didn't like Dr. Synode so close to me, but I also didn't really feel afraid of him. I was just uncomfortable as I made my way to his door.

"One last thing for today. I want you to change the code on your alarm when you get home. I want it changed tonight, Sadie. Will you do that?"

"Okay," I answered confused. "What time do you want me here tomorrow?"

"I told you I want to see you at 9:00am. Will you be here, Sadie?"

"Yes." And as he nodded at me while leaning against the front of his desk, I knew that I would. I liked Dr. Synode for some reason, and I wanted to have a doctor help me. I needed a doctor to help me because clearly I was unable to help myself.

Suddenly crying as I tried to leave his office I asked, "How do you live, when you've spent your life waiting alone?"

"I don't know yet Sadie, but I'll try to help you find that answer," he nodded.

"Thank you, Dr. Synode," I mumbled from the doorway as I opened the door to leave.

"I'll see you tomorrow, Sadie. Have a good night."

And I left him.

CHAPTER 20

Leaving the Psych Quad buildings on campus I remember feeling absolutely exhausted. Walking slowly to my car in the bright sunlight of mid-afternoon, I had hundreds of memories slamming into my brain with each step I took. I was overwhelmed and exhausted at once. I was crying and confused. It felt like it took me an hour to reach my car, but eventually I did.

5 steps away from my car, I saw Alexander leaning against presumably his own car. Looking at him, he smiled at me, then looked surprised, then upset the closer I walked to my car.

Jumping toward me, Alex made the mistake of grabbing at my arm, which made me freeze, because I didn't want to be hurt suddenly when I had felt like I might be helped. But I think he understood his mistake quickly enough to release my arm just as quickly as he had grabbed me.

"Are you okay? What happened? You look horrible, Sadie. Did somebody hurt you?" Alexander asked a little manic sounding.

"I'm okay. I have to go home, make myself comfortable, eat a healthy meal, then I need to sleep in my own bed," I answered automatically.

"Can I drive you home, Sadie?"

"Okay..." I mumbled, because realistically, I was barely more than a walking dead woman at that point. Actually, I don't know how I answered that question, and I don't think I had time to think about my answer or the ramifications of having Alex drive me home. I just said okay, and that was it.

"Let me help you," Alex offered, and I remember babbling something like, *I wish you could* to him.

Later that day, I remember being shocked by my surroundings. I was sitting at my dining room table at 4:00, with a towel wrapped around my hair, wearing a pair of sweats and a heavy sweater as Alexander dished me out some spaghetti and a piece of chicken.

I didn't remember stopping at a store for groceries, and I didn't

My Dear Stranger

remember showering. I didn't remember anything that led up to that moment at my table, but there I was being served by Alex a delicious, *healthy* meal in my own home.

And feeling suddenly overwhelmed, I began to cry as I tried to spin my spaghetti on a spoon while attempting to eat. I remember my vision so blurred that I couldn't see what I was doing. I remember trying to open my mouth for food, but an awful sound of crying exited my throat as I fought the sadness that choked me, until Alexander took over.

Gently, he took the fork and spoon from my hands and whispered, 'open your mouth, Sadie,' until I did. Filling me with food, Alexander acted like I wasn't the absolute freak show I felt like. I was nearly comatose and I knew it, but even as I knew it I couldn't change it.

And so I allowed Alexander to feed me until I thought I would throw up from the excessive amount of food my body wasn't used to. He even lifted a glass of water to my lips when my hand shook too badly to lift it.

And when I had had enough to eat, I remember shaking my head no, and the food stopped. Helping me rise, Alexander began walking me to my bedroom, but I didn't want him to go there. It was too soon to try to sleep in my bed. It was too soon to attempt to sleep throughout the night. And it was way too soon to have Alexander near my bedroom.

Stopping him, I touched his cheek and begged quietly, "Would you please leave me now? I have to get comfortable and watch some television until nighttime so I can sleep in my own bed tonight because that's what I'm supposed to do."

"Are you okay to be alone, Sadie? I can stay outside if you want? I just want to make sure you're okay tonight."

"I'm okay, but I need you to leave now. Thank you for the wonderful dinner. I haven't eaten in a really long time, so that was delicious. Thank you very much. You cook very well. Thank you. But can you go now? Please?" And then on a gasp I remembered my alarm. "You have to go Alex so I can change my alarm code. I have to! I have to change it now. Please go!" I yelled.

"Okay. I'll see you tomorrow?"

"Okay. I'll be on campus sometime in the morning, but I don't know when I'll be finished and I don't have a class until 2:00, so I don't know when. But you have to go now. I HAVE TO change my alarm."

"Okay. Good night, Sadie. I'll see you sometime tomorrow. Call me if you want to talk or if you need anything, okay?"

"Okay. I will," I said quickly, but I think we both knew I wouldn't.

Walking Alex to the door, I practically pushed him out as I turned for the security panel. Looking at the panel I had to concentrate so hard to remember how to change codes. It was weird that something so easy was going to be so hard for me, but then it hit me and I remembered. Punching in the current code, plus the counter codes, following the instructions on the panel, I finally did it. I chose a new 4 digit code, and I even had the sense to write the number down right away because I was likely to forget it by morning.

And then it was done, and I knew why I did it. I knew why Dr. Synode wanted me to do it, and I knew what it might mean.

I knew He would still find a way, but at least I could admit to myself and even to Dr. Synode that I had tried to stop Him from visiting me. I tried to stop my dear stranger for the first time in 7 years from taking any *more* of me. I tried, which was a huge step for me.

Eventually, after watching multiple TV shows which I was barely aware of, I made my way at 8:00 to my bed. It was still light out in September, but with my dark blinds I made it feel like night as best as I could.

Crawling into my bed I remember allowing the mental exhaustion to claim me. I felt the pull of sleep, and I sank into it deeply. I said good night to the audacious world, and I said goodbye to my stranger. With tears and a heavy heart, I said my good bye as I felt sleep pull me away from the lonely life I lived.

Remembering that day and night, I think that was truly the beginning of my life.

CHAPTER 21

Thinking of Alex, I remember his sweetness to me always. He just had a way about him that was so undemanding, and light, and kind, and even a little fun. He was never intense or dramatic and he never pushed me too hard.
In his special way, Alex guided me into becoming a better, healthier Sadie. He guided me with his kindness into the life I had always wanted to have.

So the following day after my horrifically honest day with Dr. Synode, and my sleeping release from my stranger, I started over again.
There is no other way to describe it. I started over. I met with Dr. Synode every single weekday for a month, I attended classes when I was able, and I walked with Alexander when I was well enough to do so.
And he never asked. Alexander met me when I was on campus and he walked me when I told him I would be there, whether for class or for my appointments with Dr. Synode.
Eventually, the pattern continued until it was just that- a pattern. Dr. Synode and I had scheduled our therapy visits around my classes, and Alex and I had scheduled our walks around my therapy sessions and classes.
And I made it this way daily until Christmas.
My parents of course had contacted me from time to time before Christmas, and I told them what they wanted to hear. I told them school was good, my apartment was nice, my car was running without problems, and my life was well.
So when Christmas came, I finally saw my parents for the first time since the summer. And I knew my appearance concerned them, which I could see all over their faces, but neither of them acknowledged it, therefore, it's like I wasn't this ugly, skinny little sallow Sadie. My mother did however tend to put more food on my plate Christmas Eve and Christmas morning, which I guess was her passive-aggressive attempt to tell me I looked like shit

without actually saying it. And I appreciated her silence.

Christmas night I returned to my apartment to a huge gift sitting at my door, and I was thrilled. I could tell from the 'Sadie' on the bag card it was from Alexander, and I was excited.
He and I continued to walk to class every single day. He spoke and I mostly listened, though once in a while I did respond or ask a question about his funny tales. But that was it. We never physically touched, nor did he ever kiss me again.
Alexander made a point of cooking me dinner every Friday night, no matter what my mood was like that day, and I always enjoyed myself regardless of what that mood had been like before he made me a meal. And after dinner he always left me. I never had to ask him to leave, he just knew to leave after the dishes were cleaned up, which was a relief.
I wasn't ready for Alexander to be more than he was then. I wasn't ready for more than the friendship and comfort he had become for me. I wasn't ready for more of anything with Alexander and I knew he understood without me having to explain my emotional inability to be more than companions.
And over the three months of slowly rebuilding my life, I had no visits from my stranger. He never came to me but His last words haunted me, always.

"I'll be back for you..."

And I was afraid almost every night that that would be the night He retuned to me, but He never did. I was without Him completely, but aware of His potential visit every single day and night.
I was aware He might come back for me, but I was no longer excited or intrigued, or desperate for His visits. I was now afraid of them- not physically of course. I still craved His touch and I ached for the sexuality He provided me.
But emotionally, I was scared to death of seeing my stranger and regressing to the lifeless Sadie I had been while waiting for Him. I was afraid always, and I admitted as much to a sad Dr. Synode, who understood but still seemed confused by my stranger's presence in my life.

So on Christmas night, I returned to my apartment to a huge present from Alexander. Opening my door, I reset the alarm in my apartment and dropped the food and gifts from my parents on the dining room table. Excited, I found myself running and jumping on my bed with my huge Alex gift bag.

Opening the bag, I pulled out a beautiful card, with beautiful words, lined in silver and purple print. The card was so touching I instantly cried. I held the card and cried before opening my gift because the card couldn't have been more perfect for me.

It was purple and silver, and the front read:
'Wishing you a wonderful Christmas season filled with hope and promise'.

And the inside of the beautiful card held a hand written note from Alex.

Dearest Sadie,

I wish you nothing but peace and happiness in the new year. I wish you some comfort and peace throughout your days, and I wait for the day you feel peace deep inside you. You are a wonderful woman, and I hope for the day you believe that to be true.

Have a wonderful Christmas. I look forward to walking beside you in the new year.

Best wishes always,
Alex
xo

And I remember that card, which I've kept all these years later. I remember the feeling I felt; one of complete happiness, mixed with a deep sadness I couldn't explain. I remember feeling like I wanted Alexander in my life always, and I remember being sad that I couldn't possibly give him back all the kindness he was giving to me.

So breathing slowly, I opened up the bag to find my Christmas gifts.

First, I unwrapped a gigantic, male sized XXXL sweater, which made me laugh because Alex always had to wrap an extra sweater around me and my winter coat when we walked to and from classes. He always told me I was way too cold and he'd have to find a huge sweater to fit over my bulky coat when we walked.

And when I pulled out the sweater, it looked like he did. Not that I would have worn the enormous sweater over top of my winter coat, but it was a thoughtful, if not funny gift anyway.

Second, I pulled out a lovely black scarf with silver thread throughout it. It was cashmere and warm, and I wrapped it around my throat feeling its warmth around me instantly.

And lastly, at the bottom of the huge bag was a book. Unwrapping the book, I was a little taken aback by its title, and unsure of how I felt.

I had never told Alex about my past, and I had never spoken about the attack. That was a very private time in my life, and I never spoke to Alex about it, so how he knew anything I was unsure and instantly insecure.

Opening the cover, there was an inscription.

You never have to talk to me about what happened to you, but I want you to know I'll always listen if ever you need to talk about it. I thought I'd give you this book to maybe help you heal, if you ever need some extra support. xo

Looking at the cover of a female with a male shadow behind her, I was scared. I didn't want to read about what I should or shouldn't feel- what I should or shouldn't do. I didn't want to know what I was supposed to do because I had tried to heal myself the best way I knew how at the time.

What Alex didn't know, and what Dr. Synode failed to understand was I had two men to overcome. I had the bad man AND my stranger, and I don't think there was ever a book written for a situation like my own.

So placing the book under my beside table, I ignored it and went back to the huge sweater and scarf. Two perfect gifts from a man who often seemed way too good to be true.

There was an undeniable attraction to Alex that I welcomed AND shied away from. I wanted him in my life, but I was afraid of what that might entail.

To say I was afraid of sex was an understatement. I was messed up over sex. I was lost and unsure of myself. I had my lover, and I had the bad man. I thought I had made love with my beautiful, charismatic, loving best friend, but I learned I was only a joke to him. I was a woman who had only ever had sex with one man who loved her, but a man who didn't love her enough to keep her sane.

I had a lover I craved every day of my life but a lover I knew wasn't good for me, no matter how wonderful He made me feel physically. And at that time, I finally understood the reality of my dear stranger- He was my soul mate and He was my destruction.

*****

So by Christmas night I hadn't seen Alexander in 3 weeks and I honestly missed him. The winter exam session had started for the holidays, and I was finished my exams the first week of December. And when I held my wonderful gifts, I quickly grabbed the phone and called Alex to thank him. Wrapped tightly in my scarf and humongous sweater, I dialed and waited.
"Hello?"
"Hi. Um, Merry Christmas, and thank you so much for my gifts. I love the scarf and sweater," I stated quickly, choosing not to mention the book.
"You're welcome. Does the sweater fit?" He asked me laughing.
"Yes. Perfectly. How did you know my size?" I teased right back.
"As soon as I saw it, I thought of you, measured the sweater, and was sure it would fit you completely."
"Well, good job measuring it. And the scarf is beautiful. I'm already wearing it and loving the feel. It's beautiful. Thank you."
"You're welcome again. I wanted to ask you, since tomorrow is Friday, can I still come over and cook you dinner? I've tried to master a new recipe and I think I've nailed it. You would actually be my guinea pig, but I think it'll be fine. Can I come over tomorrow?"
And without even thinking, I said yes. Just like that- Yes. And that was it.
"I'll see you tomorrow around 4:00?"
"Yes. Thank you. I'll see you then. Merry Christmas, Alex."
"Merry Christmas, Sadie."

After we hung up I remember feeling almost giddy. The following day was Boxing Day, so all the stores were open again, and I couldn't wait to go shopping in the morning. I had absolutely NO idea what to get Alex, but I knew I wanted to get him something really special because I felt like he deserved it.

So falling asleep eventually, I dreamt my first dream of Alexander. And though it wasn't really dirty, I did wake up from our dreamt kiss touching myself sexually to my absolute horror and shock, until I became coherent enough to stop myself.

*****

The next day, after shopping for Alex, and even for myself a little, I was as physically ready for Alexander's visit as I could be. I wore my new fitted clothing, my hair was dried and styled, and I wore makeup. Remembering, I was actually excited for his visit.

And when finally Alex knocked on my door, I was happy. Practically bouncing, I looked through the peephole, turned off my alarm and let him in.

Looking at Alexander's smile, he was so handsome, and my mood was so joyous, I jumped into his arms and hugged him tightly.

Holding on, I inhaled his clean scent and I warmed instantly in his embrace. Wearing my new clothes, and the beautiful scarf he bought me for Christmas was nothing compared to the warmth his hug gave me. I was warmed and happy instantly in his arms.

Eventually, when reality set in, I pulled away from Alex with an awkward 'hi' thrown at him, while looking anywhere but at him.

"Well that was the best hi I've ever received," he replied with a grin, and suddenly my awkward vanished as quickly as it came to me.

"Please come in. I have something for you. Um, I hope you like it," I mumbled as I walked into my dining room.

When Alex entered my dining room he was still grinning, but now he looked like a little kid, well, at Christmas, I guess. Walking directly to his large gift on the table, he smiled a 'may I?' as he dropped his grocery bags on the floor when I nodded.

When he began tearing open the large gift ribbon, and unwrapping one present at a time, I found myself almost bouncing beside him. God, he was being so slow and methodical,

I wanted to just rip each present apart quickly, but I didn't. I waited, as he unwrapped each of the beautiful cook books I bought him. 10 stunning books from 10 different countries with photos of each country and a recipe per 100 page book. They actually cost a fortune, but I couldn't decide on which countries to buy him, so I ended up with every one available.

When Alexander suddenly plopped down into a chair, I knew I had him. I could tell I had picked the perfect gift. Just the way he held each book with such care told me he loved them.

"Sade... These are way too much, but I love them. Honestly, this is the best gift I've ever received. Thank you so much," he said as he suddenly grabbed my side into a half hug as he held the book on England in his other hand.

Fighting retreat, I stayed still until he finally let me go to look closer at each book. Quietly, he flipped through the pages as I waited. Sitting next to him in a chair, I waited for him to rejoin me.

And I was thrilled. Alexander being happy made me happy, I realized. I didn't know what an awesome gift making someone else happy felt like. I had always been alone, so I had never tried to make anyone happy before, and it was an amazing feeling. I felt alive, and I felt good looking at a happy Alex.

"Sadie, these are so cool. I can't wait to try some of these recipes. Look at the book from Greece. Every recipe looks delicious, doesn't it?" And I nodded as he flipped through. "Look at Australia. I don't know about some of these ingredients, but the food looks so good it makes me want to go there right now," he chuckled. "I really do love these cookbooks."

"Well, I hoped you would. I couldn't decide on a country, so I bought them all."

"Thank you. I guess this means I better start cooking for you more frequently than Friday nights, huh?"

"Oh! That wasn't why I bought them–" I panicked.

"I know, but it gives me the perfect excuse to cook for you more than once a week. What do you say?" He asked looking so charming and handsome I couldn't resist him.

"Okay," I answered because honestly, that's all I wanted to answer.

A few minutes later I picked up Alexander's grocery bags and walked them to my kitchen as he continued looking at his new books. Putting the food in my fridge, I bent for the crisper drawer and rose to Alex standing right beside me. Startled, I made myself breathe and I made myself stay still as Alex leaned down to me slowly.

And then he kissed me.

Finding myself leaning into him, Alex kissed amazing. He kissed me deep and beautiful. He nipped at my lips and took my tongue into his mouth. He held me around the waist and by the back of my head. He held me to him as he kissed the fear and awkward right out of me. He kissed me in a way that spoke of forever.

Pulling away, Alex once again leaned his forehead against my own. Whispering, he asked, "No tears or panic this time?"

To which I cheekily replied, "Not yet."

"Good, because you need to get used to me kissing you. Okay?"

"Okay," I agreed. And that was it.

Alexander pulled away from me, smiled at me, and started unpacking the other grocery bag. He asked me if I wanted to help him cook, and I nodded yes.

And so we began cooking together. Well, he began cooking, and I began trying every teaspoon he held up to my mouth, and stirring everything he asked me to stir while he prepared more and more food for our dinner.

An exhausting 45 minutes later, we finally sat down to eat.

And after an hour and a half sitting at the table, with his Christmas stories over, browsing through his new cookbooks together, Alex and I began cleaning up the dishes. Beside him washing dishes, I felt the awkward post kiss- is he going to kiss me again? -anxiety creep up. But I shouldn't have worried. Alex asked if he could leave the cookbooks at my house with the exception of one each time he came to cook for me, and I agreed.

Leaving 15 minutes later, Alexander pulled me into a hug at the front door and whispered, "Thank you so much for the wonderful Christmas presents." And I smiled as he walked out the door without a kiss goodbye.

After getting ready for bed by 7:30, I jumped on my couch and realized I really did love making Alexander happy. I also realized I wanted to make Alexander happy every chance I could, because I felt happy when he was happy.

CHAPTER 22

So Alexander fast became my best friend. I rarely discussed personal things with him, which seems weird of a best friend, but with Alex I didn't need to. I was sure he knew about the attack based on the book he gave me at Christmas, but he never pried or asked invasive questions of me.

If I did mention something about the last 7 years of my life that sounded sad or telling, he would pause and listen until I finished the statement. He never gave his input, nor did he try to make me discuss further what I may have slipped and told him. But he listened, clearly. I could see him stop and inhale, and almost suck up any little information I gave him.

Sometimes he would hold my hand, and other times he gave me a little hug if I spoke. We were at the point in our best friendship and slight relationship where Alexander kissed me hello and goodbye every time we met up or walked together, and I was okay with that.

*****

But a few months later I woke in a panic. I remember thinking for sure my stranger had been in my apartment as I slept. Waking, I scrambled through my apartment looking everywhere for him. I felt His presence everywhere. I smelled His scent all over me. I *knew* His presence and I was sure it was all over my apartment. I remember calling out to Him and crying over Him and even begging Him to come back to me.

I couldn't explain my actions, or my desperation for His love, other than to say it was a relapse of sorts. And so I relapsed completely.

Grabbing a bottle of vodka, I drank it down with a splash of orange juice and I waited. I took my drink to the shower and scrubbed and shaved my body, and then I waited. I sat up waiting and drinking again until I passed out hours later sitting at my dining room table.

And Alexander found me like that a few hours later.

He always stopped by to take me to school, but never unexpectedly. We always spoke the night before and discussed when he would be over, and this visit was no different, except for the fact that the day itself was very different. This was a special day. This was April, and Alexander was graduating from University.

Hearing the knock, I remember remembering Alex was coming over to take me to a Graduation brunch, so I hurried, stumbling to my front door. I stumbled, and even hit the wall in the hallway. I was hammered, and a little surprised by how drunk I actually felt as I threw the door open.

Forgetting to look through the peephole with my drunken eyes, I made my biggest mistake yet with Alexander, and it was one that has haunted me for years. I threw open the door in my drunken excitement and then everything stopped for me as I looked at my mistake.

Mr. and Mrs. Hamilton stood beside Alexander in my doorway waiting for me. Pausing, I stared at Alex in shock, even as I watched his charming smile fade into one of disappointment and even hurt, I think.

Faking, as best as I could, I opened my door further, and leaned against the wall as I accidentally yelled, "Come on... *in*." But no one moved. Smiling at Alex, I tried to hug him hello, but he held a hand out to my arm instead, and kept me away.

"Hi, Mrs. Hamilton. Welcome to my home! It's nothing like yours, but it's nice and clean," I heard myself say way too loudly again.

And to her credit, she spoke to me like the wonderful woman she was. "Hi, Sadie. It's lovely to see you again. Mr. Hamilton and I are going to go wait in the car for you to get ready. But please don't take long, dear."

Yet after she spoke kindly, I remember looking at myself and seeing what they saw and I almost died on the spot. Looking at my long, practically see-through t-shirt, which barely covered my body, I was mortified. Leaning into Alex, I tried to cover myself. Leaning into Alex, I wanted a hug. Leaning into Alex, I needed his support.

Begging, I whispered, "I'm so sorry, Alex," and finally he hugged me back.

When he turned to his parents and asked them to wait in the car, I saw Mr. Hamilton studiously looking down the hallway, not in my direction at all, so I knew my humiliation was complete. I must have looked trampy and ridiculous, or like a drunken whore to him. I was an embarrassment to myself, but especially to Alexander.

Crying, I apologized to them all.

"I'm so sorry for this. I don't drink anymore, I swear, but I needed it last night, and I made a mistake. I promise I don't drink anymore, but something happened last night and I drank by mistake because I was stressed out."

And with those desperate words, Alex seemed to startle as he held me and quickly told his parents he'd be down as soon as he could. Still holding me, Alex led me back into my apartment and closed the door in their faces.

Turning me in my dining room, he held both my arms and asked the question I didn't want to answer.

"What happened last night? Were you hurt?" And I wasn't.

Shaking my head no, I told all I could. "I thought someone was here and I panicked, that's all. Sometimes I drink when I'm scared."

"Who did you think was here? Who? Why didn't you call me? I could've driven over and kept you company?"

"I didn't want you to be tired today, and I didn't want to ruin your day..." And then it hit me. "I'm really, truly sorry. I didn't want this, I swear. I made sure everything was perfect for you today. I bought a new dress and I had my hair done yesterday, and I have a gift for you and I was going to make you happy today, I swear. I'm so sorry, Alex," I cried, and I meant every word I had just confessed.

I had met his parents once before when Alex and I went out for dinner on St. Patrick's Day, and they were lovely to me. And this second time was supposed to be perfect. I would look good, and I would support Alexander at his Graduation brunch, at the ceremony, and later at his parents' home for the party they were throwing him. I was going to be perfect for Alex.

"What can I do to help you?" Alex asked, cupping my cheek in his hand. And as he looked at me with nothing but concern, I felt worse.

Alexander had made me dinner on New Year's Eve, dinner on Valentine's Day, and even on my 24th birthday in March. He had made no advances, but to kiss me hello and goodbye, which I loved and waited for. He was always a constant support for me at school and at home. And now he offered me the same, even as I ruined his special day.

"I need you to leave and go to your brunch. Please explain to your parents that I am beyond sorry, and that I will make this up to them, but especially to you. I'm so sorry, Alex."

"I know you are, Sadie. Do you want me to stay?"

"No. Please go and have a great brunch. I want you to have a great day and please forget about me and all this crap. God, I'm embarrassed, and so sorry. I just made a mistake."

"I know, but I really wish you had called me. I could've-"

"I should've, but I really didn't want to ruin your day, which I did anyway..."

"It's okay. I'll call you later, okay? The ceremony doesn't start until 3:00, so I'll have a little time in between."

"Please have a great day. I really want you to because you truly deserve it. I'm so sorry," I mumbled crying again. I could actually feel myself sobering up even as we stood in front of each other. "I have a gift for you I think you're gonna love."

"I'm sure I will, but I don't care about that. I care about you, Sadie. What can I do to help?"

"You can go, apologize to your parents for me, and please have a great day. I'll talk to you later, okay?"

"Okay," he said walking back toward my door. Turning, he looked as awful as I felt. "You can tell me anything, Sadie."

"I wish I could Alex. But I don't know how to tell you some stuff," I admitted sadly.

"Well, maybe one day you'll try," he replied as he walked out my door. "I'll talk to you later," he said again as he left me.

To say I was devastated that day is an understatement. I was mortified, and lost, and drunk, and broken. Alex had been nothing but amazing to me, and the one day he actually asked me to do something for him, I blew it.

Alexander asked me for one thing. He asked me to be with him on his special day, and he asked me to meet his family and friends on his special day. He asked and when I panicked, he promised me there would be no pressure, and that we could, or even just *I* could leave as soon as it all became too much for me. He only asked that I be there with him for as long as I could handle, and I screwed it all up.

Walking into my bathroom, I relieved myself, and then I remember looking in the mirror. And I was gross.

Just my physical appearance alone should have sent him running, I looked so disgusting. My T-shirt really was mostly transparent, and my face was grey and haggard. My eyes were just a flat, lifeless, bloodshot brown. And my hair, which I had had professionally styled the night before was a stringy dirty blonde mess, because I had left it as is after my drunken shower.

I remember feeling dirty and ugly.

So crying again, I hopped back in the shower. And making a serious effort, I remember wanting to be clean for Alexander because he deserved it.

After my shower I made a decision. I called Dr. Synode and gave him the scoop over the phone and listened as he guided me into forgiving myself and moving on. He told me what I already knew- I made a mistake. He asked me to go pour the contents of my vodka down the sink. He told me to lie in my own bed and take a little nap. Then he told me what I already knew. I was to wake up, prepare myself and move on with my day. I was to go to the graduation ceremony, and I was to offer my support to Alex, on *his* special day.

So after my nap, I dressed in my new black and navy dress with matching striped pumps, curled and styled my hair, and I tried to make myself less pale with my make-up. I finished with a final smoke for probably a long time, and I drove to the University for the ceremony.

And I remember the look on Alexander's face when he finally saw me in the huge auditorium. He had already accepted his diploma, and he'd walked down the aisle and thrown his cap with his fellow graduates. He was done, surrounded by family and friends, and then he saw me waiting in my chair closer to the back of the large gathering alone.

Suddenly smiling, he walked right past his friends and even his parents to get to me. He walked up to me and then he took me into his arms, bent my back and gave me a Hollywood style kiss in front of everyone. And I was shocked, but happy. I was embarrassed but I also didn't care. I wanted Alex to kiss me and forgive me and from the depth of the kiss I received, I think I was clearly forgiven.

When we resurfaced, I wiped my lipstick as casually as I could, and then I waited.

"Thank you for coming. You look beautiful."
"You're welcome. I'm really sorry I disappointed you earlier. I made a mistake."
"I wasn't disappointed, I was sad. I hated seeing you look like that again, and I couldn't really help you and that's what bothered me the most," Alex said while pulling me into his arms. Whispering in my ear, "I don't like to see you struggle, Sadie. It kills me to see you so messed up. That's all."
"But I am messed up," I whispered back.
"But you're getting better."
"I know, but I'm not great."
"But you're getting better," he said again.
And I was.

When he let me go, Alex took my hand and led me to his parents. Dying of embarrassment, Mrs. Hamilton again showed me a grace I would have never had. Smiling, she actually told me I looked beautiful, and she said she was glad I could join them. Then she asked if I was still coming to the party later, to which I mumbled, "If you don't mind?"
"I don't mind at all. And Alex wants you to come, so we'll see you at 7:00?"
When I nodded, Alexander told his parents he would see them later and then he pulled me out of the auditorium.

Once at his car, Alex shifted me to lean against his door and then he kissed me again. He kissed the life right out of me. He kissed me until I was nearly gasping for breath. He kissed me until I didn't even remember where we were.
Whispering against my lips, he asked, "Where's my present, Sadie?" Making me laugh. And once I told him it was at my apartment, we were instantly on our way to my place in his car.

Opening my door, Alex turned his back as usual when I shut off my alarm by code, and then he pushed past me rubbing his hands together while looking around for his gift. Smiling, I nodded toward the dining room table.
When he was seated he picked up the 2 gifts and said, "I know what these are," with a big grin and proceeded to open up the last 2 cook books I had ordered from another store to complete his

collection.

"These are great, Sade. Did you see some of the recipes?" He asked while browsing through.

"I peeked once, but I saw a gross one with liver, so I closed it quickly," I smirked. Alexander knew liver for me was off the menu. "You know you're supposed to open the card first, right?" I said handing it to him.

When he opened it, it was a generic looking graduation card in black and silver, but I had inscribed the inside just for Alex.

Reading it, he looked up at me with his handsome face and nodded. "I look forward to cooking for you for years to come too, Sadie."

So handing over the last special gift, I was excited. It was a little envelope I knew he would love. I knew he would love it, and I knew what it meant. I knew the implication of my final gift, and I was nervous and excited to give it to him. I was scared, but I also wanted to do this.

When he opened the little envelope, he read it, placed it gently on the table under his hands, and then he looked at me. He looked at me with every question I expected on his face. He looked at me a little stunned. He looked at me and I knew he understood I was trying.

"A 3 day culinary seminar in Toronto at the Harbor Front hotel with Chef Mancini?"

"Yes..."

"Are you coming with me?" He asked quietly.

"Yes..." I breathed through my fear.

"Are you sure?" He asked just as quietly.

"No, but I'm going to be sure in 3 weeks."

"Okay." And then a silence descended on us as he flipped the card back over and traced the embossed invitation confirmation with his fingertips. "This is an amazing gift, Sadie. I love it. Really, I can't thank you enough for this," he finished looking back up at me.

"I wanted you to have something special from me because you're kind of special to me," I said lamely.

"Well, this is pretty special. I can't believe you did this. Do you remember when we saw the commercial-"

"Yes, that's when I decided to get it for you. That night."

"And when did you decide to come away with me for 3 days?" He suddenly asked bluntly.

"Um, I think officially today. But I was trying before. I thought about it all the time. Actually, I obsessed over it but I couldn't do it. Then today when you were nice to me when you should have been mean to me, I decided I was going to go with you, for sure. I think I am. I think I will. I want to..." I finished kind of babbling, as I finally sat in the chair facing him.

"I will never be mean to you," Alex stated while taking my hand.

"I think I know that, but I fear it. You're pretty important to me. You're all I really have, and I'm scared of you being mean, or leaving me, or not being my friend anymore."

"Do you like when I kiss you?"

"Yes," I blushed.

"Good. Because I love kissing you. It makes me happy, and I won't be mean to you, and I won't ever end our friendship. Because I want more, Sadie. I want more than this friendship with kissing benefits," he smiled. "I want you in my life so I'm patient with you. I know I have to be, and I *will* be. I'm not going anywhere, okay?"

"Okay..." But I was starting to panic a little, I could feel it. I didn't want to, but I was uncomfortable, and nervous, and unsure of my decision and of Alex's confession, and of the 3 day trip in 3 weeks, and of everything else. I was starting to panic and I needed my space.

"Alexander, would you drive me back to campus so I can get my car?" I asked a little too abruptly.

"What's wrong? Did I freak you out? Tell me."

"A little, but I'm okay. I'm trying."

"I know you are. What freaked you out?"

"All of it, the potential, the future, us, *everything*..." I choked out. "What if I make a mistake again, or do something wrong, or I'm not very good for you, or-"

"Stop, Sadie. I said I would be patient, and I will be. We've spent nearly a year talking and walking with each other, and other than a kiss, have I ever asked for or taken more from you?"

Thinking, I knew the answer. "No."

"Right. So if we go away and you're not ready for anything more, we just have a great time in Toronto, and I learn some amazing cooking skills I never would have learned on my own. That's all I want. Well, I *want* more, but I'll settle for just your company if that's all you can give me."

Trying to calm the panic while looking at Alexander, I believed him. And he was right. He had never taken more from me than a kiss which I actually liked, so he wasn't so much taking, as giving me a kiss. He was right about his unbelievable patience with me, and I believed him.

Catching my breath, I took his hand again, as he squeezed my own, and I tried to relax. I looked at his beautiful blue eyes that matched his tie, and I tried so hard to push the panic and fear away. I tried to not ruin this day again with my panic.

But honestly, He kept barging into my brain. Memories of Him were invading my mind. I thought of the way He made love to me, and all the sexual intensity He held in my life, and I was overwhelmed with need. Feeling myself turning back to that time, I was in a haze of sexual need. My body was craving sexual touch, and I was desperate with the need to release.

Moaning, I closed my eyes as I rocked my body into the feelings He gave me. Breathing faster, I touched my body until I could feel myself building. I knew I was close, but I knew I needed more. I knew I just needed a little more pressure and touch and speed to help me release.

Building, I felt His fingers inside me, and I felt His thumb rubbing against me. I felt the speed and strength of Him entering me, and I felt the pressure of His demand. I was so close.

When I opened my eyes, Alexander was watching and he had his hand over mine in between my legs. My leg was on the table and the other over the arm of my chair. Alex was helping me tease and impale myself, and in that moment of time I was unaware of Alex and myself or anything else, other than the feeling between my legs as I sped towards my climax.

Arching, and spreading my legs wider as I pushed back into my chair, the release suddenly slammed into me.

Crying out, my body weakened even as my legs shook uncontrollably. And finally I was saved from the horrible need clawing at me, as Alexander lifted me and took me to my bed.

And I remember the journey, and I remember the strange nostalgic feeling I had of being carried to my bed by my stranger. I remember the feeling of being small in His arms. I remember being carried back to my bed to heal by Him.

Rolling to my side, I felt a blanket wrapped tightly around me. And I felt myself passing out, but I couldn't fight it. I was exhausted emotionally and physically. I had released for the first time in a year and a half, and I was done.

"That was the sexiest fucking thing I've ever seen in my life, Sadie. Go to sleep, baby. You have an hour until we have to leave for my parents' house," Alex whispered into my ear.

And nodding, I was soon unconscious.

*****

When I woke up later it was 5:00 in the morning to my absolute shock. I had slept for 11 hours. I had slept soundly for almost 11 hours. 11 hours had passed in a solid, heavy, deep sleep, and I was relieved for this sleep and the solitude I had had while I slept.

Looking around, I found a note from Alex on the pillow beside me.

Sadie,
I tried to wake you but you were sound asleep and I figured the night you had before exhausted you, so I decided you needed your sleep.
Don't panic, I'm not mad or disappointed. I wanted you at the party, but really, it's a party of all my family, and even I would love to bail on it. Plus, I'm sure you'll meet my sisters and brother eventually.
I hope you sleep well. I'll call you tomorrow. And I'm still coming over to cook for you tomorrow night.
Thank you Sadie for the amazing gift, but I don't have any demands or even expectations. Whatever happens happens, and if nothing happens, I'm okay with that, too. We'll be in Toronto together cooking with a master chef, which is pretty cool.
Have a great night and day tomorrow. I'll see you soon.
Alex xo.

Rereading his note, it really did seem like he wasn't mad or disappointed in me for not going to his party. But I would have. I didn't want to meet his huge family all at once, but I absolutely would have made myself go to his party for him. Alexander deserved it.

When I looked around my room, I was a little grossed out that I was still wearing my new black and navy dress from the day before, and I could even feel my makeup all caked in and nasty around my eyes.

But when I stood up to use the washroom the memory of what I did slammed into me like a train.

I remember being humiliated, and embarrassed, and aroused at once. I was disgusted and turned on. I hadn't had an orgasm in so long, that I couldn't believe how easily it had come to me in that moment. I couldn't believe how much I had needed that moment. I couldn't believe how much I had *enjoyed* that moment.

But I was also overcome with the need for Him. I missed Him and His touch. I missed the sexual history we shared. I missed having a man in my life who brought me such sexual pleasure and release. I missed Him. Still.

Showering, I remember crying and shaking with my embarrassment, especially when I cleaned myself between my legs. I remember wondering how I was going to face Alexander. I remember wondering if he would look at me differently.

And so I spent the day obsessing.

*****

When Alexander finally knocked on my door at 4:00, I was beside myself with anxiety. I could barely open my door to him, but I did. Bracing myself, I looked through the peephole at his smiling face, and I slowly allowed him to enter.

But before I could even speak, Alex took me into the deepest, longest, sexiest kiss we had ever shared. Gasping and shaking, I allowed him to kiss the anxiety right out of me again.

When he eventually pulled away, Alex breathed against my lips, "Was yesterday about me at all?" And I died. What could I possibly say to that? "It's okay if it wasn't. But one day that will be *all* about me, Sadie. You will want ME to make you orgasm like you needed me to help you get off yesterday." And then he kissed my lips quickly, and moved past me for my kitchen.

Stunned, I remember standing in the doorway. I couldn't believe he didn't hate me, and I couldn't believe he wasn't disgusted by me. I think he should've been. I think I would've been disgusted by him if he was fantasizing about another woman while with me.

Eventually, Alexander walked back up to me, took my hand and led me to my dining room table to sit. Smiling again, he shook his head at my confusion, kissed my lips quickly and walked back to my very active kitchen. Cooking and smiling, Alexander kept looking back at me like he was afraid I'd bolt on him or something. But I didn't.

If there had ever been a moment I questioned his loyalty and care for me it was rapidly vanishing in that moment. I remember thinking, if my sexually ridiculous behavior from the day before didn't scare him away, I realized I was honestly starting to believe he would stay with me through anything.

An hour later, Alex served me a fabulous meal. And I remember moaning once, then quickly remembering the last time I moaned in that exact chair. And as I instantly quieted with my total embarrassment, Alex's head snapped up, he looked at me like he was going to jump me then and there, and then he smiled and said, "I love that sound from you, Sade. Please don't stop moaning on my account," as I nearly choked to death on my veal when he grinned. And then he continued eating.

After dinner and the tedious clean up, thankfully, Alex acted the same. He kissed me and he left. He said he'd call me the next day and that he wanted to make plans with me over the weekend.

He acted normal, and I found myself acting normal in return. And we were. For the next three weeks, he came and went, while I stayed sober, and quiet. He did most of the talking, and all of the planning, and I agreed to follow along.

For the next 3 weeks we were normal... until our trip to Toronto.

CHAPTER 23

After much discussion about no expectations, Alexander finally picked me up Thursday afternoon to drive the couple hours to Toronto. We had the hotel booked for three nights because the cooking seminar went from Friday through to Sunday afternoon, after which we would drive back home Sunday evening.

Before the trip we discussed the seminar, and the food, and the beautiful hotel we were staying in. We talked about the places we would walk and visit after the seminars. We talked of dinner in the hotel and at a few of the local restaurants. We spoke about everything trip related, except for the obvious.

We discussed no expectations- until the lack of expectations actually *became* the expectation.

When Alex picked me up, he carried my small luggage to his car, while talking excitedly about the seminar. He had looked up the requirements and the planned menus and food preparation we would be required to participate in. He teased me mercilessly about my lack of cooking skills and how he would pick up the slack for us if we were partnered up, which I hoped we were. To my humor, he even offered to help cook my own menu items when Chef Mancini had his back turned, so we didn't accidentally kill anyone.

Alexander was in good spirits as usual, and I found myself relatively light hearted as well because of his mood.

To say I didn't think about the sleeping arrangement would be a lie. I did. Frequently. *Always.* When I least expected it, I thought of all the potential and the fear almost got to me, but then I was distracted by something Alex said and I would forget momentarily my sexual anxiety. Regardless of my perpetual thoughts, eventually we arrived, and Alexander was wonderful as usual.

When we made our way to our room, Alex held my hand while carrying his duffel bag, and wheeling my small luggage. He opened our door, looked inside, smiled, and pulled me in with him. After dropping our bags on the desk in the corner, he immediately walked us to the window, which I had assumed from the name, had a beautiful view of the harbor front, and it did.

When I stood in front of the window, Alex turned himself until he was behind me, wrapped his arms around my stomach, leaned into my shoulder and whispered, "Thank you for this amazing gift, Sadie. I promise you won't regret it." But immediately I did.

I don't know why, but my whole body tensed up and I felt sickness grow inside me. I felt irritable, and confused, and shaken. I was too anxious suddenly, and I think Alexander picked up on my change of mood quickly.

Letting me go suddenly, he kissed my cheek, took my hand again and started for the door. Following, I was curious as I tried to even out my mood.

"Let's go to dinner. I made us a reservation when we checked in. Sound good?" And I nodded because the alternative was crying at that point. So we left for dinner.

Once in the restaurant, I remember being totally restless. I didn't know why, other than the obvious- I was nervous and overwhelmed by my situation.

I remember believing this was it for us- one way or the other. I think I truly believed I had to be with Alex to keep him at that point. I think he needed something from me emotionally and sexually to keep him interested. I think I was sure that would be our last weekend together if I didn't put out. I think I was sure he would abandon our weird, pseudo-friendship with kissing benefits if there wasn't more for him, no matter how many times he had said he had no expectations.

So after ordering, I excused myself feigning a need for the washroom after the long drive, but I bee-lined for the bar near the entrance instead. Quickly ordering a double vodka and orange, with 2 extra shots of vodka, I kicked them back as quickly as possible. I remember even dribbling the drink down my chin in a bid to swallow as quickly as I could. Afterward, I casually walked back to Alex as I felt the alcohol warmth radiate through me.

When our dinner arrived, I ordered a glass of wine suddenly. And though I saw Alexander quickly look at me, like he was gauging why I ordered wine, he didn't say anything.

And so we ate, as Alex spoke of his family, and friends, and his graduate studies, and I was interested in all of it. I wanted to know what he was going to do, and what he wanted in life. I was interested to know what his lifelong goals and expectations were.

Just before dessert, I actually did have to use the washroom, so again I excused myself. And repeating the process, I used the washroom first, and followed with another stop at the bar. Ordering the same, I drank the 2 shots first, then thought I would finish with the drink. And I almost made it.

But halfway through my double vodka and orange, Alexander suddenly held me from behind and took my glass and hand into his own when I went to lift it back to my parched mouth.

"Why, Sadie?" I remember was all he whispered in my ear.

And totally busted, I panicked. I absolutely panicked in his arms with his breath next to my face, and his weight holding me against the bar, while his warmth and the warmth of the vodka threatened to strangle me.

Crying out a choke, I couldn't even speak. I remember having no words in that moment. I had no excuses, nor events to blame, like I used to. There was nothing. There was absolutely no external factor to cause this mistake except for weakness- plain and simple. And I *was* weak.

With tears sliding down my face, I held it all in until Alex moved to my side and sat on a barstool close to me. Still holding the drink, I pulled it away from his hand, and like a disgusting lush, I quickly kicked back the liquor straight down my throat as he watched.

Bracing myself, I finally turned my face toward his and what I saw in that moment broke me. He wasn't mad, and he wasn't disappointed. He wasn't disgusted or embarrassed. And he wasn't even judging me. Alex was simply waiting for my answer because he honestly wanted to know why. He was trying to understand me, which actually felt worse.

"I don't know..." escaped my lips, because that's all I could say.

"You do know. So tell me. I want to know why."

"I don't, I swear," I pleaded.

"Tell. Me. Why." He suddenly demanded while getting very close to my face. "Talk." But I still couldn't explain. "Tell me WHY," he demanded again, but I still couldn't move or speak.

When Alex suddenly raised his hand to the bartender I was surprised. Asking her for a bottle of Vodka, she told him she couldn't do that, so he demanded instead 5 shots of vodka and 2 vodka and oranges, which apparently she *could* do.

Still not speaking, I didn't move. I had no idea what he was up to, and I couldn't figure out his intentions. I didn't know what to do, so I stayed perfectly still as she poured the shots and drinks in front of us.

When the bartender finally walked away, Alexander handed me a shot and barked, "Drink it". And I would love to say that I didn't. I would love to remember a moment of strength. I would love to recall me taking a stand and declining the shot, but I didn't.

Like the weak idiot I was, I took the shot he offered and drank it, quickly followed by another one. I even grabbed for a third, but Alex put his hand over the shot glass, and waited for me to fight him I think. But I didn't fight him because I really had no fight in me. So after the shots I just waited for him to make a move.

"Tell me why you needed to drink," he again asked right in my face. But I shook my head no. "Sadie, I want you to tell me, right fucking now."

And when he raised his hand from the shot, I quickly snatched it up and drank it because I had no shame in that moment. I had no shame left.

"Tell me why you did this?" He asked again as I kicked back the 4th shot.

And it was that shot that I knew was going to kill me. I remember that feeling. I remember when I would drink until I felt the last drink that was going to mess me up. The drink that was going to make me puke or pass out. That one drink, be it the 8th or the 15th drink that was going to send me over the edge of numbingly drunk, to hammered without control. And that last shot was the one.

"Alex... I'm going to be sick soon," I pleaded.

"Good. Talk." But I still couldn't. "Sadie, I want to know why you had to get drunk and hide it from me. I want to know what I did to make you like this." Oh, god.

"You didn't. I wasn't. It's not you..." I moaned.

"Why?"

"I'm fine. Sorry. I made a mistake," I again stated even as my body shook and my mind struggled between one reality and the next.

"Answer. The. Question. What happened?"

And then my stomach started turning, and my hands began shaking, and my legs were bouncing on the barstool rung, and everything was starting to spin, and I felt lightheaded, and hot and chilled, and I tried to remember what I drank, and I remembered the first double and two shots and the glass of wine and then the 2 shots before the second double and then the shots with Alex and then I wanted to cry and scream and hit him, and beg him to like me anyway.

And finally, unbearably, the pressure grew and grew with his light blue eyes staring at my face even as I tried to not look at his, and then everything just grew and built and grew until I was choking on the alcohol and gagging down the words, and begging him with my eyes to leave me alone, even as I tried to get off the barstool that his leg and arm had me trapped in, until I just exploded.

"I was scared you would fuck me or rape me or hate me and leave me after this weekend. I DON'T *KNOW!*" I screamed as I suddenly pitched backward trying to escape.

"Sadie!" He yelled as he caught me and pulled me into his lap as I suddenly threw up on the floor.

When I heard the bartender yelling at us, and Alexander trying to lift me into his arms while trying to kind of drag me away from the bar at the same time, I wanted to help him. I really did try to help, but I felt my feet drag behind me, even as I tried to work my legs. When Alex pulled me into the women's washroom, he forced me into the stall, and pushed my head into the toilet. Gagging and throwing up again, I was a mess, and I knew it.

Begging, "I'm so sorry, Alex. I didn't mean to," I cried.

And I remember I really didn't mean to do anything like that. I just wanted to take the edge off my worry. I didn't mean to get that drunk, and I probably wouldn't have been if he'd just left me alone to drink. But he made me drink those last shots. He made me get that drunk, so I thought it was his fault.

"You did this to me," I moaned.

"Yup. **I** did this," he answered sounding bored.

"You did. You made me drink those last shots," I gagged out as I threw up again.

"Yup," he replied like he was humoring me.

"Stop saying yup. You did! You did this!"

"Okay," he again replied.

"I want to go home, Alex. Right now."

"Okay." He conceded, and then he stood up as he kind of

dropped my head onto the toilet. And walking away from me, he actually had the nerve to say, "Find your own way home. I'm done. You thought I would leave you this weekend, and I am. You were right, you fucking alcoholic Psycho," and then I jumped as I heard him hit the door hard when he left. Listening, I heard the door slowly squeak shut, and I was relieved to be alone, until I wasn't alone again.

"Are you okay?" I heard a female ask from behind me. Lifting my head off the side of the toilet seat, I was humiliated looking at a waitress from the restaurant.

"Um, yes. I'm fine. Sorry about all this. I'll be fine in a minute," I said as another gag hit me. Turning for the toilet bowl, I gagged again, but thankfully didn't throw up in front of her. "I'm leaving in a minute. Sorry..."

"Do you need any help getting to your room?"

"No. I'll be fine in a minute. Sorry."

"Is your boyfriend going to hurt you?" She asked quietly. And I remember knowing what she thought of Alex.

"No. He's not really my boyfriend, but kind of. And no he won't hurt me, but he *is* leaving me which hurts. But I deserve it," I admitted to a total stranger.

"Has he, ah, raped you before? Because that's not okay, even with a boyfriend," she stated to my back, ramping up my humiliation to a degree I couldn't have known existed.

"No. He's never hurt me, and we don't do that."

"Sex?" She asked me with surprise.

"Yes. We don't have sex. So he won't hurt me that way."

"Then why did you yell that in the bar? Everyone heard you, and a few customers asked that we check up on you. You can tell me if you're scared. My Manager sent me in here and he won't let you get hurt, I promise."

I remember trying to stand, as she grabbed for my elbow until I was steady. Leaning against the stall wall, I looked at her, straight in the eyes and confessed, "Alexander has never hurt me, and I don't think he ever would physically, but I hurt him all the time because I can't talk to him, or be normal, or be what I should be with him. Did you see him?" And when she nodded, I followed up with, "Did you think he was good looking?"

"Very," she answered.

"He's very good looking, and he's so good to me and nice and really fucking patient with me and all my bullshit, but I just can't be with him like that, even though I want to be, I think. Sometimes..."

But I had lost her, I could tell. She was no longer sympathetic, but confused and I knew the questions that would follow, so I walked away from her and made my way to the sink. Looking in the mirror as I washed my hands, I was disgusted again. I had vomit on the right side of my face, and my hair was matted with it on that side of my head. My skin was the sunken sallow shade of Sadie past, and I looked a little like death again. I didn't look like the kind of woman an Alexander Hamilton would be with.

So scrubbing my face, I wiped off the smeared mascara and finger brushed my teeth with nothing more than water, all while the waitress stayed silently beside me.

"I'm fine, you can go now. Please tell your Manager I'm sorry for the mess at the bar, but I'll be leaving the hotel soon."

"Are you sure?" She asked again, and I remember wanting to scream in that moment.

"Yes," I snapped, as I stumbled toward the washroom door.

Once I was in the lobby, I stumbled outside for a smoke. Asking a stranger for one was awkward, but mine were hidden upstairs in my luggage and I really needed one for my nerves. I knew I had to go back to our room just for a minute and I hoped Alex wouldn't be a jerk about it, but I needed a smoke first.

Smoking, I thought of nothing but Alexander. I hoped he wasn't too mad at me and he would just let me in so I could at least get my purse before I left. I hoped, though I had little faith left.

After my smoke, I made my way upstairs again shakily. I remember knocking on the door, and I remember the relief when Alex did answer the door to me. But after the relief came upset when he just stood there looking at me indifferently while waiting for me to speak, I think.

"I just need my purse. I'm sorry to bother you."

"It's no bother," he replied somewhat automatically.

And it hurt. I remember wishing his indifference didn't hurt, but it did. He walked away from the door at that point and sat in a chair near the window while browsing at the seminar pamphlets we had grabbed from the front desk. Ignoring me completely, I walked in, grabbed my suitcase off the desk and wheeled it into the bathroom.

And sitting on the edge of the tub, I remember my confusion. My head still spun, and I was totally drunk still, but at least the humiliation had subsided somewhat because I didn't know what to do about leaving. I could call a cab to take me to the train station, or to the greyhound station, but I was nervous. I didn't like walking around in the dark by myself, and certainly not in this town. I was insecure here at best, and adding in the fact that I was still drunk, desperate, alone, and confused, spelled absolute disaster for me emotionally.

Reaching for my purse, I wanted to know how much cash I had on me because I needed to do something. I needed to figure this out. I needed to get myself home so I could be alone again. I needed something to stop all this stuff in my head all the time, because the pressure was building, and the pain was intensifying, and the memories were swamping my brain and the constant mistakes I made were hurting Alexander which was killing me. And the constant thoughts of Him were driving me insane so I needed to figure something-

"OW!" I screamed when I was suddenly pulled by my hair.

"What are you doing?" Alex yelled at me.

"What?" I screamed again, trying to rip my hair out of his grasp. I didn't know what was happening but I was scared to death of Alexander instantly.

"DROP IT, SADIE!" Alexander screamed in my face, as he pulled me up by my hair. Looking, I saw the nail file drop from my hand as he twisted my wrist.

"What are you doing?" I cried. But I was suddenly thrown into the shower by Alex who jumped in after me and landed on me. Panicking, I remember fighting as best as I could. I fought him even as the cold water poured down on me. I fought him hard, but just like before, I didn't win.

So I stopped fighting. I let Alexander Hamilton hold me down. Sobbing, I closed my eyes, turned my face to the wall, and I let him hurt me without fighting.

"Sadie? What's wrong, baby? Talk to me. Why did you cut yourself up? Why would you *do* that? Am I really so bad that you need to get drunk to be around me? Am I really so awful that you need to cut yourself? *Please.* Explain it to me, Sadie."

God, I remember the sound of his voice that day. Even with my eyes closed, I knew he was crying. I could hear it in his voice. I could hear his pain and upset and it sobered me up as nothing else could.

And I was suddenly awake.

"It's not you, Alexander. And I know I say that all the time, and I know you must be sick of hearing the same thing from me, but it really isn't you, and that's why I don't make you go away. I should tell you to go away but I can't. I like you in my life, but I don't know how to be with you."

"Be with me how? Sexually? Emotionally?"

"Both. Every way. I don't know. I love your voice, Alex. I love it, and I love how easy and light you are, but I don't know how to be with you because I'm not very good emotionally, or like mentally, in case you haven't noticed-"

"I've noticed," he said so deadpan I choked out a laugh.

"I just don't know what to be with you," I admitted once again. And it was true. I still didn't know what to be for him.

"I've told you this a hundred times- just be you."

"I know, but that's such a stupid thing to say; no offense. Just be myself? I don't know who that is. So how can I be myself with you?"

"Okay, I have a question," he paused until I nodded. "Am I the world's best non-boyfriend boyfriend?"

"Yes..." I admitted.

"And what have I done to you that was so bad in a year?"

"Nothing, but-"

"Nothing. I've done nothing, but given kisses and held your hand. I've never made a move. And I've never lied to you about it. I told you there were NO expectations this weekend, and I meant it. I told you, but you never believe me. So what else can I do?" When he looked at me and paused, I realized he actually wanted an answer.

"Just be patient-"

"Not good enough. I AM patient. What else can I do?"

"I don't know. Nothing, I guess."

"Nothing? I can do nothing to stop you from expecting the worst, or waiting for me to screw up, or fuck you up, or hurt you, or ruin this relationship that I've tried to build with you? I can do nothing?" He asked again a little angrily.

"I don't know. I'm the problem. I have some stuff-"

"*Believe me,* I know you have some stuff, even if you won't tell me about it. Not good enough, Sadie. Tell me something. Give me one definitive example of what I can do to make you stop expecting me to hurt you. Tell me just one thing I can do, because I don't have a clue anymore. I've read the books on spouses and partners of victims of abuse. I've done the research and asked the questions. I've even watched Oprah, but nothing I do works with you. Time hasn't worked, and patience hasn't worked. Being a support system for you hasn't worked, neither has being just your friend. So tell me one thing I can do. I need to hear one thing, or you were right, this IS our last weekend together." And when I gasped, he continued. "It is Sadie. This is it. I've spent a year trying to make you comfortable with me. I spent a year being your friend and waiting for you to realize you feel more for me than simple friendship. I've spent a year waiting for you to eventually love me back, but you don't love me back and I don't want to do this anymore."

I remember to this day clearly the look on Alexander's face. It was a look of complete indifference and acceptance. I think he was sure I would simply agree to end things. I'm sure he thought I would tell him I couldn't think of anything he could do to make me love him. I saw in his eyes the acknowledgement of our end.

So panicking at the thought of losing Alexander, I said the exact opposite. "Can you touch me a little?" I barely whispered.

"Are you kidding me?" He asked rather abruptly.

"No. I just thought if you touched me a little, I would get used to it and maybe like it and maybe I'd get better or something."

"Now?" I remember nodding and meaning it. "I can't. You're still drunk and emotional. You've hurt yourself and all I want to do is bandage up your arms because I've been watching them slowly bleed this whole time, sitting in the tub with you soaking wet and freezing. So please don't take this the wrong way but I really don't want to touch you under these circumstances. I'm not looking for a pity fuck, Sadie. I want you to want me too."

"I think I do," I answered automatically.

"Well, let me know when you *actually* want me, not when you think you want me and we'll revisit this conversation."

And that's when I knew my words had blown the conversation. I had made Alexander feel insecure and I hated myself for it.

"Can I tell you something, Alex?"

"I really wish you would," he answered sadly looking away from me.

"I think you are *very* good looking, and so does a waitress from downstairs. And that isn't a pity compliment, I promise."

And then he looked back at me. I remember he looked at me until he slowly smiled at me. Waiting for him to speak, he surprised me with his lack of a humorous comeback, but he was smiling at least, which I would take. I hated a sad, confused, or

disappointed Alexander.
"Are you staying here tonight?" He asked me bluntly.
"If I can."
"I want you to."
"Okay... Can I get out of here and change?"
"Of course. I'll change out there," he said while standing away from me in the shower.

45 minutes later, I was warmed from a HOT shower, mostly sober, while dressed in leggings and a long T-shirt. I was also sporting bandaged arms after Alex had knocked on the door when my shower ended. He had looked at me in my towel, looked at my arms and handed me the band aids which he must have bought in the gift shop downstairs, and then he left me alone to continue.

When I exited the washroom, Alex was still dressed lying on top of the bed watching TV. Smiling at me, he quickly jumped up, passed me and entered the washroom for his own shower.

10 minutes afterward, he joined me in the bedroom wearing sweats and sat back down on his side of the bed.

"Would you lie down with me," I remember asking nervously, and he answered a somewhat breathy 'yes...' as he lifted the covers and crawled in beside me.

"Sadie. You can never drink like that or cut yourself again with me. You have to talk to me and tell me you're freaking out so I can either try to help you or so I can leave you alone, because I don't ever want to see that again, okay?"

"I'll try," I agreed as my words hung there in the silence of our room. They just floated around us like a promise. Or maybe like a pledge, until the silence was broken by Alexander.

"Try hard."

And I heard the warning in his gentle tone. I knew I would lose him if I ever made another mistake like that again. I heard the implication, and I understood the warning. So I decided I would.

"I promise I'll try very hard..." I whispered.

And that was it. I fell asleep immediately, with only Alex's hand touching my hip as we each lay side by side in the bed.

*****

And I remember how fun that weekend was. The cooking seminar was brutal. The Chef said things I had never heard in my life, and even Alex shrugged a few times when I asked what the hell was going on. We did our best; though Alexander's best was way better than mine, and we learned a few neat ways to prepare everyday foods.

Overall, Alexander took the classes seriously, with little bouts of humor between us here and there, and he helped me when I burned my hand on a handle that was scorching when I lifted the pot from the grill.

He was wonderful. And the second night, we slept side by side but a little closer, until the third night we were officially spooning each other.

I remember being wrapped in his warmth and loving the feeling of it. He was warm and I was warmed by his presence.

When we drove home Sunday night, Alexander was humorous but tired. He admitted he hadn't slept well, to which I let him know I had slept very well. Smiling at me, I think he liked that response. I think he liked that I slept well in his arms, even if he didn't sleep well in the process. But when I asked why he didn't sleep, all he said was, "it's exhausting sleeping beside someone you want, when you can't have her." And I quickly dropped the conversation.

When he dropped me off at home, he walked me up, deposited my luggage inside, gave me a spectacular kiss and left. He said he'd call me the next day, and I was relieved. I wasn't ready for a full on relationship with him, but I wasn't ready to let him go either.

CHAPTER 24

The following weekend, in the middle of May, Alexander came over on the Friday and cooked us a wonderful dinner. Everything was delicious and lovely. We were funny, okay, *he* was funny, but I got a good one in once and a while. And the evening felt light and I was happy.

I hadn't had another drink since the weekend before in Toronto, and though I still smoked like a fiend when Alexander wasn't around, I found myself smoking less and less outside on my balcony, so that it wouldn't bother him in my apartment.

After dinner, I excused myself to go have a smoke, and Alex nodded as he cleared the dishes.

Sitting on my little lawn chair, I remember how full, and good I felt. I remember the world was looking up for me. I actually felt it. I felt closer to Alex and I wanted to keep getting closer to him.

I remember turning my head and seeing him smile at me through the balcony door while I had been smiling absently looking around my balcony. I felt a little stupid sitting there with a smile on my face, but I couldn't help it. Everything felt good that night.

"I'm spending the night, Sadie. Chain smoke if you have to and take your time. Go relax in the tub if you want. Do whatever you want. Talk to me or don't. But you promised me you would try really hard, and I'm holding you to that promise. Okay?"

Shocked, I remember nodding silently.

"I'm spending the night here. But it doesn't mean anything will happen, it just means something *might* happen. Either way, I don't care. I just want to spend the night here with you. Okay?" But all I had was another nod. "Say okay, Sadie."

"Okay," I croaked while shaking. And then he left me alone on the balcony.

However long later, I don't know; my mind likes to remember hours passing, as the evening turned to night, Alexander walked out the door and unfolded the other lawn chair to sit beside me.

"What's going on?" He asked. But like a mute, I still had no words so I just shrugged. "How many cigarettes have you smoked?" A pack? Half a pack? I couldn't tell, so I shrugged again. "Would you like to come in? It's a little chilly out here. You could have a shower to warm yourself up?"

"Okay," I said, practically bolting from him on the balcony. I remember diving for the door, and hitting the screen a little too hard with my forearm. I remember stumbling like an idiot trying to get away from Alexander.

Running for the shower, I grabbed a huge towel from the closet on the way, and slammed and locked my bathroom door. Running the taps, then the shower overhead, I waited for the warmth.

Once in the shower, I did my ritual. I shaved my legs and underarms, and scrubbed my body with pumice. I washed my hair and scrubbed off my makeup. Again, I was on autopilot. I remember thinking, why am I not thinking about what this means. I remember being surprised that He hadn't entered my thoughts. I remember being confused by the ease in which I was accepting this situation with Alexander.

When I cleaned between my legs, I remember thinking of my vagina. I still had hair there because He liked it, but I wondered if Alex did. I knew it was the norm now to have it bare, but I didn't think I was ready for that. Actually, I knew at the time I wasn't ready for that. But the more I obsessed with my vagina, I decided a close trim was in order. And so I did. Not quite bare but definitely much less hair, I found myself shaving for Alexander. I shaved myself for Alex instead of keeping it full for Him.

And when that strange reality hit me, I remember laughing in the shower. I remember the strange awareness of my vagina and who I was grooming for, which seemed like a good sign. If I was wanting to make Alexander happy, who was HERE, instead of for Him, who wasn't- I was pretty sure I had made the right decision.

Afterward, I learned I was in the shower for over an hour. Alexander told me that a week later. He told me he let me stay in there, but that he had paced in a frenzy in the hallway, stopping to press his ear against the door listening for a sign of anything bad. He told me the visuals of what I could be doing to myself nearly made him insane.

Alexander confessed he thought he would eventually find a bloodied mess in the shower. He told me he was scared to death

that entire hour, making deals with himself that he would barge in every fifteen minutes, but then he would hear me put something down, or the shower curtain move, or he heard me laugh, and he kept himself from busting down the door. Barely.
    Alexander admitted that my hour long shower, preparing myself for him, was the longest hour of his life, and he was an absolute mess while I was in my shower.

When I was finished, I brushed out my hair, scrubbed my teeth, wrapped myself in the huge towel, and then realized I didn't have any clothes with me, so I panicked some more.
    I remember opening the door. I remember the steam following me into the hallway. I remember Alexander leaning against the opposite wall, and I remember his face. He was totally stressed out, I could see it.
    "What's wrong?" I asked, but he didn't speak. Instead, Alex leaned toward me, looked at my arms, and then to my horror lifted my towel to my upper thighs only, thankfully, and dropped the towel with a burst of breath. And that's when I realized he was checking me out, and he didn't trust me at all.
    Offended, I whispered, "I promised to try, Alexander."
    "You're right. I'm sorry, Sadie. Please forgive me?" And I pretended that I did.
    When he walked past me into the bathroom, I left him and went to my room to dress.
    Looking in my drawers and closet, I realized I was at an absolute loss again. I knew what I wore for Him, but this was Alex. I knew what nightgowns He liked, but I had no idea what Alex would like. Then again, I realized I didn't think I wanted Alex to like what I was wearing because if he did, I remember thinking I was giving him permission to do whatever he wanted to me.
    When I heard the shower end, I decided quickly. Jumping, I grabbed a pair of leggings and another long t-shirt. In my struggle to be quick I forgot to wear underwear, but at least I was covered by black leggings. Panicking, I threw my towel in the corner of my room and then I stood shaking not knowing what I was supposed to do.
    But Alexander did.
    Standing in my bedroom doorway with only a towel around his hips, Alex stared at me until I found myself covering my chest with my arms. Staring at Alexander in a towel was too much for me. Alex was tall and lean and muscular, and clearly took care of

his body, unlike me. Staring at Alex made me feel weak, and little, and plain. So I lowered my head, because I couldn't look at him anymore. Looking at Alexander was just too hard for me.

"Remove the pants, Sadie," he said with a gentle smile, and unbelievably I did.

Standing back up, I crossed my arms over my chest again and tried to breathe. There was something entirely different about Alex in that moment. He was looking at me differently, and I felt different about him.

"Come here," he whispered, and unbelievably I did.

When Alex turned us and sat on the edge of my bed, I remember the fear and the shaking, and the sudden *need* I felt. It was so intense for me. I actually felt the pull of need deep inside me, and in that intense moment I wanted Alex to touch me.

When he placed his hands on my hips, he squeezed gently, and then rubbed my hips as if to warm me. Looking down at him, I watched him watching me.

"Tell me to stop." But I didn't. "Tell me when you panic, Sadie. I need to know," he begged. But I didn't tell him I already was, *kind of.* I *was* panicking, but I was needy too. So I said nothing.

Alexander then moved his hands slowly down my hips, across my pelvis until his hands slid into the junction of my thighs, but he didn't stop there. Moving still, he stroked my inner thighs, until he stopped at my knees.

Holding onto me, he asked, "Who are you thinking about?" And I answered immediately.

"You..." I moaned.

"Tell me when you don't think of me. I want to know. Okay?" So I nodded yes.

Leaning forward, Alex made his way to my left foot, and lifted it onto the bed beside him. Quickly grabbing his shoulders for extra support, he held the back of one thigh, while his hand stayed on my foot beside him on the bed.

"Lift your shirt to your waist," he rasped. And instantly I did.

Knowing what he was seeing, I remember wanting to flee. Knowing he could see all of me right in front of his face, I wanted to pull my foot away and retreat. Knowing he could see the scar running down my hip made me want to close down, but I didn't. Unbelievably, I stood still while he looked at my body.

"You're so beautiful, Sadie."

But I didn't feel beautiful. I felt exposed and insecure and really quite neurotic in that moment.

"Lie down on the bed. I want to touch you a little- just a little. But you have to tell me when it's too much, okay?" And I nodded, as I pulled my leg away and turned to lie on the bed.

When Alex turned toward me and lay down next to me, I remember the feeling of fear I felt instantly. When he was leaning over me, I think wanting to kiss me, it was suddenly too much for me. Throwing my hands up from my sides, I pushed at his chest, until he moved back to my side.

And I remember almost attacking him. I remember preparing myself to fight. I remember digging my heels into my mattress for elevation and strength. I remember waiting, but he didn't move.

"Look at me, Sadie. I'm never going to hurt you, I promise," he said as he moved slowly back toward my lips.

And when he kissed me I felt it everywhere. I felt his lips kissing my own, but my entire body felt his kiss, too. He was so good, and I loved everything about that moment with Alex.

Eventually, Alex moved a little down my body and took my nipple into his mouth. Sucking and nipping me through my shirt, I found myself lifting and arching to get him closer. I felt the moisture on my clothing, and the aching in my nipples as he switched sides. I remember I enjoyed him, and I enjoyed the sensation of being with him.

And when he eventually touched my vagina I knew it was Alexander. He was gentle and slow, and he didn't invade me quickly. He took his time working his fingers inside me. He took his time, so I knew it was him.

He didn't tear into me, and he didn't throw me into a frenzy of need. He was loving and slow and careful with my body. He was beautiful and patient. And I knew it was him with me.

I remember that moment always. It was that moment that captured me, because I knew Alexander was special.

Slowly he made his way down my body. Slowly, he continued his gentle assault within me. Slowly, he tried to please me.

When he pushed my legs apart and up, I closed my eyes and waited for the feeling I knew. I waited as he engulfed my body with his mouth and tongue. I waited, feeling his fingers and tongue try to coax a reaction out of me, but no reaction came.

I tried though.

Whispering a cool breath against my body, he asked, "Who are you thinking about?" And I told him the truth.

"You. Only you, Alex," as he continued his slow love to my body.

Later when he reached into my bedside table, I was surprised when he pulled out a condom. Looking at me for permission I think, I nodded.
I remember thinking, when did he put them there? Maybe when I was in the shower? I didn't know. But I was surprised and distracted and I wanted to make Alexander happy, and I wasn't really panicked which was a first, and I wasn't thinking about anyone but him, so it seemed like something I could handle with Alex.
So we did.

And Alex was wonderful. He spoke to me the whole time, but not in a dirty way- more like to comfort me, and to remind me of him. He touched me lightly, and he kissed me heavily. When his body eased in between my legs, I didn't panic at his closeness like I had before. I didn't panic over what we were doing. I wanted to do this with Alexander, so we did.
When he finally entered me I was okay. I didn't hurt, and I didn't want to retreat. I was happy when he kissed me harder. I was happy when he smiled at me and moved within me. I was happy to be with Alex this way.
And when he whispered against my lips, "I love you so much, Sadie," I was happy to be loved by him.
I felt like everything suddenly fell into place for us.

When he had finished, I could see his disappointment that I hadn't had an orgasm. I could feel his disappointment all around us. But I was happy, so I told him I was.
I made sure he knew I was happy, and I didn't resent his inability to bring me to climax. I took that burden upon myself. I explained that I didn't orgasm often and that it was a problem with *me*, not his technique.
So after he rose to use the washroom, I remember lying in my bed with the sheets pulled up my chest thinking that sex wasn't so bad. I remember being relieved by how easy it had felt with Alex. I remember being grateful sex with Alex had been easy.
And when he returned looking happy, I actually opened my arms for him. It was such a strange thing for me to do, but I opened my scrawny little arms anyway because I *wanted* to hold Alex in my arms.

So crawling up my bed, Alex situated himself between my legs and lied his head on my chest. Squeezing me tightly, he whispered, "I love you Sadie for being with me. I promise it'll get better each time we try." And holding him tighter I nodded.

When he began pulling the sheet back down my chest, Alex whispered, "It's next time, Sade," to my shock. And laughing at my reaction, he teased, "I'm only 25, so I'm ready about every 10 minutes or so." And he was.

When Alex finally fell asleep next to me, I was truly happy. He had tried so hard to bring me to orgasm, but he never looked pissed off or frustrated with me. He just asked what I liked, when I liked it. He was so kind and loving, and really very good at sex, I'm sure.

At one point, I wanted to ask him how many women he had slept with out of curiosity. I remember thinking he had made a lot of women very happy because he was just so good at sex. But then I feared he would ask me the same and I didn't know how to answer that question.

I remember thinking about everything he had done to my body. I remembered his hands and mouth all over me. I remembered how much I enjoyed his touch; I just couldn't orgasm, but I don't think that was anything special. I think many women have that problem. So I lied in my bed with Alexander passed out beside me thinking of all the ways he was a terrific lover for me.

I dreamed of Alex in between my legs, and I dreamed of Alex kissing me hard.

And then the dream twisted as everything changed in a millisecond and I knew I was no longer with Alex. I knew it wasn't Alex with me, but I didn't tell him because I didn't care.

The need in me was so great, I found myself whimpering and begging. I found myself spreading my legs, and begging Him to touch me. I found myself touching my body as I moaned and arched into His touch.

And I was frantic with my need. I was half insane with the craving for Him to enter me. I needed His tongue, and fingers, and His body to enter me. I needed everything in that moment. And He gave it.

Pumping into me hard, twisting and biting my nipples, I arched into Him. Planting my feet on the mattress I pushed upward to help Him plow into me. Begging, I tugged and pulled at His skin.

Moaning, I rubbed myself even as He pounded into me until I was done.

And on a scream I came for us. Milking Him, I felt Him slam into me as I came over and over again. But the tide wouldn't end. I was insatiable and greedy, and I needed Him. I needed more of Him.

So when He stopped moving above me, I grabbed at myself to ease the burn for more. I fingered myself until I felt His mouth and tongue devour me. Screaming and arching again as another release slammed into me, I still felt the need. I still needed. I was restless and relentless. I needed another orgasm. I needed more still. I needed...

Until I woke to Alex calling my name. Over and over, he called to me, as he wiped my face of my hair, and tried to soothe my body with gentle words and soft kisses.

But I was too far gone to stop. Writhing against him, I pushed and pumped my body against his thigh. Begging for more, I tried to ease my own need with my own hands and fingers. Grabbing and tugging and impaling and arching, I tried to get what I still needed, but I could hear him.

Breaking into my dream, Alexander was coaxing me down. Kissing my cheeks and temple, he was trying to bring me back with his warmth. Still rubbing up against his body, my body wasn't my own yet. I still felt the need but it was slowly fading. Slowly, I was losing the intensity of need which assaulted me.

"Sadie... Wake up, baby. Come on Sade. Wake up for me..."

And then Alex entered my mind, and I woke on a gasp.

Feeling my body ache, I was awake. I knew I was awake because I had Alexander's scent all around me. He was around me and his scent was inside me. It was Alexander who I wanted to heal me.

Crying out, I was frustrated and embarrassed, but Alex soothed me back down.

"Oh, Sade... What did he do to you?" He begged quietly. But I had no words.

Struggling, I tried to get away from Alexander but he held me tightly to him. Shushing me and rocking me, he held me until he was the only thing I knew.

"I'm sorry..." I moaned.

"It's okay, baby. We'll work through this. Look, I know you're not there yet, but I love you Sadie, and I'm not going anywhere, I promise. We'll work out all this stuff with you."

"But-"

"If I have to kiss you and make love to you for the next 50 years, I'll just have to do it. Okay?" And I could hear his teasing again and I remember knowing Alexander truly loved me and he would wait 50 years for me.

"Thank you," I cried. "I do want you here, and I do want to be with you. I just can't help the dreams sometimes. But that's all they are; dreams." And that was almost true.

They *were* just dreams then, but they were based on my past reality. So I didn't lie to Alex, which I promised I would never do. I didn't really lie to him, because He *was* just a dream then.

"Can you sleep? Can I get you a drink or anything?" Alex tried.

"I just have to use the washroom," I mumbled embarrassed.

And when I turned on the washroom light, I was shocked to see myself. My lips were dark and swollen, my hair was a sweaty mess, my skin was flushed and glistening, and my body ached everywhere.

When I tried to use the toilet, my body burned. I felt swollen and full still. Everything ached. I was raw until I stopped going.

Stripping myself of my long t-shirt, I stood in the mirror and looked at my body. I had pinch type bruises all over my breasts, and my thighs had hand mark bruises. I was a mess. Grabbing a hand held mirror, I raised my leg on the tub and looked at myself, and I was swollen- very swollen and dark purple.

I remember looking at my own vagina trying to remember if I did that to myself, or if Alex had. But then I realized it didn't really matter. It was me who provoked it and it was me who demanded it. It was me who needed more than his gentle love making could provide, so I had caused it to myself.

After my shower, I walked back to my room in the early light of morning, and I crawled in next to Alex. Still wearing my towel, I eased onto my side, and pressed my back against him because I needed his warmth, and he gave it to me immediately.

Wrapping me in his arms, Alexander spooned me warm, and I was comfortable and exhausted in his arms. I was barely conscious within seconds of being held tightly in his arms.

"I love you Sadie," he whispered, and I fell asleep soundly. Again.

*****

When Alex tried to make love with me a few hours later, my wince stopped him at once.

I remember him jumping up into a sitting position while turning me onto my back as he raised my knees and spread my legs wide. Looking at me so intimately was unnerving, and rather too much for me emotionally, but I didn't move. I just watched him looking at me as I felt him spread my labia apart. When he licked a finger and slowly eased into me I couldn't help my slight wince again, and he stopped. Looking at my body he attempted to touch me once more, but as I pulled away slightly he stopped immediately again.

"I'm so sorry I hurt you," he said sadly, as he eased my legs back down.

"It's okay. I think it was mostly me. I think maybe I did that to myself when I was..." I admitted embarrassed again.

"Can I get you anything? I don't know if some ice would help with the swelling. Maybe I could go to the drugstore and pick up a cream for the discomfort?"

"No, thank you. I'll be fine," I said while pulling his shoulders closer to me. I wanted him to lay with me and not fuss over me. I didn't want to discuss my swollen body or my crazy sexual frenzy in the night. I just wanted Alex in my arms, happy. I loved when Alex was happy.

"Are you happy, Alex?" I whispered.//
"Very. I've wanted to be with you forever, Sadie."
"I'm sorry I'm not really normal with sex."
"I don't care. We'll work on it until you *are* normal with sex. I think maybe you can be with me. But if you never are, I don't care. I just want you, Sadie."
"Me too..." I admitted, and I actually believed what I said. I truly believed Alexander was the one person who would help me. And I really did want him in my life always.

"Please don't leave me, Alex," I suddenly gasped.
"I won't, Sadie. I promise I won't. And I'll make you happy too. It won't just be me. I'll make you happy, and I won't leave you. Ever."

And again I believed him. Alexander wasn't a liar and he didn't play games. He was kind and gentle and he said he loved me and he promised he wouldn't leave me. And I believed him.

So falling back asleep peacefully for a few more hours, I woke to Alex bringing me a tray of food in my bedroom.

And that was our weekend.

We had The Weekend. The weekend all new couple have. The one weekend that makes a new start into a complete relationship. The weekend every new couple has where they have sex and eat, and hide all embarrassing bodily functions, shower, have sex, eat some more, shower again, and have more sex. The weekend when they lie in bed and eat in bed and screw in bed and talk in bed. The weekend where they each tell their stories and give insights as to what they want and what they wish for. The weekend the individuals in lust become a couple in love.

That weekend.

Alexander Hamilton and I may have been skirting around a relationship for nearly a year, but that weekend we were cemented as a couple.

We made love again Sunday morning when he thought I had healed enough, and once again later Sunday afternoon before he left to return home. And I remember looking at Alexander when he kissed me goodbye after our weekend, knowing he did love me.

CHAPTER 25

But 3 weeks later everything changed between us again because I knew I was pregnant. I knew it because I had experienced it almost 2 years earlier. I knew I was pregnant and I was sure Alexander would handle it way better than I was, which annoyed me to no end.

I remember sitting in my dining room while Alexander cooked us dinner. I remember the nausea churning in my stomach. I remember the scents and aromas wafting from the kitchen. I remember Alexander talking and talking about his day at the clinic he was working at over the summer as an Intern. He was talking and talking, and I remember wanting him to shut up. I was irritable and freaked out and I felt like hell.

For 2 days I was either sleeping, trying to sleep, or trying to wake up while exhausted, or I was nauseous. But I never actually threw up which I think I wanted at that point. I hated walking around with a constant cloud of vomit that wouldn't get out of me. To make matters worse, Alexander's food was so gross smelling, it filled the room with a stink I couldn't get away from, until finally I snapped.

"Alex, could you please open the kitchen window? The food fucking stinks!" I barked.

And after I snapped, I remember Alex slowly turned around to look at me, as he leaned against the counter, dusted off his hands with a dishtowel, while staring at me silently. Raising an eyebrow, he tried to prompt me to speak. But I couldn't.

"I'm waiting," he said with annoyance. "I've been very patient with this nasty mood of yours for the past week, but I'm getting a little tired of it. If you'd like some time to yourself, all you have to do is ask for it. If you want me to cook something else, tell me what you want. If you want me to leave, ask me to leave. Just please tell me what you want because I don't think I've done anything wrong, but you're acting pretty bitchy with me and I don't know why. So why don't you spare me all this crap, and just talk to me."

"I think I'm pregnant," I blurted out as I gagged in my hand. Once again I couldn't just vomit and be done with it- I had to only gag and continue traveling on the nauseous roll coaster I couldn't get off of.

"Pregnant?" He asked quietly.

"I'm sorry."

"Are you late?"

"Of course. Think about it, we've had sex for 3 weeks straight, and never once did I have my period. Plus, I feel horrible and exhausted. And I just know it, Alex," I cried a little.

"Have you taken a test or anything?" He asked while walking toward me at my dining room table.

"Not yet, but I *know* Alex." I just couldn't admit *how* I knew.

"Okay, I'll be right back. I'm gonna go buy a test, or two, just to be sure. Here," he said turning back to kitchen. Pouring me a glass of water from the fridge, he hurried back to me. "Drink this while I'm gone, and another if you can. But don't go pee until I get back," he said handing me the water and grabbing his wallet and keys from the hall table. He then turned again back for the kitchen and turned off the stove burners and lowered the oven heat, and then ran back through the dining room for the door as he yelled, "I'll be right back. Don't move, okay?"

And when I nodded Alexander stopped, walked back toward me, leaned down and gave me a kiss. He kissed me so deeply, I had to pull away when I felt a gag ram up my throat. Turning my head quickly, I gagged again as he turned to leave.

"I love you, Sadie." And I nodded again as he left.

Once he was gone, I remember walking to the door to lock and alarm it behind him, then walking numbly to my balcony with the glass of water while lighting a cigarette. Sitting on my balcony chair, I smoked as quickly as I could in as little time as I had.

When I saw Alexander pull back into the parking lot of my little building 25 minutes later, I power dragged one last time, butted out my smoke, and ran for the washroom. Brushing my teeth as quickly as I could while gagging again, I exited with my glass refilled, but unnecessary. I already had to pee, even as Alex pounded on my door.

Looking through the peephole, I let him back in as I walked to my living room- the only place I could be at that moment. The smell of my kitchen and dining room was horrible, my bedroom got me into this mess, but my living room had the balcony door and some fresh air for me to breathe in deeply.

Sitting on the couch I shook with the knowledge of the inevitable. I was one hundred percent pregnant and I was scared. I didn't want to do this and I didn't know what Alex wanted. He was a good guy and pretty damn sweet, so I could see him supporting a decision to keep the baby, but I could also see him feeling let down if I told him I didn't want the baby. I was essentially screwed because the father of my future baby was a good guy instead of a prick, and wasn't that a mess for me.

"Can you do the test, Sadie? Can you pee, yet?"

"Yes, I can pee, Alexander," I answered annoyed by his sweetness again. How his kindness bothered me, I didn't know. But I remember thinking Alexander's brand of nice was really fucking annoying under the circumstances.

"Sadie, what's wrong? Why are you looking at me like that?"

"I'm sorry, I don't know. I just know how this is going to end and I'm mad about it, or pissed off, or scared. I don't know, but I need you to stop talking to me for a minute, okay?"

Nodding at me, I knew I had hurt his feelings. I knew he was trying to be a wonderful man for me, but I was too stressed out to appreciate it. I wanted to be angry at something, and his kindness was bugging me, which was totally irrational but I couldn't help it.

Standing, I took the bag from his hand not very gently, and stormed into my washroom. Ripping open the first package of 2 different kinds of the same test, I quickly read the instructions and squatted over the toilet as I peed on the tip of the stick and even on my hand accidentally. Replacing the cap, I stopped myself from peeing more, and I tore open another box as I re-squatted, peed on the next stick and on my hand again then placed the cap back on the stick and leaned it on the sink beside the first one.

Finishing my pee, I wiped my body and washed my hands while I waited, but the second one was already clearly 2 pink lines, and the first one was turning into a matching blue line like its window claimed it would if positive.

I was staring at 2 positive tests in 30 seconds. I was pregnant like I knew I was anyway, but at least now Alexander would know for sure.

Opening the washroom door, my bitchiness was at an all-time high. I held up the sticks to his face as he flinched, then I dropped them in the hallway as I walked to my room. Ripping of my clothes that stunk like the food he had been making, I angrily wiped at my falling tears and crawled into my bed. Waiting for Alex, who I knew would come to me, I was beyond irritated- I was pissed right off.

When I felt the bed dip, I snapped, "Good job, Alexander," as he flinched beside me.

"Why are you so mad, Sadie?"

"Seriously? Because I'm pregnant and unwed with a bastard, and I look and feel like a tramp. Your parents already saw me hammered and then 2 months later I'm pregnant? Oh, I don't know why I'm mad," I snarled my sarcasm.

"A tramp? Really? I think you're a little far from being a tramp, Sadie. And you sound really stupid right now. Unwed? A bastard? What the hell is this? The *fifties?* No one even thinks like that anymore, and we haven't even had time to talk about this yet. So why don't we talk-"

"I don't want to talk yet. I'm tried. Can you leave me alone?"

"You're tired? It's like 4:30. Are you really going to sleep, or are you just avoiding me?"

"Both! And I'm not stupid! That was really mean, Alexander."

"I didn't say you were stupid, I said you sounded stupid. Look, I'm sorry, but I haven't had any time to think about this and you keep lashing out at me. Can you just give me a minute to think about this without you barking at me?"

"Sure take all the time you need. God knows, **I** have lots of time to decide what I'm going to do."

"What *we're* going to do."

"Uh huh."

"Sadie, I mean it. This is between us, and we'll make this decision together, whatever that decision is. I'm here, baby."

"Yeah, until you're not here."

"I'm here," he said angrily, trying to turn me toward him but I fought his hands. I wanted to be on my side staring at the wall. I wanted to be alone with my thoughts. I wanted to be pissed off.

"Can you stop this for a minute and just talk to me?"

"Not yet. I want to be alone. You said I could ask you to leave me and you would. So please, just go," I begged almost crying.

"Please... Let's just talk for a minute, then I'll go. I promise. Please Sadie, I need to talk about this," he begged in return almost crying.

"I don't know what to say to you right-"

"Then let me talk. Please, I want to talk to you before I go."

When I heard his voice sounding sad I hated it. I hated it in my stomach which actually made me gag again. Alex being sad was a heartache for me.

"Okay... I'm sorry. Go ahead and talk," I gave in.

Turning, Alex suddenly spooned me and held me tightly in his arms. Pushing my hair away from my ear, he kissed my earlobe, and exhaled across my cheek. Holding me, I was warmed immediately. I remember that; the feeling of warmth he gave me, and the lack of nausea for the first time in days when he held me tightly to him. Alex holding me made all discomfort and nauseous upset go away.

"When I was at the drugstore, I went crazy, running up and down the aisles looking for the tests. I actually yelled at a cashier 'where are the pregnancy tests?!' and she blushed at me. I think she felt bad for me having a pregnancy scare at my age. But after I got the tests, I walked to her counter and paid for them with a smile on my face. I even said, 'this is a good thing,' I think," he spoke as I flinched. "Wait, Sadie. Just listen to me," and I nodded for him to continue. "I don't know what you want to do because this just happened, but I want you to know I'm in if you want to have this baby. I'm totally in. Just thinking about it makes me happy for some reason. But we can talk about it. I just want you to know that I would be happy if we had a baby together."

God, I remember that moment, and I remember hearing his voice. He sounded emotional, but so sure of himself. Alex did want this baby and I did think he would stick around. I realized he would be happy about this and I wouldn't be alone. This time I wouldn't be alone waiting for someone to help me.

"I love you, Sadie. And I know you love me even if you can't say it. But you do love me. You love having me around, and you love me in your life. I know you look forward to seeing me and I know you like me with you. We're working on the sexual difficulties, but other than that, we're doing really well together. I love you, and it would make me happy to have this baby with you," he confessed while still holding me warm and kissing my cheek.

"I just need to think. But thank you. I really don't know what I want to do yet, and I'm afraid of being alone-"

"You're not alone. I'm here."

"For now-"

"For *ever*," he stated holding me tighter. And then we stayed quiet.

Eventually I fell asleep to wake later around 7:30 with Alex still holding me. Turning to face him, a gag hit me immediately, and I turned my face quickly from his in case I finally threw up. But I didn't. Again, I just felt like I needed to, but nothing would come up.

"Let me make you something to eat," he whispered, even as I shook my head no. The thought of food was disgusting. "Just try, baby. I'll make you something you won't hate, I promise." But stopping Alex when he had a mission to help was impossible, so I gave in.

Ten minutes later he was slowly crawling back into my bed. Helping me prop up against the headboard, he smiled endlessly at me. He was lighthearted and happy looking, the total opposite of my confused and freaked out.

"I don't know what I want to do yet, Alex," I confessed.

"I know, but we have a little time, and I'll take care of you while you decide. I'd take care of you anyway, but I want to help you with this. This is ours, not just yours, and I want to help."

Placing the tray in my lap, there was toast with a foreign syrup like glaze on it and it was sweet and delicious. I didn't know what it was, but it tasted amazing. I actually ate the toast and drank the apple juice without feeling like I was going to throw up.

"What is this?" I asked wanting more.

"Just a little secret I read about. Apparently this syrup aids nausea and has a high fat content, some calories, and vitamins for the mother. Do you want more toast?"

"Yes, please. I'm starving," I said, dipping my finger across the plate to pick up the crumbs.

"I'm going to be here for you, and I'm going to take care of you, Sadie," Alex whispered against my lips as he kissed me deeply.

And he did.

For the next 6 weeks he kissed me, and held me tightly when I was nauseous and he stayed with me before and after his clinic shifts.

He was always with me. There was never a moment when I had to wait for him. There was never a moment of panic or fear. He never left me long enough to fear he wouldn't return to me. He always came back, and he always seemed to know when I needed a little verbal reassurance that I wasn't alone anymore.

For 6 weeks, Alexander fed me Special K, or plain chicken and rice, or his delicious sticky sweet syrup on toast, which was fast becoming my favorite choice for breakfast, lunch and dinner.

Alexander was amazing, and I loved him for his attention, but I still didn't know if I wanted to have a baby with him.

*****

"We have to talk about what we're going to do, baby. I've let you put this off long enough, but we need to decide now. It's been weeks, and I assume you're around 10 weeks now, so we have to talk about what we're going to do. And you *have to* see a doctor soon," he pleaded as he walked into my bedroom and kissed me hello.

"I need you make love to me," I responded instead. And when I saw his head snap up, I actually laughed at his reaction.

We hadn't touched since the day of the pregnancy tests. Well, we had once when I had had a particularly vivid dream, but Alex had only gotten me off with his hands and mouth that time. There was no penetration, and no release for him, which bothered me even though he never mentioned it or complained about our one-sided encounter.

"Make love to you? *Always.* And I even get to go bareback this time which is a first, so giddy up," he laughed, recovering quickly from my demand.

Smiling at his humor, I pulled him in for a deep kiss until he kissed me as hard as I craved. Actually, he devoured me with his mouth and I felt need rush inside me for the first time in weeks.

I had spotted a few weeks before, which we read was normal, but I wasn't spotting now, and I needed to feel Alex connected to me.

So we tried... and failed actually.

Something was different inside me. I felt like my insides were lower or something. It was like he touched against painful nerves inside me. Alex was slow and gentle, never thrusting hard or deep, but it was still painful and after a few minutes of trying different angles, we stopped trying altogether.

Looking at me, resting his forehead against my own, he asked if I was okay. And I told him the truth. I didn't enjoy that, and it had hurt badly, though I didn't know why.

So after a few minutes of silence, Alex made his way down my body and took me with his mouth and hands, which didn't hurt me. And though I climbed high, I could never quite get over and it only added to our frustration, I remember.

And so I gave my first blow job. I'm sure I wasn't very good, but I tried. I wanted him to be happy, and I wanted him to find his release since I couldn't. I leaned over his body and took him into my mouth while he held my hair away from my face and watched me.

"Go slow, Sade, so you don't gag," and I did.

Taking him in as deep as I could, I enjoyed his sounds and movements. I enjoyed his smiles and groans. I enjoyed him moving gently against my mouth, until he was ready. Pulling out of my mouth he took my hand into his and we both stroked him to climax in the sheets. He came, and as I watched him I was suddenly turned on by it.

I remember being surprised that I was so aroused. I liked seeing him pump himself with my hand as he arched into the sheets. I liked watching his stomach muscles contract as he shook and moaned his release. I was turned on by Alex coming for me.

Suddenly touching myself, I felt my own climax build quickly. Touching myself, Alex pushed me to my back and took over. Rubbing and impaling me with his fingers, he forced my own orgasm from me. Spreading me wider, he bent and licked and sucked at me as he tried to coax my release, and I did.

Arching and moaning in turn, I released into the sheets for him. I was exhausted and wore out, but I had come for Alex as well.

Afterward, slowly turning from him, Alex spooned me and we fell heavily asleep together.

But Alexander eventually woke me in a panic. Shaking me, I opened my eyes to him sitting with my legs over his knees as he looked at my body closely. Talking on the phone, he kept trying to rouse me while still speaking to someone else.

And that's when I knew what was happening. Again. Trying to close my legs in my embarrassment, Alex forced them wide open with his hands as he cradled the phone on his shoulder. Actually touching part of the sticky bloody mess with his fingers, he

explained what he was seeing to whoever was on the phone.
   And looking at my surroundings, I remember the feeling of being mortified. I didn't want this again, and I didn't want to feel this again. Strangely, I thought of my mother and a new wash of embarrassment hit me. I was exhausted. I was exhausted from all this crap all the time, and I knew my mother would think I had fucked up again. I knew what she would think, but I didn't care this time. I remember feeling bad for Alex.
   Trying to close my legs again, he shook his head no as he continued talking. And I remember that moment of feeling shut out from my own body again. Alexander was taking over my body and I didn't have the strength to fight him. I was weak and exhausted. I was so tired I closed my eyes and attempted to sleep through the embarrassment.

Waking on route to the hospital, Alex held my hand tightly as he spoke to me. He was right there beside me talking about our lives together. He spoke of our future, and he repeated over and over that he was with me and he wouldn't leave me ever. And I believed him.
   Reaching out to Alex, I squeezed his other hand and thanked him for being with me. I thanked him for being so wonderful, and I thanked him for loving me. I remember thanking him over and over for the wonderful life he wanted to give me. I remember wanting him to know that even though I didn't think I loved him the same, I did love that he loved me, which sounded convoluted, but was the truth nonetheless.
   Alexander Hamilton was everything to me then. I didn't have to wait for him, and I never questioned his intentions. He had proved himself to me completely. As I lay on the gurney I looked at Alex and knew I wouldn't ever let him go. I didn't want to.
   Alex never asked me for anything but my affection, but he tried to give me everything, and I loved that he loved me enough to try to be everything that I needed from him.

In the hospital, I was rushed to obstetrics to a waiting team of one doctor and two nurses. They knew what was happening and they were trying to stop it. I was still freaked out by my pregnant reality, but I was glad people were trying to help Alex and I, because I didn't want this sadness for him.

"I'm probably anemic again," I admitted to the busy room, and they acted accordingly.

45 minutes later I was comfortably listening to Alex relay any information he could to anyone who would listen. He told a doctor our assumed date of conception, and he explained how tired I had been. He even told them all the meals he had prepared and what I could and couldn't eat. Listening to him, I thought he was amazing.

And then the nurse asked a question I didn't think would haunt my life with Alexander. She wanted to know if this was my first pregnancy, and when he answered yes, I couldn't breathe.

But then the doctor looked into my file and stated, "Second pregnancy with previous second term miscarriage," and I flinched.

Looking away, I remember the clock on the wall. It was giant and meaningless. Time was moving so slowly as the doctor continued asking questions of Alexander. Time was irrelevant in that moment because I was sure I was feeling the end of my relationship with Alexander. I knew he would be hurt that this wasn't my first pregnancy, and that I hadn't told him about it, and that I had experienced all this before him. I knew he would be sad over my previous miscarriage and I hated seeing Alexander unhappy.

"Was he there for you?"

"No," I said to the clock.

"Did he know?"

"No," I mumbled.

"Did you hide it from him?"

"No," I breathed into the quiet of my room.

"Then I don't understand, Sadie. Explain it to me."

"He was gone. He didn't come back until I had lost it. I didn't have the chance to tell Him, and then it was over by the time He came back, so there was no point," I cried.

"That's awful, baby. I'm sorry you had to go through that alone." And turning my head to look at him, I believed him again. Alexander was looking at me so sincerely, with tears in his eyes, holding my hand to his mouth as he spoke. "When was it?"

"Almost 2 years ago," I confessed again.

"Well, I'm here, and I'm not leaving you, Sadie."

"Thank you," I choked out. Crying, I held his hand to my cheek. Tugging him closer, I needed his warmth to surround me and he gave it. Crawling up the bed beside me, he gently lifted my head so I could rest on his arm. Holding me tightly, he warmed me even as I cramped up again.

"I'm sorry if I lose it. I think I'm going to Alex, and I'm really so for you. I know you've secretly wanted this, so I'm really sorry I'm going to lose it."

"You might not, Sadie."

"I think I probably will Alex so you need to be prepared, okay? But it's not as bad as you think. I remember it was just there and then it was gone. I don't think it's so bad, really. But I don't want you to be sad," I choked through my tears.

"I'm okay, baby. If we lose it, I'll be okay. We can have another baby later, but if we don't have another I'll still be happy with you. I want you to know that, Sadie. I am happy about this baby, and I want to be happy with you. So please just try to be happy. For me? If the baby is okay, will you promise to try to be happy about it? Please?"

"Okay," I whispered and that was all I could say in that moment.

But I didn't lose the baby that time, and 2 days later I left the hospital with Alexander.

My parents weren't called, and neither were his. We were going to wait to tell them until I was in the clear which wasn't going to be for a while. I was again extremely anemic so put on medication, and I was given strict orders to limit my time standing and walking. I wasn't necessarily put on bed rest, but it was recommended that I spend more than 12 hours a day lying down and resting.

So Alexander and I took life day by day. We had essentially decided to keep the baby though neither of us actually said we were. It just became a given after the miscarriage scare that we were keeping the baby.

Alexander still worked and I still didn't attend school. We spent every chance we could together in my apartment, and eventually the days and weeks passed before us. Before we knew it we hit 16 weeks, and I was considered safe from an immediate miscarriage. I could relax a little, and I remember the relief so clearly on Alex's face when we had the 16 week ultrasound.

We decided to find out the sex, and to my humor and relief we found out we were having a boy. Alexander was ecstatic, whooping and clapping his hands together as he bent and kissed me and my stomach. He would have wanted either gender I knew, but I think he really wanted a boy.

And I wanted a boy because girls scared the hell out of me. I didn't want a girl to have a life like I did. And though I would have never allowed it, girls could be physically hurt much more easily than boys could, and I feared that every day of my life. So I was relieved that we would be having a boy.

So the day after our ultrasound, Alexander and I went to tell his parents about the baby with me nervously holding his hand. I didn't want to be there, and I didn't want to see his mother's face when he told her I was pregnant. I remember not wanting to know what they really thought of me, but after much begging from Alex I gave in and went to the Hamilton's house.

When we drove to his parents' house, I told Alexander they were going to think I trapped him. I knew they would think I did this on purpose. I said they would probably say I was a tramp or a whore and they would hate me, but he disagreed.

I was told NO ONE would ever speak to me like that, especially his family. He held my hand during the drive and I could see how excited he was to finally tell people we were having a baby.

When we arrived, Alexander's oldest sister, who was already married with 2 young sons greeted us at the door, and I knew she knew. She introduced herself, but looked right at my tiny baby bump. Leaning in for a hug, she smiled at me and whispered, "Congratulations, Sadie," and I exhaled.

When Mary hugged Alex it was for much longer and he smiled and shook his head and grinned at something she was saying to him. They were whispering together, but he kept looking at me with a wink and I knew I was safe from Mary's judgments.

When we were all introduced again, Mr. Hamilton offered me a drink which I immediately declined even as Alex stiffened beside me. And I remember feeling insulted that he would think so little of me by then. I was pissed actually.

In the 4 months since this had all began, I had cut my smoking to 3 cigarettes a day, which was completely psychological at that point, and I hadn't had one single drink, or even a Tylenol. I had tried to put on some weight for the baby and for myself. I did everything I was supposed to do, but Alex had stiffened and I was pissed.

Releasing his hand, I found myself near tears. Wanting this announcement over, I just spilled it right there in the front entranceway. Not even seated around the dining room table, I spilled our secret.

"I'm pregnant. And Alexander wants to keep it. And he says he loves me, and that's it."

And in the momentary silence that followed, I heard his brother say something that sounded an awful lot like whore and I laughed. Standing there, fisting my hands against my sides, I laughed like an idiot when I heard the word whore, because I expected it and I knew it was coming, and I was right.

"Told you, Alex," I laughed. Turning to his mother I continued. "Look, I get it. You met me once when I was too shy to speak, once when I was drunk, and now you're finding out I'm pregnant. Why wouldn't you think I was a whore trying to trap your son, but-"

"Sadie!" Alex tried to interrupt.

"But I'm not a whore, and I wasn't trying to trap Alex. I didn't even want to do this, but he did. Your son loves me and he wants to have a baby with me, and we almost lost it, but then we didn't and Alex wants this baby with me. Oh, and it's a boy," I yelled. Realizing my voice was raised, I scaled back a little. "I'm sorry for all this but I'm not a whore, I'm just weird, and I have some issues but Alexander wants to be with me anyway. And-"

"I love Sadie, and we're doing this and we're getting married." Turning my head toward him I remember thinking he probably should've asked me first. "And if you ever speak about her like that again, I'll fucking kill you. Got it, Chris?"

When Mary asked, 'When are you getting married?' to break the tension between brothers, I could've kissed her.

"Very soon," Alex replied. "We don't want our baby to be a bastard, right Sadie?" He smirked at me and I again starting laughing.

Mrs. Hamilton with her unyielding grace, once again extended me a courtesy I didn't know if I deserved.

"Congratulations, Sadie. I wish you and Alexander much happiness," and then she hugged me. Bracing for it I knew it would come and it did. Whispering, she said, "I don't think you deserve my son, but I do hope you prove me wrong."

And nodding against her hair, I replied, "I don't think I will, but I'll try," as she pulled away from me. And I then understood what

I was up against. Mrs. Hamilton would always dislike me unless I made her like me, which was going to be hard.

But within minutes, my life changed again. Mary took a liking to me immediately, and as the oldest sibling of 5, she seemed to set the tone. Alexander's other 2 sisters weren't there, and his brother Chris bolted before dinner. So Mary, her lovely husband Darrell and their 2 little boys, Mr. and Mrs. Hamilton, Alex and I sat and tried to eat dinner. I ate what I could, which wasn't much, and I waited patiently for the time to come when Alex and I could get the hell out of there.

Eventually, the conversation turned to weddings and that was it. Mary and Mrs. Hamilton had the whole thing planned for a New Year's wedding. Mrs. Hamilton got one shot in when she said I would at least be bundled up, so I would look less tacky pregnant on my wedding day, but I let it slide. I already knew what I would look like to everyone else. I would look like my mother had looked, and I hated that.

When Alex and I finally left, Mrs. Hamilton hugged me goodbye and patted my stomach while smiling. If nothing else, I did think she was genuinely happy about being a grandmother again, so I had that working for me.

Mary hugged me as well and handed me her phone number in case I needed any pregnancy advice which was nice of her.

And then after a generic goodbye to Darrell and Mr. Hamilton, Alex and I walked quietly to the car.

"Sadie, I want you to-"

"Please, Alex. I'm so tired and I don't really want to talk anymore. I'm mad that you were nervous I would drink, which was insulting. And apparently I'm getting married in 3 months even though I don't remember you asking me, so I have a lot to think about. One thing I will say though; my parents won't be anything like yours. So prepare yourself. You're going to be very disappointed if you think there will be any drama from my parents."

"I don't want any drama-"

And suddenly laughing, I couldn't help it. "Well then, you picked the wrong girl to love."

CHAPTER 26

3 months later we had Christmas Eve with my parents, and Christmas Day with the Hamilton's, and it was nice. Everyone was excited about our wedding and willing to overlook all the negatives that we were facing together because Alex and I were struggling. He was paid very little while interning, and I wasn't working or going to school, but my student loan repayment schedule had already begun. We lived in my apartment still, but dreamed of a little house of our own for us and the baby.

Alex and I knew we would be okay in the future, it was just the immediate that was a little shaky, but he never worried too much. He seemed to think it would all work out. Alex told me he would always take care of us and he wasn't worried about our long term life together.

Alex talked about my baby shower gifts, and our wedding gifts as a kind of lifeline to our future. And he worked really hard, keeping up his medical studies, and interning every chance he could to bring in more money for us.

And I did offer to help. I looked for a part time job but Alex wanted me safe at home until the baby arrived because the near miscarriage made him fear me doing too much. And though I had been given the clear to carry on about the world, Alex wasn't comfortable with it, so he took on the full burden of our finances, until our baby was born.

*****

So 2 days before our wedding, Alexander and I said our short-lived goodbye. His mother insisted he spent the night before our wedding at their home, and Alex had to work straight through the night before that, so we weren't going to see each other for 2 full nights and days until the ceremony on New Year's Eve.

And I remember being upset by that. I knew I would be lonely and freak out a little. I knew I would, and I knew Alexander knew I would. So he promised to call me hourly so I could hear his voice. He promised he would stop by in the morning after his shift before he went to his parents' house for his stag day only, because we didn't have a Stag and Doe. I had no Does except my mother and his 3 sisters, plus I was very pregnant and tired and not really the party type anyway.

I wasn't into having a Doe myself but Alexander was having a stag day/night on the day/night before our wedding because it was mandatory. Even his father and my father would be there. It was a rite of passage apparently that he HAD TO have. Everyone insisted, even my mother and Mrs. Hamilton, to my surprise.

And I wasn't mad about it because I actually understood. I knew Alex had cut off most of his friends to be with me always, so I really wanted him to have fun. But like the saint he was, Alex offered to cancel when he learned we would be apart the entire day and night after he worked a night shift at the clinic. He offered, but I felt bad enough about keeping him from a little fun, so I lied and said I wanted him to go have his last hurrah. Which I did, and didn't.

I didn't want to be alone, but I wanted Alexander to be happy, so I said goodbye.

Remembering those 36 hours, I know Alex did call me from the clinic hourly. He woke me up a few times and apologized, but I didn't care. Once again, Alex did as he promised and I was able to hear his voice through the night. He spoke to me quietly and lovingly. He promised me the world and I believed him.

I knew in less than 2 years he would be a practicing Chiropractor and he would be successful. I knew he would be a success because Alexander Hamilton made himself successful at everything he did. He made himself attain everything he wanted.

One day we would have a nice home for our baby and a nice life for ourselves. Alex promised me a wonderful future and I believed him.

The following morning after his shift, Alex did show up. With a gorgeous necklace I didn't know how he purchased, he handed me a white gold necklace with a little diamond encrusted key pendant. Holding the necklace I looked at Alexander while thinking of all the ways he had mattered to me.

I thought of all the doors he had opened with a key. I remember holding the beautiful necklace wedding gift from Alexander knowing this was the absolute best decision of my life.

Grinning, I remember Alex putting the necklace on me as he burst out laughing. And when I looked at him in confusion, he tried to speak through his laughter.

"I had all these stupid lines and pathetic clichés to say to you. You are the key to my heart. I am the key to your soul. This is the key to our beginning." Grinning back at him, he continued. "It was really cheesy. Even I laughed at myself in the car this morning," he laughed again. "It's all true, but it sounded so corny, I couldn't do it. Anyway, all that IS true, but basically I thought you would love it, so I bought it for you. I know you're not the flashy jewelry-type, thank god..." he smiled again "...but I wanted you to have a special wedding gift from me that mattered." And it did.

"I love it, Alex," I said kissing him hard. Crawling onto his lap, I kissed him thoroughly. I wanted to show him how much I loved it. I wanted to love him the way he loved me. I wanted to show my love, so I tried.

Pulling Alexander on the bed beside me, I started undressing him. And fighting his clothes, he finally helped me.

"Sadie?"

"It's okay. We'll just push this belly out of the way," I grinned.

"I don't think we should. We haven't in months. Well, we haven't since the baby. We can try on our wedding night if you want." But I wanted Alex now.

"I want you right now."

"Please, baby. I can't now. I'm scared to hurt you and I'm not ready to be gentle," he grinned. But I didn't care. I needed Alex and I wanted him.

"Alex I need you to be with me. We haven't in months, and I want to before you leave me," I begged.

"I'm not leaving you Sadie," he said sitting up on his elbows. "I'm not leaving you, I'm just not going to see you for like 37 hours or something. But we'll see each other tomorrow night at 8:00."

"I know but I want you now. I need you to be with me in case you forget me when you leave me," I cried out. And I remember thinking I was being irrational. I remember knowing I was irrational at the time, but I couldn't stop myself. I was desperate for him.

"Sadie, stop."

But I didn't. Grabbing for his crouch, I pulled at his fly as I pushed my hand inside. Feeling him stiffen the second I touched him, encouraged me. But when he moved his hips to get away, I grabbed him accidentally to keep him in place.

"Shit, Sadie! Stop it. I'm not going to have sex with you right now, so let go," he snapped. And I did.

Sitting back on my heels, I remember looking at Alexander totally embarrassed again. I certainly didn't mean to hurt him, and I never thought I would act so sexually aggressive, at least not while awake, because what I did in my sleep was different and we both knew it. I couldn't fight that need because I was sleeping, and Alexander never held it against me.

"Let me take care of you," he said moving off the bed. But I didn't want that.

"No, it's okay. I just wanted to thank you for the beautiful necklace and I wanted you to know I wanted you even though it's been months since we were together. But I don't need to be serviced, Alex," I said as he flinched at my poor word choice.

"I wasn't going to *service* you. I was going to be with you until you felt secure again. I want you too, but not now- not as a 10 minute quicky before I leave, and not when you're being all intense. Tomorrow night however all bets are off. We're going to make love on our wedding night, okay?" He asked trying to hide his anger. But I could see it. I had offended him and I was sorry for that.

"I didn't mean to say that. I know it's not like that with us. I'm just tired and frustrated and I like being with you. You're good for me and I know that and I wanted to show you, that's all," I mumbled embarrassed again.

Trying to ease down the tension like he always did, Alex sat back on the bed beside me and hugged me. Wrapping me in the warmth I needed, he kissed me. Actually, he kissed the holy hell out of me, and then he leaned against my forehead and said, "Tomorrow night, Sadie. I promise to rock your world," and I grinned. "I'll work around this huge belly of yours, and I'll make you happy, I promise."

"Okay. Tomorrow night. 37 hours away. I'll wait for you then. Do you think we could sneak out between the ceremony and the New Year's reception party?"

"Yup. We can even sound believable when we say you need to go lie down for an hour because you're tired."

"An hour?" I teased.

"An hour and a half," he teased back.

"I'm sorry I'm so weird, Alexander."

"I love you Sade- weirdness and all."

"Good," and I kissed him again. A long, deep, pull him toward me until he settled in beside me kiss. Kissing him and wrapping my leg over his hip, I remember wanting to devour him. I wanted Alexander to remember this strange morning always. I wanted him to know I was into this completely, and no longer scared or nervous, or insecure about him and our relationship. I remember wanting him to know I was into him completely, and I would try to be a really good wife for him.

"Please stop, Sade," he groaned against my lips, and I smiled.

"Sorry..."

"I've got to go. I have to, or I'll do exactly what you're trying to make me do to you."

"I triple dog dare you to do it," I laughed as he jumped up from my bed groaning again.

I remember looking at his erection in his partially unzipped jeans and wanting it so badly. I remember staring at him as he adjusted himself and re-zipped his jeans. I remember the look on his face as he watched the look on my face.

"I hope to hell you still feel this way tomorrow. If your hormones change again and you don't want me this way, I'm going to explode, just to let you know."

"I will," I breathed deeply through my arousal.

"I love you, Sadie, but I have to go. I'll see you tomorrow night, okay?"

"Okay," I said. But I couldn't hide the sadness in my voice. I remember trying, but the sadness came through anyway.

"I don't know what I'm doing today- Stag secrets and all, but I'll call you whenever I can. I know your mom is picking you up at 3:00 for your nail appointment so I'll call after that, okay?"

"Okay."

And as he started walking back for my front door, I said the best I could under the circumstances.

"I love that you love me, Alex."

"I love you too, Sadie," he replied from my doorway with a beautiful smile.

And then he left me.

Alex left me, and that night the inevitable happened like I knew it would.

CHAPTER 27

He came to me.

I know it hindsight it was expected. I know in hindsight I knew it would happen. I know in hindsight it was truly inevitable.

Remembering my time with Alex earlier in the day I know I was scared of this happening. I know I knew He would come to me. I knew He would come and so I acted out with Alex.

I wanted Alexander to make love to me so that *He* couldn't. I knew He was coming for me and I wanted Alexander to be the man I was with. I know I did. And that's why I tried so hard to seduce Alex.

But I failed.

And my stranger came back to me that night.

*****

When I woke from my sleep at 2:12 in the morning, He was standing over my bed.

He was there and I knew He had come for me. He was standing over my bed and I wasn't even afraid of His sudden presence because I had known He was coming for me. I had always known He would be back for me one night, and He finally was.

I remember sitting up slowly, pulling my comforter with me until I was propped against the headboard. I remember staring at Him as He stared back at me. I remember knowing I was awake and my stranger was in front of me in my bedroom where Alexander should be. I knew He was there and I hated Him for coming back for me.

"Don't," I said into the silence of my room. But He moved closer anyway. "Please, don't. I don't want you anymore. I don't know if I ever really did. I just didn't know any better back then. I was young and confused and you messed with my head then."

But He ignored me and sat on the end of my bed, even as I pulled my legs up close to my chest to protect Alexander's baby from Him.

And when He suddenly lunged at me, I tried. I moved as best as I could but He was so much bigger and stronger than me. He easily held me still. He easily held my wrists above my head as He forced His mouth onto mine.

Fighting and turning my head frantically, I tried to use my feet against the mattress to give me leverage. I tried to fight, but the baby was getting in the way. I tried to fight until He crushed Himself against my stomach to flatten me to the bed. He crushed Alexander's baby, and I was afraid... So I stopped fighting.

I remember I stopped fighting, instantly. I gave up and I gave in. I did nothing in that moment, so He would get off the baby.

When He grabbed my face with a hand, I used my free hand to scratch His face hard. I used it quickly to hit His face until He grabbed my hand again, pushed more weight on the baby and put both my wrists into His left hand. Using His free hand He pushed down hard in the middle of my stomach until I stilled again totally panicked and in pain.

And I remember being shocked that He would use the baby as the means to still me. I remember thinking He wasn't the same. I remember being stunned that He seemed so vicious to me, because those weren't the memories I always had of Him.

To me He had always been a glorious lover who loved me. My soul mate. My life.

So I didn't fight Him anymore, but I cried.

When He grabbed my face hard again, I let Him. I stayed still as He forced a kiss from me. I kept my mouth still but I didn't fight Him, and eventually He lifted some of His weight off my stomach.

Kissing me, He was ruthless. Biting and sucking, He made my lips bleed as I stayed still beneath Him. I was still but He remained ruthless, even as I cried.

When He moved down my body, I remember thinking I would have my chance to fight. Because I did want to fight, I really did. I remember thinking of Alexander and the life he was going to give me and I wanted to fight the stranger because this wasn't the life I wanted anymore.

With Alex I woke to a reality I had never known. Alexander HAD changed me, and I wanted my life with Alex now. I realized in that moment that I was different and it was Alexander who I wanted in my life. So I told Him.

"I don't want you anymore, I really don't. You mean nothing to me anymore. You are nothing but a nightmare to me now." But He didn't care.

Moving down my body He slowly released my hands as He stared at my face, but before I could try to fight Him, He placed a hand firmly in the middle of my stomach again with force. He pushed His hand down and I understood the threat. I knew in that instant that He would hurt my baby if I fought Him, so I stilled again, even as I cried.

Lifting my hips He settled my legs over His shoulders as He made His way down my bed. Quickly holding my stomach again, He lifted my t-shirt and to my horror, He took me with His mouth like He used to.

And I honestly felt nothing. I lied there hearing Him suck and lick at me as I cried. I listened to the sounds He made with repulsion. I listened but laid perfectly still to His moans as He tried to devour my lifeless body.

But I didn't move and I didn't react. I lay silently crying and deathly still with the weight of His hand on my stomach keeping me immobile.

And I remember lying there thinking of anything but what was happening to my body. I remember thinking of walking down the aisle to Alexander Hamilton. I remember thinking of Alexander's mouth on me. I remember thinking of Alexander's kisses, and his hands, and his body deep inside me. I remember thinking of how few times I was able to enjoy him before we couldn't any longer with the pregnancy. And I remember thinking of how long it would be until I could have Alexander deep inside me again. I thought of Alexander for the first time with my stranger.

Through all the dreams of my stranger, Alexander was just the prop I used to get me off. Alexander was the tool I used when I dreamt of my stranger making love to me. Alex serviced me while I thought of, and craved, and *needed* my stranger.

And I remember that moment of clarity.

I thought of Alexander... and everything changed for me.

Arching into Alex, I felt him lap me up. I felt him impale me and suck me and tease me with his tongue. I arched into him as I cried out with my need. I ached for more and I demanded it.

Begging and fighting, I took his face into me until the need grew and I stiffened with my impending release.

Holding him tightly to my body, I screamed out when he impaled me hard and fast with his fingers. Screaming for Alexander, I shuddered my release into his mouth. Frantic with my need I twisted and turned my body to him as he thrust into me quickly from behind.

Collapsing onto my shoulder my free hand rubbed and teased my body as he took me as hard as I demanded. Feeling Alexander bruise my hips with his hands ramped me up higher as I rubbed myself frantically. I needed and I took, fucking Alex as hard and as fast as I could.

And when I felt Alexander bite my shoulder, I arched into the pain and screamed for him in my sudden release.

"We were born for each other," he groaned into my soul.

"I know!" I screamed through my frenzy.

"You are mine."

"Always..." I cried.

The orgasm that took me suddenly was blinding. In a flash, I remember knowing my absolute reality. I loved Alexander. He was my soul mate and my love.

In that moment of divine clarity when I was left hanging between my orgasm and my death, I knew the life I wanted. I knew who I loved. And I knew He was gone.

"I love you," I cried out to Alex in the chaos of my room.

In my post-orgasmic haze, as I collapsed on my side, I was done.

As I fell into unconsciousness I promised myself I would never ache again. I knew I would never have to wait again, because Alexander was always going to be there waiting for me to need him.

I was going to be Sadie Hamilton, a wife and mother, and I decided I would never wait again.

And I tried.

CHAPTER 28

We were married later that day on New Year's Eve, just like Mary and Mrs. Hamilton chose, and it was beautiful. The night was cold but so clear we all saw stars through the glass ceiling of the hotel banquet center where we had our reception.

And Alex and the ceremony were perfect. He was gorgeous in his tux, and so charming and funny that by the end of the ceremony he had everyone half in love with him, including me.

His vows were long and loving and so specific to our reality, I choked up. And though I failed miserably trying to recite my own less beautiful, less loving vows, Alex didn't seem to care. Smiling, he prompted to me to finish my slaughtered vows so he could kiss me. He even said as much to me during the ceremony to everyone's humor.

And I laughed.

When we were formally announced as husband and wife, Alex finally kissed me deep and long, until his annoying brother cleared his throat and nudged us, again to the humor of all in attendance.

And that was it.

Alexander and I greeted way too many guests I did and didn't know, and we had our photos taken, and we waited out the crowd until we could disappear upstairs to the room waiting for us between the ceremony and reception. And we had exactly an hour and a half as he had planned.

When Alex attempted to lift me over the threshold of our room, we both burst out laughing when he feigned a back injury, but he lifted me anyway and deposited me in the middle of the room as I waited.

"You look so beautiful Sadie. I couldn't keep my eyes off you through the ceremony," he whispered as he slid down the zipper on the back of my dress.

Panicking for a second, I pulled away and shut off the light. With only the glow of the night in our room I hoped Alex couldn't see the bruises he had left on me.

I didn't know how to hide them forever, but for our wedding night I didn't want Alex to know he had hurt me, because I knew Alex would never forgive himself for hurting me.

When I walked back to Alex he kissed me deeply. Taking my face into his hands, he held me to him as he kissed away my anxiety.

Slipping my empire waist gown down my body he knelt in front of my white slip and kissed my huge stomach.

"Can we wait? Do you mind if we wait until later so I can take my time with you? I don't want to rush and I don't want to think about hurrying back to our reception. I just want to be with you later when we can take our time. Do you mind?" And I didn't for more reasons than Alex could possibly understand.

"No, I don't mind," I whispered as I held him tightly to my stomach.

"Good. Come here, baby." And taking me, Alex and I crawled into the bed and lay beside each other. We spooned, and he warmed me instantly. I forgot about everything but him and our life together. I forgot about everything until I was woken an hour later by Alex asking me to get ready for our reception.

But before we left our hotel room I took one last look at myself, and I approved.

I wore an off white, flapper-type dress which helped hide my huge stomach, with simple beige kitten heals. I looked pretty cute actually with my hair all swept up, and my makeup fresh and light.

The bruise and bite on my lip from Alex was hidden by a dark pink lipstick which seemed to make my skin glow. Looking at myself I realized I didn't look sallow, and I didn't feel like haggard, skinny, pale Sadie Adams. Looking in the mirror, I felt like pretty, newly married Sadie Hamilton, wife to Alexander.

After kissing my neck and telling me I looked beautiful again, Alex took my hand as we made the way downstairs to our huge reception. And once we greeted everyone, we were introduced by the DJ, and we danced our first dance together before Alex's friends and family.

After our first dance, I danced with my father, and Alexander danced with his mother, until we switched out parents again. And it was fine, if not slightly awkward dancing with Mr. Hamilton while he tried desperately to dance with me without touching my extended stomach. He tried, and I felt a little more comfortable with him as the dance progressed.

"I hope you're very happy, Sadie. I know Alex is," Mr. Hamilton said as he leaned down to me.

"I am Mr. Hamilton. Alex makes me very happy," I replied as he nodded.

Looking at Alex, he was waiting for me to make eye contact so he could smile and wink at me. Dancing with my mother looked awkward, but she was enjoying herself. Laughing and spinning a totally uncomfortable Alex, my mother made their dance a production for the crowd, to my father's humor I could see.

And when the third required dance was over, Alexander and I rejoined and kissed slowly in front of the crowd. He held me close and spoke to me softly, and loved me totally. He was amazing and I was happy, finally.

"You make me so happy, Alex," I breathed against his lips, as he pulled us tighter. And so we danced through another song.

Afterward, when people were lined up for the 11:00 buffet, Alex and I again made the rounds. He did most of the talking, but I tried. I tried to be friendly to his friends and family but it was hard. Of the 18 tables at our reception, only 2 were of my people. The rest were all Alexander's family, friends, and his family's friends.

I was severely, embarrassingly under-peopled at our reception, and I felt awkward when I recognized a few faces from high school. I was so different, and I felt so different, and I didn't know which Sadie Alex's friends' were thinking of. So when my mother motioned for us, I quickly pulled Alex to my parent's table.

After kissing and speaking to my Aunt Helen and Uncle Tom, Mr. and Mrs. Hamilton joined us at my parent's table, as my mother introduced my aunts and uncles, and my parents best friends Patricia and Tom, and Holly and Warren to the Hamiltons.

And watching quietly, it seemed like everyone got along well, and our reception seemed to be a real success, so I found myself relaxing a little.

Seconds before midnight, the DJ announced Alexander and I as the 10 second countdown was ending, so everyone cheered for us and the New Year simultaneously, which was pretty cool. Alex and I kissed our nuptials as everyone cheered and clapped the mixture of our wedding and the New Year, and I remember it was truly a special moment in time.

But by 12:30, Alexander handed me a plate of food and made me sit and eat. I hadn't attended the pre-ceremony dinner the other guests had, so really I hadn't eaten in close to 7 hours, and he knew it. Alex then bent and kissed my stomach and removed my heels while he rubbed my aching feet. He paid attention to things like that and he always took care of me.

When I was eating, he whispered, "half an hour," as I raised an eyebrow at his sexy grin.

Teasing, I quickly scooped a huge amount of food into my mouth like a pig and said, "Make it twenty," as he burst out laughing. And when I looked away from Alex I spotted Mrs. Hamilton watching us so I smiled at her with my mouth full. And amazingly, she quickly smiled back at me, which felt good. It felt like maybe I could prove myself to her one day.

25 minutes later, Alexander and I made our parting announcements, thanked everyone for attending, thanked our parents for throwing us our wonderful wedding, and then we bolted. Not even waiting for the exit line to be fully formed, we walked through quickly, leaving all the guests behind to continue partying away the New Year.

And so began our marriage.

Alexander undressed me and made slow love to me that night. He held himself above me by his arms and he leaned in for kisses as best as he could. We spent the night making love and talking.

We spoke about our day and night and about our future. We spoke about everything he wanted, and I even added my own wants to the conversation for the first time since we had been together.

We were happy and in love and I felt safe and loved in his arms while I slept.

The following morning was brutal however.

Waking slowly, I forgot about the bruises Alex gave me and I let the sheets slip from my huge body. Leaning into him with eyes closed, I was stunned when he aggressively pushed me away from him onto my back.

Opening my eyes, I looked up at him in shock and confusion until he reached for my hip and studied my skin. Trying to pull away, I remember the absolute panic I felt. I remember fearing he would know. I remember fearing he would leave me.

Begging, I yelled, "They're nothing. It's nothing, Alex," but he ignored me. Turning me, he pushed my body around until I had to fight a nauseous gag. Turning my face from his, I gagged into my hand as I cried.

"I'm so sorry, Sadie. I didn't realize I was so hard on you," he choked out. And I should have hidden the bruises better because I didn't want him to know, and I didn't want him to suffer unnecessarily, but I just forgot in my sleep.

"I'm fine, Alex. I loved being with you last night. It's probably the anemia making me bruise easily. That's all. You didn't hurt me at all. I promise everything was good last night. You were good and I loved being with you."

"But you didn't get off, I did! And you're all bruised, and I'm an asshole!" He yelled jumping from the bed while pacing back and forth.

"You aren't! You were wonderful. You know I can't orgasm easily. You know I can't! And I was tired and worn out, but I will. Everything's fine, Alex," I yelled desperately.

"You orgasm when you're with Him in your head!" He barked into our room.

"I don't anymore. I don't! He's gone. He's over for me. I think of you now. Totally. *Always.* I swear, Alex! It's just you. Remember you said one day I would think of only you, well I do now. It's just you, I swear!" I begged while trying to get out of the bed.

Reaching for him, he pushed my hand away, making me lose my balance. Falling sideways, I landed off the bed onto my side, as Alexander lunged for me.

"I'm sorry! I'm sorry, baby!" He yelled until his voice stopped, and the sudden silence almost killed me. "What the fuck is that, Sadie? Who the fuck bit you?" He yelled grabbing my shoulder and turning my back toward him.

"You! It was you! You bit me when you were excited!"

"I would never bite your shoulder! Are you crazy? Who bit you, Sadie?" He growled at me. "Who *fucking* bit you?" But I didn't know anymore.

"It was you, Alex. You bit me when you made love to me last night. You bruised me, and you bit me on my shoulder when you were excited. It was you. I promise..." I finished lamely.

Standing back up, Alexander slowly placed me on the bed. Turning from me he stood shaking looking toward the window. Shaking, I could see his distress. Shaking, I remember his confusion and anger.

"It was you, Alex," I whispered as he turned his head to look at me over his shoulder. Staring at me, he shook his head no. "It was you, Alex. No one else. I was with only you," I pleaded. "Please believe me. I was only with you lastnight," I tried to convince him.

Turning from me, Alexander walked away from me. He walked into the bathroom as I cried, and then he walked out of our room as I sobbed.

Alexander Hamilton walked away from me. He left me alone. He left me and I didn't know if he would ever return.

2 hours after he left me I made another mistake. Fighting off my past, I tried so hard- until I lost. Leaving my room, I went to the hotel gift shop and bought a pack of smokes. Walking back to my room, I numbly lit and relit the lighter in my hand. Walking into my room I was in a haze of pain and fear.

When I opened the door, I prayed with everything I had that Alexander was back, but he wasn't. I prayed that he would be back soon, but he wasn't. I prayed for the second time in my life, but again, my prayers weren't answered. Neither came back when I prayed for them, so I decided to stop praying altogether.

I lit a smoke in the bathroom and I drank some vodka. I raided the mini bar and used the little plastic covered glass for my liquor. I sat on the closed toilet and I drank my vodka as I chain smoked.

And I knew. I remember knowing I was making a mistake, but I didn't care. I knew I was being horrible, but I didn't care. I knew I was fucking up royally, but I just didn't care anymore.

All I cared about had walked out of the room.

When I sank into the warm tub, I was disgusted. I did have bruises all over me. My hips had faint blue yellow bruises, and a dark bruise sat right in the middle of my belly. I even had purplish blue bruises on my thighs. I was disgusting and disgusted, but Alexander shouldn't have left me. He should have known I didn't care about the bruises. I only cared about Alex inside me.

Alexander should have known he didn't hurt me and I would welcome his bruises anytime, because we were together and sometimes sex got crazy and bruises were left. Alexander should have known I didn't care about the bruises he left on me, but he left me anyway.

Sinking into the tub, I remember drinking my vodka slowly and smoking my cigarettes rapidly. I remember the feeling of floating in the water while my mind became quieter. I remember feeling like the end was slowly coming for me, but I really didn't care.

I had been married for less than 12 hours, and already Alexander had left me. He had promised me forever, but he meant only for *now*.

Crying, I remember the devastation I felt because Alexander left me. I remember the humiliation I felt because he left me. I remember hearing the phone ring in my hotel room and ignoring it. I remember thinking my mother would shake her head at me, and Mrs. Hamilton would be thrilled. I remember thinking I had tried and failed again, so Alexander had left me.

Remembering that day, I'm embarrassed to admit I didn't care about the baby at all. I had lost my ability to be logical and loving then. I had given up on pretending to be emotionally well for the baby. I didn't care about the baby anymore, and I didn't care about me anymore. When Alexander left me I stopped caring about everything.

So I poured a third small bottle of vodka and I chain smoked in the tub because I didn't know what else to do. I think I wanted to slowly destroy the body that had betrayed me with it's bruises.

*****

"Sadie! Wake up! What the hell are you doing?" I heard him, but I ignored the dream. "Wake up, baby! Come on. Wake the hell up!" I heard and felt the slap on my arm.

Stirring, I opened my exhausted eyes to Alexander leaning over me. Confused, I asked the most important question I had. "Are you real?"

"Yes. Oh, shit Sade, what the hell did you do? *This* shit again?" But I closed my eyes because I knew it wasn't really him anymore. "Sadie!"

"Please stop. I know you're gone. I know you left me. And I'm tired of being lonely all the time," I slurred.

When I felt my shoulders shaken, I stirred in the ice water. I didn't understand what the hell was happening, but I remember being so annoyed in the dream that I wanted to push it away forever.

"Come on, Sadie. Wake up!" And then I was lifted out of the freezing water as my body shook uncontrollably and my mind spun. Leaning into the sudden warm of Alexander, I threw up and buried my face into the warmth. "That's awesome, baby. Thank you for that," he said angrily.

When the glass of vodka was pushed to my mouth, I gulped it down with relief. I thought I was clearly in a dream, and I wasn't enduring Alexander's anger, or his sad return.

"What the hell?" He yelled. "Vodka? *Really?* You're fucking pregnant! What the hell are you doing?" He yelled again. And turning me I was suddenly face first in the sink as Alexander pushed a toothbrush down my throat until I gagged and threw up again.

"How could you do this? 3 smokes a day to keep you level was one thing, but *drinking,* Sadie? Even for you, that's a new low. Don't you care about anyone but yourself? What about our baby? What about us? You're such a selfish bitch!" He yelled in my face as he shook me.

And I remember my anger suddenly flaring. *Really?* Selfish bitch? *Me?* I had done NOTHING selfish in 8 years of my life! I had lived to make them happy. I had tried to make THEM happy for the last 8 years of my life. How was **I** selfish?!

"Fuck you, Alexander!" I screamed and hit. With wide eyes, I looked at his face of shock but I didn't care. "Fuck YOU! I'm not selfish. I tried to be everything you wanted and I faked it when I couldn't. You made me like this and you made me love you loving me and YOU made me fucked up again. YOU LEFT ME! And you promised me forever, but you lied to me, and now I'm waiting again and I'm sick and you did this!! I'm not selfish. You are! YOU LEFT *ME!*" I screamed as I hit him.

Fighting him, I punched and slapped and tried to get him away from me. I tried everything until he grabbed me by my arms, dragged me out of the bathroom and threw me on the bed. But when Alexander suddenly punched the wall above us, I silenced immediately. I had never seen Alexander this angry, and I was

My Dear Stranger

very afraid of his anger suddenly. I was truly scared of Alexander in that moment.

Tugging at the comforter on the floor I slowly wrapped myself in it as I shook and lay down on my side. My hands were blue and my lips quivered. And I was absolutely numb with the cold inside me.

Watching Alexander breathing hard as he tried to calm himself, I was exhausted from all this upset and fear and drama, and from the cold deep inside me.

I don't know why, but I couldn't stop myself from begging. "I'm so cold Alexander. Would you please warm me like you always do?" And then I cried.

When I was pulled into his arms, I cried harder, even as he tried to soothe me. I remember feeling that day was an absolute nightmare for me, and I was done.

"Why did you leave me?"

"I didn't leave you- I left for a while. There's a difference, Sadie."

"Not to me."

"But there is to me. I wouldn't leave you, but I needed to leave. I couldn't take all the confusion anymore. Why did you drink?"

"Because I couldn't take all the confusion anymore." I threw right back.

"You know you can't drink when you're pregnant."

"You know you can't leave when I'm pregnant."

"Sadie, I was trying to handle everything."

"So was I."

And I remember thinking I was being a total brat, but I couldn't help it. I wanted to punish him for leaving me. I wanted to be angry and bitchy and bratty. I wanted him to feel bad for leaving me. I wanted to hate him for leaving me, but I didn't hate him.

Moving my ass against him, I wanted him to make me feel better. I wanted him inside me and around me, until I wasn't angry anymore. I wanted him to love me until I loved him loving me again.

Touching myself, I lifted my leg and placed it on his hip. I wanted to feel Alexander but he wasn't touching me. Rubbing myself, I moaned and felt my arousal slowly climb. I was against Alex and he was so still behind me I should have been embarrassed by his neglect, but I wasn't. I was desperate for his love.

"Who are you thinking about?" He whispered behind me.

"You."

"What are you thinking about?"

"Us. Together. I'm thinking about only you, Alex," I moaned as I touched myself harder.

When I felt him snap his jeans, I begged. "Please, Alex. Please be with me."

"Never again, Sadie," he said as he pushed my fingers away from my body. "Never, *ever* again. I am the only one inside this body. I am the only one you think about. I am the only one left."

"Yes..." I moaned as he took me with his fingers. Pumping myself against him, I was alive for him. I felt everything in that moment. I was alive with Alexander Hamilton and I wanted to be alive with him.

"Who are you with, Sadie?"

"You, Alex," I groaned as he entered me from behind. "Oh, please..." I begged as he slowed inside me. But I wanted more. I needed more. "Please, Alex. I want you. Only you," I screamed as he slammed into me. "Alexander..." I moaned as he slammed into me again. "Alex!" I screamed when he took me harder. "Alexander! *Oh!*" I gasped when he began pounding into me from behind as his hand rubbed me from the front.

"Who are you with, Sadie?" He asked holding my hips still as he thrust inside me.

"You, Alex! I'm with you!"

And then the intensity grew and the need crested, and the climax roared as the orgasm tore through me into Alex.

"Who am I?" He yelled through gritted teeth as he came.

"*Alex...*" I moaned in my insanity.

And then the heaviest silence I have ever known descended upon us. Breathing heavily with my heart pounding, I heard nothing but I felt everything. And I knew, it was Alex I lived for.

"Who were you with the other night, Sadie?"

"You..." I moaned half unconscious, even as I felt him shaking behind me.

*****

We spent 3 days at the hotel as our honeymoon gift from my parents. We spent 3 days loving each other. We spent 3 days happily in our hotel cocoon, until we left for home.

And we remained happy. We continued our days as a happily married couple, coping and struggling day by day.

2 weeks later my baby shower was thrown and we scored. I think people felt badly for us and gave a little more than they normally would have, but we graciously accepted everything we could for the baby that was coming.

We changed around my bedroom to make room for the crib and we waited for the baby to come with a dining room filled with baby props; strollers, car seats, change pads, blankets, onesies, and an endless supply of baby powders, creams, and diapers.

Laughing at how it was possible for such a small creature to require so much stuff, Alexander and I waited happily for the baby to come.

CHAPTER 29

And then my baby came.
After an atrocious birth, filled with drama and upset, 41 hours later, my baby boy was finally born.
For 41 hours I struggled, and Alex tried to struggle with me, and doctors and nurses tried to ease the struggle inside me, but nothing worked. 41 hours were spent pushing and crying, and screaming for this little shithead to be born. And I was a mess.
Eventually, the control was taken from me, and to Alex and my mother's relief a quick C-section was given to my hundred pound body, to get the little 8 pound asshole out of me, as I was not so affectionately thinking of him by then.
But there he was. 41 hours later, my beautiful baby boy was placed on my chest with Alex standing close helping me hold him. My tiny baby boy was lying on my chest comfortably quiet, as Alex cried silently beside us.
Looking at the little prick who I had just hated, I was overcome with amazement. He was mine. He was so little and beautiful and pretty and just... Mine. He was an absolute angel to me.
And then with no prompting or knowledge of what the hell I was doing, and through my complete and utter exhaustion, I moved him a little higher on my chest and he instantly latched onto me and nursed. He nursed instantly like he knew who I was. He latched onto me in a way that I would never forget. He latched onto me in a way I hope he never lets go of.
Staring at his tiny mouth taking from me, something deep inside me shifted. Something dark died away to be replaced with the birth of something beautiful.
My son was born and I would never be the same.

Thinking of that first moment with my baby I still cry. I still remember the overwhelming feeling of love that hit me. The unbearable need to hold and love him that made me forget all of the pain and agony of his birth. The complete knowledge that I was created for this little baby in my arms.

And I still cry when I think of the tiny baby who saved me.

James Michael Alexander Hamilton was born on a cold day in late February. And he is my life.
Jamie changed me forever and made me the best Sadie Hamilton I could be. From the moment I held him in my arms I changed. I became a mother who would always love and cherish her child. I became the mother of the movies. I became the mother of any child's dreams because I live and breathe for my Jamie.
And amazingly, Alexander never resented my attention to Jamie. He was never jealous or put out by my life with Jamie.
Amazingly, Alexander accepted his place as second in my life, with pride. He never pushed for more than I could give and he never tried to take more than I could offer. Alex was amazing to me as I instantly became Sadie Hamilton, mother to Jamie first, and wife to Alexander, second.

Thinking back on those first few weeks, months and eventually years I can honestly say I changed completely, and for the better. Amazingly, I didn't suffer any post-partum depression at all. I never cried unnecessarily. I never cried from exhaustion. I never cried about anything once my baby was born.
I loved Jamie, and I felt like a switch was thrown in my heart the second he was placed on my chest.
I forgot about my past and I welcomed my future with this little baby of mine.

*****

3 months after Jamie was born, Alexander came home in the afternoon, surprising me. I remember looking like crap still in my early morning sweats, but he didn't seem to care. Jamie was asleep and Alex made me a lovely lunch while I showered and cleaned up. And then we talked.
Alex admitted he was always secretly scared I would go off the rails when the baby was born. He admitted that he had spoken to a counsellor at the clinic he had been interning at to learn

what he could do to help me in case I suffered depression after Jamie's birth. He had a homeopathic and herbal supplement ready for me in case I needed it. He was prepared to help me through my new life with our son if I had needed it.

Choking up, Alex told me how relieved and proud he was of me. He told me his love for me had grown a hundred times over and he often wondered how his heart could grow even bigger for me and Jamie, but it did.

At the time, I remember thinking maybe should have been offended that he was so sure I would freak out; but logically, I think I was always waiting for that, too. So instead of being offended, I kissed him.

And finally, we made love for the first time since Jamie was born. We hadn't moved into our first house yet, and Jamie occupied our bedroom still, so Alex walked me to the living room and we made slow love on the couch, and on the floor once we had fallen off the couch. We made love and it was good.

There was no longer back arching screams of passion, but I think we wouldn't have anyway, for fear of waking Jamie. There wasn't the insane intensity I used to get when I *needed,* but there was a need. I felt the need to reconnect with Alex, and we did.

A short time after Alex and I finished, lying in each other's arms talking about the new little house we had bought with our wedding money as down payment, Jamie stirred. And I remember Alex attempting to get him, but I jumped up quicker.

Running for Jamie, I held my little boy as he woke from his nap and I looked at the face that had changed me forever.

I admit I've always been a little obsessed with Jamie. I love him so much I have a hard time not caring for him. And there was a bit of a learning curve between Alex and I where Jamie was concerned in the beginning, but we managed.

I did everything regarding Jamie, and if Alex attempted to help, I admit I was a bit freaked out. Usually, I stayed quiet, but sometimes I would tell Alex what he was doing wrong, or what he should do, or what I would do, until he gave up and handed Jamie back to me. Usually, Alex smiled at my suggestions, and gave in. Usually, he just gave into my instruction without anger or resentment. Usually, he understood that I was Jamie's mom, and therefore I trumped him completely.

Once in a while however, Alex started an argument with me over Jamie's care, but then he backed off when I struggled to explain myself. If I struggled with my need to love and protect Jamie,

Alex backed off, because I think he understood I wasn't trying to be mean to Alex; but rather I was trying to be a good mom to Jamie. So thankfully, he stopped the arguments from escalating.

Anyway, I remember after Alex and I finally made love I brought Jamie into the living room where Alex had already straightened up the couch cushions and I sat next to Alex while Jamie nursed. We sat together as a family while I fed my baby and cuddled next to Alex's warmth. And we were happy.
Everything fell into place. The dreams stopped, and the need vanished. Jamie consumed my days and nights, and Alex allowed me to thrive as a mother first, and as a wife, second.

And 4 months after Jamie was born we moved into our first little house, and it was awful. Failure to disclose multiple issues had us scrambling just to survive. We had naively thought because our mortgage was only a little more than our current rent, we would be fine. We thought we could swing the slight increase in utility bills from my apartment. We thought we could handle the *slight* increase in our cost of living, but we were wrong.
We were broke, and Alex struggled endlessly. We were in our mid-twenties, playing house, married with a child, and we were so poor, I remember being embarrassed that we couldn't even afford to have his parents over for dinner.
And the house itself was horrible for us. The roof had a leaky spot in the corner of our bedroom and the windows actually whistled in the wind. Everything about our house sucked. Nevermind we didn't even have enough furniture to furnish it, but we tried to make it work.
We tried so hard until Alex and I talked one night 9 months after we moved in. Finally, Alex admitted we had accumulated too many bills to pay. Alex admitted he was struggling over the weight of paying one bill first, and rolling over another bill the next month. He admitted we were behind almost 2 months' worth in each of our bills. And I was caught totally by surprise.
I was surprised Alex actually told me he was struggling, so I knew it must be very bad if he was telling me about it. And I was surprised that we could be so screwed so quickly, because I thought it took people years to accumulate debt. I thought people made bad decisions with their money, or poor choices with their demands and wants. I didn't know any better because I had

always had student loans to pay my way, and very few financial demands before our house.

But it didn't take years, apparently. It took us only 9 months to put ourselves in a big hole. So Alex and I made a few decisions together. Together, we talked about what we could and couldn't do- what we would and wouldn't do. We talked together about our situation.

Afterward, Alex admitted he was so scared I would freak out if he told me we were in trouble, he waited. He was scared I would lose it if I had to think about all negatives, so he tried to deal with it all alone. He told me he had put off telling me we were in trouble for months because he didn't want me to lose it.

And again, I should have been offended that he thought I was so weak. I should have been pissed that he had put us in a bad situation without telling me for months. I should have been pissed that he always expected the worst from me, but I wasn't. He was right to fear my reactions to stress BEFORE Jamie. But after Jamie I was much stronger.

And so I gave him shit for not telling me sooner, but I kissed him and said we would figure it out together. I told him I was getting a job, and between our 2 mothers and his sister Mary we would have someone to watch Jamie while I worked. I lied to Alex and told him I was okay with going to work. I lied and said I was fine with someone else watching Jamie. I lied for his benefit, so he was happy again.

But I'll admit, the thought of anyone touching my son made me nearly violent. I couldn't stand to be away from him. I couldn't even stand Alex touching him, and he was his dad. The thought of our mothers watching my baby made me want to run away *with* my baby, but I didn't. I held it together for the first time, for Alex.

So 3 weeks later, I started working part time at a flower shop down the street from our awful house. I waited for my mother or Mrs. Hamilton to arrive at our house and I walked down the street to work. I worked my shift, trying to learn all about the beautiful flowers, while obsessing about Jamie. I called endlessly. I used the washroom way too often so I could sneak little phone calls to my mother or mother in law, but everything was always fine. There was never a problem with Jamie, I just assumed there would be.

And 4 hours after my shift began, I would run down the street to our awful house, throw the door open, and shake with my relief to hold Jamie again. Sometimes, even if my baby was sleeping when I returned home, I couldn't fight it- I had to wake him and hold him, to his grandmothers' horror. But I didn't care. I needed to hold my son. I needed to know he was okay, and safe, and alive, and safe.

Once, a few weeks after I started working, I had a particularly intense feeling of something wrong, and I paced and paced behind the counter. I smiled at customers and to my manager, but I was almost sick with the overwhelming feeling of wrongness inside me.

I remember calling my house, but no one answered. I remember calling my mother's cell but she didn't answer. I remember calling Alex, who was still working at the clinic, and he answered. I called him freaking out because I was nearly hysterical with the knowledge that something was wrong with my son.

So I left the flower shop without permission. I just bolted and ran down the street to my son. I ran the block and a half in under 5 minutes. I ran until I saw Mrs. Hamilton with my son walking down the street.

And then I made a huge mistake.

Screaming her name down the street, she turned toward me with a smile, until she really looked at me.

Screaming, I ran for her hysterically. I screamed and yelled and spit fire at her. I grabbed for my baby in his stroller until he suddenly cried out. I screamed horrible things and I made atrocious accusations. I screamed at my mother-in-law while bouncing my screaming son in my arms.

To say I lost it is an understatement. An older couple stopped to stare at us, while Mrs. Hamilton stayed silent in front of the psychotic mess I was with the screaming baby in her arms.

I yelled words like kidnapping, and murderer, and evil bitch and fucking KIDNAPPER!! I screamed until I was suddenly wretched to my left by Alex.

Looking at him, still ready to fight everyone who threatened my son, I lunged at him and almost dropped Jamie. I lunged at Alexander as Mrs. Hamilton lunged for Jamie. I lunged as Alexander pulled my hair, twisting my back sideways to make me stop my assault.

And then the world collapsed around me. I remember looking at the scene play out with a kind of slow motion confusion. I remember my confusion. I remember knowing I was confused but unable to understand what was actually happening. And then I suffered my first post-adrenaline dump in years.

Leaning over while shaking violently, I threw up on the sidewalk as the older couple watched the scene play out with fascination. I threw up my lunch, and effectively cleared out my body and my mind at the same time.

Hearing Jamie still screaming was what woke me up fully. Looking to my right, I saw Mrs. Hamilton holding my son close to her chest, bouncing him, while shushing him with kisses all over his little tear-stained, snotty face. She was ignoring my behavior completely to care for my son.

And then everything changed for me in that instant. Feeling Alex's hand on my back, rubbing me calm, I knelt on the sidewalk. I pulled him with me and grabbed hold of him for his warmth. I needed his warmth to make me better.

"Sadie? What happened?" He breathed into my hair, as I finally burst into tears.

"Let's go inside," Mrs. Hamilton demanded, as she walked away from us with my son. And looking at her back while hearing my baby cry, I quickly scrambled up and followed her, leaving Alex on the ground behind me.

When we climbed the 3 stairs to our awful house, I stayed away from Jamie. Even when he reached behind his grandmother for me, I didn't touch him. I was afraid Mrs. Hamilton would be mad at me if I touched him. And I was afraid of what she would do to him if I made her angry with me. I was deathly afraid of absolutely everything in that moment.

So after opening the door, Mrs. Hamilton walked into the bathroom with my crying son while I stood alone in the living room silently shaking. When Alex suddenly touched my shoulder, I shrugged off his hands because I really didn't want to be touched while I waited for my son. I wanted nothing but my son.

My baby was crying in the bathroom with his grandmother and I didn't know what to do. So I stood silently still, waiting.

5 minutes later, Mrs. Hamilton walked out with my quiet little boy in her arms and she handed him to Alexander. She handed him to Alex and my devastation was complete. She thought I was a bad mother, and she was going to take Jamie away from me.

"Please don't take him away from me... *Please.* I'm a really good mother. Ask Alex," I begged as my breath left me with a gasp.

"Sadie. Go sit down over there," she said pointing to the couch. "Alex, there's a bottle in the fridge. Give Jamie the bottle in his crib, and come back right away. He's very tired and he'll sleep immediately," she stated as Alex left with my son. "Sadie. Sit," she said again much more forcefully, and I obeyed at once.

"When was the last time you cried?" She asked me while standing over me.

"What?"

"*Cried*, Sadie? When did you cry last?"

"I don't know. Before Jamie, I guess," I mumbled while wiping my nose on my sleeve like a child. And when she handed me a baby wipe, my humiliation was complete.

"Come here, Sadie," she said as she sat down beside me. Taking me into her arms, I struggled to maintain my limited composure, until I just collapsed and cried all over her. Sobbing, I made a mess of her shirt, and a mess of my life. Sobbing, I let the darkness overwhelm me until she spoke.

"14 months is a long time to not cry, Sadie," she said, as I tried to stop my sobbing. "I know you love and respect Mary; do you know what she did after Tyler was born? Well, she dropped him off at my house and told me she didn't know when she would be back. She handed me a months' worth of stuff, and ran back to her car, even as I held a 4 month old Tyler in my arms and called for her to come back to talk to me. But Mary left me her son and took off," she said laughing. "Mary was gone one hour and then she came back hysterical for him. I didn't even have time to empty any of the bags she left before she was back for Tyler. And Kimberly? She booked a trip with Allan when Brady was a year old, then cancelled the morning they were leaving without even telling Allan. They lost the hotel deposit, and they were stuck paying all the airline fees, and then they fought the entire week because Allan was so mad at her. They spent the entire week at home fighting, until she came to move back in with us. But thankfully, Allan arrived the next morning and they spent the last 3 days of their vacation alone while Paul and I watched Brady over the weekend." Moving me slightly against her shoulder, I tried to lift my head, but she patted my cheek until I resettled.

"Okay, then there's me. I couldn't leave Mary alone for a second. No one could do anything right with her. I yelled at Paul all the time. I hated Paul's mother, so I wouldn't even let her see Mary. Paul and I lived in a kind of messy, crazy home where we didn't speak or even really like each other after Mary was born.

Well, I didn't like him and he was just trying to get through the days with me. I was suffering from post-partum depression as it's called now, but we didn't call it that then. It was simply the 'baby blues', and Doctors weren't too aware of what was happening to some of us. Back then, they just gave us Valium for everything, which I took," she said laughing again. "Well, I only took it for 2 days, but it was enough. Paul found Mary in a filthy diaper, dirty and crying on the living room floor, while I was passed out beside her on the couch. And Paul was livid with me. Anyway, I never took Valium again, and I tried very hard to get a grip. My mother in law started coming around more frequently, and I eventually relaxed a little with her. I never liked her, till the day she died actually, but I did see she was a good grandmother, and I relaxed a little with her taking care of and watching my little baby girl. Oh, I forgot the best one. Paul and I finally decided to have a date when Mary was 6 months old, and he had planned a very romantic dinner at a restaurant we couldn't afford, and he even booked a hotel room for the night because our house was so messy and not very romantic at that point. Anyway, I started crying in the car to the restaurant, and I cried in the restaurant, and I cried leaving the restaurant until Paul just drove straight to his parent's house so we could get Mary. And we did get her, and I was a little better after that. But Paul started taking more responsibility of her when he was home from work after that night. Just little things like taking her outside while I finished cooking dinner, or taking her for a quick walk on the weekend. Just little things I could handle, but then I ended up pregnant with Kim and everything changed again. I was pretty sick with her so I actually enjoyed Paul and his mother taking Mary more. By the time Kim was born, I was much better. I didn't obsess over Mary or Kim, and I learned to multitask without freaking out so much because Paul was a good dad once I let him be. And by the time Diana came, and then Christopher, I had the whole 'if it's not bleeding, I don't need to know' philosophy down," she said making us both laugh.

"And finally, I had Alexander and raising him was almost a joint effort. Mary and Kim were 9 and 10 years older than him, so they helped quite a lot. And we're all fine. Well, Christopher is still a pain in the ass, but my girls are good and Alex is a wonderful son, father and *I hope* husband to you."

"He is. He's amazing for me," I admitted finally looking at her. Sitting up, I again pulled another diaper wipe and tidied my face as I looked at her. "I am so *so* sorry I said all those things to you outside. I didn't mean them, and I don't really think that way about you. Not really. I was just so scared when I didn't know where Jamie was. I think I kind of lost it and panicked. But I'm really sorry Lynda."

"I know. It happens. But why did you think something was wrong?"

"I actually felt it at work, and then I called home and no one answered, and then I forgot you were with Jamie today and I called my mother's cell and she didn't answer, so by then I was almost hysterical thinking something was really wrong. I actually left work without telling them, and I'll probably be fired now and I really need to work," I said embarrassed.

"Alex. You can come in now. I know you've been listening in the hallway," she said smirking at me.

And like a kid caught doing something wrong, Alex walked into our living room, grinned at his mother and sat down across from us on the other couch.

"So what's going on? I won't tell your dad if you don't want me to, but I want to know. Is it finances?" And we both nodded. "How bad?"

And then Alex spoke. He told his mother everything. Actually, he told his mom a little more than he had even told me. He told her everything, but even as he spilled about this horrible money guzzling house, and our growing debt, he seemed to think it was only a short term problem. Alex was sure we would get out of this as soon as he could practice, because he was sure he would be successful and we would be fine. Alex was so positive and sure of himself, I think he convinced both Lynda and I that we would be fine soon, too.

"Okay, so I'll give you a loan to get you out of this mess, and then I'll give you a second loan to sell this house and buy a better house," she said over Alex's obvious objections. "I said a *loan*, Alex. I know you're good for it, and I wouldn't offer if I didn't think you would pay me back. I would never make this offer to Chris, or even to Diana because I know they would take the money and run," she grinned. "But you're different Alex, and I know Sadie wants my approval, so I know she wouldn't run either," she said while squeezing my hand. "But you need to dump this house first. It's awful. I don't know why you bought it and I don't know why you didn't ask your dad and me to help you first."

"We needed a house quickly with Jamie, and the Realtor was very nice so we believed everything he told us. He even set up the house inspection, which passed. So we grabbed it because we could afford to pay the down payment," Alex admitted embarrassed.

"Oh, I get it. I'm not judging. Your dad and my first house was a dive in the worst part of town. I just didn't know if there was a reason you two picked it. I didn't want to offend you if there was something you actually liked about it."

"God no. This house is awful," I said, making Alex laugh with me.

"It really is, mom. You should see the heating bills and the leaks in the roof and the weird smell Sadie and I can't find in the basement."

"And that wallpaper in the bathroom actually stares at me when I'm in the shower," I said making us all laugh.

"It does look like eyes! It's the weirdest thing I've ever seen," Lynda howled with laughter. "I can't even use the washroom here because I feel like the creepy walls are watching me!"

"I know. I'm sorry it's so awful, but Alex and I tried."

"You did try and now you'll try again. I'll ask Chris to come over and fix the roof for you, and I know Paul knows a good contractor to fix the broken fence outside. Maybe Mary and I can help fix it up a little inside. I know she has extra furniture in her garage from their remodel last summer, which will be good to use. And I can even help paint after you return from work. So we'll get this dump up for sale in no time." Mrs. Hamilton calling my house a dump sounded so funny to me I burst out laughing.

"I didn't know you could be funny, Lynda," I said sounding a little stupid. But she smiled at me anyway.

"I have 5 kids and 6 grandchildren. I have to have a sense of humor," she laughed.

After we all seemed to exhale any tension left, I stood and said I needed to go check on Jamie, but Lynda stopped me again.

"Sadie. He's fine. He's sleeping," she said in a tone which sounded a little too motherly for my liking. And looking at her, I knew it was a challenge, so I slowly nodded and went to the kitchen instead.

And she did help us. Remembering Lynda now, I'm so thrilled I lost it on her because after that horrible day she was a friend to me. She still wanted me to be better I could tell, but she was always nice to me and she helped Alex and I whenever she could.

Later that evening, she had Chris stop by and then Mr. Hamilton even arrived with pizza after work. Eating dinner we all talked about everything wrong with our awful house and Paul, Alex and Chris walked around making lists while Lynda and I played with Jamie.

And everything was better after that day. Lynda paid all our current and our in-arrear bills, and then she loaned us two thousand dollars extra to buy the supplies we needed to fix up our dump.

4 months later, Alex got a real job as a Chiropractic Practitioner, and 1 month after that we sold the dump. Alex was starting to make decent money, and he had a growing clientele, based on all his old friends, and his family. He was doing well, so I was thriving, because when Alex was happy, I felt happy, too.

Shortly after Alex got his new job, we found our current house and moved in two months before Jamie turned two. We moved into our forever home knowing what we were getting into and knowing what we could afford. We were smart with our second house. We actually budgeted and figured out actual costs instead of potential costs. We were smart, and we haven't struggled so hard since.

Money at the beginning was still thin, without much extra for extras, but we managed.

I worked part time until Jamie started Kindergarten and I loved my job, eventually. I spent as much time with Jamie outside in our own garden as I could, and I've managed to make him a little gardener as well. He loves being outside with his mommy, and I love having him with me.

I'm still a little obsessed with his health and safety, but I'm much better now. I actually let Alex and Jamie out of my sight for short trips to the store, or to grab a pizza in town. I just don't let them go too far. I can't.

Jamie is everything to me, and Alex knows it. Alex accepts that I need Jamie to make me the best Sadie Hamilton I can be, and he's okay with that.

CHAPTER 30

When Jamie was 4, my mother called to tell me my father died unexpectedly from a heart attack in Florida. My father died and I was kind of sad about it. I was sad because I was never very close to my parents and I realized I had missed my chance with my father. But mostly, I was sad that my mother would be alone, especially because I knew how much she loved my father.

My father was buried in Florida, and Alex was amazing. Alex booked the flights and made all the arrangements. Alex took over everything while I continued doing my things in a little bit of a fog. I went to work, and picked up Jamie, and I waited for our flight the following morning.

And Lynda and Paul Hamilton made the trip as well. With a grace I was long since used to, Lynda showed up at our house, packed our bags, and took care of Jamie while I went for a little drive. I drove away and had a smoke, which I thought under the circumstances was completely justified.

And when I returned home Alex was with Jamie, because his mother and father had left. Alex explained that we were being picked up by the airline shuttle at 6am and his parents would be at our home by 5am to help us.

The funeral was lovely- almost festive. My mother and her Florida friends had made a quick funeral wonderful.

And my mother looked amazing. She was charming and delightful, and she was warm and friendly to Alex, Jamie and I, and to the Hamiltons. She opened up her condo to us and we all got along well.

My mother was so good natured considering the loss I know she was suffering deeply, that she even made the crass joke that my father always wanted to die in bed, he just wanted to be doing something naughty when he did it, to Lynda and Paul's humor, and Alex and my horror.

2 days later when it was all over and the five of us were going to fly back home without my mother, she pulled me aside and handed me a check, and I remember thinking, already? And then honestly, I remember thinking, we could really use this. Not to imply I would take the money over my father, but he was dead anyway, whether I received the money or not, so I took it gratefully.

And with her typical behavior, my mother gave me the check and joked that it was too bad I was flying out or we could go shopping together. She told me she *desperately* wanted to update my wardrobe which she said was way too old for someone my age. And I remember a rare moment of weakness when she looked at me almost like she was asking me to stay longer with her, but I didn't.

I thought about it though, I honestly did. Then I thought, *why?* She and I are basically acquaintances at best, and I'd probably just feel weird in Florida surrounded by her and all her friends, so I hugged her goodbye and we left on the fourth day after my father's death.

I remember when we returned home Alex being all wonderful as usual, and it almost annoyed me because honestly, I felt fine. Truly, I felt fine. But Alex thought I was devastated, or maybe should have been devastated. Alex thought I must be heartbroken. Alex thought I should feel something. But I felt almost nothing for the death of my father which is awful, and not.

I saw my parents every couple weeks in the summer and every year at Christmas since I was twelve. I spoke to my mother once a month while they were away for months at a time, for years. Jamie barely knew them. And quite frankly, I barely knew them.

If I was to be really honest, I would say that the wonderful Hamiltons had far become better parents to me than my parents ever were. So I didn't feel as bad as maybe I should've, but I just didn't feel much for them living or dead, sadly.

I remember the night we returned home putting Jamie to bed, then walking to my bedroom to a waiting Alex. Alex was waiting for me with his arms outstretched like I needed comfort, but I didn't. I needed some warmth though, so I gladly jumped into his arms to warm myself.

"How are you feeling?" He whispered into my hair.

"Good. I have some good news. My mother gave me money from the inheritance."

"Really?"

And leaning up on my elbows, I turned to him with a smile. "I figure we can split it and I'll pay off my student loans and make a small down payment on the flower shop, and you can pay your parents back, and maybe pay into your Practice. What do you think?"

And he couldn't hide his grin or excitement, even under the circumstances, though I'm sure he tried to. Alex was a good guy and he took death much more seriously than I did. Actually, he would be devastated if one of his parents died so he probably felt for me the way I should've felt about my own father's death.

"Can I ask how much?" He asked slightly embarrassed.

"A hundred thousand. So we could split it and take 50 thousand each. Is that okay? Or should we sink it into the house or something?"

"Whatever you want, Sade. We're fine paying the mortgage, but we could certainly pay off some of our debts, and I'd love to finish paying back the loans from my mom, especially for the down payment on this house."

"Okay…"

"Plus, I think it's a great idea for you to buy the flower shop. I don't think Heidi is looking to make a killing. She told me at Christmas she just wants to retire comfortably. Do you want to pay my mom back, and use the rest on your loans, and for the flower shop so you won't have any debt either? I'm fine with that. This is your money from your father, baby."

"I know, but I think you should have some too." And I did.

Alex had always supported me, and Alex had always taken on the financial burden of our relationship. Even when I started working, it was part time and it barely helped. He's the one who took care of me financially and emotionally when I couldn't take care of myself. He's the one who worked and studied and continued his schooling until he graduated and succeeded, all while caring for me physically and emotionally. It was always Alex.

"How about I see what Heidi is asking, and then we decide on the leftover money, after we pay your mom back for sure? I want you to have some of this too though. You deserve it, Alex," I said into his neck as I kissed him.

And then we made love. Again, slow and beautifully. Alex took his time and he made me happy. Alex had long become a good lover to me. He had figured out what my body liked and needed to be pleased sexually. He had figured me out eventually.

All my quirks and issues were addressed and either we had moved past them, or we had moved through them.

Alex had become the best husband he could be, and the best friend I had ever wanted. The intimacy between us was natural and loving. He could look at my body with affection and I could watch him look at me with a sense of happiness and love.

And I loved him, there was no doubt. Over the years he had made me love him with his strength and unyielding ability to keep going with me when others would have walked away.

He had changed me.

I was sober, successful, and comfortable with myself. I no longer used crutches or tools to self-destruct when I was stressed out or lonely. I knew what was wrong with me and I acted accordingly. I took care of myself the way Alex had taught me to. I no longer waited for more, but lived happily with what I had- my husband and my son.

So 5 months later I did end up buying the flower shop from Heidi, and Alex and Jamie were so cute about it. They had a party for me and made me cut a ribbon across the door. My party was small obviously, but I still loved that they were excited for me.

I loved that Mary, Kim, and even Chris came to my opening with their spouses and children. Diana was traveling, but otherwise, all the Hamiltons came, as did my mother. And I remember Lynda was especially proud and happy for me, which felt good. I had always wanted her approval, and I had worked really hard to get it over the years.

And Jamie had it in his little brain that we were millionaires because his mommy owned a store, and he mapped out his entire future around it. Jamie was sure he would build flowers with his mommy when he was older.

And joking, Alex said he had been an owner at his Practice for a while, so he was a millionaire too, but Jamie just shrugged. Even though his dad was clearly better than his mommy, being in the healthcare industry, Jamie only saw the dazzle of a storefront, and the sound of the bells over the door.

In the end, I spent just over 60 thousand of the money on the store and on my loans, and I made sure Lynda was paid back, leaving Alex with just over 25 thousand to use on himself, which he sunk into his Practice. 2 new Chiropractic tables were purchased, and the whole office was given a facelift, which his 2 partners loved.

And so we continued.

I set my hours around Jamie's school, and I have worked every day from 10am until 2:30 so I pick Jamie up by 3:00 after school. I don't work evenings, though I'm always available to come in if my small staff needs me. And I never work weekends because weekends are for my boys.

My life is really good now.
My life was really good then.
My life changed a few days ago.
My life started spinning on Wednesday.

*****

My Dear Stranger

I received a letter on Wednesday that prompted this entire weekend. A letter I didn't expect. A letter I read in shock which made me send Jamie and Alexander alone to Mary's. A letter which has left me teetering between the sane and insane which I'm struggling to navigate through at this very moment.

Crying the entire day, I didn't go to work on Wednesday, and I faked illness when I called Alexander to pick up Jamie from school at 3:00 because I was unfit to drive my little boy. I faked illness to excuse the crazy that has claimed me.

2 days later they left because I sent them away without me. Jamie and Alexander are gone so I can say my goodbye and figure out where I go from here.

I sent my baby away to protect him from the me I might become.

On Wednesday after driving Jamie to school, I spoke with a few parents about a fundraiser we're throwing for the school and I carried on about my morning. I never arrived at my small flower shop before 10am, so nothing was amiss when I returned home, collected the mail and made my way inside my home for my waiting coffee.

Tossing the mail on the counter, I grabbed the heavy Manila envelope I mistakenly assumed was for Alex's Practice, and I tore it open.

But when 'The Story of SMA- Her Story' fell out in paperback form I stood deathly still. I saw the book, and my world suddenly faded away. Everything became dark and fuzzy as I stood holding the counter for support.

And after an endless amount of time I looked back inside the envelope to find the letter that has changed my life.

Again.

CHAPTER 31

Looking at my blue Asian silk journal I'm reminded of everything from my previous life. I feel everything I ever felt, and I remember everything I was put through.

I remember the years I feared everything.

I remember the sounds of the man who hurt me.

I remember the sounds of the man who loved me.

I remember the feeling of hating my body and trying to destroy it.

I remember all the years I spent waiting for the man who loved me to come back to me. I remember waiting. Always.

I know I thought He would be back for me one day. I know I thought He would be back to love me again, even after I tried to push Him away.

But He never came back.

I have lived a good life, with a wonderful husband and a beautiful son. I have made myself change. I have made myself better. I have made myself. But I always wait for Him, still.

I think I always thought enough time would pass until He would fade into a memory. I think I thought enough time would pass until He was no more than a reminder of days long since gone. I think I always thought I would forget the feel of Him so that I could move onto a nostalgic youthful memory of Him.

But I've always been wrong. And I wait still.

I think deep down I still wait so I can finally say goodbye to my dear stranger. I think that's why I still wait.

But He has never come back, so I have never said goodbye. And I wait still.

"Where is He?" I beg my empty garage.
"Where are you?" I scream out into the silence of my garage.

*****

Seeing Alexander suddenly standing in the garage doorway, I can't believe I'm looking at him. When did he get back? When did he open the door? Did I hear the alarm? I don't know, but I'm looking at him suddenly, and he looks so sad to see me.

"Oh Sadie... What did you do?" Alex seems to moan.
"What's wrong, Alex?" I whisper.
Opening his hands in front of his chest he begins to move slowly toward me. Actually, his hands are shaking and he looks really bad right now. What the hell happened?
"What's wrong, Alex?" I whisper again.
Looking, my neighbor Cheryl is behind him in the doorway. Talking quietly on her cellphone, Cheryl isn't looking at me and I don't understand what the hell is going on?
"Why is Cheryl in my house?" I whisper.
When Alex shakes his head I don't know what he means. *IS* she in my house? I swear I'm looking at her.
Confused, I yell, "Cheryl?!" And then she looks right at me. Smiling and lowering her phone, Cheryl looks right at me as she starts walking into my garage slowly, but I still don't get it.
"Why are you here?" I whisper.
"Hi Sadie. I thought I'd stop in for a minute when I saw Alex come home. How are you?"
"Fine. Why are you here? You never come over 'cause I think I'm too quiet or weird, or something..."
"Oh, that's not true. I think you're great, Sadie. We always talk outside, so I thought I'd drop by for a coffee. Is that okay?"
Looking at her, I shake my head no. Not now. Not when I'm in the garage. Why is she here? Oh! Grabbing my pack of smokes, I hide them between my legs. Stuffing them all the way into the space of my thighs, I'm sure I was fast enough that Alex didn't see them.
But no one is talking anymore, and no one acknowledged my smokes as Alex shuffles closer to me with his hands still out. He looks really sad though, and I don't know what the hell is going on?
Trying to break the silence, I look at Cheryl again. "It's nice to really meet you, Cheryl. What kind of nurse are you?"
"I'm a Labor and delivery nurse. I bring babies into the world," she smiles. Actually, her smile is beautiful. She looks very happy with her career choice. And why shouldn't she be? Her career choice is noble. She's a delivery nurse who brings life into

the world, and she's lovely.

"That's wonderful, Cheryl. Do you have a doctor?" I smirk with an eye brow wiggle.

Smiling back at me she says, "Nope. The Doctors at my hospital are way too arrogant, and I can't stand a man who acts like he's god, which most Doctors do. So I stay away from them."

That makes sense. I would hate to be with a man who had a god-complex.

"How do you know Alex?" I whisper. I wonder if...

"Just from the neighborhood, Sadie. Alex called me when he hadn't heard from you, that's all."

"Oh." Wait. He called her? "Are you having an affair with my husband?" I whisper.

"No," Cheryl replies. Without emotion I think she lies to me, and it looked like such an easy lie I actually feel embarrassed for her.

"Then why does he have your number?" And there it is. I've laid down the challenge. I know the truth and now they know I know the truth.

Quietly, Alex speaks from 2 feet in front of me. Why hasn't he touched me or kissed my cheek, or even smiled at me? Why is he still standing 2 feet away from me with his hands outstretched and shaking? Why is he 1 foot away from Cheryl, but still 2 feet away from me?

"Sadie. All of us on this street have each other's numbers. Just like you have the M's number from across the street, I have everyone's too. We all do and it's nothing. It's just a fail-safe in case one of us on the street have an emergency or something, I promise. I can show you my phone. I have every single neighbor's number and contact information, not just Cheryl's. Would you like to see my phone?" Would I? No, not really. Staring at Alexander I'm at a loss and I don't know what else to say to that. "Sadie? Can I hug you, honey?"

"Why? I mean, why *can't* you? What's wrong with you?"

Looking at Alex, he seems so weird to me right now. He's still not moving closer, and Cheryl isn't moving at all. They both seem trapped or something.

"Can I get you a blanket Sadie? You look very cold. Would you like a warm blanket?" Cheryl asks me so calmly, it's strange. It's like her lips aren't moving, but sound and words are coming out of her mouth anyway. She still hasn't moved, and I don't think I saw her mouth move. Is this a trick?

"Are you a ventriloquist?" I ask suddenly laughing. How strange is this conversation?

"Sadie. Can I have the screw driver? Please, honey?" What?

Looking at my hands I see I'm holding it. Oh god... I didn't know. Oh, look what I've done! Suddenly jumping in my own skin, I look. I see what I've done. I see it all. It's been years, and I didn't know.

"I'm sorry, Alex. I didn't know. I didn't. Sometimes, I just don't know and I didn't know this time. But it's the pressure, you know? I don't know what to do about the pressure, and sometimes I don't know until after what I did. But it's just the pressure. I promise I'm good. I didn't know, and it doesn't hurt."

Looking I see what I've done. Covering my bare breasts with my hands, I still hold the screw driver, resting it under my chin with my arms crossed. Why am I topless? Oh right, because I couldn't breathe earlier with my clothes on.

Looking at my legs, again I admit, "I didn't know. Alex? What's *happening?*" And finally, he moves.

Walking the 2 steps toward me, Alex slowly crouches in front of me and begins to raise his hand to my face. Slowly, I watch his hand shake as it comes closer to me. Waiting, his hand finally touches my cheek and he's so warm, I love it. Exhaling, I close my eyes and rest my face in his hand and suddenly I feel warmth for the first time in forever.

"Sade?" He whispers.

"Alex... You're so warm all the time. You're always warm. I love lying next to you in bed because you warm me up all over."

"Sadie, you know I'll *always* warm you. Are you cold right now, baby? Would you like Cheryl to get you a blanket?"

"Yes, please. Thanks, Cheryl. I'm really cold, and a blanket would be great."

Looking, I see Cheryl smile and nod once as she turns from my garage. Walking back into my home, I watch her. She's never been over before, so I'm not sure how she knows where to find the blankets.

"Has she been in our house before?" I ask Alex, and I think I know the answer but I don't want to know the answer.

"Not that I'm aware of. Have you ever invited her over?" Alex asks me gently.

"Then how does she know where to find the blankets?"

"She'll probably look in the hall closet upstairs. That's where most people keep them, so I'm sure she'll start there. They are in the hall closet aren't they?"

"Yes, of course. I'm sorry to distrust you. I'm not sure why I think you've done something wrong, because I don't usually, I just do right now, but not really, I don't think."

"It's okay, honey. Would you like to get out of the garage now? I could warm you up inside."

"Not yet, I..."

When Cheryl suddenly opens the door again, she smiles and holds up a blanket. Well, I wouldn't have chosen that ugly one, but it looks really warm so I guess it'll do.

Turning to Alex I see him give Cheryl a strange look with a head nod towards my home. What was that? Are they talking about me behind my back? I think they are. They have to be. Cheryl seems to know what Alex wants. Well, good for her!

"Cheryl? Are you and my husband sleeping together?" But both answer no a little too quickly I think. "Because I get it if you are. He's very attractive. Alexander Hamilton, of the wonderful Hamiltons. And he's still good looking, and in terrific shape, and really hot even years later, so I get it. If I wasn't already married to him, I'd probably try to sleep with him too."

"Sadie... Alex and I..."

"It's okay. He's a very good lover, I know that too. He's much better than he was when we were younger, aren't you honey?!"

When Alex tries to pull the screw driver away from me suddenly, I fight back and nick my own throat. I felt it. Through all the cold and the sadness, I felt the nick this time. I wonder why this time I felt it, but I didn't earlier. I wonder if it's because he's gonna hurt me this time.

"Please Sadie?" Alex whispers as he falls backward onto his ass. "Please don't do this."

"Don't do what? Talk to your lover?"

"She's not my lover. You're my only lover. You're my wife, Sadie. I love YOU."

"I know. You've been telling me for years."

"Cheryl, do you think he's a good lover?"

"We're not lovers. We've never been lovers, I swear. Alex and I have never even really spoken until this weekend. And he only spoke to me because he was trying to get to you- his wife."

"I KNOW I'M HIS WIFE!" I scream into the silence of the garage. I think I even heard an echo following my words.

Pushing Alex's chest further from me, I reach in between my legs and pull out my smokes. Mumbling 'I'm sorry', I don't even look up as I pull out a new smoke and my lighter. This is so bad, I know, but I really need one.

Once lit, I inhale deeply and exhale slowly. Alex hasn't seen me smoke in years, since we were first married, when he made little comments about my health and the smell, and made me feel so insecure about smoking that I eventually stopped, mostly. At least in front of him.

"I miss smoking, Alex. I know you don't understand, and I know you hate it, but I miss it. I wish you understood, so you'd let me have a smoke when I need one."

"*I* know, Sadie. I love smoking, too. Can I have one?" Cheryl asks from the doorway.

Stunned, I smile. "But you're a nurse! You're supposed to be all healthy and stuff."

Smiling back, she nods. "I know. But I hide it pretty well so my co-workers don't see me, and I only smoke when I'm drinking with my friends which isn't often, or when I've had a bad day at work." She confesses as she walks into the garage and sits down beside me. Handing me the blanket, she places it around my legs as she asks, 'May I?' while taking a smoke from my pack.

Sitting beside Cheryl, I feel comfortable suddenly. I'm warmed by her presence I think. Before I know what's happened, I see Cheryl casually moving the screwdriver out of my reach. Huh. That was smooth.

"I saw that," I say looking straight at her eyes, but she only grins and shrugs like it's no big deal, and suddenly it doesn't really feel like a big deal.

"What are you doing in the garage, Sadie?" Cheryl asks while lifting the blanket around my shoulders.

"I can't really talk about it, but I had some important stuff to do, and the garage felt like the perfect place to do it, you know?"

"Oh, I get it. I have a room downstairs where I do all my important thinking. I even have a punching bag in there for when I've had a really bad day."

"Really?" I ask surprised. Cheryl just seems so normal and nice, and totally not like the kind of woman who would have a punching bag in her home.

"Yup, and I love it. My nephew showed me once at my brother's house how to beat the hell out of it, and I loved it. Anyway, for Christmas a few months later my brother and sister in law bought me one and my nephew Mark put it up for me. You should get one, they're really fun. And whenever you're stressed you can beat the hell out of it. One weekend when I had a few girlfriends over because my best friend Paula from Oklahoma was visiting, she taped a picture of my ex-husband on it and we all laughed and took turns beating the hell out of *him*. Paula especially," she says laughing.

"You were married?"

"Yeah, for 2 1/2 years. But thankfully it ended almost as quickly as it began. He wasn't a very good husband."

"Oh, I'm sorry, I would hate that. Alex is a really good husband so I'm very lucky that way. Right, Alex?"

"I hope so, Sadie. I've always wanted to be a good husband to you."

"Oh, you have been. Do you remember the first time we met? Well, started speaking, anyway?"

"I do. We were on campus and you looked beautiful walking in the afternoon, so I smiled at you, and you smiled back."

Nodding, I feel very happy remembering Alex like that. He was so sweet to me. "You were so sweet, Alex."

"I hope I still am, Sadie. I try to be."

"You are..." I say tearing up.

"Alex is just so lovely, Cheryl. He is everything I've ever wanted in this life- attentive, and kind, and loving, and he really cares about me."

"I do. So much, Sadie. Please, honey, tell me what's wrong. I'm here, and you can tell me anything," he says leaning closer to me and Cheryl.

"I don't think I can tell you this, Alex. I don't think you want to know this. We never talk about this and I don't think you want me to tell you this."

"I do. Honestly. Tell me what's wrong. You seemed fine when we left, and then something happened, but I don't know what and I can't help you if I don't know what happened. Please, baby. Just tell me."

"I can leave you two alone if you want," Cheryl whispers beside me.

But grabbing her hand, I don't want her to go. Cheryl warms me like Alex does, and I like having her here with me.

"Can you stay, Cheryl? I think I like you here 'cause you kind of warm me up. Is that weird?"

"No, not at all. Can I give you a hug? Can I warm you a little more? You look very cold, Sadie." And she's right. I'm absolutely freezing.

"I can warm you, Sadie. I always do, don't I?"

"Yes." But I find myself moving right up against Cheryl's side, as she puts an arm over my shoulder and hugs me tightly to her, and I'm finally warm. It feels like years since I've been warm, or maybe just days, I don't know. But I want her warmth for a minute."

"What's wrong?" Alex whispers.

"Where's Jamie?" I cry.

"I dropped him at my mom's. He's staying there for the night."

"But what about school?"

"My moms going to drop him off in the morning. Everything is fine with Jamie."

"But what about his uniform?"

"She has a school sweater from a few weeks ago when he visited after school when you were running late. Do you remember that?"

"Yes, but what if she forgets to hug him goodnight?"

"She would never forget to hug him. And Jamie would just ask for a hug, like he does with you."

"Is he okay, Alex?"

"Yes. He's-"

"I've done a good job with Jamie, haven't I? I mean I'm a really good mom, right?"

"Yes, you really are. You're amazing with Jamie. Everyone thinks so. You've done an amazing job with him."

"Oh! Thank you, Alex. I get scared that I'm not doing enough, or spending enough time, or being the best mother. I get so afraid of fucking him up, even though I think I'm pretty good at being his mother."

"You could never fuck him up, Sadie. You love him too much to ever fuck him up," Alex smiles at me. And I think that's the kindest thing anyone has ever said to me.

"Thank you. God, Alex, I love him so much. Jamie is everything to me. He is all I think about. And I love him so much, I would do *anything* to protect him. Jamie is the best thing I have ever known because he's just so sweet to me and never mean, and he has such a beautiful soul, and I love him, Alex, so much."

"I know you do. Everyone knows you do."

"Cheryl? Have you met my little boy?"

"I have met him and he IS very sweet, Sadie. He was playing outside once when Alex was in the garage, and he tidied up the flowers between our houses, and when he saw me he picked one of the pink roses and handed it to me. It was so sweet, but when

I thanked him, he smiled a little cheeky grin at me and said, 'you're welcome, but those where from *your* side anyway, not my mommy's.'" Laughing, I can actually picture his cheeky grin. "Anyway, he was so sweet, and once in a while, I find a flower on my front steps waiting for me when I get home." She smiles again. "But they're always from MY side- the little buggar."

Bursting out laughing, I like Cheryl even more. She makes jokes, and she seems so nice and normal. She called my baby a little buggar and I don't want to rip her face off. I'm actually laughing with her, because he is a little buggar sometimes, but I always love it.

Crying suddenly, I miss my son so much it's like a physical pain in my chest.

"What is it? Tell me," Alex begs.

"I miss him, Alex. Please, please, *please* don't ever take him from me again. I won't survive it. I won't. I'll die if you take him from me again."

"I didn't take him from you. I took him skiing at my sister's place. That's all. I took him skiing WITH your permission. I didn't take him from you. I would never take him from you. I know how much you love him. And I know how much he loves you. I would never be so cruel to either of you, Sadie."

"Please don't ever take him from me again, Alex."

"I just said I wouldn't. I have never taken Jamie from you. YOU said we could go. YOU told us to go have fun. YOU were the one who decided to stay home this weekend. I didn't take him away, Sadie. I would never take him from you."

"Alexander, if you ever leave with him again, I'll slit your fucking throat, I swear to god!"

"Sadie! Jesus! Listen to yourself. I just said-"

"I know what you said. I can *hear* you, Alexander. I'm just not sure you're hearing me. So I'm being very clear. Do. Not. Ever. Take Jamie from me again or I'll fucking kill you! Are we clear, Alexander? Do you HEAR me?"

"Sadie, I think Alex promised he wouldn't-"

"Oh, you don't know shit, *Cheryl!* The best thing Alexander ever did to me was knock me up. He was smart. He did what my mother did. He knocked me up so we had to stay together."

"That's not true!" He yells, looking totally embarrassed.

"Yes it is! You know it is, Alexander. Do you really think I believe a condom broke? Do you really think I believe it was an accident? Well, I don't. I found the other condoms in your jeans that weekend, and amazingly, they all had a hole right through the middle of them. I saw them. When you were in the shower after the first weekend we had sex, I was tidying up your clothes and the row of condoms fell out of the sheets and I actually saw a pinprick hole. I *saw* it. So I held up the row of attached condoms, and I couldn't believe it. They all had a hole in the center! I saw it! I know what you did. I've always known what you did!"

"Sadie... I-"

"You have nothing to say, Alexander. I know you're probably embarrassed with Cheryl here, but that's not MY problem! I didn't trap you. *You* trapped me!"

"Sadie... Maybe you would like to speak with Alex alone. I could step out if-"

"No. Please stay, Cheryl. I realize this is probably very embarrassing for Alex, and maybe even really uncomfortable for you, and I'm sure this is super tacky seeing as we just spoke really, but I need you to stay to hear this, because I'm not crazy, and I have things to say and I want you to hear them. Okay?"

"Um, I think maybe-"

"Tell her, Alexander! Tell her you're not embarrassed and she can stay! Tell her!" I scream.

"Um, you can stay Cheryl. If Sadie wants you here, you can stay," Alexander mumbles looking down at his hands.

"Do you want me to tell you what's bothering me? Should I finally talk, Alexander?"

"Could you stop calling me *Alexander* like I'm in trouble or something? You're not my mother, Sadie, and I'd appreciate it if you'd stop speaking to me like you are. I'm Alex. I'm your husband, ALEX."

"Okay, *ALEX*. Let me say this- I forgive you for trapping me. I forgive you for getting me pregnant when I wasn't ready. I forgive you for letting your family and friends think I got pregnant on purpose. And I forgive you for making me have Jamie."

"I didn't trap you! I didn't plan the pregnancy at-"

"Then how did you know about the syrup? How did you know it would make me feel better? How did you know about the calories and the fat and the vitamins for women?!" I scream, knowing I've got him.

"I *didn't* know, but I suspected because you were talking in your sleep about another baby. You were moaning you didn't want another baby, and you were so moody and freaked out that week, so I looked up signs for early pregnancy and that's when I found that recipe! That's how I knew! That's the *only* reason I knew..." Alex says sadly.

"I know you're lying, and you never lie. So you probably thought getting me pregnant was the best thing for me or something. You probably thought I would be better if we were together forever or something romantic like that. And I can almost understand why you did it. I couldn't commit or decide anything for myself back then. I couldn't make a single decision about my life- so you made the decision for me."

"Sadie..." Alex moans, and I feel heartbroken.

Breathing deeply, I hate this tension between us. I hate anything sad between Alex and I.

"I forgive you for making me have Jamie."

"You love Jamie."

"I know I do! That's why I forgive you! You're lucky I fell in love with him the second I met him. You're really lucky I loved him the second he was placed on my chest because I don't know what I would have done if I hadn't loved him."

"What do you mean?" Alex asks as he leans in closer to me and touches my hand.

"You know EXACTLY what I mean."

"I don't."

"You do. I know you do."

And now we're at an impasse. I know he knows. And he knows I know he knows. We each know the reality we pretend we don't know, but we know. We know, but neither of us wants to say it.

"What do you mean, Sadie?" Cheryl asks quietly beside me. Staring at Alex I forgot Cheryl was even here. Staring at Alex I see him sitting there and I feel so sad for him. He loves me so much more than I love him. We are not balanced with our love and we both know it. I think Alex must have always known it.

"I mean I probably would have left Jamie with Alex and took off. I probably would have started down my dark path again. I probably would have left to fall apart or something. Right, Alex?"

"But you did love him and you stayed and you're perfect now. You're a wonderful wife and mother and you own your own flower shop, and we made it."

"Yes we did. We made it Alexander."

"Sadie? Would you please come inside with me? It's freezing out here and you're very cold."

"I'm not ready yet," I mumble as I light another smoke slowly. I think I'm waiting for him to object, but he doesn't. Alexander is smarter than that. He ignores me smoking because of the larger picture we're seeing- I think he knows I know.

"Cheryl, I think you should leave now. Alexander and I have a few things to discuss, privately, and I think we should be alone now. I believe Alexander won't hurt me, so I don't need you here anymore. Alexander and I need to be alone now, and I really don't want you to think we're bad people, because we're not. Well, not really. Right, honey?"
"We're not bad people at all."
"Why did you think Alex would hurt you," Cheryl whispers in my ear.
"I don't. Sometimes I expect the worst, but Alex isn't the worst."
"I don't know what you mean," Alex looks at me and begs.
"Cheryl? Do you think you could just keep all this between us? I know this is strange, and I'm strange, and this situation is strange, but could you please keep it between us. I don't want the neighborhood to know I'm strange. Oh, god, I really don't want the M's to know from across the street. She'd love it if I wasn't perfect."
"I won't tell anyone anything, Sadie. I promise. Especially the M's because I find them really annoying," she grins.
"Me too," I smile back.
"Why don't you and Alex talk and maybe later, or soon, I'll come over for coffee?"
"That would be lovely. Thank you Cheryl," I nod. And I mean it.

As she rises, she readjusts the blanket over my shoulders, covering most of me in its warmth. Smiling one last time, Cheryl makes her way out my side garage door without even a quick glance at Alexander. Looking, I guess I was wrong. They don't seem like they're having an affair at all, and I was probably a little offensive assuming they were.
"I'm sorry for all this," I whisper as Alex sits watching me.
"What is it, baby?" He whispers in return while taking my hand.

CHAPTER 32

As soon as Cheryl walks out the side door of our garage, I really look at Alexander for the first time in ages, and sadly, he looks confused and tired. He looks kind of like I feel; worn out and tired and confused by life.
"When's the last time you ate, Sadie?"
"Do you remember me singing, Alex?"
"Sadie. When did you eat last? Friday night?"
"I don't know. I think so. Why?"
"Because you're not taking care of yourself. You don't look very well, Sade. Can I make you something to eat?"
"Okay. Soon. Thank you. I had coffee though yesterday. No, Sunday. No, Saturday," I admit confused. I'm sure it's Monday. "Do you remember me singing, Alex?"
"I do. I remember in high school you sang Somebody by Depeche Mode, and everyone in the auditorium was silent while you sang. You sounded beautiful. I may have even fallen a little in love with you then like everyone else did," he smiles.
I remember that day. I felt beautiful and amazing and whole that day. I couldn't believe I worked up the nerve to sing for the talent show, but I did. And I was so good that day. Everyone was surprised by my voice, even me, I remember. It was just one of those rare days someone has where absolutely everything works out; from their clothes, to their hair, to the sound of their voice. Everything was perfect for me that day. I loved that day.
"Do you remember me ever dancing?"
"Not really. I remember once at a bush party you and a few girlfriends dancing to something but I was with my group of friends drinking, so I didn't pay much attention. Sorry."
"It's okay. But I remember, Alex. I always sang and danced when I was a teenager. I think I was happy before I was sixteen, and maybe even a little after that, but then my life started changing. Do you know why I stopped being happy? Do you know why I hate music and noise?"
"No," he breathes into me.
"Because He always had music playing when we were together. And then He turned it off when He left."

"Who?" He questions.
"You know who," I call his bluff.
"I don't know. Why don't you tell me, Sadie," Alex says calling my bluff in return.

Staring at Alex, I take out another cigarette. With shaking hands, I try to light it but my thumb and fingers are so numb I can't. But amazingly, Alex takes the lighter from me slowly and sparks the flint. Holding out the lighter to me, I'm shocked he would, so grinning, I ask why without asking, as I inhale.
"It's fine, Sadie. If smoking in the freezing garage makes you talk to me, I'll take it," he responds deadpan.

Looking at Alex sitting in front of me I wish I could just hug him. I don't like this distance between us and I don't like the feeling of being alone anymore. I wasted too many years alone waiting for something more.
"I received a letter on Wednesday," I say as Alexander stiffens in front of me.
Recovering quickly though, he asks, "From who?"
"My old friend Patrick. My awesomely gay former friend Patrick. Do you know him?" I ask watching him. But Alex answers without answering- his silence is answer enough for me. "How did you know him?" But when there is more silence, I continue. "It doesn't matter anymore. Just tell me how you know Patrick. Please?"
But he still can't speak.
"I grabbed the mail on Wednesday and there was a Manila envelope with a book in it and a letter from Patrick. Would you like to hear it?"
And he nods. Not looking at me, he actually looks down at his hands and nods. He looks guilty as hell about something, and I want to know so badly what's going on that I'm shaking with the need to know.
"Should I read it?"
"If you want to, Sadie. Go ahead," Alexander mumbles, still looking down at his hands.

Moving to the side of the garage, I shimmy on my butt with the blanket and lift my old hatbox to remove the letter and book. Holding the book feels like everything dark in my life. Holding the book feels like saying goodbye and staring at only darkness as you jump into the sea. Holding the book feels like a goodbye for us and I'm scared.

"Can I read it to you?"
"Please..." Alex whispers, finally raising his head to look at me. Staring back at his lovely blue eyes, I feel a dark goodbye all around us.
"Why didn't you tell me?" I beg.
"Please just read his letter," Alex says with stiff shoulders and a sad nod.

Leaning against the garage wall, wrapped as best as I can in my warm blanket, I look at Alex one last time and begin reading the letter from Patrick with a fear I can't even hide. The fear is in my voice, and it's in my shaking body.
  This is it, I think.

Dear Sadie
I hope this finds you well. I want you to know I kept watch on you until very recently when I was sure you had finally found your way to happiness.
I love you still, and I don't blame you for ending our friendship when you found my thesis. I was actually proud of you for doing that, because back then I was sure I could've convinced you to forget all about it, should you ever find out at the time. I thought you were too weak and I was too fabulous then, for you to push me away. But again, you surprised me with your response. When you almost destroyed my University career and subsequent studies I was totally pissed, but quite proud of the nasty little bitch inside you, too. You surprised me with that. But when you moved and never saw me again I can admit I was truly heartbroken then. You were very important to me, and I loved you very much, even though I'm sure you find that hard to believe. I know you won't believe me but I never did anything to intentionally hurt you. Every part of our friendship was true- my only wrongdoing was documenting it without your knowledge and using it to further my

studies. Admittedly, that was a shitty thing to do. So for that I'm very sorry. But I'm not sorry for anything else we experienced together. I honestly loved you and I loved our relationship for those few years I had it. And I wish you would believe that, because it's true.

I want you to know that I'm publishing my book in a few days, maybe already by the time you receive this letter. So I'm extending you the courtesy of a (signed) copy first, so you know what to expect. I did amend it slightly from the original draft you read years ago, and I added a more thorough psychological synopsis of the events and your reactions to them, but fundamentally it is the same. I even included the night we slept together to bring to my book the full honesty of the story.
I want you to know that I have followed your progress and I know where you've ended up, which is also in the book. I know everything, and I've included it. I know of your marriage to Alexander and I know of the birth of your son, Jamie. I have included in the epilogue where you ended up, though obviously I changed all necessary names.
I have finally included the ending, Sadie.

You are beautiful Sadie, and I honestly wish you nothing but the best in your future. You have been a constant source of pride and anguish for me since our friendship ended. I have wanted to reach out to you nearly every day of these years we've been apart, but it was actually Stephen (who I'm still with incidentally) that convinced me to let you go.

Therefore, this is a courtesy, and I have been advised by my lawyers that no legal action can take place because of the disclaimer I included and because all our names have been changed. I'm only telling you about this so you don't stumble upon the book one day unaware, because I don't want you to suffer any undue stress from this book or from the story it tells.

There is one thing I MUST say to you now though. And it's very important; so please listen to me Sadie.
I want you to talk to Alexander. He knows more than he's ever told you, but that's all I'll say on his behalf. He knows Sadie. And you need to ask

him the question so you can say goodbye to your past once and for all. You need to ask him so you know his part in your story. Remember I told you once, the best friend always knows- well, the husband always knows too. Trust me.

With my sincerest heartfelt love,
Patrick
xo

P.S. I've included a check given to me by my Publisher and I want you to have it. If you don't want it for yourself, than keep it for Jamie as a University trust or something. But whatever you decide, I beg you to please keep the money, because this is your story, and you deserve something for the life you've lived.

In the silence that follows the letter, I can barely breathe. I feel so lost and scared of what I may face with Alexander that I feel like I'm suddenly drowning. My throat is tight and my chest is pounding, and my body is numb with the cold that has settled deep inside me.

"It's not what you think, Sadie. I didn't do anything wrong..." Alexander breathes into the silence suffocating me.
"Tell me," I beg on a gasp.
"I knew Patrick."
"How?" I barely breathe. How could he possibly? HOW?
"I knew him casually through Diana. They were friends for a while, and then I met him again in University. We were never friends but just casual acquaintances back then."
"I don't get it. What's the connection to me? He's so much older than me?"
"What does age have to do with it? He was friends with all Di's artsy friends and they partied together, so I met him a few times. That's all."
"But?"
"I had one class with him in my third year. I took an elective Psych course and he was the T.A., so I chatted him up looking for a better grade. We talked a little, but it was nothing."
"Until?" I ask while pulling my blanket tighter. I'm just freezing

deep inside, and I can't stand this cold much longer. At this point I don't even remember why I'm doing this anymore.

"Sadie, I will *never* hurt you."

"I know."

"Can I sit next to you and warm you up a little?" He asks me sadly. And because I hate a sad Alex, I nod and wait for him to warm me.

Sliding over to the wall, Alex wraps the blanket tighter around me and keeps his arm over my shoulder, as we relax a little with each other.

"Did you know who I was? Did Patrick tell you everything?"

"No. Not at first. I mean I always knew you from high school, but we weren't close back then. You remember- we just ended up at the same parties sometimes, but we never hung out because you were younger than me and my friends."

"But?"

"Patrick and I were talking casually once about our weekend, and he mentioned being at his friend Sadie's apartment. And I told him I knew a Sadie from high school so he described you to me and told me your last name and we realized it was you. I think we were both a little surprised that I knew who you were. But I mean it makes sense. We went to the same high school, just a few years apart, so he knew my sister and I knew you."

"But you never told me you knew him."

"He asked me not to."

"Why?" I ask stunned by all this history. I didn't even know Patrick attended the same high school as I did, not that we would have been there at the same time, but still. I know I mentioned my high school to him but I don't remember him ever telling me he went there years before me as well.

"When you and Patrick had your falling out, he called me and asked if I knew your parent's number, which I didn't. He asked if I knew anyone who knew you and I really didn't. I remember at the time telling him you really didn't have any friends anymore. I remember hearing rumors about you and people talking about you like you had simply vanished shortly after college. So I told him I didn't know how to get in touch with you. Which I didn't at the time."

"But that day? The day on campus?" I ask breathless.

"Patrick asked me to meet you to see how you were doing. I guess he had already been called by one of his Professors, and he was to see them later that day. The Professor told him they were speaking to another student about his thesis and that they may have questions about the thesis for him later. It was actually pretty stupid of them because Patrick obviously knew you were the student. He knew you were why he was being asked to meet with his Psych Profs on campus. So he called me again."

And then Alexander pauses like he's trying to think of what to say. He pauses but his arm tightens around my shoulders and I can barely breathe from the stress and fear of what he's going to say.

"Just tell me..." I whisper.

"Patrick called me and told me what was happening. Well, actually, all he said was he had fucked up royally, and you wouldn't speak to him anymore, and he didn't want to upset you more by meeting you on campus, I think for your benefit, and also because he didn't want to make things worse for himself if you freaked out. Anyway, he called me and said you were probably going to be on campus that morning because his meeting was suddenly cancelled with 3 Profs, so Patrick thought for sure you were going to be there again to talk to them. He told me you were usually walked to your car by the security campus teams, even in the daylight, and he asked me to make sure you were okay. He told me what your car looked like and he told me you were probably around or in the Psych Quad. He even told me where I could wait on campus so I would see you leave the buildings before getting into your car."

"But I don't understand. Did he want to hurt me? Did he want *you* to hurt me?" I cry out.

"No! Not at all. He actually just wanted me to check up on you so I could tell him if you were okay. I didn't know exactly what had happened, but he wanted you to be safe. That's all. Patrick asked me to make sure you were okay. I don't think Patrick would have ever hurt you, Sade. He loved you, I think."

"So you knew I would be there?" I ask ignoring his last statement.

"Yes. But that's all I did. I waited for like 2 hours by that fountain to see if you were okay and to come up with something to say to you, because the whole thing was so weird to me. I didn't even know if you would still be there. I didn't know if I would even see you, or if you would remember me. So I almost left a few times but something made me stay put."

"What were you supposed to do to me when you saw me?"

"Nothing! Jesus, Sadie. Patrick wouldn't hurt you and I sure as hell would never hurt you. I was only supposed to check up on you and then call Patrick and let him know when you left. That's it, baby. I swear," Alexander begs while shaking me a little in his arms.

"Then what happened?"

"You know the rest. I started talking to you, and I started walking you to and from class, and that's it. Patrick didn't ask me to do that- I wanted to. I liked walking with you. Do you remember that?"

"How could I not? You slowly pushed your way into my life."

"That's not true, Sade. I didn't push my way in- I patiently waited until you *let me* be in your life. Until I kissed you. Remember?"

How could I forget? Alex kissing me changed my entire life? Alex kissing me upended my life. Alex kissing me was the start of my new life, I think.

"I loved it when you kissed me and that's what almost destroyed me," I cry as Alex holds me tighter.

"I didn't almost destroy you, Sadie. You were already destroyed. I just helped you get better," he says angrily. And I suddenly realize he's right. I want to mad at this betrayal of sorts, but he's right. He didn't destroy me. I WAS destroyed.

"Why did you lie to me? Why didn't you tell me?"

"I didn't know how and it really didn't change anything. Patrick may have asked me to look out for you one specific day, but everything after that was all me. I didn't want you alone and sad anymore. I didn't want to see you look that way, especially since I remembered you from high school."

"Do you still talk to him?"

"No."

"When did you stop?"

"Shortly after you and I starting talking again the summer you freaked out. After I kissed you."

"But why?" I still can't wrap my head around any of this. Patrick and Alex? I had NO idea they knew each other.

"Do you really want all the truth, Sadie?"

"Yes. I think it's time. I'm pretty freaked out by his letter and by you knowing him, and by everything else, actually."

"Please, don't be freaked. There isn't anything else to tell. I knew Patrick. He asked me to look out for you, and I did. Then I fell for you, and you and I moved on together. That's the end of the story."

"Why did you stop talking to Patrick?"

Pausing, Alexander takes a deep breath and says, "Because Patrick didn't want us together."

"What? Why? What's so bad about me? Patrick always said I was better than I thought I was. Why wasn't I good enough for you?"

"Actually, he didn't want ME with you. He loved you very much Sadie, and he wanted you to be happy, and apparently he didn't think I could handle being with you."

"What does *that* mean? Because I was so hard to handle?" I ask pissed.

"You *were* hard to handle, but that's not why. Patrick thought I wasn't strong enough to overlook all the stuff in your life, and he thought I would eventually hurt you, emotionally. Patrick was sure I was just a player looking to get a piece of ass and he didn't want that for you. He even said as much which really pissed me off at the time. Patrick knew nothing about me really, but he thought I couldn't handle being with you? So I proved him wrong."

"What? Like I was a game to you to-"

"Not at all. I just knew I could make you happy so I told Patrick to leave us the fuck alone. And then I kissed you and you disappeared again and I knew you were bad because you stopped going to your summer courses, and I didn't know what to do because I told you I would wait for you to contact me and that I wouldn't do anything, so I asked Patrick what I should do about you. And that's when he told me about his thesis."

Stiffening, I'm almost sick with my upset and anger. Patrick showed him that garbage. Patrick told Alexander about his theories of SMA? Patrick told Alexander and Alexander never told me! Suddenly pissed, I push his arm off of me, and grab for my smokes. Shaking and trying to light a smoke, I actually hear myself moaning out loud. I hear myself and even feel myself rocking, but I can't seem to stop either. I'm officially a mess.

"Sadie?"

"Don't. I want to think for a minute."

"But I need you-"

"Shut UP for a minute," I bark while power dragging on my smoke, as he silences immediately.

Alexander knew everything and he didn't tell me. Alexander knew and he let me think I kept all my secrets. He knew what Patrick thought of me and he never let on that he knew all the details I could NEVER discuss with him. Alexander always knew.

"So you know everything..."

"I know Patrick's version of everything, not yours. So I ignored it."

"Really? You *ignored* it?"

"Yes."

"That seems fairly unlikely Alexander. You were with me and knew all these things about me, but you *ignored* them?"

"I did. I waited to see if you would ever talk to me and you didn't. You never talked about all the stuff before me, so I chose to ignore it. I chose to leave it in the past where it belonged as far as I was concerned. You didn't ever talk to me, so I assumed you didn't want to talk to me about it. So yes, Sadie, I *ignored* what I knew."

Turning my head I stare at Alexander. Staring, I try to see if he's telling me the truth. I try to understand how a man could know all the sick and twisted that was me, but ignore it anyway. Looking, I try to understand Alexander Hamilton.

"I don't understand you, I really don't. You make no sense to me. You have always been so kind and attentive and loving toward me. You have always been such a miracle in my life but now I know you always knew and I don't understand you at all anymore."

"You understand me-"

"I don't. I'm more confused than ever. I thought if you didn't know everything I could understand why you wanted to love me. But you *did* know and you said you loved me anyway. So you really don't make any sense to me anymore."

"What doesn't make sense? Tell me. I love you and I've always loved you and I chose to ignore your past so that I could love you."

"Nobody loves the damaged girl. *Nobody.* Especially if they know *why* she's damaged."

"I did, and I do. Nothing matters about before, Sadie. I only care about where we took each other. I care about the life we live together- the life we created together. I don't care about your past anymore."

"Anymore?"

"Fine. It's a bit of a shock to find out you slept with Patrick. *That* I didn't know. I guess that part wasn't in the thesis I read years ago," Alex snaps angrily.

"It was just once. And it was a very strange night."

"I'll say! How is that even possible? Patrick is very, *very* gay. So I find it hard to believe you had sex together though you've both stated you did. I can't even imagine Patrick with a woman. Not just you. So yeah, that's a bit of a shock I'm going to choose to ignore."

Alexander says all that while visibly angry. I'm not sure if it's because he knows I had sex once before him, or because it was with Patrick. I don't really know anything anymore.

"It was only once and I had a particularly bad night, and Patrick was there and I just needed to connect with someone, and he and I connected," I say lamely.

"Connected. Yes you did," Alexander says sounding really mad or maybe jealous. I don't know.

"Look, not that I have to justify anything to you, but I've slept with 3 people BY CHOICE my entire life- you being the third. I know you slept with many women before me but I don't care. So why should you?"

Leaning toward me, Alex takes my hand again and exhales.

"You're right. I'm sorry. I am jealous and for some reason it bothers me to think of you and Patrick like that- maybe because it seems like he took advantage of you or something. I don't know. It just pisses me off that he thought I wasn't good enough for you, but that he could sleep with you-"

"Once!"

"*Once,* and that was okay. But you're right. It's none of my business. It was before me and we don't talk to Patrick anymore, and we never have to see him again so I'll ignore it."

"But I don't know if I can ignore that you lied to me all these years. I don't know how I feel about any of this. I don't know how I feel about this book coming out, or about my life in print. It's all so weird, and I think I'm mad at you for not telling me all of this in the beginning."

"Again- there was nothing to tell. A mutual friend asked me to check on you, which I did. Then I watched out for you because I wanted to. Then we started a relationship and I never talked to Patrick again. The end, until his letter."

"I don't know... I feel kind of betrayed or weird about you now. Then again I feel weird right now in general," I laugh.

"Would you please come inside with me? Please? I want to make you something to eat, and you need to clean yourself up. Please let me help you? I was frantic to get to you and you scared the hell out of me when I found you. I just need to fix this so we can move on. *Please?*" Alex asks me so desperately, and he looks so shaken, and I feel so awful physically AND emotionally, I just give in. What's the point of staying here any longer?

"Okay..."

And moving slowly, I realize just how cold and stiff my body really is. Rising slowly, I realize just how weak and tired my body is. Standing slowly, I realize just how drained and exhausted my mind is.

I did what I thought I had to do this weekend, but nothing feels finished. I still don't have a sense of closure, and I don't feel like I said goodbye to anything or anyone this weekend.

CHAPTER 33

When Alex and I finally make it to our bathroom he starts the shower instantly. Placing me on the toilet seat, Alex grabs towels and checks the water, opens the overhead cabinet while studiously ignoring me as I sit shivering.

Ignoring me, I feel cold and alone. Even with Alex beside me, I feel totally alone in my head until he suddenly turns back to me and crouches on the floor before me.

"Sadie? Why did you take your clothes off?" He asks gently.

"I couldn't breathe."

"From the smoking?" He asks stupidly.

"No, Alex. From the stress and pressure," I answer sharply.

Nodding at my explanation, Alex slowly removes the blanket from my shoulders. Slowly, he uncovers me. Slowly, he makes me colder until the shivering becomes almost a whimper.

"I want to look at your legs before you get in the shower," he says as we both look down.

Looking, I feel so dirty suddenly. Filthy, actually. I have on the same underwear since Saturday, and nothing else. I know I look deranged. I know I look dirty and abused. I think I look like I remember I must've looked years ago.

"Do you know who raped me?" I ask as the air suddenly leaves the room.

Slowly sitting on his heels, Alex places his hands on the uncut part of my thighs and looks at me sadly. Wow, I can't believe he knows this too. I guess all the secrets I've stressed over for years were for not.

"Yes..." he exhales.

"How did you find out?"

"He told me and Doug Brock at a party when we were in University. He was hammered and he told us like it was no big deal. He told us like it was nothing."

"He told people?" I ask shocked. "Why would he do that? He was in the clear."

"Like I said he was very drunk. So was Doug. But even Doug

sobered up the second he told us. Doug was actually the one who punched him first- before I even had a chance," he says with a slight scowl.

"What happened? Does anyone else know? Does everyone know?!"

"Calm down, baby. I don't think he told anyone else. He was just being a fucking idiot with his buddies. He told us because Doug was talking about a woman he had slept with the weekend before. It was typical guy shit; bragging about who you had nailed on the weekend. It was normal... until he said your name. And then all hell broke loose."

Gasping for breath, I feel the tears falling down my face onto my legs. I feel them falling, but I can't wipe them because I'm too cold to move. I don't want this anymore.

"I don't want to hear this," I whisper.

"Are you sure? Maybe you need to hear what became of him. Maybe you need to know so you can move on."

"Did Patrick tell you I saw him once?"

"No! When did you see him?"

"I don't know, years ago. I was with Patrick and he was waiting for me on the street. He was standing there and I lost it. I hurt myself and freaked right out and Patrick had to take care of me. I saw him though, and I never knew why."

"When was that? When did you see him?"

"I don't know when. Before the Patrick thing. Before I met you again. Before... you." Panicking, I grab for my throat. Fighting the fear, I gasp for breath until Alex pushes my head between my knees. Rubbing my back, Alex is shushing me and rubbing circles into my skin as I try to fight the fear.

"Where is he?" I croak.

"He's in jail actually. He was caught selling drugs. He's in jail for years, so you're safe from him, baby. I swear you are. He will never hurt you again. Never, Sadie."

Nodding, I can't talk. Shaking, I can't function. Moaning, I can't breathe.

"Listen to me. I ruined him, Sadie. I made him quit school and I made him go away. I turned all our friends against him, and Doug and I destroyed him. Doug and I made it impossible for him to continue at school and we made it impossible for him to stay around us. Doug threatened to tell the Police what he did if he didn't stay the fuck away from you, forever."

"Why? Why did you and Doug do that?" I mumble as I slowly lift my head. Looking at Alexander, I'm once again shocked by what he knows. I never knew he knew so much. I never knew he was always aware of everything because *I* never knew anything.

"Well, I know Doug was pissed because he had a bit of a thing for you in high school. He mentioned you more than once over the years and I know he felt sickened and disgusted by what happened to you. When he told us what he did to you, Doug lost it. He punched him viciously until I had to pull him off with a few others at the party. Doug had always liked you in school and when he found out we knew who hurt you he went crazy," Alex admits shaking.

"I don't want to hear this, Alexander." I beg.

"Sadie. There's more. Are you sure you don't want to hear it so you can move on?"

"Why didn't you tell anyone? Why didn't you tell the Police?" And I realize my words sound like an accusation as Alex stiffens in front of me. "No! I'm not blaming you, I just don't know why you didn't tell."

"Because *you* didn't. I don't know. Doug and I were going to, but then we talked and realized you didn't tell the Police and we didn't know why you wouldn't, so we figured there was a reason. I knew you knew him because of the Prom party a few years before, so I thought you had a reason for your silence. That's the only reason, Sadie."

"Okay."

"Why didn't you tell on him, Sade? Why did you let him get away with hurting you?"

My amazing friend. The boy who knew I had an older lover and therefore thought it was okay to rape me. The boy I trusted. The boy I stupidly told about my stranger. Therefore, I had to protect my secret with my silence. Always.

"I was afraid," I choke. Sobbing suddenly, I hold tight when Alex pulls me into his arms. Holding tightly, I cry on him. Holding tightly, I'm warmed by him. Holding on tightly, I'm exhausted by everything in my head.

"Of what, baby? Him hurting you again?" Alex asks gently.

"Everything. All of it. He was so popular and friendly, and I was Sadie the Prude and I was young and I was afraid of everyone finding out and blaming me for being a dick tease, or whatever else I might be called. I was afraid of all of it." Pausing, I remember his words until I cry out, "Alex, he kept saying he loved me and that he was making love to me and that he was showing me his love and stuff like that. And I had all this other stuff in my head, and I was confused and-"

"It's okay, Sadie. I get it. You can stop if you want to."

"I need to sleep, Alex," I moan.

"You need to get clean first. I don't know how long your legs have been like that. Let me help you. Let me hold you up," he asks as he stands.

Lifting me by my arms, Alex actually leans down and slips my dirty underwear from my body, as I stand humiliated further in his arms.

"I'm so sorry for all this. I don't know what happened anymore. Patrick's letter made me think of lots of things, and then I was afraid of you because I didn't know what part you played in my life, and I was so confused, and the pressure was just too much this time. I didn't mean to be so gross, and I didn't mean to be like this again."

"It's okay, Sadie. Lean on me," Alex say as he steps into the shower with me fully clothed. Lean on me, and I do. Lean on me like I always do. Lean on me…

"You're so good to me, Alex."

"Because I love you, Sade."

"Why?" I beg.

"Why wouldn't I?"

Almost laughing I picture what I must look like, and smell like, and seem like, and I shake my head with a grin. "I can think of a thousand reasons why you shouldn't."

"Well, I can't," he says as he pours shampoo into his hand.

Standing, I place my hands on the tiles in front of me for support. Smiling, the feel of having my hair washed is amazing. Smiling, because everything seems better in the shower, I can almost breathe fully. I can almost feel peace or something in this quiet moment in the shower with Alex.

"I hate Kyle," I whisper as Alex stops washing my hair and pulls me closer to his chest.

"Me too, baby." And that's it. What else can we say?

10 minutes later, Alexander has cleaned me from top to bottom. And when he cleaned between my legs I was mortified, but he was so clinical about it, I just waited him out. Waiting, I knew Alex wouldn't dream of taking advantage of me, and I knew he would never hurt me when I was so weak. Alex would never hurt me.

"I believe you won't ever hurt me, Alex. I know I never tell you that, but it's true. I actually believe I'm safe with you," I whisper.

"It's about time, Sade," he says in my ear. "I've proven myself to you for years, and I've waited for you to finally believe in me."

"I know you have. I'm sorry, Alex."

"Better late than never I guess," he whispers in my ear, and I know he's teasing me. We're okay. I've made another mistake, but Alex and I are okay.

When Alex helps me from the shower, I'm wrapped in multiple towels, until he finally strips himself of all his wet clothes. Stumbling for our bed, I can barely walk I'm so exhausted. Stumbling, I'm exhausted completely.

"Don't fall asleep, honey. Please? I want to grab you something to eat first. Can you please stay awake?"

"I'll try. But I'm exhausted, Alex."

"I know, but I'll be quick. Just sit upright until I get back," he says in our doorway with a towel wrapped around his waist.

But I know I failed because the dreams stole any peace I felt with Alex as soon as I closed my eyes.

CHAPTER 34

Feeling Him inside me, I moan and writhe as my body begs for more from Him. I need more. I need release. I need to feel this again as I pump and push for the release I need.

I *need*, but Alexander's voice forces its way slowly into my brain. I hear Alex, not Him. I feel Alex, not Him. I know Alex, not Him.

"Please..." I beg.

"Sadie. Wake up. Sadie!" And I don't want to wake from this, but slowly I do.

Turning to Alex, I feel my climax on the brink. I feel myself. I know I'm touching myself, and I'm almost there. I know it, but all I see is Alexander's face of disgust watching me.

Sliding my hand out from between my legs, I can't even speak through my embarrassment. I pause as I try to return to the real world. I pause as I try to come back to my current bedroom with my own husband in the house we love with the memories we've built together.

"I'm sorry..." I cry. And I am. I don't know why this happens and I don't know why it's happening now. I wish it didn't happen, honestly. I wish that feeling of need would go away forever.

"Was it Him?" Alex asks darkly.

"No," I lie. But I can see he doesn't believe me and I can feel his hurt all over our bedroom. "I'm sorry. I don't know why that happens. I don't know why..." I cry again as my arousal fades away completely.

Staring at Alexander I feel like I know something. I feel like *he* knows something. I feel like there is something greater than this room and the reality within it.

"What's wrong, Alex?"

"Nothing," he says a little too angrily.

"I'm sorry for that. I don't do it on purpose and it's only when I'm sleeping. I never do that when I'm awake," I say, neglecting to mention the time in the garage a few days ago.

"I know. And I'd like to say it's okay because you're asleep, I really would. But it's not okay for me. I hate it and it makes me feel used and disgusted when you get off in your sleep to someone else."

"But I don't know-"

"Yeah, I know. You don't know because you're asleep. And when we were first together I helped you and I *serviced* you when you were thinking of someone else, but I thought that would change. I thought given enough time you would only think of me when-"

"I do!"

"You *don't*. You might not do it much anymore, but you still do sometimes. Sometimes I wake up and you're having a full out orgasm in your sleep, and I watch with both fascination AND disgust- or maybe with sadness. I don't know. But it hurts, Sadie. I hate it because I feel like just the piece of shit you're married to but not the lover you want, and I fucking hate it!"

Pushing onto his back, Alexander stares at the ceiling as he throws an arm over his face. He's shutting me out and he's right but I don't know how to change it. I wish I could change it.

"I don't mean to hurt you," I whisper as I touch his chest.

"I know, but it does. Think about it in reverse, Sade. Think about how YOU would feel if I was getting off in the night, in my sleep, moaning and writhing in our sheets while thinking of another woman. Think about it..." He says while turning his head toward me.

"I swear I don't mean to do it. I just-"

"I know, Sadie! Jesus Christ, I know. You can't help it, but that doesn't make me feel any better. We've been together for 8 years, and you still think of someone else! It makes my skin fucking crawl. And yet, I'm still hot for you. I think that's why I would just fuck the hell out of you years ago when you were all keyed up. I wanted you so bad, I didn't care who you were thinking of when we screwed like that. Plus, I knew when you weren't sleeping it was about you and me making love together, so it was all okay or something. I just tried to ignore all the sleeping bullshit with you. I ignored it because we were together and you love me, and we have a good life together now. Well, until this weekend hit, we've had a few really good years. But I hate it, Sadie. I really fucking hate it and Him."

Looking into Alexander's eyes while he rants I'm struck with the feeling again of sitting on a ledge. I feel like we're right there but we need a push. I feel like I'm teetering on knowing something more but I don't know what it is.

Wrapping my arms around his chest, I ask the question.
"Alex? Do you know why He never came back for me? Do you know? I know you don't want to know about this, and I know you don't know who I'm talking about, but I can't believe He walked away. I know I told Him to, but I can't believe He left me. He was everything to me for almost 7 years and He left me just because I told Him to? It doesn't make sense. Do you know why He left me Alex? Do you?"
Begging, I squeeze Alexander tightly. Begging, I need him to hug me back. Begging, I need Alex to make me Sadie Hamilton again. "Please, Alex. Do you know where He went?"
"Sadie... I don't know who you mean?"
"You know. I know you know. You know everything, remember. You told me you knew everything so I never had to tell you anything, and you DID know everything. You *know*, Alex. So please, just tell me."
"Sadie, I don't know what you mean."
But he's lying- I can tell. A wife always knows when her husband lies to her, and mine is no different just because he doesn't lie very often doesn't mean I don't know when he does. I know he's lying which means he knows what happened.

"Alex, please... Tell me why He left me? I need to know. I mean I know I told Him to leave because I did, but I had told Him before to leave me and He always came back, even when I didn't want Him to. I asked Him before and He always came back. And He said He'd come back. He left but whispered He'd be back, even though you and I were together and I really didn't want Him to come back anymore. But that last time He came to me right before we were married He left me forever and I don't know why. Do you know why He left me?"
Staring at Alexander's face I can barely breathe. My lungs are gasping and my heart is thumping in my chest. I feel my tears dripping on his chest, but I can't move with the fear. I think we're about to jump off a cliff together.

"Please Alex... I've always loved Him. Do you know why He left me?"

"You've loved Him...?" He chokes.

"I always have. I can't help it. Do you know what happened? Do you know why He left me?"

"You've always loved Him, huh? Really? Well, fuck you, Sadie! How could you say that to me?" He yells, shoving me off his chest. "How could you say you've always loved Him? I'm your husband and I'm fucking good to you. How could you say that to me?" He yells while jumping out of our bed.

In our room the sudden explosion of sound threatens everything within me. Alexander yelling makes me aware of the reality of this moment. I need to fix Alexander before he can jump.

"Oh, I love you too. It's just different from-"

"Different? *Really?* Like I'm just the asshole you're married to, but He's your soul mate or something?"

"Yes. No! Not like that! Do you know what happened?"

Crying, Alex stops pacing and says, "Yeah, I know."

Whispering, I beg, "Tell me..."

Struggling to sit up slowly, I don't want to spook Alexander because I want him to talk. I want him to tell me what he knows. I want this...

"Jesus Christ! I almost lost my mind when I saw Him leave your apartment one night thinking, 'no way, not Sadie. She wouldn't have a lover. Not her. She's much too innocent and messed up to put out.' But then I saw Him leave your apartment and I looked in your window and I saw you naked and recently fucked and I didn't know what to do, so I watched Sadie. He was 37 years old for fuck's sake. 37 and you were 22 and fucked up and He was fucking you, Sadie. So I watched you and then it was over a fucking year until I finally saw Him leave your apartment again, and you and I were already talking and walking on campus until I kissed you. But you freaked out and wouldn't talk to me after the kiss, and you wouldn't screw me even though I was good and I loved you, and there He was in your apartment that night and I waited and I watched from your balcony window you and Him in your bathrobe, and then in your bed hugging each other, and then finally I saw Him leave in the early morning without fucking you and I thought maybe you didn't fuck Him because you knew you loved me. And I needed him to go away Sadie. For you!"

"I don't understand," I cry pulling the sheets tighter. "You saw us?"

"Yeah, I saw. Once by mistake and the second time on purpose that summer. Actually, it was quite good timing on my part- but you didn't fuck Him that night."

"I didn't. I told Him to leave me alone because-"

"You finally realized how sick and screwed up it was?"

"No! Because I wanted to try to be with you," I yell desperately. "But how did you see us? I didn't know you then. That was before Patrick asked you to spy on me," I ask confused again.

"When I found out Patrick knew you and I knew where you lived I checked up on you sometimes. That's all! It wasn't spying- I didn't do anything wrong! And really, what were the Vegas fucking odds of me seeing Him in your apartment? Very fucking unlikely, but I did!"

"But you saw us, so that was way before Patrick asked you to check up on me."

"So! I just wanted to make sure you were okay. You were like a weird little rumor after high school. Everyone knew you just kind of vanished after you were attacked, and when I found out where you lived because of Patrick I checked up on you sometimes."

"But-"

"Look, it doesn't matter when I saw you. You needed Him gone and I made that happen and we've been fine. You haven't cried for Him or asked about Him in years. And I thought you were fine. You haven't had your dirty little dreams about Him in a long time, so I thought you were finally over it."

"What did you do?" I gasp.

"I read your sick journal when we started dating, and I knew how long He had been fucking you and I made it stop for you…"

"What did you do, Alexander?"

"Nothing! Everything!"

"What does that mean?" I scream to get his attention.

"When I saw you the day after we were married, I freaked out. I drove back to your apartment and I read your book again and I knew He had been there. I knew He had been there the night before our wedding. I knew He hurt you and I read how you fought Him. For the first time I read what He did to you and I read how you protected our baby. I read it all, and I freaked out. Then I made Him go away."

"How, Alex? How did you make Him go away?"

"I drove to your parent's house and had a talk with your father."

"WHAT?! *Why?!*"

"Because I love you and I've always loved you, just like I told you the first time we made love. You needed me to help, so I fixed things. I fixed YOU. We're fine and I did that for you. I made Him go away, FOR YOU!"

Choking, I beg, "What?"

"I didn't know what to think because I knew you weren't close to him, but fucking him? No wonder you were such a fucking mess when I finally got to you!"

"Why? I don't under-"

"Because I told you I loved you and I would wait for you forever. I just didn't know I was waiting for you to stop fucking your goddamn BROTHER! Do you know how fucking sick that is? Your *brother*, Sadie?"

"*What?*" I whisper.

"Your *brother*, Sadie. Jesus Christ! You were fucking your brother."

"What...?" I whisper again as everything spins around me.

Looking at Alexander there is darkness everywhere. But Alex looks like a spotlight in my vision. He looks like he's glowing in the room. Every sound has faded, and every object has disappeared. I am in a tunnel of Alexander. I am looking at Alexander as the world falls away.

Shaking, I hear His voice all around me. Shaking, I remember His voice all around me. Shaking, I feel His voice inside me.

We were born for each other...

You were created for me...

You were born for me to love...

Oh god.
My brother.

When Alexander moves slowly toward me I shake my head no, but he continues anyway. Walking with his hands outstretched, he slowly kneels on the bed beside me.

"Sadie?" He whispers.

"I didn't know..."

"You DID know."

Shaking my head frantically, I know I didn't know. "I didn't know...." I whisper again.

"I think you *did* know Sadie, but you didn't know what to do about it. He raped you when you were a tiny little 17 year old and he was a 31 year old man, so I think you chose to make it beautiful so you could deal with it. You chose to make it love instead of a nightmare. I know you knew Sadie, you just couldn't handle it, I don't think."

"I didn't know..."

"You DID know, baby. But I think you chose to pretend you didn't know."

"I didn't know..." I moan.

"Fuck, Sadie! Think about it. How didn't you know? After I'd been to your parent's house once I saw His picture and I knew for sure. I saw the picture your dad had of Him in your house. Granted there was only one grad picture, but it was His picture, and it was right there in their living room. I didn't know who he was when I saw you two screwing, but I knew by the time He came back and hurt you before our wedding night. You *knew*, baby."

"I didn't know..." I mumble shaking my head.

"You knew. And by the time we were together, I knew who it was, but it looked like you had sent Him away that night before we were officially together, so I chose to ignore it. I convinced myself that whatever was going on between you two was over. Whatever sick fucking thing was between you both was totally over that summer, so I ignored it. I loved you and you looked like you said goodbye to Him, so I waited for you to come back to me. I waited until school was starting up again and I couldn't wait any longer, and then I called you again to make our walking dates. I thought it was over between you two, so I chose to ignore how disgusting it was. I ignored it and pretended I didn't know what had been going on in your life, Sadie, even though I didn't know who he was yet. But you always knew," Alex says again. But he's wrong.

Pulling at my hair, I find comfort in rocking back and forth. I know I didn't know. I *know* it. How could I? I never really knew Him. I met Him twice when I was little and my Dad was trying to stay close to Him after the divorce, but that's it. He was before mom and me. He was part of my Dad's before us life. He wasn't part of my Dad's after us life. I didn't know.

Suddenly jumping in my own skin I remember the first time He came to me.

He hums to me a lullaby as I slip into a comforting trance of early childhood. This lullaby is familiar, yet I can't place it.

Together we were alive. Together we were born for each other.

Oh my god...

"I didn't know..." I cry out.

When Alex suddenly grabs my arms and pulls me to him I can't help but collapse onto him. Holding tightly to his shirt, I keen a cry of repulsion.
"I didn't know... I didn't know... I didn't know..." I rock.
"Sadie! Stop. It's over."
"I didn't know... I didn't know..."
I think Alexander is speaking but all I hear is an ocean sound of one thought only. Crashing into my brain like waves... *I didn't know. I didn't know. I didn't know.*
"SADIE!! Enough, baby. It's over. You didn't know, okay? I believe you. I believe you didn't know, okay? Stop!" And I do. Alex believes me, so I can stop talking now.

But I can't stop thinking. I was 16 when He came to me. I was 17 when He fucked me. I was 22 when He impregnated me. Oh. My. God!
Suddenly gasping and gagging on our bed I think of that baby. That baby was going to be His. It would be His and I would have had a lifetime with a child of *His*.

"Sade! What is it?"
"That baby..." I croak.
"I know. But it's over, honey. The baby didn't happen, and you're so much better now. We have Jamie now. It's over."

Quickly standing, I just have to get away from Alex for a minute. I have to. It's not his fault, but I'm so disgusted and shocked and freaked out I don't even know what to do with myself. Actually, I know exactly what I want to do to myself, but I can't. And I won't. And Alexander shouldn't have to suffer through any more of my crazy because I can't handle all this pressure weighing me back down. Alex shouldn't suffer any more with me.

"You have to leave me. I'm disgusting," I cry.
"That's never going to happen, Sadie. That was all before us and it's over now," Alex says angrily.
"You have to leave me. You have to take Jamie away from me," I moan desperately.

Walking to my closet as Alex calls to me from the bed, I ignore him as I pull out my warmest jogging suit and dress myself. Pulling out a huge sweater I place it over top my hoodie. Grabbing my first Christmas present from Alexander I pull over the huge XXXL sweater he gave me. Walking to my drawers, I pull out 2 pair of wool socks and walk back to my bed to dress, even as Alexander keeps talking to me.
But I feel dead. I'm the old Zombie Sadie. I am lifeless with this reality.
When Alex pulls at my arms as I sit, I fight him. I don't want him to hold me, or warm me, or even love me anymore.
"Please Alex, understand. I need to have a smoke, and I need to understand what's going on. I need this."
"Okay, I'll come with you. I don't mind," he says scrambling for more clothes. But I can't even acknowledge this kindness of Alexander's because I feel nothing but the shock of my reality crushing me.

My Dear Stranger.
David Adams.
My half-brother.

CHAPTER 35

Walking past my quiet kitchen and living room I walk directly to the security panel because I need to make sure we're safe. I have to be sure because I need us to be safe again.

Entering the garage, I hear the beep of the door and I know the rest of our house is still armed. I know we're safe inside again. I know we're safe right now.

Sitting in my lounge chair, Alex follows me almost immediately while pulling on his winter coat. Not even pretending he doesn't know what I'm doing, Alex leans down and picks up my smokes and hands them over to me.

Lighting a smoke in silence, I see Alex grab another chair as he props it up right beside me. I see him with me, but I can't even acknowledge him.

"Alexander? If the start of a relationship is forced but the situation of the force changes, is the relationship still tainted forever?"

"I think so," he answers immediately.

"But if I thought I loved Him, does that make the relationship change?"

"I don't know. Maybe you just changed the relationship in your mind so you could deal with it. Maybe it was just a coping mechanism, or something. You could always talk to a Psychiatrist, or a counsellor about it. Maybe you could get the answers you need with some counselling," Alex says softly.

But I don't think so. I don't think I told Dr. Synode who He was because I don't think I really knew, but he was already judgmental about my 'unconventional' relationship without even knowing who He really was to me. I don't think a different Psychiatrist will feel any differently, and then I'll never get an objective answer to my question.

"My father knew?"

"Yes. And after some convincing he called David and I left it with him. Your father told me we would never see him again.

Your father was absolutely sickened and distraught by what I told him. He felt guilt and shame, and I know he was almost murderous with his rage. And just before he phoned Him, he asked me to keep this between us. He told me he would make it so He never saw you again, and he would deal with it totally. He wasn't sure if he even wanted your mother to know, but I don't know if he did or didn't eventually tell her. He-"

"Oh, god... No, he wouldn't. How could he? No, she would have freaked out, right?"

"Well, as I said, I didn't know if he would or wouldn't tell her, I just wanted to get the hell out of there. I needed to get back to you, and I needed to be with you. I felt differently about the pre-wedding night stuff after I read what you chose to do for Jamie's sake. I read how you only gave into Him to protect my baby. I read how you thought of me instead of Him during the act, so I realized you really did believe it was me with you the night before, because you couldn't face being with Him anymore. And I needed to get to you because I loved you and I was so devastated by what happened to you. So after your dad assured me this would be dealt with I returned to the hotel to take care of you."

"And I was a mess. Again," I admit calmly.

"Yes. But with reason, Sadie. I think that's why I've always stuck around. You always had a reason to be messed up. It wasn't like you were just some psycho who couldn't deal with life. You were a woman struggling to deal with her *horrible* life. And somehow that made every freak out or *mistake* as you called them tolerable. I never resented your freak outs because I knew you were trying desperately to deal with so much. I was just angry at what you *did* when you freaked out."

"Does anyone else know?"

"I doubt it. I'm pretty sure your father wouldn't have told anyone else, and *I* sure as hell didn't. And I don't know who else knew about it. I know Patrick thought you were delusional, even after everything he did see, maybe because he didn't see David ever. I don't-"

"Don't ever say His name again. Like *EVER*, Alexander," I speak through my exhale, and I realize this is by far the most calming cigarette I've ever had in my life.

"Sorry, Sade. I'll never-"

"Is there anything else, Alexander?"

"No," he says way too quickly. And again I know he's lying.

Will this weekend never end? It's like 6:00 in the morning on Tuesday and it's not over yet. There's more. Alexander is still holding back, and he's still lying to me about it.

"Don't talk, Alexander. If you're going to sit with me I want silence while I think," I say kind of bitchy to him. And maybe surprised by my sudden hostility, he simply nods and looks down at his hands.

Think!

What did Alex say to me? What was it he said?

Reaching for my blue Asian silk journal, I hold it tightly in my hands. I know Alexander stiffened beside me when I picked it up, but I don't care. It's my journal and I can hold it if I want to.

Feeling the silken thread beneath my fingers, I'm again reminded of my youth. I remember always rubbing the cover after His visits when I would write about our night together. I remember holding my journal as I cried for Him to come back to me. I remember crying on my journal when He would leave me. I remember crying, all the time.

But I never cry anymore. I don't have to. Everything is good and safe now. Everything is as it should be. Everything is as I always wanted it to be.

"What if He comes back again?" I choke out. I feel so scared suddenly by that reality, I shake uncontrollably.

"He's never coming back, Sade."

"How do you know? He *always* comes back."

"He's not," Alex says taking my hand.

"But what if He does? Will you hate me forever? I can't seem to get Him to leave me alone. I can't seem to be without Him. He's just always waiting in the background for me," I admit crying.

"He's not coming back, Sadie. Ever," Alexander says with a complete confidence I don't have.

"But He-"

"*NEVER*, Sadie."

Crying, I look at Alexander and the confusion swamps me again. I know he knows more. I can tell there is more to this- again.

Crying, I am exhausted from all this. This has been the longest weekend of my life, and I can't make it stop.

What did he say? What did Alexander say to me?

'And I needed Him to go away Sadie. For you!'

'You needed me to help and I fixed you. We're fine and I did that for you. I made Him go away, FOR YOU!'

Oh FUCK! What did he do?

"What did you do, Alex? Tell me," I beg.
"What do you mean?" He whispers beside me.
"What did you do to Him?" I ask. There I've asked the question I should've asked when this all started. "How do you know He won't come back?" Oh god...
"What do you mean?"
"You know what I mean. Please don't screw with me. I know you know what I'm asking. What. Did. You. Do. To. Him?" I spell it out clearly.
"Nothing."
"So then He might come back one day. He might come back to claim me. He might hurt me again."
"No, He won't," Alex says shaking his head. But he knows. I can tell he knows more.
"Please, just fucking tell me what you did. I don't care anymore, and I won't be mad. I just need to know. What did you do to Him?"
"Sadie, I swear I didn't do anything to Him. Just drop it, baby. Let it go now. It's over."
"It's NOT over! Don't you get it!? It will *never* be over! If I'm not fucking Him in my sleep, I'm waiting for Him to come back to fuck me awake. It never ends for me! What the fuck did you do?"
"I didn't do any-"
"JUST TELL ME!"
"There's nothing to tell. I swear I didn't do anything!" Alexander yells back visibly shaking.
"Okay. Well, I don't believe you, and I don't want to live like this, and I can't keep doing this with you. I know you did something, and I know you won't tell me, but I can't keep doing this. I WON'T keep doing this, Alexander!"
"What the hell does *that* mean? You don't want to be with me

because of Him?"

"No! I don't want to do this anymore with you because *you're* the one I'm supposed to trust, and I don't trust you because you won't tell me what you know, or what you did. And if I can't trust you, then we have nothing left. You've never hurt me, but I keep learning more and more I didn't know about you, and I feel like I can't trust you, and I always did trust you because you proved to me you wouldn't hurt me, but you keep hurting me. And this weekend of reality has been awful and exhausting, and I don't love you enough to fake it if you won't be honest with me."

"So that's it? I don't know what happened to Him, but I'm sure He won't be back for you, and that's enough to make you not love or trust me? That's all it takes after the years we've been together and the life we've built together? That's all it takes for you to not want to be with me anymore?!"

"Yes. That's all it takes," I say shocking us both I think. Actually, I AM shocked. I never thought I would want to live without Alex. I love him, and he makes me happy, and he forgives all the disgusting in my past, and he loves Jamie, and he's happy with our lives which I love. And I don't want to be a single mom, and I don't want to live alone anymore, and I love Alex, but I don't want to be like this anymore.

"I don't think I trust you because you won't tell me what you did."

"But I didn't do anything!" Alexander yells at me, while shaking my chair with his hand.

"You did!" I scream in our garage. Screaming, I push his hand away and jump up. Standing, I look down at Alexander and I want to beat the shit out of him I'm so frustrated. I don't even care that he's 6 foot and I'm 5 foot 2. I don't care that he's all fit and muscular, and I'm an ugly, emaciated waif at the moment. I don't care that he could defend himself without so much as a scratch landing on him, I still want to beat the shit out of him! I want to hurt him, and I'm shaking with the need to hurt him.

"Don't even think about it, Sadie. I'm not the bad guy here. I'm your husband and I love you."

"I can do whatever I want! And I know you know more than you're telling me!" I yell as I lunge for him.

But as I knew would happen, I am quickly subdued. I am twisted and thrown back into my lounge chair, even as it almost tips over to the side. With his hands holding my arms, and his lower body pressed against my legs, I am completely subdued again.

"Do it!" I spit in his face. "Take me, Alex! Why not? Fuck me like they did!"

"Holy *Fuck,* Sadie! You've really lost your fucking mind this time!" He yells back into my face. "Sit there! And don't fucking move! Just light another fucking smoke and sit there! I mean it! If you fucking move out of that chair, you'll see me really fucking pissed! Do you understand?!"

"Yup! Take your time, Alexander! You fucking murdering asshole! I know exactly what you did!" I scream as he releases my arms.

Shaking his head, he storms back for the house, but not before threatening me again.

"Don't you fucking move, Sadie, or else you'll see what a murdering asshole I can be!" And then he throws the garage door open as it slams against the inside wall.

And I don't move. Just the novelty and shock of Alexander's anger is enough to keep me seated. I called him out, and I can't wait for this to end. No matter how it ends, I'll just be glad it's over. I'll miss my baby boy forever, but I need this to all be over. And even though things are looking really bad for me, I can still strangely admit I don't think Alexander would ever hurt Jamie.

Ironically, I think whatever Alexander does to me, he would never do to Jamie. I just hope I gave Jamie enough good memories of me that he'll never forget how much his mommy loved him. Crying, I hope Jamie knows how much I have loved him from the moment he was placed on my chest 6 years ago. I hope he always remembers me with love.

Still crying, I jump when Alexander walks back into the garage.

Staring at his face of rage, I feel my tears fall faster down my face, even as I lift my hand for one last drag of my smoke. And the scene is suddenly very funny to me. I feel like I'm actually smoking my last cigarette like a death row last request. It's too bad I didn't have time to request my last meal though- toast with Alexander's thick sticky syrup.

Suddenly laughing. I find this whole thing beyond my ability to cope with. If I had a knife I'd slit my legs to release the pressure. If I had alcohol, I'd drink until I was numb and didn't care. If I had pills I'd down them until I passed out.

But at least I have my smokes with me.

"Pick up your journal," he barks. And I do. "Look in the back," he yells again, and I open it quickly. Skimming through, I see nothing but my last entry from the night before our wedding.

Impatiently, Alexander grabs the book from my hands, and flips to the end. Opening the journal wider, he places 2 pieces of paper against the missing edge, and I'm stunned.

"Read it," he suddenly whispers and in that change of his voice alone I am blindsided by my panic.

Looking back up at Alexander, he hands me my smokes again and moves to lean against the wall with his arms crossed against his chest and his eyes looking downward.

So I read.

CHAPTER 36

But the torn out page is blank but for one stain and one sentence.

"Today the stranger died before he killed me."

Flipping the page quickly, I see a stain of lips on the middle of the second page with only one sentence below.

"But I kissed you goodbye... stranger."

Looking at the lips, I'm sure they're mine. I'm sure they're the same shape as my own. I'm sure this is my kiss on the page. But I've never worn brown lipstick in my life.

Looking at Alexander I breathe my confusion of reality in this moment.
"I don't understand..."

Shaking his head, Alex finally raises his head and stares at me. Staring at me in silence, I find I can't breathe. I don't understand any of this, and I don't understand the look on Alexander's face.

"I found Him in the septic tank of the old house, Sadie," Alexander whispers again while choking up.

"What?! What do you mean?"

"I mean, when Chris and I were in that shitty old basement trying to figure out what the hell reeked down there, I found Him in the septic tank."

"Why? What did you do to Him?"

"Sadie, you need to think for a minute," Alex says very calmly. "You need to really think about this. I let you pretend you didn't know until the nightmares stopped, and then I think you really didn't know after that. I think you forced yourself to forget Him because you needed to not know what happened. I don't know. But now I need you to think really hard. I need you to remember so we can get back to normal. I need you to remember what happened so you stop thinking I did something wrong. Because I didn't do anything wrong. I didn't do anything but clean up what YOU did."

Gasping, I'm in shock at his accusation. "What **I** did? I didn't do anything!"

"Yes, you did. You did this. Not me. I did nothing but clean up afterward. And you need to remember Sadie so you let this go once and for all."

When Alexander walks toward me and crouches in front of me, he takes my face into his hand and forces me to look at him. I know my eyes are wide, and I know my mouth is open. I know I'm breathing heavily and shaking uncontrollably. I know there's more, but all I see is Alexander's beautiful eyes in front of me.

"I found Him in the septic tank, Sadie. Do you remember that?" And shaking my head, I know I don't remember. "Think Sadie. You freaked out for 2 weeks. You were a fucking mess. You acted so deranged, I hated even leaving Jamie with you, but somehow I still trusted you wouldn't hurt Jamie when I went to work. Do you remember those 2 weeks?" And shaking my head I know I don't remember. "You were so messed up. And you were still moaning for Him in your sleep, but you were screaming out and crying as well. You were horrible, and I didn't know what to do. I was exhausted from the nightly rituals with you. I was exhausted and so tired of all the drama at night with you. We starting fighting every night after you woke up, and you wouldn't tell me what was wrong, but you kept saying it was over between us, over and over again and I didn't understand why. And I fought you back and told you we weren't over and we would make it. And I thought you were just losing it because you had started working a week before and I thought you couldn't handle being without Jamie, so I tried to make you quit working. I tried to make you quit but you argued we needed the money, which we did. You were so screwed up at night, but totally lucid in the days when we'd talk. Do you remember those 2 weeks?" And shaking my head no, I know I don't remember.

"Think! *Please,* baby... Think about it. That was when you freaked out on my mom and called her a kidnapper and a murderer. That was when you totally lost it on her in the street. Do you remember that day?" And nodding my head, I know I remember that day.

"That was when you got better though. After my mom calmed you down and we decided we would sell the house, you calmed right down. You still cried a lot at night, but I thought it was just the change in our circumstances. You've never handled change well, and I thought because you had to go to work for a few hours a day you were struggling. Do you remember that?" And nodding, I know I remember that. I WAS struggling with being away from Jamie. I hated it.

"I would find you sitting on the bottom steps of the basement and I had to physically carry you back to bed. I would find you crying in the bathroom, and I had to coax you back to bed. I would find you all over the house crying, and I would have to kiss you until you stopped sobbing. You even once told me my kisses were magic for you, which under the insane circumstances I suddenly found us in almost overnight, was such an innocent, sweet thing to say to me, it made me keep fighting for you to get well. Those simple words made me try to love you more so you would get better again."

Looking at Alex crying in front of me, I'm heartbroken. I hate him feeling sad, and I hate him crying.

"Your kisses *have* always been magic to me..." I whisper against his mouth, as he leans his forehead against mine.

Breathing in Alex's scent I'm reminded of all our years together. Not even a decade together that feels like 2 lifetimes. He has been so good to me over and over again. He has been such strength for me for years, I'm sure I never would have survived my life without him.

"You're so strong all the time, Alex. Don't you ever get tired?"

"All the time. But I don't think I'm as strong as you think. I think sometimes it's almost a weakness that keeps me with you..." He admits sadly.

And he's probably right. What kind of person stays with someone like me for years? What kind of man waits on such a weak woman for years? Why would he wait around when I have given him so little in return?

"Sadie, I need you to think hard about what happened. I need you to try to remember. Do you remember the septic tank? Do you remember the smell in the basement?"

"What did you do?"

"A week after we decided to sell, Chris had left our house after helping with the roof, but I was still in the basement looking for a dead rat, or something else to explain the smell. But that's when I found Him in the tank," Alex says as he gags. Pulling away from me, he sits back on his heels and looks like he's fighting either crying or gagging again, or maybe both. "I found Him and I ran upstairs but you were sleeping on the couch with Jamie, so I ran to our room and found your journal under your sweaters in our closet. I tried to find out if you wrote about it, and that's when I found the 2 pages at the back of the book which really didn't tell me much. So I panicked," Alex says painfully.

Staring at me, he seems to be waiting for me to say something, or remember something, or do something. He's waiting for me but I'm clueless.

"What did you do?" I ask gently, as he shakes his head again.

When the house phone suddenly rings, we both seem to jump together. Standing quickly, Alex orders 'stay here' and I do. Then again, lighting another smoke seems to be about the full extent of my physical capabilities right now.

Waiting seems to be the theme of my life.

When Alex returns, he looks exhausted. He looks like shit, and though he doesn't say anything, I know the smoky garage is bothering him.

"Are you ready to go inside now?" He asks gently as I shake my head no again.

"Who was it? Jamie?"

"Yes, and he's fine. He had a great night at my parents' house and he doesn't want to go back to school. He says he loves you and he can't wait to see you at 3:00."

And then I'm done. "Oh god, I miss him. He should be home

with me. He should be here. What if he needs me today, or misses me, or feels abandoned or something? What if something bad happens to him and I'm not there?!" I cry.

"Sadie, please. Please baby, stay focused. Jamie is fine and it's already 8:30, so we'll pick him up in 6 1/2 hours. He's absolutely fine. And I called the office and said I wouldn't be in today, so we have all day to figure this out, but I need you to focus."

"I am, but I don't remember anything. I really don't. I remember the meltdown on your mother, and talking about the house, and deciding to sell, but that's it. I don't remember what happened other than that. What happened, Alexander?"

Exhaling, Alexander straightens his spine and continues. "2 weeks later, I found him and then I covered him up with concrete in the septic tank. I drove to Home Depot and picked up bags and bags of concrete mixture, and when you were sleeping, I unplugged the tank, and then I filled it in. I filled it and filled it but it took forever and it wouldn't harden or fill in completely, no matter how many bags I poured. And I felt like I was losing my mind. Then I remembered there was that weird drain thing by the side of the house, so I ran outside, and I almost cried when I saw concrete coming out of it. So I found that thick silicone spray stuff Chris used in the attic and I filled the bottom of that drain, then I had to wash away all the extra concrete mixture which was all over the place outside. But by then it was 3 something in the morning, so I had to wait until the morning and I drove back to Home Depot to buy more bags of concrete and a small plastic tarp to wrap around the drain spout and then I waited until you went to bed again and I continued filling it in. I continued the second night and finally, the septic tank started filling. I think the concrete in the pipe hardened in the day, so the concrete stayed in the tank. Maybe even the bottom of the tank hardened. I don't know. But it started filling up, and eventually, after close to thirty bags of concrete, the tank was filled with wet, dark grey concrete."

Alex sits down on the garage floor in front of me as he exhales the stress of his story. Looking at him, I feel awful. I wish I knew what happened but I honestly don't.

"Then what happened?" I beg.

"I showered, my back and arms were killing me and I made my way to bed. But you were in the throes of another fucking nightmare and I was so tired, I felt like I wanted to just leave you. I really felt like leaving you in that moment because I didn't know why you did it, or what exactly you'd done, but there you were freaking out again, and I was just so tired, and I wanted to leave you. For the first time since we had been together, which was only like 3 years at that point, I wanted to leave you. And I would've left that night I think. But as I thought about what I would do, and if I took Jamie with me, and where I went, and who I told, you screamed for me to help you. You actually screamed out 'Alex, PLEASE!! Help me!' And once again I found myself drawn to your side.

"I actually found myself unable to move or breathe as you struggled in our bed. I watched you with a sick fascination for a minute or two, and then you begged me again to help you, and you begged me to run with Jamie. You screamed for me to save you, and you were acting like you were being raped and hurt, and that's when I snapped. I grabbed you from your sleep, waking you almost violently. I woke you aggressively, and after a few seconds of fighting me, you calmed instantly and wrapped yourself all around me and then you asked me to make Him go away. And I didn't know what I could say or do to help you, so I whispered, 'I buried Him, Sadie,' and you relaxed in my arms at once. You calmed in my arms instantly and you thanked me for taking care of you again, and then you moved out of my arms, turned to your side, and slept. And I just sat there on the bed beside you; emotionally numb, physically exhausted and so tired of all the crap that came with you, I didn't know what to do anymore. But I looked at you as you slept soundly and even though you were covered in sweat, and your hair was a tangled mess, I realized I didn't want to leave you. I didn't want to not be with you, and I didn't want to not love you. I realized that no matter how crazy your past was, and how crazy you could be, I loved you anyway, and I never wanted to leave you. And I haven't."

"Alex, I-"

"And you were better after that. The very next night you slept like the dead, and the night after that, I finally slept like the dead. You even joked that I snored so loudly you had to sleep in Jamie's room on the floor. And you were normal again, relatively speaking," he grins. And I can't help but laugh a little as the tension starts to drain from my body.

"I don't remember Alex, and I don't know what to say. Does anyone else know? Do we call the Police?"

"No. We do nothing. Nobody knows, and I wouldn't testify

against you anyway, not that I'd have to as your husband. And once I had convinced my brother I was just a home improvement idiot for sealing up the septic tank, he helped me build that smaller one at the back of the garage using other outflow pipes he found."

"But what about... Him. What- did no one look for Him?" I ask totally shocked again by my reality. How are we even having this conversation? Why are we so calmly discussing a death? I just can't get my brain around anything, and maybe that's why I'm so calm. I don't know anything, but everything is so strange and so surreal in this moment with Alex.

"Sadie? Don't you remember? About 4 months later, we were questioned as were your parents. You were asked if you had seen or heard from Him in months, and you told the truth- You hadn't. And the Police didn't push because they had spoken to your parents first, and your parents had told them you hadn't seen Him since you were a child. Your dad lied, then called me without asking any questions and told me what was said. We were warned that the Police had some questions, but that we were in no trouble. And from your dad's tone of voice I think he *did* assume something had happened, but he seemed to be protecting you anyway. I don't know. But the Police came and asked us less than 5 questions and then they left. And that's it. I think that's why you received all the inheritance because as far as I know He's still listed as a missing person."

"But I should-"

"It's over Sadie. You can't remember what happened and I don't *know* what happened. All I have are these 2 pages that tell me nothing. And until you remember, there is nothing we can do. It's over, baby, and I need you to leave it alone."

"But it feels wrong or something."

"Do you know what happened?"

"No."

"Then how do you know it was wrong? For all we know He killed himself because you pushed Him away or something. I don't know. I like to think that's what happened. I don't know though and I've spent 4 years dealing with this alone, and if Patrick hadn't sent that fucking letter, you'd still be fine, and we'd be fine, and none of this would be upsetting you. Right?"

"I guess. It's just weird to think He died in our home and we covered it up. Literally," I say without humor.

"Sadie. Think hard. Do you remember what happened? Any of

it?"

"No. I don't remember anything about that time except the freak out on your mom."

"So please stop all this. Just stop. We're fine, and we're going to be fine. We don't know what happened and you might never remember, so I'm begging you to let this go. Please?"

And looking at the desperation on Alex's face, I want to let it go for him. For Alex's peace of mind, I want to bury all this crazy shit. I need to give him a little peace for a change.

I still have this little doubt about all this. There is this tiny nagging suspicion in the back of my brain wondering if Alexander knows more than he's telling me, but I mostly trust him. I trust him almost totally.

"Is that it, Alexander? Is there anything else you know? Is there anything else you've always known that I didn't know you knew?"

"No," he says firmly while looking directly into my eyes.

Nodding, I try to accept his answer. And as I think about it, I wonder does it matter if he did anything, or knows more than he's saying? Does it really matter at this point? He's gone whether by my doing totally, or with Alexander's help, and nothing really changes either way. I'm free of Him, and Alex has kept me safe. He has covered up and protected me and Jamie. So even if he does know more, or even if he does know what happened exactly, in the end it doesn't really matter. I'm safe from Him. And I'm safe from being haunted by His visits.

"Okay, I'll try to let this all go. And I'm really sorry for all this. This weekend has been brutal for me, but I'll try to get better. I'll try very hard, Alex."

"Thank you. I need you back. You have scared me and tortured me, and put me through hell this weekend. But I need it to be over. Please?"

"Okay," I nod.

And I will try to forget any suspicion and any doubt I may have because in the end I think I've decided it really doesn't matter anymore. All that matters to me now is Alex and Jamie, and all of our safety.

CHAPTER 37

A half an hour later, Alex and I have finished our toast with the sweet sticky syrup I love, and we're crawling into bed for a nap.
 Setting the alarm for 2:00 in the afternoon feels weird, but we're both afraid of sleeping past picking up Jamie from school. We're both exhausted and we both just want a little calm between us. I need Alex's warmth, and I think he needs me needing his warmth, too.
 So closing my eyes, I feel the pull to sleep immediately. I feel the need to sleep in Alex's arms. I feel the need to sleep away the horrible reality I can't remember.
 And I did.

 3 hours later at 2:00, Alex jumps up and offers to pick up Jamie for me after a quick shower. Alex offers, but I insist on going with him.
 And sitting on our bed waiting for Alex to shower quickly I realized I'm not afraid anymore. I realized when I woke from our nap I didn't feel afraid for the first time in 16 years. For the very first time since I was sixteen I wasn't anxious about sleep. I didn't perform my cleansing ritual, and I didn't sleep with the overwhelming sense of anticipation followed by disappointment which was all I had known as a younger girl. But I also didn't sleep with fear of His return followed by relief when He hadn't come for me. I just slept. I slept in Alexander's arms in the middle of the day and I felt free.

 Picking up Jamie at 3:00 is amazing for me. I feel like I've been without my baby for years. I feel like I haven't heard his sweet voice in years. I feel like I haven't hugged him in years. But everything fades inside me when I see him walk out of the school while looking right at the safe pole we always meet at. Jamie sees me and walks quickly right to our safe pole to be in my arms.
 And I'm happy. I am truly happy with my life, especially in this moment. Alexander is standing beside me with his hand on my back, and Jamie is letting me smooch his whole face as I hug

him. Jamie is giggling and talking a mile a minute about everything he did over the weekend even as I keep kissing him. Jamie is in my arms and I'm happy.

When I'm through attacking my son with kisses, Alex offers to take us all out for an early dinner and we agree. In the car Jamie talks the whole way to the restaurant, in the restaurant, and then in the car after the restaurant, and it's good for me. I need Jamie's sweetness and innocence to wash away all the darkness from our lives.

In the restaurant I heard noise everywhere but I didn't start shaking or let the irritation of sound distract me from my boys. I heard all the noise, and I didn't like it still, but I wasn't overwhelmed by it like I would've been even yesterday.

And after we left the restaurant, I asked Alex to stop at the coffee shop I love, and he did. Quickly hopping out before I could, Alex returned with a coffee for himself and a large cup of my absolute favorite coffee for me because he knew. He remembered what a complicated coffee I liked, and he pleased me again with such a little thoughtful gesture.

When we three return home, I see Cheryl in her driveway wave at us, and I have a moment of absolute panic until Alex takes my hand. Jamie jumps out immediately, and I collect myself enough to grab my coffee and purse as I slowly get out of the car. Waving back at Cheryl, she walks over to my side of the car as I pause half in and half out. Pausing, I'm embarrassed and scared, and...

"How are you, Sadie?"
"Good. I'm good," I reply automatically.
"That's good. I was going to see if everything was okay with you after I settled in."
"It is. I'm fine. I'm sorry for yesterday," I hear myself pleading.
"No need to be sorry, and *nothing* happened yesterday," she says loudly enough to convince me of her loyalty. "Just remember-punching bag. It'll do wonders for stress and pressure. Okay?" And as I nod, she leans in and smells my coffee, which shocks me a little. "And when I come over for coffee, none of this flavored crap, okay? I need good solid black tar, preferably Columbia, because I've been living off it for years at the hospital. Okay?" And again I nod wordlessly. Hugging me suddenly, Cheryl whispers, "Anytime you need a friend, call me or just knock on

my door, Sadie. I'm either at the hospital or at home. So anytime..." she says kindly.

And that's it. Choking up, I hug her back and thank her for her kindness, as we pull apart.

"See ya kiddo. I miss my flower surprises," she says to Jamie as she walks back to her home.

And I'm okay. I'm still a little embarrassed thinking of Cheryl seeing me physically AND emotionally naked in my garage, but she didn't seem to mind, so I'm going to try to forget it too.

After a few tense seconds Alex wraps his arm around my shoulder and whispers, "you're doing really well, Sade," and I exhale. Finally able to move, I walk to Jamie on the porch who is patiently waiting to get into our home, while still talking endlessly about his trip.

2 hours later, Jamie is bathed and in bed. And after a quick story, he passed out immediately, even as I drag myself to my own bedroom to pass out immediately.

After a quick shower, I brush my teeth and crawl into my bed. I'm done, without even the energy to walk downstairs to say goodnight to Alex, but I should've known he would come to me as he always does.

Crawling in next to me, he picks me up and over his chest as he hugs me tightly. Bathing in his warmth, I exhale and feel myself falling.

"Are you okay?" He asks quietly, and I nod because I *am* okay.

And I'm free.

After years and years of anxiety, depression, insanity and fear, I am totally free. I can breathe. And I can live, finally.

I have Alexander who has proven himself a hundred times over, and I have Jamie who loves me unconditionally. I have a husband I love and a child I live for.

I am finally alive. And the world remains audacious.

*****

My Dear Stranger

EPILOGUE

"ALEX!! ALEX, WAKE UP!" I scream jumping on him in a panic. Pounding his chest, Alexander wakes by throwing me off him onto the floor in his own panic. And after scrambling with the sheets, Alex jumps to the floor and he's almost at our bedroom door before I've stopped screaming.

"Wait! Wait, Alex!"

"What the hell's happening?" He yells as his head whips around the room. Looking around frantically, I realize he's ready to fight. He's ready, and I've scared the hell out of him again.

"I'm sorry. I didn't mean to scare you. I'm so sorry, Alex," I cry. "But I wrote about it. I wrote in the other journal, so it wasn't in the same as what I thought was the beautiful journal. It's in my hatbox!" I scream again as our room suddenly silences.

Watching Alex, I see him try, figure out, then comprehend within seconds. Watching Alex, I see him grasp what I'm saying, even as he tries to understand what I mean. Watching Alex, I'm shaken to my core.

He doesn't look right. He doesn't look like Alex. He doesn't look like my husband.

"What other journal?" He asks shaking.

"The stupid one with all the deaths and stuff. The scrap book of dead singers, and my friend, and my teacher and those kids from Margaret Mary High. The OTHER one!" I yell, as I scramble off the floor and run to the spare room.

Feeling Alex behind me, I dive under the bed. I even bang my shoulder on the wheel post underneath, and scrap my elbow on the carpet. Reaching, I tug out the Christmas bags I reuse, and toss aside the extra shoe boxes I don't use but have to keep for some reason. Reaching, I'm just desperate. Halfway under the bed I reach until finally I feel my hatbox.

Tugging at it, I scream, "Help me!" As Alex pulls my legs back out. Scrubbing my chin on the carpet I don't care. He pulled me out in a millisecond and I'm still holding my hatbox tightly even as I shake.

I have it!

"What's wrong, mommy?" And as I whip my head to the door, Alex grabs for Jamie. Scooping him up, Alex looks at me like he has absolutely no fucking idea what to say to him. Looking at me desperately, I can't help him. I am wordless as Jamie stares at me still half asleep.

"Nothing's wrong. Um, I was just looking for something for months now and I finally found it. Sorry I woke you," I say while giving Alex the help me out here look. And thankfully he does.

"We're sorry for waking you but everything's fine. Let me take you back to bed now, okay?"

But Jamie just stares at me like he knows we're full of shit. Jamie is looking at me like he knows we're lying to him. Jamie looks at me like he's almost offended we're lying to him.

"Please, baby. Let daddy take you back to bed. *Please...*" And even as I hear the desperation in my voice, I know Jamie hears it, too.

"Okay. Goodnight. But can I have a hug first?"

And that's it. I'm done. Looking at my little boy, I'm just done. He knows me and he knows I'm messed up and he's going to go easily, but he's going to hug me first because he knows me.

"...yes, please," I whisper holding in my sob as best as I can.

As Alexander slowly releases Jamie from his hug, he looks at me like he's begging me to keep it together, and I will. Jamie is too young for all this bullshit. He is too young to know what a whack job his mom can be. He's too young, and sweet, and beautiful for me to willingly damage.

"Goodnight mommy," he breathes into my ear as he hugs me. And I keep it together. For Jamie, I can do anything.

"Let daddy take you back to bed, okay? You have swimming tomorrow right after school so you'll be super tired in the morning. I love you, baby. Sleep tight." And as he nods against me he gives one final squeeze before pulling away from my hug.

Walking back to Alex, who again scoops him up, I know I did good. Jamie doesn't look freaked out anymore, and he's going back to bed without a fuss.

"I'll be right back," Alex says, and I know he will.

"Take your time," I say as Alexander stares at me a little too long.

And once they're gone. I know where I have to go.

Running down the stairs as quietly as I can, I rip out the treat drawer and grab the stale pack of smokes at the back I think I left half full. I think I have enough for this.

Opening the garage door, I forgot the sensor and immediately the warning sound goes off, even as I dive for the main panel in between the front and garage door.

Shaking, I punch in the code, and try to remember how to take it off the garage door to the house again. Thinking, I try to remember how to change the sensor. Thinking, I remember the code.

My dad's birthday so we would all remember it. My mom and dad, and me. We didn't pick MY birthday because that was too obvious, so we picked my dad's birthday. 0508. May 8th. My dad's birthday.

And when I did change the code in my second apartment I used the year my dad was born. I used my dad again because he paid for the security and because he was my dad. I used his year of birth because we would all remember it. My mom and dad. Patrick. Alexander. The Hamiltons. We all knew the code that was my dad's birthday, and then I used the year of his birth.

My dad.

Our dad.

Oh my god...

"Sadie?" Alex breathes behind me as I jump.

"My dad was 37 when I was born, and my mom was 25 when I was born. So my dad was May 8th, 1943. I was born in 1980. I was born in 1980 but that was too obvious," I can't help but laugh.

"I don't understand, Sade. What does that matter? Your mom was his second wife, so-"

"What's our code, Alex?"

Though I'm not looking at him, I can hear the absolute comprehension when Alex suddenly inhales. He totally gets it.

"I made it so easy for Him, and I didn't even know I was. I made it soooo easy. I gave Him the codes without giving Him the codes. My dad's birthday, and then the year he was born. I gave Him my dad's information, which He *always* knew."

And again I can't help but laugh a little. It's so clear to me now. Now that I know how He got to me, it's so clear to me. I always wondered how He stood over me while I slept. I always wondered how He could get to me, time and time again, but now I realize I gave it to Him all along.

Crying out, I'm shocked again, and I just can't stand much more of all this shit.

Opening the garage door, I throw myself on the floor as I rip open the hatbox and grab for the stupid journal at the bottom.

Sensing Alex moving around the garage I can't even look at him. I don't care what he's doing. I don't care about anything but this stupid journal.

And suddenly the journal is in my hands, and I feel the texture of all the glue, and the staples, and the tape. Stretching it across my lap, I feel the bumps of folded newspapers and I remember younger Sadie.

For months, Alexander and I have carried on. We've been happy and we said we put the past behind us. We've pretended like the past WAS behind us. But it wasn't.

We're still going through the motions of being totally sane and together. We're pretending our lives are perfect. We're pretending. And I'm scared to ruin the facade.

I don't want this to end us.

Lighting a smoke, I take my time while smoothing the journal across my lap over and over again. Inhaling my stale smoke is the only thing I'm capable of in this moment. I can't open the journal, and I don't want to know what's inside.

Why tonight? There was NO reason. There was nothing different about tonight. Alex and I were normal and we went to bed normally. We snuggled and we slept. There was no drama, nor upset. We didn't have sex or talk about the past. I wasn't thinking about Him at all. He was nowhere near me. He didn't touch me, and He wasn't on my mind.

"Why tonight, Alex? Why did I remember this tonight? Did something happen in my sleep?"

"I don't think so..." he whispers.

"I'm afraid of what I'm going to find. I know it's in here, but I don't know what it says. I really don't Alex, and I don't understand why I suddenly remembered tonight to get this journal but I can't remember what's inside it. Why don't I remember?"

"I don't know, Sade. Maybe your mind is protecting you or something. But you don't have to do this tonight, baby. You don't have to do this ever," Alex begs while taking my hand.

"But I should."

My Dear Stranger

"Why?"

"I don't know. Don't YOU want to know? Doesn't it bother you knowing I might have killed someone? Doesn't that matter?" I ask turning to look straight at Alexander. Begging, I need to know if I'm going to change everything with this.

"No. It really doesn't matter to me. One way or the other, He was bad, Sadie. He hurt you for years, and I think He may have hurt you again. I think whatever happened is in the past and we should keep it there. Finding this changes nothing. I won't feel any differently towards you, no matter what happened."

"But what if I still wanted Him?" I whisper. "What if I was willingly with Him? Will you feel differently about me then?"

"No, I don't think so. I think you're finally over whatever hold He had on you, and I won't feel any differently about you because of something you might have done almost 6 years ago. I love you, and I honestly don't think this will change anything for me."

"Do you want to read it with me? Should I read it first? What should I do?" I start to panic quickly. I can feel the panic, and even hear it in my voice. My panic feels almost tangible.

"Sadie, you DON'T have to do this at all. I don't care," Alex says wrapping an arm around my shoulder. And then I'm warm.

Suddenly, completely warm, I open the stupid journal of my melodramatic youth and find the pages near the back. And it's so obviously which pages they are, I nearly laugh. They have no glue or tape, and my words are written in a beautiful script all alone among pages of scraps and newspaper clippings.

Opening the pages wide, I am warmed by Alex, and everything else fades away...

Yesterday the stranger came to me. Yesterday he came for me. Yesterday, he came to claim me.

Waking from a light rest, I heard his voice in my dreams. Waking from an afternoon nap, I heard his voice all over my home. Waking from my rest, I was startled to hear his voice surrounding me.

So jumping, I ran to the sound overhead. Jumping up, I ran to him. Jumping, I ran to the sound that had haunted me for years.

And that's when my world ended.

Lying on the floor, he held my baby asleep in his arms. Holding my baby, he didn't even see me. Holding my baby tightly in his arms, my stranger was a nightmare to me.

So I watched in my horrified silence.

I watched him cuddle my baby to his chest. I watched him sing a beautiful song of love to my son. I watched him sing the lullaby of my childhood. I watched him love my son.

And then he saw me.

Dropping my baby from his arms, he stood as my baby screamed out for me. Looking at my son I tried to see if he was hurt. I tried to see pain or injury on his face, but thankfully all I saw were the tears of a one year old being startled.

And that's when I knew. I knew what I had to do. I knew I had to get him away from my baby. I knew I had to save my son.

Running away from my baby's screams, I took the stairs as fast as I could until I was tackled and twisted as I fell. Fighting, I tried. Screaming, I tried. Fighting, I tried... but I lost again.

When he punched my stomach hard I knew I was dead. Gasping for breath became my sole focus. Gasping for air to aid me became my life and death in that moment.

And then the stranger spoke. In a voice filled with such misery and confusion, he spoke the words that ended my life. He spoke and his calm voice broke me. He said the words, and I knew.
"You were born for me to love..."

And as I cried no, he grabbed my face hard and breathed his madness into me. "Him or me," he grieved.

"Who?" I screamed.

But in the silence that followed as he stared at my face, I knew. And it really didn't matter anymore. Nothing mattered. I would protect them both with my life.

And then I died. I turned my head and I cried. I lay there feeling my life leave me as I chose them instead of me.

When I felt my clothing torn, I surrendered. I closed my eyes and I said goodbye. I whispered my love to my boys. I whispered my love to the baby screaming above me.

And because I made a promise to try for him, I let go. And because I made a promise to be the best mother to the Angel above me, I let go. I let go and I whispered my goodbye, because in that moment I knew anything was worth saving them, even as I died.

And then I didn't scream anymore.

Lying on the floor I was torn open by his painful penetration, but again he took my pain into his mouth as I fought my scream. He again took all my pain and made it his own. He took me until I couldn't scream anymore.

"Sadie! Stop! No more! You don't have to do this. I can't *hear* this!" Alex yells shaking me. Alex yells with tears pouring down his face. Alex shakes me with tears falling down my face. Alex yells, but I'm too far gone this time.

"Don't touch me, Alex. Just listen..." I moan. And as we stare at each other in horror, Alex silences and releases my arms with a gentle nod.

And I didn't fight my legs raised against his chest, and I didn't fight his hand on my throat. I didn't fight him anymore. For them.

Thrusting I was moved across the floor. Thrusting, he tore me open again and again. Thrusting, he loved my body alone.
Groaning, he was empowered. But frustrated, he tried to arouse me as he continued but I didn't make a sound. This was not our pleasure being had, and he wouldn't get my pleasure ever again.

So silently, I listened to the sound of my crying baby as I held in the cries of my own.

Turning my head, I looked at the couch and I waited. With wide eyes I looked at the couch as I waited. I waited silently. I waited for him to finish with me. I waited for him to finish me.
And he did.

Crying silently as I felt his release deep inside me, I let go of the dream of all I ever wanted to be. Crying for all the darkness inside me, I breathed my goodbye with his release.

Crying silently, I stared at the couch as he dropped my legs painfully to the floor. Crying silently, I waited for more.

And then it was over.

I watched him startle and cry. I watched him twist and reach. I watched the stranger look at me in shock.
Wiping the blood from his mouth, I watched him cry out for me. Looking at me with love, I watched him gasp and moan. Looking at me love, I watched a single tear slowly fall down his cheek for us. I watched silently as he finished our greatest production.

I watched the shadow move away with my son even as my eyes clouded over and my body burned. I was barely alive and unconsciousness claimed me soon...

Waking, I was horrified to feel the stranger still holding me. I was held in his arms as I tried to break free. I was desperate to escape the demon torturing me.

So turning my head slowly I looked into the eyes staring at me, and they could be no other eyes than the stranger's eyes loving, killing, and haunting, me.

And that's when I knew.

Yesterday the stranger came to me. And as I watched the life leave his dying eyes, I leaned in close and kissed him goodbye.

When I awoke seemingly minutes later on the couch I held my nursing son in my arms. I held my son close as he breathed his little life into me. Holding him tight, I cried to the little face who birthed, loved, and saved me.

"Sadie..." Alex whispers as he pulls me tightly to him. Warming me instantly, I feel half alive. I hate this feeling all over me, and I hate this feeling inside me. I hate this feeling that is me.

"I'm a really good mom, Alex," I moan.

"Oh *fuck!*" Alex gasps. "I know, Sade. I know you are. You're a really good wife too. You are, baby. Sadie, you are really good." He cries again and again as he lifts me right off the floor into his arms as he rocks me. "You're a really good mom, Sadie. You are really good." He repeats over and over until the pressure starts to lift a little from my chest.

"Will you kiss me to make me forget who I am?" I beg softly. And he does.

Kissing me, Alex holds the back of my head with his fist, as his other hand twists and holds my waist to him. Kissing me, Alex makes me forget. Kissing me, Alex makes it go away. Kissing me, Alex makes me forget who I am.

When he pulls away and rests his forehead against mine, I need him to know. I need him to understand.

"Your kisses have always been like magic to me. They make everything bad go away..." I cry on a sob, as Alexander lifts me and walks us back into our house.

Walking, Alex shushes my sobs, and kisses my head as I sink further into his arms.

And when I'm placed on our bed, Alex wraps himself all around me as I finish my cry. And I can admit to myself, I want to get drunk, and I want to swallow pills, and I want to cut up my thighs. But I won't. Because for Alex, I promised to try.

After forever, Alex breathes against my cheek, "Sadie? Who was the shadow?" And I know.
"My mom. She came to watch Jamie so I could go to work, and she made him go away for me."
"But why did she-"
"That's the end, Alex. It's over. She did it before he could kill me again. And then she must have taken care of me and Jamie, and of *him*. She did this for me. So it's over now."
"But she should have-"
"She saved me Alex... She did it before he could kill me. And then she must have taken care of me and Jamie, and of him. She did it for me. So it's over," I cry again until he understands.
"Okay. It's over..." Alex agrees turning me to my back until we stare at each other in silence.

And it IS over. She never told and we'll never tell.
The stranger left me forever, so I don't have to wait anymore.

When Alex kisses me again as beautifully as he always does, everything fades away, until only one thought crashes into my brain, over and over like a tidal wave.
"I kissed him goodbye, I kissed him goodbye, I kissed him goodbye..."

THE END

Sarah Ann Walker

Sarah Ann Walker

ABOUT THE AUTHOR

Sarah Ann Walker lives in Canada with her American husband and their son.

In her real life, Sarah is a devoted mother and wife, and an absolute junkie for coffee and high heels.

Sarah can be found on Facebook
www.facebook.com/SarahAnnWalkerIAmHer

Amazon
http://www.amazon.com/author/walkersarahann
http://amzn.com/e/B00AW22K56

Goodreads
https://www.goodreads.com/Sarah-Walker

Twitter
@sarahannwalker0

Made in the USA
San Bernardino, CA
14 April 2014